I0637824

When Doves Fly

a novel by

Lauren Gregory

Echo Mountain Publishing
Colorado, USA

This is a work of fiction. Names, characters, places, and incidents are either the product of the author's imagination or are used fictitiously. Any resemblance to actual events or locales or persons, living or dead, is entirely coincidental.

Cover art by Phatpuppyart.com

Published by Echo Mountain Publishing
Colorado, USA
echomountainpublishing.com
Printed in USA

ISBN: 0996823506
ISBN-13: 978-0-9968235-0-0

DEDICATION

This book could only be dedicated to one person:
the one who made it happen.
Thanks, Mom.

CHAPTER ONE

Lily Wright departed the train before the other passengers, gripping her carpet bag tight, eager to disappear. The bell clanged their arrival as the train rumbled to a stop, and voices rose over the hiss of steam engines as travelers greeted family and friends. Lily had no one to greet, yet every face resembled her husband's and filled her with cold dread. Throwing peeks over her shoulder, she dodged and weaved until she found the station agent.

"Where's the nearest hotel and stagecoach, sir?"

"Welcome to Denver, miss." He jerked his thumb to the east, beyond the depot. "Plenty hotels within a few blocks, they can get you to a coach."

She nodded and proceeded inside. People, suitcases, and trunks littered the station. She ducked her head and wound around them. Hair prickled on her neck. Convinced eyes had followed her, she turned, but no one seemed interested. Her heart pounded faster as she skirted the ticket line and burst through the doors to the street.

Wagons lumbered past in the waning evening light. A river

of people flowed around her—men in work clothes or suits and bowlers, women in walking dresses with pert bustles—while she stood in front of the depot and searched building signs.

She wanted a smaller place, inexpensive and inconspicuous. She'd thought she would feel safe once she reached Denver, but her anxiety had grown stronger with every mile as the train chugged across the prairie.

Lily negotiated the wide, muddy road with a stream of pedestrians toward a cross-street lined with tall brick and clapboard buildings. When the group reached the other side and went their separate ways, she started up the narrower street, scanning the buildings and stopping at each corner to survey the side roads. After several blocks, a squat, wooden structure with a large sign on the roof drew her attention: The Broadwell House. Her pace picked up.

The noise and chaos fell behind as the traffic and crowds thinned. The buildings cast long shadows over the road, and the mountain sunset blared bright color on the facing side.

Her apprehension dimmed outside the crush of people, and exhaustion weighed her shoulders down. The hotel beckoned. Her hand ached, and she shifted the small suitcase to her other hand as she passed an alley.

An arm shot from the narrow void between buildings and snatched the bag from her fingers. She gasped, but shock throttled a scream in her throat. She swung toward the breach but caught only a glimpse of a darker shadow darting away. Her feet moved a few yards into the alley, but the gloom stopped her.

Wait, what if I catch up with him? Who knows what he might do.

She spun and darted into the road.

"Thief! Help!"

The street had emptied. The nearest figure, a block away, kept moving in the opposite direction. She opened her mouth to shout again but closed it with a snap.

Heavens, what am I thinking? I can't get involved with the law here. But my bag ....

She turned back to the alley, but nothing moved, the shadow gone.

"No!"

She stomped her foot and flapped her arms. *The bag. Everything. The money! This cannot be happening.*

Paralyzed by frustration, Lily couldn't fathom what to do next. The sun dropped below the skyline. Fear overcame shock. When full dark hit, the street would only present more danger.

She scuttled toward the Broadwell House, where she walked to the clerk's desk and pulled a purse from her skirt pocket.

"One night, please."

The clerk flicked her eyes up from a newspaper. "$3.00. No visitors." She returned her attention to her paper.

Lily dug the money from her purse. The remaining paltry bills and coins worsened the roiling in her stomach. She tucked the pouch back in her pocket and laid three gold coins in the woman's outstretched hand.

"Up the stairs, on the left." The clerk slid a key across the desk.

Relieved the woman hadn't indicated a guest log, Lily snagged the key and hurried to the second floor. She let herself in, slammed the door, and turned the lock.

Minimal furniture filled the modest, tidy room. She bypassed a table with an oil lamp and matches and fell onto the bed. Burying her face in the pillow, she sobbed.

I can't stay here. He'll find me here, I just know it. I have to make it to a more remote place. But what will I do when I get there? I can't start a store with no money. She pummeled the mattress. *It's not fair. All I want is freedom to do as I wish, independence with no one deciding where I can go or how I must live, the chance to be my own. Is that so much to ask?*

Dark settled, but she didn't drift off for hours.

* * * * *

Lily rose early and pulled aside the curtain. Several wagons traveled up and down the road, but few people moved along the sidewalks. The street appeared safe in the bright morning light. She let the cover fall back and groaned.

I'm so stupid! I was so worried about him *coming after me, I let my guard down. I'm in the Wild West now—what did I expect, a stroll in the park?*

Tears threatened again, but she squeezed them back and rubbed her puffy eyes.

No. No more crying. I got myself into this; I have to get myself out. I have to think. How much is left? Thank goodness I kept some in my pocket.

Digging in her skirt, she pulled out the purse and counted. $464.50. Her bag had contained another $700.00 and the few personal possessions she'd dared take when she slipped away. Gone.

That's not enough. Not nearly enough. I'll get to Clear Springs, I suppose, and then what? I have to buy land and build on it, or buy a building, and I need merchandise. What would Papa do? She closed her eyes tight to stave off a disturbing memory and focus on the dilemma. Her eyes popped open. *A loan! They must have a bank there. That'll get the store going.*

She wouldn't allow herself to think beyond that. After straightening her dress, she went downstairs and turned in her key. The desk clerk directed her to a place nearby, and she set out.

The station man informed her that the coach to Clear Springs had left the day before, and the next would leave in six days. Lily's heart sank.

"Oh dear." She stumbled away and collapsed onto a bench.

Six days. I can't wait that long. He might catch up. I have to get out of here before that. A horse and rider trotted past. *Of course. I'll have to ride. No, that's insane. But ... if he catches up with me ....*

She denied the nagging reservations—she hadn't ridden in years, never in the mountains, and never by herself—and asked for a map and directions to a livery.

* * * * *

Two horses occupied the pen, and both looked used up.

The livery operator, even harder used than his horses, eyed her with an arched brow. He wore chaps molded to his legs and a cowboy hat with holes. Tanned rifts covered his face and shifted in strange patterns as he talked.

"Where ya headed?"

"Cheyenne," she lied.

"Where's yer men folk?"

"I'll be making this trip alone."

"Missy, that's a long ride. Oughtta at least wait for a party goin' out."

Lily set her jaw. "I'll worry about that. How much for that one?" She pointed to the less-swaybacked roan.

"That's Charlie. Let you have him for $50.00. Can you even heft a saddle on yer own?"

Her lips pursed, and she walked to a rack loaded with saddles. Struggling, she lifted one over her head. "Satisfied?"

The horseman shrugged. "All right. But ain't no way you can make it all the way to Cheyenne on yer lonesome. Bandits roamin' all over now, even if the ride don't kill ya."

"Will you sell me the horse or not?"

He opened a packet from his vest and stuffed a plug of tobacco in his cheek. "I reckon."

"Do you have any mules?"

"For what?" His eyes narrowed.

She tossed him a withering look. "A pack mule, of course."

His gaze wandered. "Nope. No mules."

Lily followed his glance and walked to the corner of the building. Several mules munched hay at a paddock trough. She rounded on the man.

"Just what are those? Pigs?"

"Bad enough if I sell you the horse, but that'll only getcha in so much trouble. I ain't sendin' you out on the trail with *two* animals you can't handle."

"Then I'll have to find someone who wants to make money. Thank you and good day."

He stuck his leg out, blocking her attempt at a huffing exit. "Listen, missy. You don't look as if you been doin' much trail ridin'. I'll allow you *might* handle the horse on yer own, mostly 'cause he's too old and tired to do much but eat. But a jack's a different animal, and tryin' to lead one while you ride ain't easy, even for trail men with some miles under their belts. What do you need to pack, anyhow?"

Lily pressed her lips together to stop their trembling. She wanted to tell him to mind his business but lifted her chin. "Goods."

"Er ... you can buy goods in Cheyenne, reckon? It's a bonafide city these days. Stores and everything."

"Cheyenne isn't my final destination. Will you sell me a mule, or are you going to spend all day asking questions?" Her nails dug into her palms.

He looked her up and down. "I can't do it. Take my advice: don't try it."

She fumed but changed her tack and offered a sweet smile. "What if I take a hired man? Can I, please, have a mule then?"

"Do I look that brainless?"

"No, truly, I promise. You're right; I shouldn't do it on my own. I'll hire someone. Do you know where I can find a reliable hand?"

The cowboy considered her and wagged a finger. "I'll give ya the address. And I'll check up on it, too."

She paid him $95.00 for the horse, mule, and a saddle. As he saddled the horse, he looked at her skirt.

"You know how to ride a western?"

She didn't meet his gaze. "Of course."

When he finished, she led the animals away, with no intention of hiring anyone.

She hitched the stock in front of a large mercantile and shopped a while, her stomach dropping every time she checked a price. She bought a split skirt for riding—and blushed while buying and changing into it—a fresh chemise and set of drawers, a few personal items, food, a small revolver, and a pitifully small load of goods.

With the goods packed onto the mule, she departed near noon with $203.87.

CHAPTER TWO

Outfitted with the bare minimum, Lily headed toward the foothills. As the Rocky Mountains drew closer and grew taller, she eyed them with uncertainty. The depictions she'd seen couldn't do justice to the size. Sharp spines and rocky projections stood out in unfamiliar, stark contrast on peaks that rose from the plains as if the land had created a staircase to the heavens. When the sunset painted them purple and gold, they took her breath away, but the prospect of becoming lost sparked a new apprehension.

She pulled Charlie to a stop after ten miles and resisted the urge to make a fire, afraid of attracting anyone or anything. Instead, she spent the evening unsaddling the horse and unpacking the mule. After hobbling them and eating a cold dinner of salt pork and bread, she shivered through the night as her backside throbbed and her chafed thighs stung.

The next day, and the next, passed the same—miles of grass, sage, yucca, and scattered cottonwood and juniper—save for more soreness and more hills. She passed a few homesteads and gave them a wide berth. She savored the sense of independence, until the moon began its journey across the sky and made her wish for someone, anyone, to break the monotony.

On the third day, as Lily wound through a dry gulch and lost sight of the flat grassland for good, Lily bobbed in the saddle, close to dozing in the morning sun. A tug on the mule's lead snapped her back from the boredom. She reined the horse in and swiveled in her seat. The mule had stopped, feet planted on a sandy bank.

She twitched his lead and clicked her tongue. "Hup! Come on, Jack."

He stood resolute.

Hauling harder on the rope, she groaned. "Oh, you stupid mule. Get up!"

He'd plodded behind the horse for miles with no trouble, slow but compliant, and she'd dismissed the horseman's cautions.

With a sigh, she wrapped Charlie's reins around the horn and prepared to dismount. She hissed through her teeth as she lifted a leg over, muscles quivering with days of abuse.

The mule whirled with a burst of speed unthinkable minutes before. The lead tore through her grip and flapped behind him as he bolted back the way they'd come.

"No! Jack! Whoa!"

Lily flung herself off the horse and stumbled after the mule. After a few yards, she halted, torn. The horse craned to look back at her, unmoved. The mule slowed to a trot, and she jogged after him.

"Jack!"

At her shout, he sped up, the packs and bundles bouncing wildly. She lumbered through a hundred yards of shifting sand and dodged prickly pear cactus and animal burrows.

"Stop, you dumb lunk!"

Gasping for breath, Lily wavered. Any farther, she would lose sight of Charlie.

But … I can't lose that load. Lord, what do I do now?

The mule disappeared around a bend, and she slumped over, propping her hands on her knees. The livery operator's words echoed like rubbing salt on a wound. She shook her fist after the mule and trudged back to the horse.

I'm doomed. Why is everything going wrong? Tears wet her cheeks, and she whisked them away. *Oh, stop whining! Get yourself together.*

Upon reaching Charlie, she heaved into the saddle and tapped her heels on his sides until he turned back down the gully. She urged him to a trot—the fastest gait she could force out of him—and scanned the trail as the canyon opened onto a rocky watershed dotted with junipers.

The jack had disappeared.

Lily shook her head in disbelief. He couldn't have gone that far, and she couldn't fathom he'd leave the trail. He resisted pulling off even to camp.

"Come on, Charlie, we have to find him." She flicked the reins.

She followed the trail for miles, checking game paths and gully spurs, until sunset shadows grayed the landscape. On the hard-packed clay and gravel, hooves left few prints. She found no sign of the mule.

Every few minutes, she argued with herself whether to turn around or push on. They had crossed a creek a few hundred yards back, and she remembered the next water lay miles ahead. Gritting her teeth, she halted the horse and glared at the empty landscape. Stubborn hope finally gave way to despair and the encroaching darkness. She yanked a rein to the side. Charlie spun on his hooves and turned west.

Lily kept her gaze on the path ahead and refused to think about the mule.

I can't let it stop me. I have to keep going. Just keep going.

* * * * *

Days crawled by as they climbed through the foothills and into the tree-lined canyons. The terrain transformed, evergreens taking over the slopes and clay turning to granite and sandstone. Daily thunderstorms soaked the thin soil and brought early-spring wildflower sprouts. The air changed with elevation, cooler and somehow fresher. Lily took it all in, but worry stunted her appreciation.

She hadn't considered the many other dangers aside from her pursuer. She avoided the few other riders they came across. When people came up the trail, she slipped into the trees and hid until they passed. The roaming bandits wouldn't find an easier target than a woman alone, and she resolved not to let her guard down as she had in Denver.

The loss of the goods preyed on her, as well. She comforted herself realizing the mule's absence made the trek easier and faster. They moved on earlier in the morning and stopped later without the burden of packing and unpacking the jack's load.

The seventh late afternoon deepened the shadows as Charlie mucked through mud to ascend a canyon trail. A rocky slope rose on one side, a sharp drop on the other. A furious thunderstorm had passed with a deluge of rain and hailstones.

Lily shivered, wrung out what she could, and pulled her cloak tighter until the sun peeked through low clouds.

"We'll stop early tonight, Charlie. What do you think?"

Shrugging her wrap back, she turned her face to the warm rays. "Oh, that feels good. I'm sick of these storms." She pulled the map from her pocket and charted their progress. "Just a day or two more, if I read it right."

Anticipation made her jittery. She squeezed her legs against the roan to urge him faster. They passed a rock field and came to a small stream, a few feet of water birthed by the storm, rippling over rocks and washing out the trail. Charlie hesitated and pulled his head back.

"It's all right, boy. Hup!"

She flicked the reins and leaned forward.

With a surging, unexpected leap, he bounded over the water. They landed, and Charlie scrambled on the slick ground. Mud sprayed under his feet.

Lily wobbled in the saddle as her heart jumped into her throat. Her feet had slipped out of the stirrups, and she groped for the horn.

A sucking, slithering, grinding came behind them. The hillside slid in a sheet, dirt, plants, and stone jumbled together. The rumble grew louder with crashing rocks and boulders tumbling down the slope.

Charlie's muscles bunched again, and he vaulted ahead.

Lily bounced from the saddle, falling backward. The reins slid through her fingers. She tumbled head over heels and landed hard. A loud whoosh left her lungs, and her chest seized as if in a vise. She clawed at the fire burning her throat, desperate for breath. Dim stars danced before her eyes, but as consciousness began to fade, the pressure dissipated and allowed a shallow gasp of air.

She sat up and rasped a faint call, "Charlie!"

The rust-colored figure disappeared into the trees. Exhaustion and hopelessness drained her last ounce of strength, and she collapsed.

CHAPTER THREE

A rattle broke through Lily's misery. She tilted her head. Realization dawned, spawning a new prickle of fear and raising the hair on her neck.

She rose on her elbows until the trail appeared through the blur of tears. A patch of beige, camouflaged against the gray granite path, brought a scream to her lips, but her mouth went dry, and only a strangled whimper escaped.

Slow. Don't panic. Back away slow.

Reason harnessed her fear, allowing her to inch backward, until the coiled snake moved its head. Adrenaline pulses turned her belly liquid and spurred her to her hands and knees in a frantic crawl. Her feet caught her riding skirt, and the rending fabric imitated the rattle's hiss, sparking fresh panic. She dug into the mud. At last, her feet found purchase.

She dashed blindly up the track until her heart thundered in her ears and her legs gave out. Sobbing between wheezing breaths, she slumped to the ground, dazed and numb, surrounded by miles of silent, desolate forest. As her breath slowed, she sought her bearings.

Get up! Go find Charlie, or you'll be stuck out here.

"Oh, what's the use?" Her croaking voice fell flat in the still, cool air, emphasizing her isolation. She pushed herself up and started down the slope. "What in heaven's name was I thinking? I'm so dense! Traipsing across the country with a ridiculous plan, insisting on doing it my way. Papa was right—I *am* still an empty-headed child."

Lily winced. His image floated up in her mind and tugged at her heart, and for an instant, she missed him desperately. Her mouth set in a hard line when the thought followed its inevitable path to the last time she had seen him. She shook her head, sniffling, and rubbed her eyes.

"No." With effort, she strengthened her shaky voice. "I'll prove him wrong."

Scattered pines marched up the hill, congregating in a thick stand of forest leading to a ridge high above. An alien landscape, nothing like the Pennsylvania Alleghenies of home.

A few things had fallen off the horse, and she followed the debris, gathering pieces like fairy tale breadcrumbs.

If only they would lead me home ... but I don't have a home now.

Her old life held nothing for her. She couldn't turn back. The unknown that lay ahead had to offer something better than the misery she'd left behind. That life had ended weeks earlier, when she lay in a soft bed with her husband snoring beside her. The sour stench of alcohol had drifted over her as pain and anger brought hot tears to dampen her hair. In that moment, she had decided to leave.

She'd fled without a word. He would try to bring her back; he wasn't the sort to take such an affront lightly. She'd had to run as far as possible. He had too many connections in the East who might discover her whereabouts if she stayed near home. She needed speed and anonymity to elude him. The frontier—supposedly civilized but wide open and ready for settlers—seemed a superb place to disappear and shed her past, a place full of freedom and opportunity. With a satchel and a ticket under a new name, she'd boarded the train in Harrisburg and waited with bated breath until the train pulled out. At every stop, in every state, she expected an agent to pull her from the car. Denver had marked a triumph, but it wasn't far enough—or was it too far?

A breeze rustled the aspens, their leaves ticking as they twirled, and brought her back to the current despair. A finger of fear crept in, insisting she'd made a mistake in coming to Colorado.

Stranded in the woods, without a mount, food, or shelter. Perfect.

Lily passed an unsteady, gloved hand across her forehead, pushing aside wisps of hair and a wave of panic.

"I'll find Charlie. He'll come back. He has to."

As she neared the stream, she paused, standing well back and searching for the snake. It hadn't moved. Her bedroll had broken free of its saddle ties and lay feet from the viper. Anything else, she could let go, but the blanket might mean the difference between life and death under the crisp, cold spring night to come.

Her heart thumped. She dropped the retrieved items and picked up a good-sized rock. Air locked in her chest as she stole closer. The breeze evaporated, and the silence amplified the heavy thud in her ears.

Hiss. The rattler's tail twitched. Its tongue flicked out to taste her scent, her warmth.

The air in her lungs threatened to explode. Only the weight of the rock kept her hands from trembling. Almost close enough to strike—for either of them.

Lily shuffled forward a few inches. The snake's head pulled back. A watery moan leaked from her slack lips. She thrust the rock toward the snake and stumbled back like a marionette with clipped strings.

With a soft thump, and a great deal of luck, the granite chunk landed on the rattler's body, pinning its tail even as its head whipped toward her.

Lily fell hard, and her teeth clacked together.

The snake's scaly body writhed, coiling in knots as it tried to free itself.

Acid shock boiled over in her belly, and she retched into the grass. Quakes rolled through her, releasing the nervous tension. After several dry heaves, she wiped her chin.

The snake had quieted but still twitched in its trap.

Lily rose, eyes on the snake, and retrieved the bedroll. Fatigue doubled her vision, but she forced herself to collect the remaining debris and set off in search of the horse.

"Charlie!"

As the shadows grew longer and darker, she stumbled through the trees, cursing the snake, the horse, and the man who'd forced her to attempt this crazy flight. Charlie's hoof prints soon faded, but she pushed on.

Breathless, she crested a windblown ridge dotted with stunted pines. The trees lead down to a small meadow. Her shoulders slumped.

The horse stood at the edge of a creek eddy, quenching his thirst.

Every inch of her body ached and quivered as she plodded downhill. She reached the meadow and called softly to the horse with her approach, terrified of spooking him again. He lifted his head and nickered.

Lily sighed as she ran her hand down his neck and caught the reins dangling in the water. Relief flooded her until dizziness made her sway on her feet. She rested her forehead against the roan's smooth coat, overjoyed in finding him and avoiding a night alone in the Rockies.

She wrapped her arms around his neck. "Thank the Lord."

He lowered his head for another drink.

Lily pulled back. "Thrilled to see you, too, Charlie," she muttered. "Can we just get to Clear Springs without any more trouble? Seems travel to a boomtown ought to be a sight easier than this."

The sun slipped behind the mountain, and she set camp by the stream. For once, she built a good fire and didn't shiver all night. Despite the warmth, Lily slept little, instead replaying the near disaster and fending off a sense of foreboding. She expected to reach the town soon. Excitement fed her anticipation, but she feared the trip's bad luck—and her husband—would follow her there. She had to make a decision.

CHAPTER FOUR

After sunrise, Lily searched for the trail. When she stumbled upon it, she collapsed in the saddle, stress playing her nerves like an out-of-tune banjo. She argued with herself while Charlie stomped his feet to ward off a sluggish fly. She twisted in the saddle, first west, then east. They had come within a day or two of Clear Springs; it would take a week or more to get back to Denver.

What am I doing? I could have died. I'm risking my life for this and don't even know that I'll succeed in that town. But ... how can I go back?

"Clear Springs or Denver, Charlie?"

The horse bobbed his head, tugging the reins to reach a sprout of grass.

"What if I can't get a loan in Clear Springs? Or land? This place is a lot more remote than I thought. I just don't know. Denver .... I might find work, but he's more likely to find me there, isn't he? He'll know to come west, and Denver's the first place to look. Besides, I might not have enough food for another week, and the weather might not hold. A snowstorm could blow up any time. Oh, Charlie, what should I do?"

His ears flicked, but he went on nibbling.

As Lily considered the return trek through the canyons, she shuddered. She didn't want to endure the steep trails, unstable rocks, and sheer drop-offs again. Charlie had already started to go lame, and risking him was madness. Her goal lay so close ....

With a frustrated groan, she turned the horse westward and sank into the rocking rhythm of his gait. The hard ride had exhausted both of them and opened her eyes to the unforgiving wilderness of the Rocky Mountains she had daydreamed about since childhood. By her reckoning, they'd arrive in Clear Springs by evening. Exhaustion soon gave way to eagerness. She wanted to start her new life. Shaking off thoughts of the journey, she focused on the destination.

* * * * *

As Charlie trudged past the outlying structures of Clear Springs, Lily rehearsed the lies she had devised to go with her new name.

Lily Grace Wright, aged 21. I hail from Chicago. My parents died and left me and my brother orphaned. We intended to open a dry goods store, but he got tied up with business in Chicago, and I came ahead to get it off the ground.

The only kernel of truth lay in her desire to open a store. She hoped the story would forestall questions and garner sympathy.

Charlie stumbled, and she clutched the saddle's horn. She still found riding astride uncomfortable but had come to appreciate the western seat. Leaning forward, she steadied her breathing and patted the roan's neck.

"We'll be there soon, Charlie."

A thousand emotions assaulted her, a symphony at a crescendo, while the clamor of the bustling town grew. Riders and buggies clattered down the rutted roads, pedestrians dodging them. Horses neighed over the low rumble of wagon wheels, machines, and people. She averted her eyes from several women dressed in bright, revealing clothes, despite her curiosity. She'd seen prostitutes before, but the "soiled doves" of the gold rush town held a strange mystique.

The town's lone hotel occupied a narrow, two-story building, and she halted Charlie at the hitching rail. A young man—a boy, really—leaned near the double doors with his chin sagging on his chest.

Lily cleared her throat.

He glanced up with a bored look. His eyes grew large, and he gaped as if he had seen a ghost.

Her heart thumped, anxiety planting the impossible idea he somehow recognized her.

"S-sorry, ma'am." He scrambled off the porch, grabbed the reins, and offered her a hand while his face glowed red.

She told herself his reaction likely had more to do with her unconventional attire and saddle, and the reminder made her blush with him. Leaning on his hand, she slid from the saddle and suppressed an unladylike groan as she worked her stiff legs.

The boy hitched the horse with fumbling hands.

She pulled her purse from a saddle bag and passed him a heavy coin. "Please bring the packs in and stable him. He'll be hungry."

The boy avoided eye contact as the color in his cheeks deepened. "Yes, ma'am!" He pocketed the money and hurried to unload the animal's burdens.

Jittery and nauseous, Lily faced the doors, prepared to put her story to the test. She mounted the steps and entered.

In the cramped lobby, the tang of tobacco floated on stale air. A fireplace dominated one soot-blackened wall, and a steep staircase disappeared in the smoky haze. Huddled in front of the hearth, an older man in a threadbare suit read the weekly gazette.

A clerk surveyed her as he wheezed and puffed a pipe, arms propped on an enormous belly.

Here I go. Lily straightened and stepped to his counter with a bright smile.

"I need a room, please."

One eyebrow cocked, and he grunted. "Alone, miss?"

Her smile faltered while her queasiness grew. "Yes, a room for one, please."

"What brings you to Clear Springs? All by yerself?" He took a long draw on his pipe and narrowed his eyes, huffing billowing smoke.

Lily cleared her throat. "I intend to open a business."

He grunted again. His eyes glittered, and a sly smile grew around the pipe stem. "What kinda bizness?"

The grin confused her, but she returned the smile. "A dry goods."

Another grunt and a low chuckle. He shrugged, rippling his fleshy bulges.

What an unpleasant man! At once, she chided herself for the uncharitable thought and forced the smile wider.

"Sign the book." He jabbed at the guest log. "I'm Wilford Amos, proprietor. Jacob's gettin' yer bags?"

"Yes, he was quite helpful." Lily picked up the pen beside the book.

Amos coughed and muttered, "Ha! A lazy rip ...." He grabbed a key from behind the desk and dropped it in front of her.

She paused, the nib hovering over the paper. Her fingers trembled. She had started to write her real name. Her throat clicked as she swallowed and wrote *Lily Wright, Chicago.* Under the date column, she jotted *April 29.*

"What's yer pleasure, miss?"

"Pardon?"

He raised his voice and drawled, "How long?"

"Oh. I suppose two weeks should do for now."

"That'll be $30.00, then. You want yer meals 'ere?"

She blinked as her stomach dropped like a stone. "You must have mighty fine rooms. How much are meals then?"

Amos sneered. "The boardin' houses are full up, last I heard, but you could wait fer 'em to finish the new hotel down the road. Should be done in a couple weeks." He cackled. "Meals sempty-five cents a day."

"That will be fine." Her mouth tightened, and her chin jutted out in a confidence she no longer had. He made her feel like an awkward child. *Stop letting him rattle you! You're a lady, act like one.* She withdrew a roll of bills from her purse and counted out the money. "I'll need a bath brought up, please, *Mister* Amos."

He smirked. "That'll be a nickel. I'll send the boy up wit' the bags when he's done wit' the horse. Be awhile, I figger, slow's he is."

"Fine. Thank you."

She resolved to move from the hotel as soon as possible. Taking the key, she walked to the stairs.

His smoke-charred voice followed, "Firs' door to the right."

Lily climbed the stairs and opened the door to Room 2.

Faded, yellowed paper lined the walls with blue flowers no longer blue. A worn coverlet draped a sagging bed beside a chest with a cloudy mirror and a cracked washbasin. A dented chamber pot occupied one corner, and a ratty chair filled the other. Over the single window facing the street, stained curtains hung limp, filtering the dying afternoon light.

She grumbled, "Mighty fine, all right. I hope it doesn't take long to get the store going." Rubbing her neck, she sank into the chair and pulled aside the curtain.

The sun hovered over the mountain and shadows encroached on the town. The limited view left an impression of a fallowed garden overcome by a riot of spring growth, with new construction and temporary shelters sprouting in every direction. A few two-story buildings loomed over single-story false fronts: a stately new bank, Harlan's Hardware, a stationer, and several saloons coming to life at the end of the day. Houses crowded secondary streets, and shacks and canvas tents clustered at the edges. Pine forest and aspen groves skirted the surrounding slopes and gave way to a carpet of grass on the valley floor.

She had pored over newspapers and books filled with fanciful imagery of the West for years. Clear Springs matched the descriptions on the surface, but it didn't fit the picture in her mind. While the landscape awed her, it had a harsh, dangerous beauty. On brief acquaintance, the town felt drearier, more oppressive, than she expected. She hoped the long day and her mood only made it seem so.

This is what you always wanted: the mountains, the frontier ... the adventure. Now you've got it.

Footsteps clattered on the stairs. At a knock, she cracked the door to find Jacob catching his breath, and he hauled her things in and set them down.

"I'll be gettin' the water fer yer wash." His face colored. "It'll take a bit to warm."

"That's fine. When is supper served?"

"That'll be a spell yet, ma'am." He shuffled his feet and fidgeted with the door handle. "Cook's down with grippe, so the maid's to rustle it up."

"Oh. I see. Thank you, then."

The boy retreated, and Lily unpacked. She hung a spare petticoat and bodice over the chair and arranged her personal items on the dresser. After looking for a place to hide her purse, she settled for stuffing it under the pillow and collapsed on the bed to wait. *Why did I have to ask for a bath?* She wanted sleep more than anything.

She jerked upright at another knock on the door, realizing she'd dozed off.

Jacob's voice came from the hall, "Water's ready, ma'am. Maggie says you have jus' nuff time afore supper."

"Thank you, Jacob." She didn't think she could rouse the energy and almost called him back to tell him to forget supper, but a rumble from her stomach kept her quiet.

Lily forced herself up, gathered her things, and shuffled down the hall. After locking the door, she undressed and brushed at the filth on her riding skirt and blouse. She loosened her corset and breathed deep, savoring the liberation, and laid the clothes over a stool beside a tiny claw foot bathtub. A pang of longing overcame her. She missed the luxuries in her parents' home: a comfortable bed, the elaborate bath, and her closet full of clean clothes. She dipped her finger in the tub and grimaced at the lukewarm water.

"Better than nothing." She sighed. "I suppose I'm lucky it's not just a tin tub."

With a shiver, she folded herself into the small bath and leaned back, closing her eyes as the tension drained from her battered body and her mind drifted.

CHAPTER FIVE

The caskets lay side by side. Charlotte stood in the parlor doorway, a doll dangling from one hand. She had tried to make herself enter, but her feet wouldn't move. The black crepe over the windows rippled like ghostly shadows. A glimpse of pallid skin peeked from each coffin.

What if they wake? Maggie, their cook, said people sometimes came back to life to claw their way out of their caskets.

Charlotte wanted to touch them, to check for life, but a vague fear stopped her. She stayed rooted, cold bare toes on the threshold, eyes fixed on the open boxes, waiting for the children to move.

If only Mother would come down. Then I could go in.

Charlotte had tried to rouse her mother, but her parents' door remained locked, and no one answered. Only weak cries had come from the room in the two days since Peter and Cecilia died.

Mother had fallen sick, too, but the cholera kept her bedridden for just a day. She'd devoted the next two days to nursing Peter and Cecilia—Charlotte had felt fine. In her delirium, Mother blamed herself for taking the children to the fair, but Charlotte had been the one who pestered until she agreed.

If I hadn't, Peter and Sissy wouldn't be in caskets. Once a middle child, now an only.

After they died, Mother locked her door, and Charlotte hadn't seen her since. Maggie had arranged the wake and the coming funeral but went home sick—was it only the day before?—after assuring Charlotte that Papa would return home from his business trip any time. Charlotte waited all night, but Papa hadn't come.

Something moved in Peter's coffin. Charlotte's eyes widened, and she squeezed Dolly's arm. A fly drifted from the casket and landed again. She relaxed and released her breath. And waited.

The back door banged open. Charlotte didn't move—she couldn't. Her limbs had turned to stone.

"Eliza!" Papa's voice rang in the silence. "Maggie?" Footsteps clattered on the wood floor until he reached the hall rug. "Charlotte! Where's your mother? Why are the drapes ...?"

His hand fell on her shoulder.

She tried to speak, but her cracked lips only trembled.

A sick moan came from him, and he pushed past her into the room with the caskets and flies. He bent over the bodies and groaned.

"No, no, no," he chanted. "Peter ... Sissy ... not both ...."

Tears stung Charlotte's eyes.

Papa whirled on her. "Where is your mother?" More a roar than a question.

Her body shook. *Why is he angry with me?*

He ran past her and thundered up the stairs. Banging on a door. "Eliza ... Eliza!" More heavy footsteps, and he jerked

Charlotte by the arm. "Is your mother sick? Where is Maggie? Or Cooper?" He bent, eyes wild, and shook her until her teeth chattered. "Charlotte, answer me!"

Sound came from her mouth, but no words.

Shoving her aside, he raced upstairs. Yelling and rattling the door as Charlotte collapsed in the parlor doorway.

"Papa?"

The hall remained quiet. She fell asleep crying, clutching Dolly close.

* * * * *

On the forty-first day after Peter and Cecilia died, Mother announced the end of her self-imposed isolation. She came downstairs in a high-collared black dress devoid of frills and told the household she would strip the home of sinful excess. Her husband's jaw tightened, and he turned on his heel without a word.

Later, Mother exited Charlotte's closet with an armful of dresses.

Charlotte gasped. "Mother, no! Not my favorite. Please!"

She trailed her mother, fingers grasping at bright satin and velvet.

"Our pride and greed must be purged, Charlotte. The bible says, 'Everyone who is arrogant in heart is an abomination to the Lord; be assured, he will not go unpunished.'"

"Mama, I don't *care* what the bible says!"

Mother threw the clothes down and whirled on her, a hand flashing out against Charlotte's cheek. "Blasphemer! Just as I thought. You've already been tainted, ruined by our sins." Her eyes narrowed, accusing. "That's why God didn't take you."

Charlotte froze. Her mother had never struck her. She wanted to go to Papa and beg his help, but he'd left, off at the store again, and he had changed, too.

Weeks before, angry voices had come from her parents' bedroom.

Papa had yelled, "I won't be lectured in my own house!"

Her mother had screeched in reply, "Then get out!"

They rarely spoke to each other after that, and only between clenched jaws, and Charlotte had seen him just a few times since the funeral.

Mother snatched up the dresses and carried them downstairs to add them to the bonfire of sinful excess behind the house.

* * * * *

Charlotte knelt before her mother. "Mother, please can't I go? Betsy promised there wouldn't be any dancing," she lied.

The begging galled Charlotte. At eighteen, she had the right to go where she pleased, but her mother's penance for the deaths of her brother and sister a decade before had turned the house into a drab prison.

"Absolutely not. That sort of debauchery is wholly improper." Her mother's lips pursed as she tucked a needle in and out of a cloth held close to her face. With a cluck, she continued, "A coming out party .... It's unseemly—flaunting herself in front of everyone in those immodest dresses that are so popular. Her father should find her a husband discreetly. Remember First Timothy: 'Women should adorn themselves in respectable apparel, with modesty and self-control, not with braided hair and gold or pearls or costly attire, but with what is proper for women who profess godliness—with good works.'"

"Betsy does more good works than any girl I know." Charlotte sighed and sat back on her heels, plucking at her modest brown "respectable apparel" with loathing. Once her mother invoked verse, any plea would fall on deaf ears. She added, under her breath, "*She* can leave the house."

Mother remained intent on her needlepoint, and Charlotte stomped from the parlor.

She would miss the biggest social event in town. *How humiliating! No one will invite me to anything again.* She groaned and threw herself on her bed. *She ruins everything! How will I ever escape this tomb if I can't even go to a party?* She'd looked forward to the fete in hopes of attracting a beau. Lately, she could think of little else. Marriage, running her own house, inviting friends to dinner, making calls. Yet, she'd never find a husband and have her own life if no men knew she existed.

I'll find a way out. She can't keep me here forever.

* * * * *

Charlotte sat in the parlor reading the gazette. A whole column devoted to Betsy's party. "Saturday evening, the town's young people attended a spectacular affair to celebrate Miss Roberts' coming of age. Adorned in their finery, the lady of the hour and her entourage enjoyed refreshments, music, and dancing into the wee hours ...."

"It's so *unfair!*" She threw the paper aside.

The door banged open, and the groom shuffled in with a bucket of coal. Charlotte scowled at the interruption.

"Pardon, miss, I dinna know ye were in here. Want I should come back?"

She waved a hand toward the stove and snatched up her sewing.

He shuffled to the coal box and knelt to stoke the fire. Her father had hired him a week before, but she'd only spoken to the young man once. Handsome in a coarse way, with big shoulders, thick black curls, and muscles rippling under his shirt. Warmth sparked in her belly.

He turned as if he sensed her eyes on him. "How are ye today, Miss Charlotte?"

She swallowed, fumbling with her needlework. "Fine, Duncan, thank you. Are you well?"

"Aye, I be grand. 'Tis a fine day to run deliveries." He dumped the rest of the coal and stood, flashing a bold smile. "And even finer for bein' in a lovely lady's company."

Her stomach fluttered. The forward comment demanded a rebuke, but the magnetism in his eyes stifled her. When he moved toward the door, an impulse struck, and she jumped up.

"Deliveries today?" She made a pretty pout. "I hoped you could bring some things up from the cellar. Papa invited the Smiths and Moores for supper."

"To be sure, I have time if ye need help."

Duncan moved closer, at the edge of a respectable distance. His masculine scent, redolent of horses and leather, enveloped her. She inhaled, savoring it, and heat baked her face. Had he noticed?

She stammered, "Oh, g-good. I'll go down with you and show you what we need."

Charlotte had no excuse to go with him, but the words had come before she could stop them. She couldn't explain her improper behavior, but she wanted more time with him.

"I'd be glad for it."

"Let us get to it then." She waved a shaky hand at the door.

They approached the cellar door, and Duncan stopped to light a lamp. He held out his hand and steadied her as they descended. His skin seared her palm—or did the heat come from her? She couldn't tell.

At the bottom of the stairs, he stooped under the low ceiling and retreated to allow her in. The casks and shelves left little room to maneuver, and they stood inches apart.

Charlotte cleared her throat. "Well, then. Let me see." Her mind went blank, overwhelmed by a giddy lightheadedness. Words tumbled out, "We will need some of the sweet potatoes, a ham, green beans, honey, the canned cherries, likely some lard, as I think we are almost out in the kitchen ...." Warm puffs of breath tickled her ear. She pored over the shelves, not daring to look at him. "Eggs! But those are upstairs, of course. Some jelly—apple, I should think ...."

Her pulse thumped in her ears. The seconds dragged out. She couldn't think clearly. She waited—why didn't he say something? When she couldn't bear the tension any longer, her face turned toward his. His steady gaze mesmerized her. She couldn't move or breathe.

Duncan lifted a hand, his fingers nudging her chin up. Her lips parted. He paused, his mouth hovering over hers.

She had to stop him, berate him for taking liberties, but she couldn't. She wanted a kiss more than anything. When his lips grazed hers, his fingers holding her chin steady, excitement spread through her.

Have I fallen in love already? Nothing else could feel this good, could it?

His tongue flicked along her lips and dipped between them. He tipped her chin down, teasing her mouth open. Their tongues entwined, and the contact shot a bolt of pleasure and excitement to her core. Her knees weakened, and he slipped an arm around her and pulled her close. As the intensity peaked and Charlotte feared she would faint, he broke the kiss. She opened her eyes to his dazzling smile.

"Aye, a fine day, lass."

Her nervous titter made her feel silly. "Yes ... I ...."

He touched a finger to her lips.

"I must see ye again, soon. I've thought of nothin' else since I met ye. Tell me ye'll meet me. Tonight." He smirked and shook his head. "Look at me, beggin' a girl for but a few minutes. But I canna help it. I believe ye've enchanted me."

Her stomach flipped.

How can I tell him no? Nothing so exciting had ever happened in her life. Her parents would be furious—but they didn't have to know. *No one can deny love's unstoppable force, all the poets say so. I can't help who I love, can I?*

She nodded, unable to speak.

Duncan grinned. "Grand! I couldna bear it if ye denied me." He kissed her again, a light touch that left an ache deep inside her. "Meet me in the stable at ten o'clock. Make sure ye don't get caught. Go on up now, before anyone comes. I'll get the things ye need for supper."

He released her, nudging her toward the stairs, and turned to the shelves.

Charlotte moved up the steps in a daze. She peeked out onto the empty hall with a shaky sigh of relief, raced to her room, and fell onto the bed, laughing. Her skin tingled, and her pulse thrummed. Something inside had reached its boiling point, like a volcano ready to erupt. Her sensible side insisted she shouldn't go, couldn't go.

But that kiss, his touch. I want more.

Rational thought vanished. She *would* go. What could a little kiss hurt, after all?

CHAPTER SIX

A knock startled Lily awake. She shook her head, disoriented and cold. The bath, the hotel, Clear Springs. How long had she sat in the chilled water?

"Y-Yes, I'll be out in a moment," she stammered.

Shivering, she climbed from the tub, dried with a thin, dingy towel, and pulled on clean drawers. She let out her breath to tighten her corset. Frowning, she tried to smooth her wrinkled, old skirt, but it was hopeless.

Oh well. I doubt the supper crowd here includes dignitaries, and I can't wear the riding skirt.

After pinning her hair in place, she slipped into the hall. She dropped off her soiled clothes and found the cramped dining room.

The lodgers quieted when she entered. Six men stared.

"Please excuse my tardiness," she murmured. She felt like a child again as she moved to an empty chair.

A young man to the left gaped, wide-eyed. Lily cleared her throat and smiled. He shook himself and fumbled out the chair.

"Pardon, ma'am. We just ain't used to feminine

company."

The rest of the men rose and followed with a chorus of "Welcome, Miss" and "How do you do?"

Lily nodded. "Thank you, I'm well."

The men fiddled with their silverware and shifted in their seats.

"I'm Lily Wright, from Chicago." The lie came easier each time. "And you gentlemen?"

The older man she'd seen reading in the lobby smiled from the end of the table. "Henry Warren, an attorney from Virginia. Pleased to make your acquaintance, Miss Wright."

The men proceeded with names as the maid and Jacob brought dishes piled with steaming food. The fare passed around the table, and everyone turned to Lily. She suppressed a laugh, doubting they would bother with grace outside of "feminine company," and bowed her head to offer a short prayer. Little talk interrupted the meal. The men made an attempt to mind their manners, but it was clear most didn't have much to start.

As they finished, the atmosphere relaxed. The men talked about a supposed gold strike in a nearby camp. When conversation lagged, a man across from Lily spoke up.

"Don't aim to pry, Miss Wright, but what brought you all the way to Clear Springs? Long trip from Chicago." He wore a suit and a dour expression. Mr. Lawson? She couldn't recall.

"My brother will be starting a business here, and I came to assist him."

"And what kind of business is that? I haven't heard of any Wrights in town."

Lily bristled. "My brother hasn't arrived just yet. We'll have a dry goods."

Lawson's interest piqued. "Where's his land?"

"Oh ... we haven't bought it yet." Her heart pounded. She hadn't prepared for such questions.

Lawson snorted. "Pardon, Miss Wright, but I sure hope your brother has a load of money then. Prices are high, and going higher every day."

Another man broke in, "I hear tell it's up to $500 for poor lots."

One retorted, "That was last week!" The men guffawed.

The room whirled as her stomach heaved. *That can't be true!* She couldn't afford a plot at that price, loan or no. The men's laughter quieted, and she forced a tight smile.

"I am sure my brother can buy what we need."

"Well, I wish you and yours good luck, miss." Lawson's pointed look told her he didn't expect her to have any. "This is a hard place for them that are used to it ... and harder for them that aren't fit for it."

"I appreciate the well wishes," Lily murmured. "I'll excuse myself now, gentlemen. I am quite tired."

The man who had seated her jumped to pull out her chair, and they all bid her a good night. Upstairs, she unlocked her door and dropped into the chair, trembling as tears stung her eyes.

They have it wrong. Land can't cost that much. How will I get a loan for that much?

Exhausted, she undressed and slid between the sheets of the hard bed. She would go to the bank and land office in the morning. They would help her. They must. She had come so far, she couldn't fail.

* * * * *

Lily rose early and stretched, still sore from her days of riding. *At the least, I won't be on a horse today.* She dressed to look as respectable as possible, brushing the wrinkles from her dress, and tried to salvage her bonnet. They still looked like she'd dragged them across the prairie, but she had nothing else.

Outside, she shivered. Clouds loomed over the mountains, threatening a late shot of winter. She strolled down the plank sidewalk and turned away from the stares that followed her. Anyone new—especially a woman—would draw attention in a small mining town, she assumed. No soiled doves or dancing girls wandered the sidewalks at that early hour, and she felt conspicuous. She pushed on, lifting her skirts to avoid the mud as she crossed the street.

Few lamps dotted the real estate office, and she hesitated while her eyes adjusted to the dim room. A low divider separated the large, chilly office into sections. Two desks occupied one side, with two agents addressing paperwork with applicants. Benches filled with men sat in rows on the other side. In the closed space, bodies and wool and tobacco overwhelmed, and she held a kerchief to her nose.

A man who clearly hadn't washed in weeks offered her his seat.

She took it, forced a polite smile, and prepared to wait.

* * * * *

Hours later, a clerk called her up. He glanced at her from behind stacks of paper and ink bottles. Racks of deeds hung behind him, waiting for ink to dry.

"Yes, miss?"

"Good morning. I need to purchase a town lot."

"What size lot?"

"I'm not entirely sure. For a small store."

"We have lots of twenty-five by one hundred for $300.00."

Lily went numb. "But ... that's outrageous. Nothing cheaper?"

"Sorry, miss, that's the smallest lot in town." His face remained blank, his voice bored and detached.

She closed her eyes and breathed deep to regain her composure. "What about a loan?"

"Clear Springs has two banks. I can't say whether they will loan to you or not." At her heavy sigh, he softened. "Miss, it won't hurt to ask, but if they don't offer you a loan, don't seek out others who will. Clear Springs is full of scoundrels these days. You might find a position in town for a wage. Once you've gathered your funds, then we can help you."

Lily worked to hide her trembling chin and rushed out. She stalked up the street to an imposing brick building. The lobby bustled with activity, and she started toward a desk near the back. A handsome man with a big smile came around to shake her hand.

"Francis Warburton, at your service. How do you do, Miss ...?"

"Wright, Lily Wright. Fine, thank you."

He held her hand a bit too long as his eyes swept over her. Upon releasing his grip, he gestured to a chair. "Well, please have a seat, Miss Wright."

Lily perched on the seat while her fingers plucked at her skirt.

Warburton sat behind the desk and leaned forward. "What can I do for you today, Miss Wright?"

"I'm seeking financing for a new business."

"Splendid! There's no better place. What kind of business?"

"A dry goods."

"I see. I assume you have collateral or a letter of credit and reference from your bank?" Warburton's kind tone contrasted the seriousness on his face.

Oh dear. She scrambled for an excuse.

"Not at this time, no. I believe my brother will be bringing a letter when he arrives. I'd hoped to get started sooner. Time is of the essence during a rush, as I'm sure you can understand." She pasted on her most charming smile.

"I see. What kind of financing do you need?"

Lily wished she'd looked at the prices of wholesale goods and shipping. She guessed, added it to the land price, and blurted out a number. "$1000.00 will be sufficient." She held her breath.

Warburton raised an eyebrow. "That is quite a sum, with no letter or collateral." He paused, eyes running over her again, before smiling. "Perhaps I can speak with the bank manager."

"Please, Mr. Warburton, it's very important. My life—I mean to say, our business depends on this."

His lips pursed. "I'll see what I can do, Miss Wright. Please wait here." A grimace twisted his face when he returned. "Miss Wright, I spoke with the manager and, unfortunately, we cannot offer financing at this time. Perhaps once your brother arrives, we can revisit the matter."

Lily suppressed the urge to plead further. "I, I understand, Mr. Warburton. I appreciate your time."

Her nerves hummed with tension as she exited the bank. *One more chance. One last chance.* Her mind raced for alternatives in case the other banker denied her, while she told herself he wouldn't.

She picked up her skirts and barged into the street. A horse barreled toward her. Lost in thought, she pressed ahead into the animal's path. A shout from behind shattered her daze, and she stopped. A pair of hands hit her back, shoving her forward. The horse thundered past as she hit the muddy ground. She lay stunned when a pair of boots stepped in front of her.

A man held out his hand. His clothing differed from the miners she'd seen; he wore a dark blue shirt, heavy jeans, and boots with spurs. Sandy-colored hair curled beneath a wide-brimmed cowboy hat instead of the standard bowler.

Lily took his hand, and he pulled her up. Wincing as she put weight on her leg, she found her skirt mud-caked and torn. Tears spilled while she brushed off the mud and picked at the ripped fabric. *What else will go wrong?*

He tugged her to the boardwalk, on the porch of a small restaurant. He led her inside, sat her at a table, and dragged a chair up in front of her. She couldn't stop crying.

A deep southern drawl rumbled from him, "Ma'am? Are ya hurt?"

He must think I'm a perfect ninny, crying over spilt milk. She sniffled and shook her head.

In the café, without the sun glaring in her eyes, she had a chance to appraise him. His face would have been too delicate, if not for sharp angles and sunburned wrinkles that gave him a severe expression. His blue eyes bored into her, exposing her, until he smiled and offered her a handkerchief. The smile erased the stern cast and crinkled his eyes. Her heart stuttered.

"Then ya might as well dry them tears. Ain't no sense cryin' over a dress."

"No, it's not the dress. It's just … a difficult day." She wiped her nose and dabbed at the tears.

"It almost got a sight more difficult. New here in town?"

"I just arrived yesterday."

"Have to learn to watch where yer walkin'. It can get a bit rowdy."

Lily smirked. "I can see that." She remembered the bank. "Thank you very much for your help, but I really must be going."

Disappointment flickered before he offered a hopeful smile. "I can't persuade ya to stay with an offer of supper, then?"

"I'm sorry, no. It's very important."

"Will ya at least tell me yer name?" The rumble of his voice made her melt.

"Oh. Yes. Um, Lily Wright."

"Luke Jackson. Mighty pleased to meet ya, Miss Wright."

She stood, and Luke held out his hand again. Like an awkward schoolgirl, she hesitated, lost in his eyes. She blinked to break the connection and shook his hand, reminding herself the bank would soon close.

"I guess I'll just have to hope I see ya around town." He grinned.

"Perhaps, Mr. Jackson. Good day."

Lily limped to the door, and he ducked around her to open it. On the sidewalk, she made a point of looking for traffic, but as she started across, she swiveled her head back to him. Still standing in the doorway, he chuckled and motioned for her to watch the road. She jerked her gaze away and hurried to the other side. Embarrassment almost made her hope she wouldn't see him again. Almost.

She found the Western Miners Bank and walked to the back of the deserted, drab lobby, frowning at a dozing teller. After knocking on both rear doors with no answer, she sighed and sat back to wait.

CHAPTER SEVEN

Breathless, Charlotte entered the barn.

"Ah lass, I'm glad ye came." Duncan grinned. "Ye've made me quite daffy, I'm afraid."

Charlotte giggled. "I couldn't disappoint you."

He took her hand, grabbed a lantern, and pulled her to the loft ladder. She balked and withdrew her hand.

How far does he intend this to go? I'm not ready for ... that. But if I say no ....

"Just in case they look for ye. They wouldna look up there." He shrugged.

"Oh. Clever!" She smiled, but the doubts remained.

She climbed, feeling for each rung with her feet, with his hand steadying at her waist. The contact jolted her like lightning. He drew her to a pile of bedding, and she sank onto the blankets, curled her legs under, and arranged her skirts. Duncan dropped beside her and leaned against the wall, stretching out his legs.

"'Tis a lovely night, made even more so by a lovely lass."

Charlotte smirked and tapped his arm. "I think you aim to flatter the lass!"

"True, I do." He grinned. "But I do mean every word. Ye are the most lovely lass."

He ran the back of his hand down her jawline.

A shiver coursed through her as she lowered her head. "Thank you. I hope you don't think me terribly juvenile. I've never ... done something like this."

"Nay, I'm flattered. Truly, I thank ye for comin' out in the cold. Ye must think me a terrible scoundrel ...."

"Hmph! I think no such thing. It is cold out tonight, though," she chided.

Duncan pulled her to his side, slipping an arm around her shoulders. "Sure, and I'll just be havin' to keep ye warm then."

Her heart skipped a beat and galloped ahead. The warmth of his arm brought goosebumps.

Duncan leaned in and brushed his lips on her forehead. Moving lower, a light kiss on each cheek. Her eyes closed when he pressed against her pursed lips.

A dart of fear surfaced. *I'm alone in the dark with a man.*

As he caressed her shoulder, the anxiety faded. A bit of pleasure wasn't the end of the world. She relaxed against him, surrendering.

He ran his tongue along her bottom lip. She gasped. When her mouth opened, he dipped his tongue in, exploring, darting around hers. His hand slid from her shoulder to cup the back of her head, and he deepened the kiss. The intensity surged until Charlotte pulled back to catch her breath. Duncan ducked his head and nibbled her exposed neck.

Passion overwhelmed her, and her heart hammered. The soft kisses on her neck stopped, and she opened heavy lids, his eyes locking onto hers. His breath quickened while his fingers tugged at the clasp of her cloak. He slid the cover off her shoulders and traced her prim neckline, tickling the skin. Her breath caught as his hand glided over the swell of her breast, down to her waist. He rested his hand on her hip and smiled.

He whispered, "So beautiful. I dinna think I can control meself."

"Don't, Duncan. I want you." She cast off her earlier assertion.

His eyes widened with a dubious look. "Lass, do ye even know what lovemaking means? I dinna think yer ready for that."

"N-no, I don't know, not really." Defiance sparked at his condescension. "But I'm an adult, a grown woman, and I want to know."

Duncan shook his head. "Charlotte, sweet, that should be reserved for a husband. I canna take something I canna give back."

"But, I thought .... Don't you want me?"

He took her hands in his. "I dinna mean that at all. I dinna deserve such a fine lass. I have great ambition, and I aim for a wife like you, with a fine family to help us settle down." His lips tightened, and his eyes darkened. "But that's just a dream. No one gives a lad like me a chance. They treat us like the slop in the street. Without a good marriage, we dinna have no hope. Yer parents are nice folk, they treat me good, but I'm not what they want for their lass. I'd love to be yer husband, sweet, but ...."

He spoke the truth. Her parents would never allow it. *Nonsense! I'm eighteen now. They can't stop me. I'm in love, that's what matters.* The more she thought of it, the more she determined to do as she wished.

"I'll convince them! You're an honorable, hard-working man. They'll see."

"And if ye fail, lass? Then yer spoiled for another man, and I'm to blame."

"No! If they don't agree ... I'll run away with you." The words thrilled and terrified her.

Duncan's eyes opened wide, questioning, hopeful.

Charlotte nodded, a smile spreading on her face.

He grasped her shoulders and pressed his mouth hard against hers. She responded, opening and inviting him in. His tongue captured hers as his hand cupped her breast.

A whimper escaped her at the unfamiliar throbbing centered in that most private spot. Charlotte trembled with desire and fear of the unknown, her senses overpowering her until she could think of nothing but the building need for ... something.

He broke the kiss, and she opened her eyes.

"I feel so strange, Duncan." Her voice quavered.

"'Tis normal, lass. Ye must trust me."

His fingers found the buttons of her blouse and deftly unfastened them. Before she realized it, he'd tugged the chemise off. His gaze commanded hers while he loosed her corset. She stiffened as he slipped fabric off her shoulders, the chill air contracting her nipples.

He whispered, "Perfect."

Cupping her breasts, he rubbed his thumbs over the peaked tips. Charlotte gasped and shuddered. Duncan smiled and leaned in to take her lips again. He left a trail of kisses along her neck, down between her breasts, before pushing her back. She swallowed.

What comes next?

He reclined beside her and lowered his head, pulling a nipple into his mouth, suckling it, sending sharp needles of excitement through her. He switched to caress the other with his tongue. Capturing it between his teeth, he gently tugged, lowered his mouth and sucked harder. His fingers played with the other point.

Charlotte's breath came faster. An unbearable ache grew in her chest, her belly, her sex. His wet mouth pulled darts of pleasure through her breasts, but a torturous fire followed in her core. It filled her with a painful craving—but for what? She didn't know, couldn't imagine, what would quench it. She writhed under the assault, fearing she would go insane.

He pulled her skirt and petticoat up, bunching them about her waist, and she didn't care. His hand scorched her thigh and inched higher. It found her mound and snaked through the opening in her drawers, between her thighs, inside, tickling the soft down. He pushed a finger down, between the folds. Charlotte cried out and tensed, a strange, new sensation startling her. She squeezed her legs together, but his finger moved in a tantalizing circle. He lifted his head until his face hovered above hers.

"Hush, lass. 'Tis all right."

His mouth covered hers with a light touch, and she kissed him back. She calmed under his lips. His finger stroked the sensitive point on her mound.

As her apprehension diminished, Charlotte focused on the growing pleasure, but a throbbing torment tempered it. Emptiness, a profound hunger, she couldn't believe it would ever find satisfaction. He massaged the little bump, and she seemed to float. Her body twitched, an overwhelming spasm. She screamed against his mouth as every muscle contracted.

Charlotte lay still, eyes closed, breath coming in quick gasps. Duncan groaned, nudged her legs apart, and kneeled between them. She felt lightheaded, her limbs heavy.

"Charlotte."

She turned her head and opened her eyes as he hovered above. Hot, firm flesh touched her core.

"Now ye belong to me, Charlotte."

He pushed into her, breaking through her barrier. Charlotte uttered a sharp cry and jerked. After a moment, she stopped struggling, but her whole body trembled. When she opened her eyes, Duncan loomed over her. His gaze penetrated the fog in her mind.

He bent to kiss her, licking her lips until they opened for him, and began to move within her, and the sensation changed. Fullness replaced pain. Heat rose within her once more. His movement brought more desire. Her hips tipped up to meet him, a movement of their own. The aching need returned, and she moved faster to satisfy it.

Her body quaked. He buried himself within her one last time and erupted. Charlotte cried out, and his deep voice joined hers. Collapsing upon her, he shuddered as both gasped for air.

Tears rolled off her cheeks, dampening the hair at the sides of her face, as emotion overwhelmed her.

"What's wrong, Charlotte?"

"Nothing." She smiled, dazed but content.

CHAPTER EIGHT

A door slammed, and Lily's head snapped up.

A voice boomed, "By God, those bastards in the capitol are gonna ruin me!"

Lily blinked. The light had faded, and rain pattered outside. The teller had disappeared. A man stood near the bank's front door in a rumpled, old-fashioned suit and several days' growth of beard. He shook water from his jacket and hung it on a rack. He muttered a curse, jerked his hat off, and plunked it beside the jacket. The man turned, still grumbling under his breath, and walked toward the doors near Lily. When she cleared her throat, he stopped.

"Oh. Evenin', ma'am." He coughed and mumbled, "Sorry, I didn't know anybody was here."

Lily stood and forced a smile. "Quite all right, sir. Are you the manager?"

"Yes, ma'am, manager and owner. Silas Barnes, at your service." He stuck a grimy, moist hand out.

She shook it and wiped her hand on her skirt, disguising a grimace with a cough. Sour whiskey floated between them.

"Yes, well ... I'm in need of financial services."

As she spoke, his eyes wandered over her and settled on her chest.

"Uh—yes, yes." He wrenched his eyes back to her face. "C'mon in my office here, and we'll discuss it."

The dark, cramped room held a small desk with papers scattered on every surface and two rickety chairs.

He fumbled with a lantern. "Have a seat, ma'am."

A crack of thunder rattled the building. The ceiling dripped with a steady, quick leak, forming a puddle on the floor. She settled gingerly on the seat.

He plunked into the chair behind the desk, shuffled papers, and gave her a wide smile.

"And your name, ma'am?"

"Lily Wright."

"How can I help you, Miss Wright?"

"I'm looking to start a business."

"Uh huh. What kinda business?" He plucked a match from the box by the lantern and used it to pick his teeth.

"A dry goods store. Clear Springs is growing fast and will need more stores."

"Yeah, likely." He studied the match end, tossed it on the desk, and gave her a dubious look. "So, you're gonna open up this store on your own?"

"Well, no." She pulled her shoulders back. "My brother will be joining me soon."

"Uh huh. What are you puttin' up?"

"Pardon?"

"You got somethin' to guarantee the loan? Or a credit letter, at least?"

Lily sighed. "No, Mr. Barnes."

He scratched at the scruff on his chin. "How much you need?"

"I believe a thousand will get it started." She continued, before he could cut her off, "I understand it's a lot to ask on just my signature. But please, Mr. Barnes. It is vital that I get this money, and I.... Well, I have no where else to turn."

Barnes shook his head slowly. "Miss Wright, no disrespect, but ever'body says that. I'll need more to go on than that."

"I, I have experience with running a store. My father owned one for many years. I can make it successful."

"Unless he'll be runnin' it, I still don't have much faith I'll get my money back." His eyes narrowed as he sucked at his teeth. "Now, I'm not averse to helpin' someone out to get their feet under 'em, but if I gave you that kind of money, the terms would have to be pretty hard."

Lily seized on the ray of hope, nodding. "That would be fine, Mr. Barnes. Whatever interest you feel is fair."

He snorted. "Wouldn't be just interest, Miss Wright. I can't afford a loss like that. That kind of risk on me.... Well, I'd have to take it up a notch." He gazed at the ceiling. "I think I'd be lookin' at holdin' the deed. First missed payment, I take over. And, say thirty percent interest."

Her jaw fell.

Barnes shrugged. "Take it or leave it. That's what I can offer."

Lily didn't know much about business or financial matters but knew she'd be mad to accept the proposition. The idea of doing business with such a man made her skin crawl. *I can't refuse him. It's my only hope for the store. I'll just have to make it successful. With the boom, it won't be hard.*

She took a deep breath. "Fine, Mr. Barnes, I'll accept your terms."

He grinned, a flash of yellowed teeth. "I'll get the paper

drawn up. Come back in the morning, and I'll have it ready."

By the time she left, the rain came in a deluge, and the street had turned into a swamp of mud and debris. Lily, exhausted, wet, and cold, found Jacob leaning near the door and told him to let the cook know she wouldn't need supper. Amos watched from behind his cloud of smoke as she passed through the lobby, but she rebuffed his curiosity and trudged up to her room.

Shucking off her muddy boots, she heaved a sigh of relief. At least one thing had gone right. She could buy the lot, hire a builder, and order merchandise. The contract would give her new name legitimacy. Only one problem remained, and she had no control over it. She could only trust her trail would remain cold and hope a familiar face didn't appear in Clear Springs. Without undressing, she collapsed on the bed and slept hard.

* * * * *

Lily woke with a start, soaked by a cold sweat. Her heart thundered as she gasped for breath. She sat up and lit the bedside lamp.

Shadows danced on the walls in time with the flickering light. She couldn't remember her dream, but stark flashes of loss and fear left her on edge. She tried to banish it.

I'll have my own place. Mine, and mine alone. No more people to lose, no one to answer to. A brand new life. Maybe then the nightmares will go away.

As dawn brightened the room, she rose and attempted to smooth the wrinkles from her rumpled, torn skirt. She had to buy a new dress first thing and have the old clothes washed and mended. Once she had a decent dress, she'd be off to the bank and the real estate office. A long, busy day, but at the end, she would own a piece of the Rocky Mountains. The idea cheered her, and she hummed as she went down for breakfast.

The dry goods had only a few dresses to choose from, and she picked the best of the lot; a plain, brown cotton at least a size too large. She rushed back to the hotel to change and grumbled at the baggy fit, but chided herself for her vanity. After sending the soiled, ripped clothes to the laundress, she returned to the bank.

She arrived after nine o'clock but found the door still locked and leaned against the clapboard to wait. Wagons and horses lumbered back and forth, flinging mud from the night's rain. Men trudged up and down the planked sidewalks. Only two women walked among them; one older and stooped, leaving a shop and heading toward the shacks up the hill, and the other in a low-cut, silk dancing dress entering a saloon. Lily turned away, taken aback at seeing a soiled dove—and her own curiosity about the women.

Silas Barnes, still disheveled, came up the walk carrying a scuffed leather bag.

"Good morning, Mr. Barnes."

"Miss Wright." A sluggish nod.

She followed him inside, where he ushered her into the office, and she sat as he lit the lamp.

"Miss Wright, give me a minute, and I'll get the paperwork finished up." His pen scratched on a paper. "All right, this is it then." He pushed the papers across the desk and spoke quickly in a bored monotone. "Like I said, thirty percent interest for a year, payments due first of the month. First missed payment, I'll take over the deed. The land has to be improved and remain so during the term of the contract. You can't get insurance for wood structures in boomtowns, so that's on you. I already told the real estate feller to send the deed over here, and I'll hold it 'til the final payment. Just sign there."

Lily took the pen and skimmed the paper, her pulse thudding in her ears. She signed in a stilted script.

"Right, then. You go over to the land office, and they'll be waitin'. Take care of business there and come back. I'll give you whatever's left in cash."

She took a shaky breath and smiled. "Thank you, Mr. Barnes. I appreciate your faith. I promise I'll pay on time."

His face split in a wide, sly grin. "Pleasure doin' business with you, Miss Wright."

Lily shuddered but shook it off and left with thoughts jumping from one idea to the next in a frenzy of giddy planning. At the real estate office, she purchased a lot on the south end of Main Street. The agent gave her a few builders' names and congratulated her. She returned to the bank, where Barnes issued her the remainder of her loan. The building would cost—she hoped—around four hundred, leaving enough to buy a small starting inventory.

She called on the recommended carpenters and found one who would build a shop for $425.00. He told her he could have it finished in a couple of weeks.

By late afternoon, her feet ached and her corset dug into her sides, but she made herself stop at the stationer's for paper and ink so she could start writing suppliers. He prattled as he gathered her purchases at a glacial rate, in particular about his annoyance at a Mrs. Durand who was a hermit and forced him to deliver. Lily fidgeted, annoyed at his sluggishness and wishing he'd stop his chatter. She ached to retreat to her room for peace and quiet to work.

When she exited the store, Luke Jackson stood near the door. Her stomach fluttered.

"Evenin', Miss Lily Wright."

Despite a mild exasperation at another interruption, she returned his smile. "Ah, hello, Mr. Jackson. What are you doing here?"

"Ya don't figure I can write?" He frowned, eyes boring into her.

"No, I didn't mean that ...." She turned tongue-tied.

"I'll have you know I'm an educated bumpkin. I went to school all the way to sixteen, even if it *was* only in Houston." He cracked a smile and shook his head. "I am still a bumpkin, though."

She clucked and scowled. "You made me feel awful."

"My sympathies." He grinned. "I saw you go in. Wanted to ask if I might buy you supper." He bent in a mock bow and gestured toward the café.

"That's very kind, Mr. Jackson, but no."

His scent drifted past, a whiff of leather and sweet grass, and she almost changed her mind.

"Kind? Ain't tryin' to be kind. I just aimed to have a nice supper with a pretty lady." He shrugged, a smile playing at the corners of his mouth.

She willed her heart to slow its pounding. "Really, I can't, Mr. Jackson. I have a lot of work to do."

"What kind of work? Maybe I can help." As he leaned against the rail and tipped his hat back, his eyes twinkled with mischief.

Lily denied the jolt of attraction that turned her hands clammy. She let out an irritated sigh. "No, you can't help. I'm preparing to open a shop, and I have a lot to do."

"A shop, huh? What kind of shop? Where at?"

She changed her tone, trying for curtness. "A dry goods, on Main. Now, if you'll excuse me."

"I'll be your first customer." He chuckled and tipped his hat brim.

"Wonderful. Have a good evening, Mr. Jackson." She turned on her heel and strode up the walk.

"Oh, I will, Miss Wright. I will."

She resisted the impulse to look back.

At the hotel, she had Jacob bring her supper to her room and spent the evening perusing supplier advertisements in newspapers and magazines. Luke interrupted her concentration; the way his eyes made her breath catch, the way his deep, smooth drawl sent a shiver up her spine. She pushed them aside with an annoyed huff and refocused. After several hours, her ink-stained hand ached from writing letters of inquiry, and her eyes burned. When she crawled into bed, Luke crept back into her thoughts, and she lay awake for hours.

CHAPTER NINE

After the first night, Charlotte had met Duncan often. She would slip out after everyone had retired and race to the stable. Duncan had created a comfortable retreat with a makeshift bed and washbasin—their own lovers' lair.

The affair, and the resulting joy, guilt, and fear, kept her on edge. She acted silly under the spell of newfound love. In the middle of a task, she often found herself humming, and her mother would scowl at the noise. The house seemed less suffocating. She stopped scanning the papers for news of her peers and the parties she couldn't attend. Instead, she daydreamed of a fancy wedding and a house for just the two of them.

Despite that happiness, the worry of getting caught subdued her schoolgirl crush. After a close call, Charlotte told Duncan they couldn't keep meeting, but he sulked and accused her of being ashamed of him. She reassured him and found herself naked in his arms once more.

Adding to the tension, the ease with which she abandoned her virtue made her uneasy. She couldn't silence her mother's puritanical voice in her head as it reproached her wanton, immoral behavior. Each time doubts crept in, she justified the sin with their intention to marry.

As winter gave way to spring, she devised a plan to invite Duncan to dinner and announce their love to her parents. She and Duncan would convince them he would make a fine husband, a good, responsible man, despite his humble beginnings. If she could make them understand she was in love, they would agree to the marriage. If all else failed, she would point out her father's immigrant background and poor financial standing as a young man. He wouldn't want anyone thinking him a hypocrite, unwilling to give a young man a chance, would he?

Charlotte sought out her parents in the parlor. James read while Eliza worked on her sewing. Charlotte entered with a cheerful air, trying to mask her nervousness, and sat on the sofa between them.

"Hello Papa, Mother."

"Charlotte." He glanced up from his paper.

Her mother focused on a new piece of embroidery depicting Christ on the cross. She registered no awareness her daughter had come in.

Charlotte asked, "How was your day, Papa?"

"Fine."

She hesitated, fidgeting. "Papa ...."

"Yes?" He didn't look up.

"Um ... may I invite a friend to supper tomorrow?"

"What friend?"

"Just a friend I'd like you to meet." Charlotte held her breath.

"Tomorrow? No, not tomorrow. I've already invited a guest."

"Oh. Who, Papa?" She frowned. He limited business

guests to Fridays.

"A fellow who moved his shop into the building next to mine. He's a stationer from New York. Very successful. I think you'll like him."

Her mouth went dry. She managed to squeak a question. "Why is he coming to supper?"

He turned the page and smiled. "He's coming to call on you. He's a fine suitor."

"No!" The cry escaped before she could stop it.

"What? Why not?"

"I, I just don't think I'm ready for that, Papa. And a man I don't even know ...."

"Nonsense, Charlotte. That's hardly an excuse not to meet one. You are more than old enough to find a suitable fellow. You can't stay shuttered up in this house forever. You need to start courting."

Her mind raced, but she couldn't think of a counter to his assertion. She considered telling him of her affair but hadn't the courage without Duncan beside her. She'd find a way out of it later. Duncan could help her come up with an excuse.

"I, I suppose you're right, Papa."

Her father nodded. "That's a good girl. You'll like him."

"Yes, Papa. I think I'll retire now."

She dashed to her bedroom and paced through the evening.

* * * * *

Charlotte woke drained and nauseous. She had settled on feigning an illness but found she wouldn't need deception.

After spending the day in bed, she sent word she couldn't

attend supper. She expected her father to come up and chastise her, but he left her undisturbed. Her father would invite the man again. She had to find a more permanent solution.

She felt better the following day and stole away to meet Duncan. When she relayed the conversation with her father, he laughed heartily.

"What is so amusing? Don't you care that he's trying to marry me off to some boring stationer?"

"Silly Charlotte! Of course I care. But he canna force ye to marry the man. Ye're gettin' upset over nothin'. Calm yerself. Put yer father off a bit longer on this suitor, until ye can convince them to let ye marry me."

"I'm not so sure, Duncan. I don't know how long I can stall. Once my father decides something ...."

"Dinna worry yer little head. Yer father even asked me into his office the other day for a cup of coffee. He's comin' around."

"You think? Oh, I hope so. I am so tired of sneaking out. I want *you* to court me, to take me on walks and sit in the parlor and come to dinner. I want to marry you."

"Dinna worry lass. I will."

* * * * *

Her father cornered her in the parlor several days later.

"Charlotte," he said as he entered, "there you are."

She tensed and laid her sewing aside. "Yes, Papa?"

"Mr. Kinney will be coming to call on you this evening. Make sure you are ready to receive him." He sank into his favorite chair and tamped tobacco into his pipe.

The words sucked the air from the room. He wouldn't let her out of it this time. She had to tell him.

"Papa ...."

"Yes?"

"Papa, I can't receive him."

"What now, Charlotte? You are not ill *today*, are you?" He frowned. "If not today, then I'll tell him to come tomorrow."

"N-no, I'm not sick. I mean ... I cannot receive him at all." She shot out of the chair and paced. "I don't want a suitor. I'm in love with someone else."

Her father laughed. "Charlotte, enough of this ridiculous skittishness. Goodness, I can't believe you are so worried that you're willing to lie to avoid him. Kinney is a perfectly nice gentleman."

"Papa, I'm not lying. I'm serious."

He turned to look at her. "What? What are you talking about?"

She *did* feel ill now. Her throat tightened, and she had to force the words out. "I am in love."

"With who? You don't even know any young men."

She took a deep, shaky breath. What had possessed her to start this conversation? "Duncan, Papa."

He picked up the gazette and shook it open. "This has gone far enough. I'm not in the mood for childish pranks."

"Papa, it's not a prank, and I'm not saying this because of Mr. Kinney. I truly am in love with Duncan."

He lowered his paper and studied her. "If you're serious, you've made a naïve mistake. You know very well that Duncan Fitzgerald is beneath you." His voice sharpened when she started to object. "He is not a proper suitor, and I will not allow any relationship between the two of you. Whatever he's claimed, I'm sure he's just using you for position and money. You'll have to forget whatever girlhood crush you think you have for him." He waved a hand. "If what you say is true, all the better that you meet someone else to help you realize how foolish you sound. I won't hear any more about it."

Charlotte knelt at his side. "Papa, please," she pleaded in a rush, "you don't understand. Duncan is not beneath me. He's a fine gentleman. He's a hard worker and will do well for himself. You even said yourself not long ago. I love him, and I want to marry him. You must understand!"

"Young lady, that will do. Go get dressed to receive Mr. Kinney." He returned to his paper.

"No! I won't." She stood, crossed her arms, and stamped her foot. "You cannot force me to accept some stranger. Duncan is just as good as you. He's no different than you when you were young. Mother came from a much better family, yet you didn't think you were beneath her. I can't believe you can be so arrogant and hypocritical."

While she spoke, his face had gone pale. He sprung up and slapped her. She gasped and backed away.

His eyes blazed. "How dare you speak to me that way! Has the boy already dragged you down to his level?"

Anger, stronger than she'd ever known, rose inside her. She turned and fled.

* * * * *

Charlotte locked herself in her bedroom and refused to answer when her mother, and then her father, knocked and told her to come down for supper. Unwell again the next morning, she slipped downstairs to find something to settle her stomach. In the kitchen, the cook stood at the table kneading dough.

"Miss Charlotte, how are you?"

"I don't feel well, Sarah. Perhaps I just need to eat something."

"Ah, I have some fresh, hot bread here."

"That sounds good. Thank you." Charlotte slumped in a rocker in the corner and nibbled on a hunk. "Is Papa gone to work already?"

"Yes, he left early this mornin'. Said he had to place an ad for a new groom on his way to the store. Miss Eliza hasn't been down yet."

"What?" She jumped up, tossed the bread on the table, and raced out.

"Dear? My goodness, what's wrong?"

Charlotte ran to the stable.

"Duncan!"

"Mornin', lass." He offered a weak smile. "You told him?"

"Oh Duncan, it was awful! He said I better forget you, that you only wanted me for his name and money, and he wouldn't listen. He was so angry. I don't know what we'll do now."

Charlotte burst into tears, and Duncan held her..

"He's wrong. We'll think of something, lass."

Charlotte sobbed against his shoulder as he tried to comfort her. All at once, her stomach rebelled, and she jerked away from him. She ran into a stall, bent over, and vomited. After a while, her stomach settled a bit.

Wiping her face on her apron, she came out to find Duncan eyeing her with a strange look.

"I haven't felt well this morning. All this trouble, I suppose."

"Charlotte, when did ye have yer last course?"

"What?"

"Your monthly?"

"Duncan!" Heat flushed her face, and she turned away.

Grabbing her arm, he spun her back to face him. "When?"

"I, I don't know." She counted on her fingers. "A couple of months perhaps?"

"Ah, lass!" Duncan grinned. "Our problem is solved."

"What are you talking about?"

"Charlotte, dinna ye realize what's happened?"

"What? Goodness, just tell me!"

He laughed. "I'd gamble yer expecting."

"Wha—No, I can't be ...."

"Aye, Charlotte. And now yer father will have to let us get married."

Charlotte struggled to comprehend the words, but she couldn't focus. Her knees buckled, and all went black.

CHAPTER TEN

Lily stood in front of a skeletal structure, making plans for the store layout. Mist swirled in the creek bed at the edge of the valley, and frost covered the grass. She shivered and pulled her cloak closer.

The carpenter had completed the frame for the clapboard shop ahead of schedule, with one story, a large room in the front for the store, and three smaller rooms at the rear for storage and living space. It sat on the western end of Main Street, between a blacksmith's shop and an empty lot.

Anticipation vibrated through her. Everything had started to fall into place.

A small man in a crisp suit, out of place amid the workmen scurrying through the town in the early morning, left the boardwalk and walked toward her.

"Miss Wright, isn't it?"

She recognized him from the hotel. "Yes, Mr. Warren. How nice to see you."

"A good morning to you. Your store is coming along? Has your brother arrived yet?"

Her guard went up, like sliding a mask over her face. "I'm afraid he's been delayed, but I've been able to manage a start." He watched her closely, and she pointed to the unfinished building to divert his attention. "It should be finished in a week or so."

"Very good, very good." He glanced at the building but turned back, looking up at her over his glasses. "I hope you are finding Clear Springs to your liking?"

"Oh yes. It's lovely."

A look of regret crossed his face. "Less so than it used to be. It is changing a bit too fast for my taste."

"Yes, I suppose it seems strange to long-time residents."

He nodded. "I am tempted to move on. The rowdy elements may take over."

She chuckled. "It can't be that bad, can it?"

"Sadly, it may be. Clear Springs stayed small for years. Ranchers came in about sixty-one; some were Fifty-niners who stayed. They surveyed for yellow, but no luck. There is good pasture for sheep, however." Warren pointed up the valley. "They built a stage stop and a general store, and Clear Springs was born. It stayed quiet until seventy-six, when they found silver over on Chapman Hill."

"Where is that?" She shifted her chilled feet, anxious to go back to the hotel but afraid of appearing rude.

He waved to the north. "Just a couple miles. But it wasn't a real boom. Samuels—the one who owns Clear Springs Ranch—leased out some land, added a hotel, saloon, and sawmill. That's when I arrived; my firm sent me up here. I liked it so much I resigned and stayed on." He smiled. "Within a year, the silver played out. Most of the miners drifted out. Town quieted down, but it's been a way point. Nice atmosphere, good people.

"A year ago, Samuels' men went to round up sheep and

stumbled on a vein." He took off his spectacles and cleaned them. "Samuels started mining. The strike produced a fair amount of ore and began attracting attention. Many were skeptical, since they had scoured the area long since, but a new strike always lures a few dreamers. Clear Springs started growing again, another saloon, a few shops, and a bank. I should have guessed when they spent such a bundle on the bank." He sighed. "Two months ago, they hit a large lode, the news leaked, and I fear now it's changed forever. Too many people running from the law." His eyes scanned her face, and he seemed about to ask a question.

Lily spoke before he could. "I'm sure they won't let it become seedy, Mr. Warren."

An account of the latest strike had spurred her choice of Clear Springs, and she hoped for exactly the change he predicted, as long as lawlessness didn't take over. She counted on that transformation to assist her own. His concern made her uneasy.

"I'm not. There are ... unsavory characters." He gave her an earnest look. "Take care to steer clear of them, Miss."

"Thank you, Mr. Warren. I will."

Pressing a card into her hand, he said, "I must tend to my office now, but if you ever need anything, please call. Good day." He scuttled back to the boardwalk, carefully avoiding horse droppings.

What a strange little man. Lily shook her head and turned her attention back to the building.

Over the previous week, she'd written to suppliers and evaluated her competitors. She browsed the shops to see what they lacked and noted their prices. Newcomers arrived each day to stake claims in the hills and buy supplies. More tents and cabins sprung up at the edges of town. Wagons filled with tools, machinery, food, and liquor filed down Main Street. Impatience hounded her. She wanted to open the store and capitalize on the money flowing through Clear Springs.

Meanwhile, Lily stayed alert. No matter how remote the possibility, she worried luck might allow her husband to happen on a clue to her destination, so she people-watched.

Men held the overwhelming majority and showed keen interest in a new lady. She brushed off a few gentlemanly advances and ignored the more crass comments. Several dozen women lived in Clear Springs, more than half of them fallen women.

While the men eyed Lily with interest, the women treated her with suspicion and didn't bother to conceal it in their prying questions. She provided the false biography but deflected their curiosity. She welcomed the distraction of readying the store.

As she returned to the endless list of preparations, a voice from behind startled her.

"Miss Wright! A sight for sore eyes."

She turned as Luke strode toward her.

"Good morning, Mr. Jackson."

"This is your shop then?"

"It will be." She couldn't help an elated smile.

Luke stared for a long moment. "Lord, but ya are pretty when you smile." He sighed, a wistful exhale.

Her heart responded with a stutter, but she caught herself and shot him a disapproving look. "Mr. Jackson, mind your manners."

He took off his cowboy hat, giving her a sweeping bow. "Yes, ma'am. I shouldn't have ever said yer pretty. My deepest regrets, I'll never say those words again."

She gasped and opened her mouth to protest but snapped it shut. Refusing to give him satisfaction, she crossed her arms and turned back to the building.

"Don't you have work to do, sir?"

"Why yes, I do, as a matter of fact. I'm in the market for some dry goods."

"Then you should go *to* the dry goods, I should think," she snapped.

He chuckled. "Naw, I ain't impressed with none of 'em. It's an important order I'm puttin' in. I want real special care taken with it. Thought ya might like some business."

"Perhaps you didn't notice, but my store isn't open yet."

Luke whistled low. "Yer far too sober, Miss Wright. Yer in need of some relaxation, I'd wager. I could help with that, if yer of a mind sometime. I'm real good at relaxin'." He held up a hand at the sharp look she shot him. "Just an idea, now. A picnic, maybe. No impropriety intended." He put on a serious face. "I did notice about the store, but I don't need the order right yet. Won't need it for a month or so. And I wanted to make sure I was yer first customer, like I said."

She smothered a laugh and beat down her growing attraction. A pang of loneliness tugged at her. She missed the excitement and joy of love, and Luke stirred that memory. *No. The last thing you need is a man.*

She pursed her lips, impatient. "I can't take orders yet. The place doesn't even have walls. You'll have to go somewhere else."

He pulled a piece of paper from his pocket and held it out. She took it without thinking and unfolded it.

"Well, that's my order, and you took it." His mouth curved in a smug smile. "Just let me know when it comes in ... unless ya want to see me before then." He ambled off.

Lily couldn't think of a clever retort and scowled at his back. Her eyes widened as she read the list. It contained a good number of items and would result in a substantial bill.

She went a few steps after him, but he'd disappeared.

* * * * *

In the evening, Lily retired to her hotel room. The usual delivery of newspapers from the coast had arrived that morning with two-week-old editions. She pored over them, eager for a taste of home. Ladies' columns couldn't satisfy her loneliness, but they maintained the tenuous, familiar connection.

Once she'd exhausted the fashion and gossip, she turned to the advertising and made notes on possible suppliers. The Philadelphia paper carried dozens of offerings, and she read them with interest, passing over unrelated ads and missives. As her tired eyes scanned, one drew her back, and when she read it, a cold hand gripped her heart.

Search for a Missing Wife: Mr. Fitzgerald of Jefferson City seeks news of his wife Charlotte, who disappeared some days ago. He gives her description as tall, dark-haired, green eyes and says he fears an illness has left her insensible. He asks anyone who may have seen her to relay information to him at 46 West End Lane in the same city.

Fear and anger mingled in her belly. The clamminess on her hands left dark smudges on the paper. He hadn't given up. He wouldn't let her go.

Insane .... He's telling people I'm insane.

Her fingers scratched at the words, tearing them from the paper until shreds littered the room like snow. She collapsed on the bed and sobbed until she fell asleep. She collapsed on the bed and sobbed until she fell asleep.

CHAPTER ELEVEN

Charlotte winced at the pounding behind her eyes. Hay, dirt, animals, manure …. The odors assaulted her, and her stomach rolled. She blinked, trying to sit up.

"Easy, lass." Duncan pushed her back.

"What …?"

"Ye fainted. Rest a bit." He kneeled over her, holding her hand.

It came back in a rush. Pregnant. He'd said she must be with child. What on earth would she do with a child? A bastard child …. Images flashed before her: an infant lying in a cradle, being rocked to sleep; the child beginning to cry; the mother looking for help—with no one there.

She bolted up. "No! I can't be with child." She gripped his hand, trembling. "I don't want a bastard child. I, I'm not ready to be a mother. What will my parents say?"

"Calm yerself, Charlotte. Don't be daft. Ye won't have a bastard. Don't ye see? This solves everything." A smile lit his face.

Her eyes widened. "Solves? Are you mad?"

"Lass, now yer parents must let ye marry me. They won't allow their first grandchild to be a bastard. We can be together and have everything we want. A family, a home, money ...." Agitation flickered across his features, and he rushed on. "'Tis perfect, don't ye see? Our love has made a life, and we can be a family. We'll get married straight away, and there'll be no disgrace."

She caught the hesitation and put it down to surprise. "But Duncan—"

His eyes darkened. "Don't ye want to marry me? To start a family with me? Ye said ye loved me. I thought ye'd be happy."

The pain on his face wrenched her heart. "No, Duncan, it isn't that at all. I do love you. I want to marry you." She pressed against him. "This is all so sudden. I am happy, I suppose. I *am*. We'll get married. I'm sure it'll be fine." She repeated the words in her mind, over and over.

"That's a good lass." He pulled back and grinned. "We'll have everything we want."

Forcing a smile, she let him embrace her until she remembered what he'd said before. She asked how he'd known she'd told her father. Duncan explained James had come out to the barn early and interrogated him. He'd accused Duncan of seducing her. Duncan, of course, had denied any impropriety, but James told him he had one week to find a new employer—and to stay far away from Charlotte.

"Oh dear. He will be so angry."

"He'll get over it, lass. Once they're used to the idea, they'll just be thrilled for a grandchild."

She nodded, but her chest tightened, as if a huge weight had settled on her and would suffocate her. "I hope so."

Childbirth and children .... Fear of the unknown threatened to overwhelm her. She loved Duncan, though, and wanted to marry him and make him happy. Joy transformed his face and pushed her fears back.

"Take care of that wee one, Charlotte." He rubbed her belly, a grin lighting his features.

She gave him a weak smile while her insides twisted. "I will."

In a daze, she left the stable.

* * * * *

In the evening, Charlotte gathered her courage and knocked on her mother's bedroom door.

"Come," Mother answered. She sat at her dressing table, pulling pins from the hair piled atop her head. "Yes, Charlotte?"

"I need to talk to you, Mama."

"What is it?"

"I ... I need help."

"With what?" Her mother ran a brush through her tresses, and her lips moved in a silent recitation of verse.

Odd, I didn't realize how gray she's become. Charlotte swallowed and turned to the wide window, unable to look at her. "I'm going to have a baby, Mama."

"Of course you will."

Charlotte threw up her hands. "No, Mama. I am going to have a baby *now*."

"Don't be preposterous, Charlotte. You aren't even courting. Though your father did say he found a nice gentleman for you. From the store, I think."

"Mama—"

"I suppose it *is* best that he find you someone. I certainly won't allow one of those hedonist parties. And none of our friends have boys for a girl your age. Though, I don't think there is any rush. You aren't that old, and I don't think you are quite ready to handle your own house. And children! Goodness, that would be ...." Her voice caught.

Charlotte knelt in front of her mother and took the brush from her hand. Mother blinked and lost the faraway look in her eyes.

"Mama, listen to me. I am with child. Now."

Her face went blank and her lips moved, without sound.

"Mother, I know this is a shock. But I'm in love. I want to marry him." She squeezed her mother's hands.

Her lips curled. "Fornicating, rutting like an animal. I should have known. Who?"

"Duncan."

"Duncan who? Is that the young man who works for Doctor Alexander?" She frowned. "A doctor? I don't know, they have difficult schedules and—"

"Mother, you know Duncan. Our groom." Charlotte suppressed her irritation.

"What in heaven's name ...? Marry our driver? That's absurd." Her mouth set, and she shook her head. "Your father won't have it. Imagine what everyone would say. Goodness, no."

"Please listen to me, Mother. There's no other option. I am with child. Duncan is the father of my baby. We must get married. As for what everyone would say, well," she took the plunge and tilted her head, "I expect they will say a lot more if I have a bastard child." She refused to acknowledge the twinge of satisfaction in needling her mother.

Her face went white. "Don't you dare use that language with me."

"What language would you prefer?" Charlotte trembled. Opposing her parents, she still felt like a small child about to catch a scolding. *I must start acting like a grown up.* Steeling herself, she pushed on. "If I am not married, my baby will be a bastard. No one else will have me. You must help me convince Papa, or we'll be forced to run away. And you'll never see your grandchild."

Mother pulled away, and her lips narrowed into a thin line, all but disappearing. "I will pray on it, Charlotte. Leave me."

Charlotte rose and backed from the room, numb.

It's done. There's no going back now.

* * * * *

As the sun peeked in and frost sparkled on the trees and grass, Mother stalked into the dining room. Charlotte sat with a cup of broth while she battled nausea. Her mother hadn't dressed her hair, and wrinkles stood out on her colorless face.

Her voice cold, Mother spoke without looking at her. "I will speak to your father, Charlotte." She left as Charlotte buried her face in her hands.

Charlotte walked a tightrope through the day, anxious but hopeful, and ended up in the parlor shortly before supper. As she worked on her knitting, the front door opened and closed. Mother called to Papa from upstairs, and his footsteps echoed on the steps. Charlotte sat in silence, straining for a hint of their conversation.

Mother can reason with him; Papa always lets her have her way.

Someone descended the stairs, and she stood and faced the doorway. Her body had gone cold.

Papa's face showed nothing when he entered. Her heart raced. He stopped a few feet away, his head down, as still as a statue. She couldn't decide if she should say something or wait. An unbearable tension rattled her.

Charlotte started to speak, to tell him she was sorry, that she hadn't meant to disappoint him.

He lifted his head. Empty eyes stared out, as if he didn't recognize her. He raised his hand, holding out a small purse.

She backed off, confused.

"Take it."

Charlotte reached for the purse and opened it. A large roll of paper money and some coins. She nearly dropped it. "What is this?"

His voice came out tight. "You're an ungrateful, empty headed-child who thinks she can do as she wishes. You never stopped to think what it would do to your mother and I, did you? After what we've been through .... You have disgraced us—my own daughter a shameless whore." His lips curled. "Well, you can do as you wish now. Take it and go. Don't show your face in this house again ...."

A whore? Charlotte gaped, stunned. The word echoed with stark clarity in her head, carrying his revulsion. She'd never considered he might send her away. Angry, for certain, but she'd had no doubt he would give in and accept Duncan.

As she reeled, her lips trembled. "Papa, please. I'm sorry. You can't—where will I go?"

"Ask *him*." He turned and left the house, and the door slammed behind him.

Charlotte collapsed on the floor. She stayed there for a long time, trying to comprehend what had happened. After a while, a loud thump shook her from her disbelief. She stood and tilted her head. Silence.

She called up the stairs. "Mother?"

Intuition whispered in her ear. She gathered her skirts and bounded up the stairs two by two. She threw open the door to her mother's room.

Mother swayed in the air, appearing to float, suspended from a transom over the dressing room door.

Bewildered, Charlotte stepped closer.

A cord circled her mother's neck, a chair tipped over underneath her.

Charlotte moaned in horror and ran to her mother. She struggled to lift her, but it was no use. The body flopped limply in her arms. The eyes bulged in a pale face, unseeing.

A sheet of paper lay on the dressing table. Two lines, centered on the page in a careful script:

Fear God, and give glory to him;
for the hour of his judgment is come.

Shuddering, Charlotte recoiled and fled the room. She pitched down the stairs, stumbled and nearly fell to the landing, clutching the handrail as her feet slid on the last steps. Tears blurred her vision. Shock echoed in weak sobs. She fumbled a cloak from the coat stand and tore out of the house.

CHAPTER TWELVE

"No. I'm not crazy. I'm not like her." The words came out in a moan, and Lily bolted upright. She shrank back, certain her mother's body hung over her with blank eyes staring. Lily blinked. Nothing marred the empty room. The dingy curtain filtered bright sunlight that shone on scraps of paper scattered on the bed.

Her body quaked as a tortured groan left her. She swatted at the black and white shreds.

"Damn you! Leave me alone."

They wouldn't let her go. Her mother and father would haunt her. Duncan would hunt her.

How close had he gotten in the weeks since the paper's printing? Had he reached Colorado? If he'd stumbled on her trail, he could arrive in Clear Springs any day. Fear mounted, but she closed her eyes and slowed her hitching breaths.

He's not here yet. It's no use borrowing trouble. Focus on what needs doing today.

Maintain vigilance. She had no other defense. He might not find her, and if he did …. She would deal with that when—if—it happened. She cleaned up the paper and tossed it in the trash.

"I have to focus on the store."

She dressed and hurried through the morning traffic to the building site.

* * * * *

Days later, Lily stood on the stoop among piles of sawdust while the builder installed the door. She fidgeted with anticipation.

"Inside'll be ready in a few days. Stoves ain't here yet, and I still got to put up the shelves," the carpenter told her.

"I can close and lock the doors now, though?"

He said she could, and she squealed like a child at Christmas.

"I can sleep here tonight, then."

The man raised an eyebrow and shrugged. "If'n ya want to I s'pose, but there ain't nothin to sleep on, and it'll be mighty cold."

"Oh, I don't care about that," she said with a dismissive wave.

She walked inside and twirled in the bare room. The crisp tang of fresh wood permeated the air. She whirled and ran out.

The builder called after her, "Where ya goin'?"

Lily rushed to the hotel and raced upstairs, colliding with two men at the top. She muttered an apology, entered her room, and started packing. Within half an hour, she'd gathered her few belongings, and she went downstairs to find Jacob. She asked if he would help carry her bags to the store. He agreed with a shy grin—he still blushed every time they spoke—and left to bring her things down.

Lily turned to the desk and beamed. "I'm checking out, Mr. Amos."

He grunted and sneered, "I couldn't tell. You keepin' the horse here?"

Even his odious manners couldn't dampen her enthusiasm, and she laughed as she slid her key across the desk. "Yes, I will. Jacob has taken good care of him, and I may need him again."

"I'll give you the rest of the week, but I'll have to keep tonight's. And it'll be two-fifty a week for boardin' the horse." He counted out her change. "Sign out."

Lily jotted in the book, without hesitating at the false name, and took the money, still smiling.

"Thank you, Mr. Amos. I hope I never have to stay here again."

He grunted and waved her off. She laughed and met Jacob coming down the stairs.

When they arrived at the store, she tipped the boy and thanked him. He blushed and mumbled something before ambling off. Realizing she had no lantern, she dashed to the hardware store. By the time she returned, the evening light had faded. She traced a hand along each wall, holding a new oil lamp high, marveling at every board and nail. *My own store. My own place.* As the lamp ran low, she arranged her spare clothes on the floor in the back room, curled up on them, and slept soundly.

* * * * *

Lily scoured the town for cast off items to furnish the shop and her room. She found some wobbly chairs and a table, bought some crude dishes, and had the carpenter build a bed frame. The back room was spare, but all hers.

The carpenter put in shelves, and as orders arrived, she stocked the store with tins, bottles, and boxes. Bolts of cloth, sewing items, and household things—matches, candles, lamps, and toiletries—filled half of the store. She awaited more shipments of cloth, ready-made clothes, shoes and hats, and kitchen items that would take weeks to arrive.

On the day before the grand opening, while the sun hovered over the mountain and painted the sky with red, orange, and gold, Lily sat at the counter making signs and tags for prices. She had scavenged a broken stool from one of the saloons, and the carpenter repaired it. She wrote out numbers in a neat script. When the ink well ran dry, she went over a long to-do list again. The carpenter poked his head in to announce he'd finished his last task: a modest sign hanging out front.

She rushed out and stood in the street.

WRIGHT DRY GOODS

Goosebumps pebbled her skin, and tears pricked her eyes. The name on the sign, painted in bold black, signaled another phase of her metamorphosis. She'd grown beyond the helpless girl dependent on someone else for everything. She had become a different person—not merely a runaway playacting—and the sign cemented her determination.

The last rays of sun winked out, and she sauntered inside. With a sigh, she pulled a ledger from under the counter. She had designated it for special orders, and she flipped to the first page. The only entry said *Luke Jackson*, along with the list of items he'd ordered. She'd sent off his orders and set aside those that arrived. Wondering at his purpose, she returned the ledger to its spot and pulled out another for pending shipments. She pulled out a fresh ink bottle and made notes on items she still needed to order, humming as she worked.

A loud rap on the door pulled her from the task.

She yelled, "Not open until tomorrow."

"I have a delivery," a deep voice replied.

Lily stretched and pushed herself up. Fatigue had set in, and she trudged to the door, annoyed at the disruption. *Who would deliver at this time?* She almost turned back to the counter to retrieve her revolver. Answering the door after dark made her uneasy.

She unlatched the door and opened it a crack. A man stood on the walk, draped in shadows, holding a large wooden box. She couldn't identify him, and a sliver of fear needled her.

"What delivery?"

"Just this box, ma'am," the man said.

Lily squinted and held her lamp higher. "Step into the light."

The man moved closer, and the weak light settled on Luke Jackson.

Lily exhaled in a rush—she hadn't realized she'd held her breath—and scowled. "What in the devil are you doing here?"

He shifted the box in his arms. "Pardon, Miss Wright, but would you mind yellin' at me after I put this down?"

Lily rolled her eyes and opened the door wider. He walked past and set the box on the counter.

She snapped, "Now, what are you doing here? What is that box?"

Luke chuckled and took his hat off. "And here I thought you'd thank me."

"Thank you for what?"

"Supper, of course."

Lily eyed him with suspicion and lifted the box lid. Inside sat a crock of stew, steam rising with a hearty aroma, half a loaf of bread, and a jug of liquid. When her stomach rumbled, she remembered she hadn't eaten since early that morning.

She turned back to him. "What ...?"

"Haven't eaten yet, have you?"

She shook her head.

"Figured since you won't let me escort you to a supper out, I'd be obliged to bring one to you."

Lily wanted to refuse but didn't want to offend him; his business meant a great deal for the store. He seemed a perfectly nice gentleman. *It's only one meal, after all. Besides, it smells wonderful ....*

"Oh. Well ... thank you."

Luke grinned and lifted the dishes from the box.

She stood by, fidgeting. "I, I'll bring another chair in."

He pointed at a large barrel near the counter. "Don't trouble yerself, I'll pull that over. Just have a seat. Supper'll be served directly." He arranged the meal on the counter and nudged the barrel over.

Flustered, she sat on the stool and waited. *I should say something. Why can't I think of anything to say?*

He finished setting up and squatted on the drum. "I take it tomorrow's the big day?"

"Yes. At least I hope it's a big day. I'm afraid my inventory isn't what it should be, but I couldn't wait any longer."

"It won't matter what's on yer shelves. Ever'body will come in just to see somethin' new."

Lily smiled at the domestic scene. He ladled stew into bowls, tore a hunk of bread for each, and poured mugs of beer.

"Couldn't find nothin' else for drinks. Hope ya ain't a teetotaler."

"No, it's fine." She didn't care for beer, but she could hardly complain. "It all looks wonderful."

Luke tossed his hat on the counter, lowered his head, and closed his eyes. Lily followed suit and said a short prayer.

As they dug in, her eyes widened. "Heavens, this is wonderful. Where did you get it?"

"My stove."

She chuckled. "You cooked this? I'm impressed."

"I'm flattered. Pays to learn how to cook decent out in the hills. Else ya get stuck eatin' pretty poor. Took more than a few burnt meals, but I can put on a feed now."

Lily took the opening to satisfy her curiosity. "Where is home? How long have you been here?"

"Texas, but I've wandered a bit the past ten years. Reckon I'll be here a good while now; it suits me. Never did care for the flatlands."

"You aren't a miner, though. What do you do?"

"No, ma'am. I'm a cattleman. I'd rather deal with somethin' that ain't so hard to find."

She laughed. "Call me Lily, please. This isn't exactly cattle country, is it? I thought the beef ranches were all east, on the plains."

"Not right here, no, but there are big valleys up in these mountains that can keep a good herd. Hope to have my own, someday soon. 'Bout the best thing I can imagine is havin' my own place, in a nice wide valley, with mountains all 'round." He gazed toward the tiny window by the counter with longing, smiled, and returned his attention to her. "And yerself, Miss Lily? Don't seem like yer from these parts. What draws a refined lady like yerself out here?"

Lily hesitated. "I've always wanted to see the West, so I came. It seemed so … wide open. Full of possibility and independence. I didn't have much freedom growing up, so I read a lot. The stories in the papers and magazines—they make it sound like a paradise. I guess the West and the mountains stuck in my head. That probably sounds naïve." She smiled, embarrassed.

He studied her, and she waited for him to press for more. Instead, he asked, "What do ya think now that yer here?"

"It's a different world. Not really what I expected." She sighed. "I haven't had a chance to see much of it, though. I've been so busy I've hardly had a chance to catch my breath."

"I hope you'll let me show you some of it, then. 'Bout the only thing prettier is you," he said with a lopsided grin.

She groaned. "That's a dreadful flirtation, Mr. Jackson." A laugh escaped. His charisma pulled her in, and she reminded herself to keep her distance. As much as she tried, she couldn't deny how much she enjoyed his company.

He laughed. "Reckon it is, but I can't hold back my opinion."

They finished their meal and chatted, but when she stifled a yawn, he apologized for keeping her up, packed the dishes away, and bid her goodnight. Lily closed the door after him and leaned against it.

The evening left her torn. She liked him. Everything about him turned her resolve to jelly, and that made the pang of regret worse. She had no time for courting; she had to focus on the store. More important, she couldn't fall in love again. Her love for her husband had blinded her to his selfishness and cruelty. Luke seemed a gentleman, but who knew what he kept hidden beneath the surface? She couldn't give in, couldn't lose herself again. But a harmless friendship wouldn't hurt … if she kept him at arm's length.

CHAPTER THIRTEEN

Charlotte ran down the street, blinded by tears and desperate to escape the images in her head. Slowing, out of breath and dizzy, she trudged to where she'd arranged to meet Duncan. She waited for an hour and paced the sidewalk, her mind reeling.

My family is gone. How can that be? Where will I go?

Duncan came around the corner. Charlotte ran to him, crying hysterically.

"What happened, Charlotte?" He pulled her behind the building and took her in his arms. "Calm yerself and tell me what happened."

Between sobs and sniffles, she relayed the morning's events.

"Damn him. What a selfish, heartless .... Sorry ye had to see yer ma like that. " His jaw clenched, but he smiled and squeezed her shoulder. "We'll find a room for ye to stay at. Dinna worry, lass. It'll be fine."

"Duncan, you're all I have left. I don't know what I'd do without you."

He led her to his neighborhood and found a cheap lodge.

The room's condition—filthy, with rats skittering in the walls and shady characters loitering even in daylight—disgusted her, but she held her tongue, relieved to have someone to love and take care of her.

* * * * *

In the morning, Duncan arrived early.

He picked up her cloak and held it out for her. "Yer goin' to see yer da."

"What? No, I can't go back there. You didn't see how angry—the things he said ...."

"Charlotte, with yer ma gone, he'll come to his senses."

"He won't. It's my fault; she's gone because of me. I, I can't face him again." She shuddered.

His face turned stony as he gripped her arms, his fingers digging in. "Ye dinna have a choice. I won't take on a lass and child by meself. I canna support ye. Unless ye want to end up at the poorhouse, ye better convince him."

The threat astounded her, and a harsh alarm sounded in her head. The wretched workhouses, filled with disease, violence, and despair, meant death. She panicked.

"You can't leave me. I, I don't have anyone else. The baby needs a father. I'll go, I will, just please, don't leave us." She clutched at his chest, shaking, hating the desperation in her voice but unable to hold it back. "I need you, Duncan. I love you. Please ...."

"Then ye must do this." He softened. "I won't leave ye. I love ye, but we must face reality. I would go with ye, but I fear it would only make it worse. He'll listen to ye, dinna worry. And once yer back in his good graces, we—the baby—will have everythin' we need."

Charlotte let him pull her cloak over her shoulders and

left him in the hotel room. As she walked, his words replayed in her mind. The hardness in his eyes had chilled her. Had she judged him wrong? What if he didn't love her? She stopped.

That can't be. He's always been kind with me. He risked his position for me. He was thrilled at the news of the baby. She started walking again. *No, he must love me. Why else would he do those things? He just wanted to warn me of the peril we face, to make me bear up and do what I must.*

Within minutes, she stood at the gate. The house looked different. She'd seen it as a prison for so long, but now that she'd left, she wanted to go back. No, she could never go back—it would never be a home again. She'd escaped, but the price was too high.

If I could just .... What? What would make everything all right? Nothing.

Tears streamed down her cheeks, but she barely noticed.

I can't face him. He'll blame me. He was angry before, but now ... now it's so much worse. I can't bear his hatred.

The cold spring breeze stung her fingers, and she tucked her hands in her pockets. One curled around a lump of cloth. She gasped.

The money.

In her grief, she'd forgotten it. It could keep her out of the workhouse, if she planned well. If they both worked until the baby came, they might not even need it. She could use it as a safety net and keep it to herself. And she wouldn't have to face her father.

Guilt tweaked her conscience. She shouldn't—couldn't—hide it. She sighed and set her jaw.

It's for the baby. The baby is the most important thing. I'll protect my child, whatever it takes.

The house loomed, accusing, and she turned away.

* * * * *

Charlotte told Duncan no one had answered the door and that she'd go back in a few days, after they'd laid her mother to rest, though she had no intention of returning.

The next day, they found a preacher in another town who would marry them and had a quiet ceremony with the preacher's wife as witness. Charlotte hadn't imagined her marriage starting that way. She had a moment of doubt, but when Duncan took her hands and said his vows, her heart raced, and she told herself whatever troubles they encountered, they loved each other and would make it through.

Duncan gained a position at a tavern and rented a small, run-down house. Charlotte took in sewing to earn money and made clothes for the baby at night. She found the radical change a difficult adjustment. To distract herself, she worked to make their new home comfortable; she cleaned until her hands bled, made what repairs she could, and added curtains to the tiny, drafty windows. Soon, it felt more like a home.

Charlotte continued her deception. Every week, Duncan badgered her about reconciling with her father. Every week, she lied. She pretended she'd called on him while Duncan worked and that he'd refused to see her. In truth, she never returned to her childhood home. When shame and guilt nagged at her, she told herself she had no other choice.

They settled into married life. Duncan seemed anxious for the baby, but he worked long hours and gave her little attention. She kept busy and held her loneliness at bay.

Her real complaint came with Duncan's insistence that their lovemaking continue. As her body changed, she became self-conscious. More than that, her mother's influence hadn't faded completely—Charlotte felt it must be shameful for a woman with child to engage in "that business." She put him off for a few weeks with excuses, but late one night Duncan wouldn't accept them any longer.

Charlotte lay in bed knitting when he came in from work walking unsteady. He had only stayed at the tavern after work a couple of times, and she didn't begrudge him time with the boys, but she felt unwell and irritable.

"Ah, me lass. What a wonderful sight!" He stumbled to the bed.

"Did you have a good evening?" Her false smile escaped him.

"Most fine!" His grin turned sheepish when he looked at the clock. "I'm awful sorry to be so late though, lass. I dinna mean to stay so long." He plopped on the edge of the bed and began undressing.

"Yes, well, I suppose a man is allowed a bit of fun sometimes."

"Aye, we had fun. Me boys came in, and we were catching up."

She smirked. "Catching up on your drinking, I think."

Duncan laughed. "A bit, aye." He kicked his pants off and slid in beside her in his drawers.

"But I missed ye, Charlotte, and yer more fun than those sots."

He leaned over to kiss her, and she gave him a quick peck, recoiling from the alcohol on his breath.

"Oh ho, what sort of kiss is that for yer lovin' husband?" He pulled her close and kissed her firmly.

She didn't resist, hoping that would satisfy him. Instead, his kiss deepened, and he slid a hand up to her breast. She stiffened and pulled away.

"Please, Duncan. I'm tired."

"Oh lass, come now, I want ye," he groaned.

"Not now, Duncan. Tomorrow."

He bristled and dropped his hand. "Charlotte, how come tomorrow never comes?"

"I'm sorry. Please, just not tonight. I don't feel well."

"I'm tired of hearin' that. A man has needs and a right to be with his wife."

She flushed and turned her head away. "I, I just can't. Not when I'm with child. It's vulgar and sinful," she whispered.

"Nonsense! 'Tis no more sinful than when we were nae even married."

He took her arm and turned her toward him, but she couldn't look at him.

"Lass, love ain't sinful. 'Tis nothin wrong about lovin' me own wife. A wife is made for a husband's pleasure." His quiet, stern tone brooked no argument. "I won't be turned away from mine."

Charlotte wavered, trying to reconcile his logic with her inhibitions. She wanted to keep him happy, but it seemed wrong to take pleasure while a child grew within her. Remembering their previous couplings drew a flush of warmth. She wanted the ecstasy he provoked in her—no matter how sinful—and she couldn't refuse him anyway. She pressed her lips together. With a bob of her head, she untied the ribbon on the high collar of her night dress.

Nervousness tangled her fingers. Her body no longer seemed hers, an unfamiliar and awkward imposter.

Duncan pushed her hand away. He tipped her chin up and moved in to kiss her. Charlotte opened for him hesitantly, but he thrust his tongue between her lips. He shoved the blankets off and found the hem of her gown. His impatience and intoxication made him clumsy, and she tried to help as he moved over her and bunched the fabric up. He groaned and fell upon her breasts, sucking and kneading.

Uneasy, she pulled back at his abrupt roughness, but when his mouth found her sensitive nipple she gasped at the stab of desire. Her hands caressed the back of his head, and she squirmed under him.

He had already grown hard and scrambled to open his drawers. He freed himself and thrust into her without waiting.

Charlotte tensed and cried out at the pain of sudden invasion.

Too frenzied to notice—or too drunk to care—he continued to move, driving in and pulling out.

The pain subsided, and she tried to move with him as her own desire built.

Duncan reached his peak, groaning and shuddering his release. His body went limp, and he rolled off her.

The withdrawal left her empty, and she let out a strangled cry. Frustration stirred as her breathing slowed. Duncan began to snore. She tugged her gown back into place, rolled over, and closed her eyes.

She told herself it was better that way, she shouldn't enjoy it. Only a wanton woman would. She would do her wifely duties without complaint, but as she drifted off, she couldn't quite forget that moment of pain—or his indifference.

CHAPTER FOURTEEN

The grand opening wasn't as grand as Lily had dreamed, but as Luke predicted, almost everyone came in. Some miners remained absent, still on their claims in the hills, and the soiled doves—dance hall girls, saloon waitresses, and prostitutes—stayed away. Many citizens came to satisfy their curiosity about the store and its proprietor, though few made purchases.

Weeks went by in a blur. She worked from before dawn until well after dark. More stock filled the racks and shelves. The number of actual customers—rather than curious gawkers—slowly grew. The sales spurred hope, but the meager profit wouldn't provide anything like a decent living. She needed more customers.

Clear Springs grew, too. New businesses opened almost daily—mostly saloons and hardware stores. As a few miners' and businessmen's wives joined their husbands, tensions brewed. The wives, and a few men, vocally opposed the rowdy and improper diversions. The majority of the men appreciated the dancing, drinking, and easy feminine entertainment and helped them flourish. While those who objected recognized the necessary outlet protected wives and daughters from lustful attentions, they couldn't admit it out loud. They insisted the bordellos remain out of sight and the painted ladies remain at a distance. The staid residents couldn't eradicate the businesses, but they confined them to certain areas and controlled them through fines that acted as heavy taxes. The tensions divided the town, and the balance of power wobbled.

A saloon had opened across the street from Lily's store, and its proximity made her uncomfortable, especially once she'd seen the girls in their scant attire. Her frantic work consumed her attention, but before long, she had her first encounter with a soiled dove.

Early in the morning, a knock startled Lily as she stocked new merchandise. She hesitated, wishing she had the pistol. She'd carried it for a couple of weeks, but it unnerved her and got in the way, and it ended up under the front counter. Each day left her more confident Duncan hadn't picked up her trail. She still jumped at shadows, though, and chided herself for being a ninny.

"I'll be open at nine," she called.

A feminine voice responded, tight and urgent, "I need a corset ... please?"

Lily opened the door and tried to disguise her surprise.

The woman—hardly, she looked much younger than Lily herself—stood on the stoop in a low-cut bodice with breasts threatening to spill over. The blouse bared her arms, and her skirt hung open on one side, exposing colorful petticoats and stockings.

Lily cleared her throat and stepped back.

The woman smiled and rushed past, leaving a waft of strong perfume and chatter trailing behind. "Obliged. I'm desperate for a new corset. My stays broke last night, and the other stores won't let us girls shop 'til after hours, and my boss'll have my hide if I'm not workin' durin' busy hours."

The bright, heavy paint and dyed blonde hair fascinated and repulsed Lily. The dove stopped at the counter and turned with an expectant look.

Lily shook herself. "Oh, certainly. A corset? I only have a few just yet …. Not many women in town, so I haven't ordered many …." She led the way to the back corner.

She had seen saloon girls and a couple of crib girls from a distance but hadn't spoken to any. A gossipy customer explained the crib girls worked out of cabins or tents, usually disguising themselves as laundresses. They held the lowest rank of the doves in Clear Springs. Lily didn't exactly revile the prostitutes—she pitied them—but their activities disturbed her. Her mother's prejudice lingered. A woman who would allow such things done to her ….

Realizing she'd been staring, she whirled toward the discreet shelf of corsets and fumbled through them. They found one to fit, and the young woman quickly paid and left.

Afterward, Lily recalled what the woman said about the other store not allowing them to shop during regular hours.

Poor girls can't even buy clothes when they need to. That's absurd. I suppose I might gain a lot of business if I let it be known I'll let them shop.

The idea occupied her, and near the end of the day, she closed early to visit the saloons and spread the word that she would give the women extended shopping hours.

Sounds and smells buffeted Lily like a wave when she entered the Golden Eagle Saloon. A piano jangled over the conversation and laughter. Her nose wrinkled. The odors dredged up memories of her husband: beer and whiskey, pipes and cigars, perfume and sweat. Smoke hung in a thick layer at the ceiling, a gray pool of swirling, acrid fog. She squinted to scan the room, shuffling her feet and looking for a table. Eyes crawled along her body and peeled away her composure.

Five o'clock. She hadn't expected a crowd, but dozens filled the barstools, and games occupied the tables. Men ate, played cards, argued, and flirted with girls serving drinks. The women sauntered amongst the men, chatting and flaunting their wares. Paint hid faces and dresses revealed acres of skin.

Lily lowered her head and sank into a chair. She averted her eyes, carefully smoothing her skirt, but still the stares sought her attention.

Eventually, a short, plump woman with ample cleavage and pale skin sidled up to the table with a smirk.

"Missus, what's yer pleasure?" Her tone betrayed her curiosity.

Lily cleared her throat, seeking a good place to start. Buying something might break the ice. With a hesitant smile, she said, "A lemonade, please."

The woman tilted her head, shrugged, and walked away.

Most patrons had returned to their activities, and Lily observed them with hooded eyes. She'd chosen one of the better establishments to start. Clean, well-groomed men, dressed in work clothes rather than suits, talked and gamed. Many sported wedding bands on their left hands. The serving girl huddled with the barman, whispering, and Lily squirmed.

The woman returned with a glass of cloudy liquid and plunked it down. She had a vague prettiness, with bright red hair and a wide smile. Lines creased her eyes and mouth, and Lily guessed she was at least forty.

Lily laid a coin on the table. "Thank you." She faltered but spoke quickly as the woman turned away. "Sorry to keep you, but I ... well, I hoped to talk to one of you—one of the girls."

The woman spun back, an eyebrow raised as her lips hardened into a thin line. "Listen, missus, we don't need you ladies comin' in here to harass us about your man. If you can't keep him home, that's your trouble."

Lily blinked. "M-my man? What—" Her mouth formed an O as comprehension settled in, and she put up a hand in protest. "No, you don't understand. I'm not here about that. I, I don't have a man."

The woman looked sideways at her. "Then you're here to get one?" She cackled.

This will be harder than I thought.

"No, no. I'm looking for business." That sounded even worse. Lily stammered, "I mean to say, I own a store. A dry goods. I wanted to let you all, the women working here, know that I ... well, I'm happy to let you shop ... at regular hours. I won't limit the hours you can shop, I mean." She felt like the snake pinned by the rock, writhing and looking for a way out.

"Why? What are you aimin' at?" Suspicion sharpened her voice.

Lily smiled and lifted her shoulders. "Customers, for dry goods. I have the new store, across the way. I'd like your business."

"Why you tryin' to get us in there? That'll only make them prissy ladies mad. They don't like runnin' into us." Still eyeing her askance, the woman shifted and folded her arms.

"Some, perhaps, but there are more of you than there are of them. May I ask your name?"

The woman regarded her, shrugged, and offered, "Ellie. You know, that'll rile up a lot of folks, caterin' to us. Might just backfire on you."

Lily tilted her head. "I suppose it might, but I think it's worth the risk. Without you girls, I may be out of business pretty fast, anyway. Ellie, it's hard to get started here, as a woman."

A small smile touched her lips. "True that." She glanced around the room and clucked. "Hell, I expect you'll regret it, but I'll tell the girls."

Lily laid more coins on the table, enough for a generous tip, and pushed them toward Ellie. "I'd appreciate it. I hope I'll see you soon, Ellie."

"Maybe," Ellie hedged, plucking the money from the table and moving off as a man across the room bellowed her name.

The sun had gone down, and Lily stood on the boardwalk in the twilight, contemplating trying her luck at another beer hall or waiting until the next day. Dusk lent the street a sinister feel, and roaming the town after dark made her uneasy. The saloons would get rowdier in the evening, too, and she would only interrupt the girls in their work.

A warm hand on the small of her back brought a yelp, and she whirled on the offender.

"Just what do you think—"

Luke grinned down at her. "I think yer a bit jumpy, miss."

Her shoulders slumped with relief, but she swatted him. "With rough characters like you around, no wonder," she teased.

A wounded look passed over his face. "Rough, am I? I've never accosted a woman on the street."

Lily arched a brow. "Where, then?"

Luke couldn't hold the pout and broke into a hearty laugh. "In the appropriate places, miss. I reckon I better stay on guard around you." He made a face, throwing up his hands. "Don't know what yer complainin' about. I'd be thrilled if someone accosted me. I courted the Samuels girl not long ago, but she turned out not to appreciate my gentlemanly charms, and I had to cut the ol' girl loose. Haven't found anyone else willin' to listen to me."

"Perhaps you ought to try a different tactic." As their laughter trailed off, she noticed how close he stood, and her pulse quickened. "How are you?"

"I've been right good. Gettin' ready to head out on the trail soon. I'll be pickin' up my supplies in the next few days, if that's all right."

She hid her disappointment with a half-smile. "Oh. Well, I'll make sure to have things ready for you."

"I'd be mighty grateful. Need to get things packed. I could mosey over and take some off yer hands now, if it's no trouble."

Lily hesitated. *I'd best get back to the store, anyway.*

"No, no trouble. I have several things you could take with you." She denied the accusation from her sensible side that desire had made her decision.

"I'd appreciate it."

They turned to cross the street. Lily slid her hand into the crook of his arm, and a jolt of excitement shot through her when the firm muscles under his jacket tightened. She almost pulled her hand back, as if she'd touched a hot stove. They walked in silence, but tension crackled between them.

In the store, Lily consulted her order ledger. "Much of it's here. There are only a few things I'm waiting on, and they should arrive in the next day or two." She pulled out the parcels she'd set aside for him.

"Perfect! Really do appreciate ya handlin' it. Set my mind at ease knowin' it'd be done up right." He gathered packages but turned back. "Mind if I take ya to supper before I pick more up tomorrow?"

"Ah, no." As her mouth formed the word, her heart pounded out a different answer. She combed her mind for an excuse. "I can't, really. I ... have an appointment tomorrow."

"Have ya eaten yet tonight, then? Just want to thank ya for takin' good care of me. Don't make a poor cowboy beg." He grinned, put the goods down, and laced his fingers together in a gesture of appeal.

Her breath seized. His smile unraveled her resistance. *No harm will come of a quick dinner. Then he'll leave town, and I can focus on the store.* She denied the crazy aching crush at the thought of him leaving.

"Very well. Really, I should be thanking you."

"I'll let ya do that another time." He winked and retrieved the packages.

Luke stopped a boy and paid him to take the parcels to his place, and they walked up the street. He proposed the restaurant in the new hotel, but she protested that she didn't have a proper dress. He brushed aside her objections, but she insisted, and they went to a quiet tavern. The food was dubious, but they enjoyed themselves, and she lost her self-consciousness in the rough surroundings. He regaled her with tales from his cattle rides. Her attraction deepened as she listened, finding him more interesting than anyone she'd ever met.

After they pecked at the meal for a while, he walked her back to the store. Holding his arm didn't make her as uneasy as the first time, and they chatted as they dodged people on the boardwalk. She unlocked the door and stepped inside before turning to him with a smile.

"Thank you for a lovely evening, Luke."

"My pleasure, Miss Lily. I hope you'll let me take you out again once I get back off the trail," he said, taking her hand.

Thrown off by gesture and awkward again, she dropped her key. They stooped to retrieve it at the same time. When she straightened, they stood close, almost touching.

She giggled and waved a hand. "I, I'm sure you'll have forgotten about me after all that." Her voice wavered.

"Reckon I'll have to do this now, then." He bent to press his lips to hers.

Her sensible side railed, back away, stop the pointless flirtation. Beyond this point, it would only cause her heartache, one way or another. He would be gone for months and might never return. She had no time for pining over a man and didn't want to pick the wrong one again. He would complicate everything. The reasons to stop faded in the background as her lips softened for him. It felt right.

He rested his hands on her shoulders, but didn't open his mouth or try to coax hers to part. She wondered why he stopped there. His hands stayed still, barely touching her. He had made his offer, and seemed to wait for her to decide what should happen next. She sensed no pressure or guile in him, but she'd been wrong before ....

Abandoning clear thinking, she opened her lips. His mouth mimicked hers. Their tongues entwined in a tentative caress as she leaned into him.

Luke pulled back slowly, breaking the heated connection. His eyes glittered in the ethereal moonlight.

"I'll be back tomorrow." He turned and strolled away.

Lily stood in the doorway, waiting for her body and emotions to calm, and after a long time, she wandered off to bed.

CHAPTER FIFTEEN

On a cold day in early December, Charlotte woke after a night of little sleep. Her back ached, and she could find no comfortable position as her pregnancy neared its end. She guessed the baby would come in a few weeks, perhaps at Christmas. Ambivalence unsettled her. She wanted to see the baby and have the pregnancy over with, but the birth and caring for the baby scared her.

When she couldn't hide her growing belly, she'd begun her confinement. She had kept herself occupied, but loneliness had brought on a heavy depression. In the tiny house she shared with Duncan, she and her husband passed like neighbors late at night, and silence filled the days. No voices chattered in the kitchen, no one sat with her while reading or sewing. The stillness let in painful memories, guilt, and anger. She'd retreated to her childhood daydreams of adventure in the mountains of the West and often sat reliving old stories.

The isolation contributed to fear of the impending birth. Charlotte had no idea what to expect. Embarrassment kept her from speaking of it with Duncan, and she had no women friends. The more the baby grew, distorting her belly and kicking at all hours, the more alien it felt.

Shivering, she rolled from the bed and shuffled to the chamber pot. Balancing in an awkward and painful squat, she relieved herself. Wind whipped through the trees as a light snow fell, and she stoked the stove and put water on for coffee before settling in her rocking chair to sew until Duncan woke.

He'd acted distant and distracted more and more. She feared he'd been unfaithful. He often came home tousled, washed in perfume. She had confronted him once, but he dismissed it as paranoia. She told herself his restlessness was anticipation for the baby. He showed more interest in it than he did in her. His eyes lit up if the baby kicked when he touched her belly, and he'd already chosen names. Charlotte was glad he cared about the baby, but she'd begun to doubt his love for her.

Hours had passed when Duncan shuffled from the bedroom.

"I'll get your coffee, dear." She pushed herself up with supreme effort.

He grunted.

She poured him a cup and started breakfast, though the clock showed almost noon. They usually ate around midday since he often didn't get home until well after midnight. As she fried potatoes and eggs, the wind howled under a leaden sky, rattling the windows and huffing through cracks around the leaky stovepipe.

"You'll want to bundle up. The storm is bad," she said as she brought him a plate.

"Aye, I heard it. Wish people had the sense to stay home on a day like this, so I wouldn't have to go out."

"You'll get home early though, won't you?"

"Ought to, if it keeps snowin'."

"Can you get more coal before you go? The bucket's almost empty."

"I know it, no need to nag."

She held her tongue and started washing up.

"Ye ain't eatin', lass?"

"Not now. I don't feel well. I didn't sleep."

He grunted.

She finished cleaning, and Duncan finished eating. He dressed and went out for a load of coal from the bin behind the house while Charlotte returned to her rocker. A blast of snow swirled in when he came back. He dumped the coal in the bucket and shook the snow off his coat.

"Damn me, 'tis cold out there. Ye dinna need nothin' else? Ye canna go out today."

"Thank you. I'll be fine."

"I'll be after goin' to work then." He gave her a perfunctory kiss on the cheek.

"I'll wait up for you."

Quiet settled like a shroud once he'd gone. Charlotte finished mending a shirt, set it aside, and heaved up to stoke the fire and make a cup of tea. She winced as the pain in her back intensified. The mound at her midsection hardened. When the spasm faded, she added coal to the stove and had tea before returning to bed. She managed to doze as the storm raged on.

A knot of discomfort, tightening in her core, woke her. She held her breath until the ache lessened. She rolled to her other side with a groan and closed her eyes, but her stomach curdled as a notion snuck into the back of her mind.

No, it can't be. It's too early.

She pulled her covers closer and dismissed the idea.

Some time passed before the pain returned, and her belly tightened. After it tapered off, she slid from the bed, lit the lamp, and went to the window. The snow had grown heavier. A foot of powder covered the vacant road, shadowed blue as night fell.

Terror rose up like a living thing, and she squashed it. Five o'clock. Duncan would come home early. Soon enough. From the little she'd overheard of the gossiping cook and maid in her childhood, a birth took longer than a few hours. She nodded emphatically, as if the act would make it so.

She grabbed the broom. Perhaps activity would stave it off, or at least slow it down. She seized on the idea, and it echoed in her mind.

Slow it down. Slow it down. Slow it down.

As she swept the front room, she paused to catch her breath. A spasm came and bowed her over with a whimper.

"No. Please wait. I, I can't do this now."

When the cramp released her, she frantically pushed the broom back and forth. Tears stung her eyes. She focused on action, denying what she already knew. The pain hit. She waited and gritted her teeth, then continued her frenzied attack on the floor and swept over and over, long after it was clean. Pick up Duncan's clothes, more coal in the stove, a kettle on to boil, make bread for supper.

All at once, her body gave out as another contraction struck and forced her to her knees. She cried out, torment, fear, and anger combined in a wretched wail. Wetness slicked her thighs. A spreading blot on her nightgown lacked color.

"No, oh no."

Charlotte hauled to her feet while she searched her memory. The liquid was the "breaking of the waters." The pains would get stronger and closer together, and at some point the baby would come out, but her understanding of childbirth stopped there. She went to the window.

The snow blew sideways, and the street remained dark, lifeless.

Should I get dressed and find help? That old woman lives a few houses up.

Duncan had told her he knew a midwife he would fetch when the time came, but he wasn't there to fetch her. She debated, her thoughts scattered like broken glass, but the vise twisted through her belly again. The force sucked the air from her lungs. She waddled to the bed and sat on the edge. Her mind filled with panicked chatter.

Where did I leave my dress? No, the baby can't come—I haven't finished the booties. Did Duncan get more coal? Oh yes, I hung my dress by the stove to let it dry.

As she prepared to dress, another contraction slammed into her. She lay back, gasping for breath, until the wave ebbed.

I'll never get the dress on. My cloak. I'll put it on over my nightgown. Modesty be damned. Just rest a minute longer, then I'll go.

Charlotte didn't go. The pains came faster, doubled, trebled. She sobbed, begging the baby to wait. The pressure became constant, spasms wracked her body, and the urge to push took over. She strained with each convulsion, clutching at the bedsheets, sweating and moaning. With a final searing torment, she screamed and collapsed.

A vague realization came: the baby was out.

It was covered in bloody mucus, wrinkled and tiny—too tiny. She attempted to focus and wipe the blood from the infant's face.

Why isn't it crying?

Only then did she find the cord around its neck. She unwound it, but the form remained still, ashen under the smears of red. She patted it, rubbed it, shook it gently. The baby wouldn't move.

A dull, black horror swept over her, swallowing her up. Blood spread under her and darkened the sheet, a tide of oblivion to carry her away. She fainted.

*　*　*　*　*

Charlotte woke.

Duncan sat propped in a chair near the bed, dozing. Her eyes refused to stay open.

She whispered, "Duncan."

His head snapped up, and he leaned close. "Charlotte."

"Where is the baby?"

His face fell. "The baby ... dinna make it."

"Oh," she said. "I'm sorry."

Another death, another loss. Anger and sorrow and emptiness engulfed her. Her eyes closed, and she fell asleep again.

*　*　*　*　*

A week passed before Charlotte could leave the bed. She gradually regained her strength but spoke little. Duncan nursed her when he could and slept in the chair beside the bed.

When she could move around, he set her up in the rocking chair beside the stove, piling blankets around her and arranging everything within easy reach. She sat, staring, a world away. He tried to interest her in sewing or reading, talking or playing games, but nothing sparked her attention.

Duncan called the doctor again.

The doctor checked her eyes and her breath. "Do you have any pain?"

"What did you do with the baby?"

He patted her hand. "That's not something you need to worry about, miss."

"I want to know. Was it a boy?"

"You must forget the child. It'll do you no good to dwell on it. Are you sleeping well? I can give you some laudanum to help."

Charlotte turned her head away. After a moment, the doctor rose and stepped out. Voices drifted in.

"Physically, she's recovering well."

"Then what's wrong with her, Doc? She is nae herself."

"It happens sometimes after such an ordeal. She'll pull out of it. She should have a child again as soon as possible. That will take her mind off it."

"Aye, I need a bairn quick, else she's little good to me."

No, I must have heard that wrong. But the words haunted her and fueled resentment and blame.

At first, Charlotte spoke little and flinched at any contact. Duncan returned to the bed, but she squeezed as close to the edge as she could and lay awake, night after night. Though he complained, he didn't press her. She eased back into caring for the house while Duncan worked each day. As the winter passed, she resumed the housekeeping, shopped and ran errands, took in sewing. A shadow of normalcy.

Her mother had allowed grief to poison her mind, to steal her life long before she died. Charlotte determined to do what her mother couldn't: remake herself and become stronger. With a goal in mind, she banished the past and focused on a plan for the future. When memories surfaced, she resolutely turned them back, refusing to acknowledge them, and marshaled all her strength to concentrate on something else. But every time she looked at Duncan, she couldn't help the anger, the blame. If he had cared, if he hadn't left her alone ....

* * * * *

Charlotte lay sleeping when Duncan returned from work late, bumbling in the dark and knocking things over. She'd had a busy day; early hints of spring had arrived, and she wanted to plant vegetables on their tiny plot. Exhausted, she resented the intrusion and stiffened, gritting her teeth.

He shed his clothes and slid into the bed. She lay on her side, facing away from him. He ran a hand over her hip and up to her breast, cupping it as he leaned in to kiss her neck. She stirred and mumbled to feign sleep. He shifted closer and pressed against her, groaning as he ground his groin into the cleft of her cheeks.

His voice penetrated the dark, slurring, "Shhh. 'Tis just me, wife o' mine."

The words did nothing to calm her. Instead, panic gripped her. She tried to jerk free. Duncan's arm tightened around her, and he squeezed her breast.

"No!" She twisted to escape his hold, but he held her firmly.

"Charlotte, 'tis past time. I'm tired of waitin'. And the doctor said—"

"No! I don't care what the doctor said. I don't want a baby."

His fingers dug into her tender flesh. "I dinna much care what ye want. Ye're my wife, and ye'll do as I say. I want a child, and soon."

She blurted, "Then I won't *be* your wife. I'll run away."

Flat laughter met the declaration, and he turned her face to his with a rough paw. His eyes flashed in the moonlight, dead calm in his voice. "Ye won't get far. I'll kill ye before I let ye make a fool of me."

"You can't stop me." She clawed at his arm and tried to lunge off the bed.

"Ouch! Bitch! That's enough of yer insolence."

He grabbed her arm and shifted his weight onto her as she struggled. She sobbed and begged him to stop. Forcing her onto her stomach, he straddled her squirming legs and pinned her arm behind her. Charlotte screamed and flailed with her free arm as he tugged her nightdress up. He shifted to pry her legs apart and kneel between them while she writhed. His anger reached a fever pitch, and he twisted and yanked her arm back until she screamed.

Brutal and excited, he entered her roughly, and Charlotte wailed. She still squirmed to escape, but he imprisoned her. It didn't take long for him to release his seed, and he rolled off, collapsing beside her.

Charlotte bolted up on the edge of the mattress as soon as his bulk freed her. Disgust, fear, anger, and pain competed within her, bile burning her throat.

She hissed in the dark, "I hate you, and I'll never forgive you."

In a flash, his hand connected with her cheek, and she fell sideways. Quiet settled as his breathing slowed.

Then he spoke, low and cold, "Ye're mine. I dinna care if ye forgive, but ye dinna ever forget that."

She sprawled at the end of the bed, sobbing. When his snores grew loud, she dropped to the floor and crept from the room. She spent the rest of the night in her rocking chair.

The next day, Charlotte refused to speak. Duncan ignored her silence and acted as if nothing had happened. She couldn't tell whether he thought the incident didn't matter, or if he simply didn't remember it.

She would find a way out. The idea of running off alone terrified her, but she couldn't stay.

The money. With the money, I can go anywhere. As far away as I can.

She devised a plan after reading about a small town out west with a new gold strike. The journalist painted the town, called Clear Springs, as an Eden in the mountains, teeming with frontier freedom and opportunity. Charlotte reasoned that a boomtown, with its rapid growth and an influx of wandering souls, would offer anonymity as well as the chance to make a living. She'd be careful and cover her tracks. With a head start, a new identity, it would work. It had to.

Duncan violated her again, Charlotte shut down her mind, lying cold and unresponsive beneath him. She retreated into a trance to escape the torment and went over the plan in her mind. Afterward, she lay next to him, tears burning her cheeks, whiskey tainting the air.

She resolved to leave the next day.

CHAPTER SIXTEEN

Lily woke with a start. Her heart pounded, and sweat dampened her hair and nightgown. She sat up, hugging her legs and rocking.

Another nightmare. During the day, she'd learned to keep the memories at bay, but at night, the fear, anguish, and rage of the previous year crashed through the barriers. She dreamed of her mother and father, or the baby. She dreamed Duncan had found her and dragged her back, determined to punish her for escaping—the one she'd awakened from.

They are gone, in the past. I can't let them rule me.

Darkness blanketed the room, and she couldn't tell the time. She shook off the disquiet of the dream and lit the lamp, pulling her bedspread closer in the morning chill. By the time sunlight peeked in the windows, she'd turned her focus to work and gaining customers.

In the afternoon, she visited another saloon. Her jitters had subsided once she knew what to expect, and she entered with more confidence. The woman she talked to promised to pass the invitation on, giving Lily hope for more customers. When she arrived back at the store, a boy informed her that Luke had begged off due to an unavoidable delay and would pick up the goods the next evening.

Her heart sank, but she made a quick supper and worked while she ate. She stayed up long into the night, going over paperwork, occasionally distracted by the image of his smiling face.

Sunday morning, Lily walked to a small church, arriving late on purpose and slipping into the back pew. The preacher spoke about the dangers of consorting with the devil. Afterward, as she lined up with other members to thank the preacher, the women gave her a cool reception; no one spoke to her, and they avoided eye contact. She wondered if scandal had already arisen over her invitation to the saloon girls.

Lily returned home and cleaned until Luke arrived. He stood on the steps as another man hitched a horse at the rail. Her stomach fluttered, and she invited them in.

Inside, she pointed out a pile of crates, packages, and tins. The men carried the load out and tied the crates onto the animal and packed loose items into saddle bags. Luke returned as the other man led the horse away.

Luke leaned against the doorframe. "Can I persuade ya to join me for supper again, to make up for missin' our appointment yesterday?"

Lily didn't even consider refusing. *I might as well enjoy his company before he leaves. Nothing has to come of it. Once he's gone, I can go back to my quiet life.*

They took supper at the quiet diner where they'd first met. Lily asked about the cattle drive, and Luke's eyes lit up.

"We'll be up north, almost Wyomin'. We gather up the beefs from their winter feedin', brand 'em, and drive down to Denver. Takes a month or two. Some rough country, but nothin' prettier." His voice softened. "These mountains .... There's somethin' special about 'em. They get under a man's skin. When he wakes up at dawn and the sun's comin' up over the tops, through the trees, the light's so soft and so brilliant it hurts, all at the same time. Makes him feel like he's the only person on earth. The wind in the trees is like a special song nobody else ever heard before. It calms all those worries that plague a man.

"And ya can build a life here, all on yer own, just off the land. Nothin' else ya need. But then in a flash the land can turn dangerous, almost like the mountains are tryin' to see if yer worthy. They test ya, and keep testin'. Makes ya know yer alive. And if ya pass muster, the reward is somethin' ya can't find no place else: Ya get to keep seein' that beauty and hearin' that song.

"I see these fellers flockin' here like pigeons, thinkin' they'll find a big hunk of rock, and that'll solve all their troubles and make 'em happy. I ain't seen one yet that happened to. Mostly they wander around lookin' lost, and tired, and desperate. Most of 'em never figure out the fortune in these hills ain't somethin' ya can pick up and take with ya." He glanced at her and looked away, as if he expected her to laugh.

A shiver raced up her spine as he talked, and the passion in his voice made her breathe faster. She realized hiding and setting up the store had so preoccupied her, she hadn't paid much attention to the landscape—though her troubles on the trail explained a lot of that. Was that the test? After dreaming of it for years, she resented the fact that her circumstances had drained the wonder from the experience. The mountains had become an obstacle to overcome, the backdrop to her liberation, rather than a destination. Luke's perspective made her want to see her surroundings with fresh eyes.

"I never thought of it that way, or I suppose I did a long time ago, when I could only dream of seeing it. I like your version" She smiled. "You don't miss Texas?"

He tilted his head, contemplating. "I miss some of it, and the family. I reckon I'll head back for a visit eventually, but for now, my heart's here."

Lily's heart fluttered in response.

After eating, they chatted, but a palpable energy lit the air. The conversation lulled, and Luke studied her a long moment before speaking.

"Mind if I ask ya something?"

Unease tightened her chest. "I suppose that depends on what it is."

"Tell me why yer really here."

Lily swallowed and broke eye contact. "Does it matter?"

He scanned her face as he paused. "Yep. Not the way ya think, but it does." The lamp's wavering flame threw light and dark across his face.

"I left my husband." She lifted her chin.

"Can I ask why?"

"He … didn't treat me well." She couldn't suppress a shudder. "I ran away. The marriage was a mistake. I was young, naïve, wanted to escape my parents' house.

"I left him without saying anything. He would have stopped me … one way or another. He'd told me that. After he left for work, I gathered a change of clothes, some food, the little bit of money I'd hidden. I tried to disguise myself and stuck to alleys. A family let me ride with them to Philadelphia. They let me off in the city, and I bought a train ticket for St. Louis and then Denver. I rode from there to here, on my own. That was stupid, really, and I almost didn't make it. But I was desperate." Luke's face showed concern without condemnation, and she continued. "I changed my name and tried to make sure he couldn't follow. But he'll try to."

His eyes darkened. "So, he don't know where ya are?"

She shook her head, afraid she'd break down if she spoke more.

"Good. Some men don't deserve to call themselves that. Hittin' or houndin' a woman never makes a man bigger, though some of 'em think it does." He reached for her hand, and his voice dropped lower. "I won't let a man do it, if'n I can stop 'em."

Lily forced herself to meet his gaze. Tenderness softened his sharp features. In the blink of an eye, everything became clear.

They left the restaurant and walked to the store in silence. She unlocked the door, took his hand, and led him inside. In the back room, he sat while she lit the lamp. Dim light filled the small space, and she took his hands to pull him up.

"Lily, ya don't have to do this. Ya don't have to prove nothin' to me. I'm happy to wait."

She lifted a finger to his lips. "I'm not trying to prove anything. I want this, you. I don't care what happens later."

Rising up on her toes, she drew his head down, meeting his lips with her own, and melted into him. She pulled away to unbutton his shirt. He watched, smiling. Her arms slid up, and she entwined her fingers behind his neck as she laid her face on the soft mat of his chest. Soap, leather, and a faint musk. She relaxed against him. From the first touch, it felt right.

They moved toward the bed. She sat him down and stood before him as she undressed. She smiled as she realized she didn't even feel nervous or shy. Her chemise fell. She tugged her drawers down and stood nude.

Luke's gaze slid up her legs, studying each curve and dip, every rise and shadow. He rose and pulled the pins from her hair. His fingers ran through her auburn curls and let them fall over her breasts. Breathing deeply, he buried his face against her neck. A hand came up to cradle her head.

Lily waited, unmoving. She wanted it to last, though her core already burned.

His body heat warmed her as he undressed. Her attention followed his hands. She smiled at the stark contrast between the pale flesh of his body and the sun-darkened skin of his face and hands. Hard ridges of muscle played between supple clefts, a mix of power and tenderness. A long scar ran from his shoulder, down over the bicep to his elbow, and made her wince.

He stood naked with her. Her pulse raced, and a primal ache throbbed deep in her belly, tempered by a dart of apprehension.

Lily tilted her face up. Rising on her toes, she kissed him, and their bodies met. His arms slid around the small of her back. They sank onto the bed, kissed and explored with their hands and mouths. Her fingers found his member pressing against her belly and caressed it. He followed, sliding his hand over her mound to the warmth between her legs. His finger settled over the firm button and stroked it with a soft touch.

She gasped and arched toward him. Her belly tightened as she trembled against him. She lifted her leg over his hip, opening herself to him.

They rocked together, hips tilting back and forth in a slow rhythm. Neither looked away. Heat built between, within, around them. Their bodies melded, seeking the same release. On a final, deep thrust, intense pleasure overcame them.

As their breaths slowed, contentment settled in, and her fingers traced the lines of his face. He watched her and smiled. They fell asleep without words.

* * * * *

Lily woke and reached for Luke, but his spot had gone cold. She lay still, fixing the memory of his taste, smell, and touch in her mind. Dawn had come. She lit the lamp, pulled out the chamber pot, and relieved herself. Taking her dressing gown from a hook near the bed, she slipped it on and sat at the table. A sheet of paper lay there.

> *Lily,*
> *I wish I didn't have to go. I couldn't bring myself to wake you. Didn't want to have to say goodbye. Leaving now is hard, but I have to if I want to save enough for my ranch. Reckon I'll be back in 2 or 3 months. I'll be thinking of you and counting the days til I see you again.*
>
> *Yours Truly, Luke*

Tears filled her eyes and spilled over. Leaving the note on the table, she rose to dress.

She'd known he had to leave and couldn't fault him for it. She had made the choice and didn't regret the wonderful night. Luke wasn't Duncan.

Can I trust him? Or myself? Love doesn't have to mean losing myself, does it? I can love him and be my own person. When he comes back—if he comes back—we'll see where it goes.

CHAPTER SEVENTEEN

Lily sat at the counter in the quiet store, mulling strategy and trying to forestall a creeping gloom. The second payment would come due soon. She'd paid the first installment—Luke's large order helped ensure that—but she needed more income. She drummed her fingers on the countertop.

She'd focused on work and avoided dwelling on Luke as spring advanced with grasses and flowers splashing color into the valley seemingly overnight. She'd priced new stock, organized displays, and completed orders for more merchandise. The shelves had filled in, and she surveyed them with muted satisfaction.

Now, if only I had customers!

Business had dropped off after the initial excitement of the opening. As summer closed in, the miners drifted farther from camp, ranging over the mountains to find new claims. They only came into town every week or two. The slow season compounded her newcomer status.

While some respectable wives ventured in, they didn't stay to chat. Clusters of women whispered when she passed them on the boardwalk, and she couldn't shake the feeling they whispered about her. People had to suspect the ruse about her "brother" by now. Gossip always spread like wildfire. They would invent their own scenario for a young, single woman in a rowdy gold rush town. Their version would titillate, and it wouldn't take long for rumor to become fact.

Would she have to choose between the powerful and the numerous? She waited to see if sales would improve as word spread of her willingness to serve the saloon girls.

The door opened, and a man held it for an older woman in a stylish walking dress. If not for his clothing, Lily would have thought him a child from his height—at least a head shorter than his companion. His fine, tailored suit, with a cutaway jacket displaying a gold watch chain, dispelled the impression. He hung his bowler and the woman's umbrella on the hat rack, and they perused the window merchandise.

Lily smiled and called, "Can I help you?"

His eyes touched on her, and he gave a curt nod. As he looked over the items, his chin thrust forward, and his hands slid up, curling over the narrow lapels of his jacket. The woman sniffed and turned to a rack of clothes. He finished his examination, offered the lady an arm, and they stepped up to the counter. She raked Lily's dress with a smirk and looked away.

"You are Miss Wright?" His clipped nasal tone reeked of Eastern high society.

Lily tensed. She found her voice, but it came out strained. "Yes ... and you are?"

"Samuel Beckett." He inclined his head to the woman. "This is Mrs. Samuels, one of the founders of Clear Springs. We represent a group of businesses and social organizations in Clear Springs. We are circulating a petition to present to Marshal Parker to propose decency laws for our growing city. I assume you would like to join the petition." As he spoke, he'd produced a piece of paper from his pocket. He unfolded it and thrust it toward her.

Relief surged, tempered by caution. Eastern accents always made her think of Duncan. Still, the man's officious manner grated on her. She gave the paper a cursory read. Several signatures followed a brief appeal to the marshal, with no mention of which laws the group sought.

Beckett's gaze had wandered, a bored scowl tugging at his mouth.

Mrs. Samuels took up the address. "I'm sure you're a good Christian woman, Miss Wright, and as such, you know we must not tolerate those elements of society who would drag good people into sin. We must help them see the errors of their ways or encourage them to move on. As Galatians says, 'Now the works of the flesh are evident: sexual immorality, impurity, sensuality, idolatry, sorcery, enmity, strife, jealousy, fits of anger, rivalries, dissensions, divisions, envy, drunkenness, orgies, and things like these. I warn you, as I warned you before, that those who do such things will not inherit the kingdom of God.'" She breathed deep, seeming enraptured by the words. "We must cleanse our town of these people. They will bring the wrath of God to Clear Springs." Her lips curled, and her eyes flashed with a crazed zeal.

Just like my mother. Lily suppressed a tremor and offered a polite nod. Turning her attention back to Beckett, she tried a smile, but it felt weak.

"Mr. Beckett, pardon me, but may I ask what decency laws you propose?"

His gaze snapped to her, and his mouth tightened. "The customary laws desired by a town that does not intend to let the depraved rule, Miss Wright." His tone made it clear he didn't appreciate being questioned.

She hesitated. Beckett surely had some influence in town, and she had no desire to alienate him, but she resented the overbearing attitude. In the past, she would have capitulated to such a demand without thought, if only to avoid unpleasantness. Instead, she found herself speaking before she could rein it in.

"I'm afraid I don't have your experience with the depraved, Mr. Beckett. Which laws are considered customary?"

He squinted at Lily, as if a strange animal had mysteriously appeared before him.

His voice sharpened. "Liquor laws, laws regarding where and when certain businesses may operate, as well as laws limiting the presence of certain persons in respectable businesses during normal business hours. Laws, Miss Wright, which protect decent citizens from those who are not." He pointed toward the ink bottle on the counter and waved a hand. "We have much to do, so if you do not mind, I would appreciate it if you would hurry it along." He moved to study an array of cloth.

Lily gaped at his dismissal. Her nails dug into her palms, and her jaw clenched. Was it a test? Perhaps the "decent" segment wanted to find out more about her and her intent, or maybe they simply wanted her on their side. Would she gain their trust—and their business—if she joined their campaign? She questioned whether that would overcome any doubts about her. If she didn't sign, would the petitioners cause trouble? It felt like a trap.

She considered Beckett as he fingered a bolt of flannel and tapped his foot impatiently.

"Mr. Beckett, thank you for the information, but I believe I must decline to join this petition." She slid the paper across the counter.

His head swiveled, and his blank stare spoke volumes. "I believe you misunderstand, Miss—"

"I understand well enough, Mr. Beckett. Good day."

He thrust his jaw out and snatched the paper off the counter. He turned, walked to the door, and plucked his hat from the rack. Mrs. Samuels shot Lily a sneer before whirling to retrieve her shade. Beckett opened the door, glanced around the shop, and settled his gaze on Lily with a chilly smile. He ushered Mrs. Samuels out.

Lily let out a ragged sigh. Her throat burned with indignation and sickening memories. Her mother's voice snuck into her mind, railing at sin. A stab of satisfaction buoyed Lily at the thought of defying the years of self-righteous dogma her mother had heaped on her.

Why would God care who I let shop, or when? And they seem to forget "judge not, lest ye be judged." I have to take care of myself, and I'll do what I must to make it on my own. No one else will do it for me. She swallowed and straightened her back. *I'll be damned if I'll let them bully me.*

Underneath the anger, anxiety festered in the back of her mind as she wondered where the choice would take her.

CHAPTER EIGHTEEN

While Lily turned the "Open" sign to "Closed" after locking the door, a soft knock stopped her. Again, she wished she could have afforded a door with a pane. The display window sat too far back to see a person at the door. The knock turned insistent, followed by a hissing whisper.

"Please, let me in! Ha' mercy ...."

Why did I leave the gun under the counter again?

The voice pleaded like a child, high-pitched and frightened. "Ma'am, please, I got nowhere to go."

Lily cracked the door. A girl cowered on the stoop, wrapped in a shabby shawl. Her head hung between her shoulders, her face hidden by disheveled, dirty hair.

"What do you want?"

The girl raised her head. A battered face emerged in the dying twilight. One eye had nearly disappeared under a swollen lump distorting one side of her face, and a trickle of blood leaked from a split lip.

Lily threw the door open and pulled her inside. "My goodness, what on earth?" She scanned the empty boardwalk and slammed the lock home.

The girl's eyes darted around the store, but she didn't move.

Lily bent close. "Who did this? You need to see the marshal about this."

The girl's good eye grew wide, and she jerked her head side to side. "I can't."

"Heaven's sake, why not?"

The girl merely looked away.

Lily huffed, gestured for the girl to follow to the back room, and sat her at the table. After dipping a cup of water from the kettle, she grabbed a clean cloth and a tin of salve. She knelt and tipped the girl's face up, brushing her hair back. Lily wet the cloth and dabbed at blood and smudges of dirt.

"What's your name?"

"Jessie." Her swollen mouth turned it to a lisp. She kept her gaze lowered.

Lily nodded and applied ointment to her lip and a scrape above her eyebrow. The bulge on the left side had grown even larger and darkened to purple. A plain girl, with mousy brown hair and hazel eyes, though she didn't appear as young as Lily first thought.

As Lily worked, Jessie calmed, and her hands loosened their grip on the shawl. The wrap fell open and revealed a small breast under a torn blouse, but Jessie made no move to cover herself. Distinct finger marks reddened several spots around the breast.

Those will be bruises later.

She brushed hair from the girl's face. "How did this happen, Jessie?"

"I was robbed."

"By who?"

Jessie considered Lily, eyes narrowed. "A customer," she

said after a long pause.

Lily sighed. "You aren't in one of the houses?"

A spark of derision lit her good eye. "I ain't pretty 'nuff fer them."

"So, you don't have a madam?"

She shook her head. "I got a crib over at South Street. Bed and a stove." The esses came out mushy.

"Oh." She could think of nothing else to say.

"Bastard took all my savings. Stupid, keepin' it in my crib."

"But, why did he ...?" She gestured at Jessie's face.

"He wanted the extra without payin', and I told him to shove off. He boxed me a cheap shot when I wasn't lookin' and near knocked me out," Jessie grumbled. "He kept goin', though. Mean cuss. Finally quit and said he would take my stash 'cause he wasn't teachin' me a lesson for free."

Lily's stomach rolled, and she looked away. "Why is it you can't go to the marshal? It's not illegal here, is it?"

She shrugged, winced, and pressed a hand against her ribs. "Got my own difficulties. It ain't worth the trouble. He won't do nothin 'bout it. Ain't nobody takes the word of a dove."

"I see." Lily dabbed at an ooze of blood on the girl's lip. "Why did you come to me?"

"Some of the gals been sayin' you're friendly with us."

"Oh. Well, yes, I guess so."

"You was one?"

Lily blurted, "Goodness, no!"

A flash of hurt painted Jessie's face.

"I, I'm sorry. I didn't mean to ... say it like that. I've never ... been a dove. I just—I don't think you girls should be condemned for it."

"I ought to go," Jessie mumbled.

"No. I'm sorry. Really. You can stay." The words tumbled out in an awkward rush.

Jessie shook her head. "It's all right. I ain't mad. I ought to get back to my crib, or someone will chisel the rest of my stuff."

"Well ... okay. Are you sure you'll be all right? That's a nasty bump. Do you have enough to eat?"

"Ain't the first. I'll mend, and I can feed myself. "

Jessie rose and pulled her shawl around her. She walked through the front room, stiff and slow. Lily followed to unlock the door and stood aside while Jessie stepped out. The girl didn't turn back, but a muffled, "Obliged," drifted back as she shuffled off.

Lily locked up, went back to her room, and slumped into the chair.

That poor girl. How did she come to such a state? Just one mistake?

Her heart skipped a beat, and she swallowed hard. Jessie's disfigured face kept coming to her. Her mind conjured images of a desolate room with a stained mattress. She shook her head, but the disturbing picture wouldn't recede. Shuddering, Lily jumped from the chair.

She scrambled to light a fire in the stove, desperate for action to chase the vision away. She busied herself tidying up, made a quick supper, and ate, but had to force the food down. Sleep was out of the question.

She'd never really considered the notion she could be doomed to such a fall. It wouldn't take much. The possibility stunned her.

Looking for another task to distract herself, she started for the front room.

The shattering of glass startled a cry from her. A thump and rumble of something rolling on the floor followed.

Lily stood rooted in the doorway, mouth ajar.

She waited, minutes crawling by in silence, until she dared to investigate. She picked up the lamp and tiptoed into the front room. Chilled night air wafted through a blank hole in one of the window panes, and glass littered the floor underneath. Several feet away, a lump lay next to a rack of clothes. She crept to the window. The street lay dark and deserted, the only sound a faint tinkle of piano from across the road. She picked up the bulky object and turned it over. Twine bound a slip of paper to a rock the size of a child's shoe. Fingers trembling, she untied the string, set the rock aside, and unfolded the paper. A bolt of horror rocked her.

One word, scrawled in bold letters.

WHORE

CHAPTER NINETEEN

Lily paced the back room. The paper, rock, and twine lay on the table and drew her gaze on every pass. The glass remained on the floor, the litter of broken shards flashing in her mind. Her hand groped for the gun in her pocket, and its weight reassured her.

The smashed window had rattled her, and the word on the paper brought back her father's stinging accusations. She still carried deep shame and hurt from him. She ran a hand over her face and pushed her father from her mind. The window had nothing to do with him, and dwelling on it would only distract her. She needed to focus on the problem at hand. Perhaps the assault involved the girl.

No, that makes no sense. Even if anyone knew of Jessie's visit, they wouldn't wait until she left. Who, then? Children? A drunken fool?

"Beckett?" Her soft voice interrupted the scrape of her shoes on the boards.

He'd acted like a bully, but this? He carried a chip on his shoulder. Fastidious, pretentious. The sort of man who remembered small transgressions and let them fester and repaid the offenders. Had he added her to that list? Possibly. He wouldn't expose himself to the risk of dirty work himself, though. He'd use a hired man. Beckett had the capacity for coarseness, but it didn't suit his style. He'd pride himself on appearing "civilized" and carry out intimidation and punishment through more sophisticated means. Still, she couldn't rule him out.

The most frightening—and she hoped least likely—possibility remained. Her blood went cold.

Duncan. Perhaps, despite all her efforts, he'd found her. A multitude of clues could lead him to her. She didn't know how she knew, but she felt sure he would come. With persistence, cleverness, and luck, Duncan could have found her trail.

Lily stopped pacing. Memories flooded her mind in jumbled fragments, like a river jammed with debris. Duncan's face, smiling as he talked of his ambitions, laughing and gesturing as he described the house he would build for her when he achieved success. She watched him turn more serious, desire highlighting his full mouth and deep-set eyes. Then his face transformed, a magician's trick. The smile faded, his lips tightened to a colorless line, nostrils flared. His eyes went dark. Rage emanated from him as waves of scorching heat.

"No, no, no," she moaned, rebelling against remembered fear.

What would he do when he found her? She wanted to believe he would simply confront her, angry but concerned, and beg her to come back. A voice inside insisted he wouldn't make it that easy. He would need to punish her. He would want to see her cower. He would make sure she never rejected him again. Could he harness his rage, use it to terrorize her? Might he start by intimidating her with an anonymous attack, followed by another, and another? He might. Rattle her, keep her on edge. Take her confidence away, piece by piece. Make her afraid of the enemy she couldn't see. Duncan always planned ahead, and she'd seen his cruel streak. She imagined him watching her, waiting for her reaction. She imagined he would relish that.

Sickening fear crept in, tightening her chest until she couldn't breathe. A trickle of sour sweat ran down the curve of her spine. A weight tugged at her hand. Without realizing it, she'd taken the gun out of her pocket. The metal gleamed. Heavy for such a small thing, as if its potential added to its weight. Her hand shook. Could she—would she—use it, when the time came?

* * * * *

When the sun rose, Lily sat hunched in the chair. Her hand cradled the gun in her lap. The slip of paper lay on the table, an accusation. Grainy sand coated her eyes, knives twisted her in back.

She would go to the marshal. Perhaps he would say several such incidents had occurred, and the culprit sat in his jail; but she expected he would say he couldn't do anything and she should let it go. Perhaps a deadly mistake.

Lily slid the gun into her pocket and gathered the paper and rock. Revulsion sloshed in her belly as she put the items into a bag. The window's jagged hole mocked her as she skirted the debris in the front room. Her nerves thrummed with apprehension. She arranged her features into a calm façade, opened the door, and stepped outside.

A mongrel dog trotted down the street. A man swept dirt off the saloon's porch across the way. One wagon idled up the road, the horses twitching and shaking their heads as flies buzzed them. On her side, a stooped form shuffled along the boardwalk, moving away. An ordinary bucolic morning, nothing out of place, but the town didn't feel the same. When she'd arrived in Clear Springs, the source of her fear seemed distant, remote. Now, it surrounded her.

Her jaw clenched. *No. No matter who is behind this, I will not give in. I won't let them take this from me.*

She smoothed her rumpled skirt and started up the boardwalk. As she neared the marshal's office, she spotted Jacob leaning against the hotel's hitching post. She called to him and beckoned.

He grinned and loped across the street. He acted more comfortable with her, but his shyness still made him awkward, and he stuffed his hands into his pockets.

"Mornin', Miss Wright. Can I do somethin'?"

"Hello, Jacob." How to ask the question without seeming nosy? *Might as well be direct.* "Have any men checked into the hotel in the past few days? Any newcomers?"

"Just one, ma'am."

"Can you ... describe him? Do you know anything about him?"

His head tilted. "Uh, he's an average fella, I guess. Don't really stand out. Think he said he was from up north. Came in two days ago." He shrugged.

"But what does he look like? Dark-haired? Dressed fancy or ...?"

"Huh. Dark, I s'pose." He paused. "I wouldn't say fancy, but not workin' duds."

That could be Duncan.

"Somethin' wrong, Miss Wright?"

She forced nonchalance. "No, no. Someone I know is expected any time now, but that doesn't sound like him." *He could be watching me now.*

"Oh. Sorry." He shuffled his feet. "I better get back, or Mr. Amos will hide me."

"Yes, I'm sorry to keep you. Thank you for your help." She smiled and squeezed his arm.

His eyes widened, and he looked at her hand. "Take care, Miss Wright." His head bobbed as he spun away and loped back to his post.

More people had stirred, and she scrutinized each one before entering the marshal's office. Three jail cells lined the back wall. The marshal sat at a battered desk, sporting a curled mustache, a wide-brimmed hat tilted on his head, feet propped up as he studied a sheet of paper.

Lily cleared her throat. "Pardon me, Marshal Parker?"

He lowered the paper and appraised her with a heavy-lidded gaze.

"I, I need to report a crime, Marshal."

His eyebrows lifted in a disinterested query.

Lily pulled her shoulders back and stomped to the desk, annoyance overcoming nervousness. She began to understand Jessie's opinion of him. She dropped the bag on his desk with a thump.

He snorted. "What's that?"

She bit back a nasty reply and kept her voice neutral. "*That* is what shattered my store window last night."

Parker pulled out the contents, unfolded the paper, and smirked. "What do you expect me to do with this?"

"Find out who did it, of course!"

He looked at her under heavy brows and returned the items to the bag. He held it out, but she stepped back.

"Ma'am, there's nothin' here to tell me where this came from or who might've wanted you to have it."

Her apprehension welled up and spilled over. "Marshal, this may have come from someone who wants to harm me.

141

Post a guard, or, or something. I need help. Please."

Parker propped his chin in his hands. "I can't stand around guardin' everyone who thinks someone's out to get 'em. It's probably nothin'. Now, if you can bring me some proof that somebody in particular threw this, I can charge 'em with disturbin' the peace, and they'll have to pay a fine or spend the night in jail. But I don't got time to go lookin' for some fool. This ain't a resort, ma'am, and it'll only get rougher. Keep your wits, bar your doors at night. Otherwise .... Well, it might be best if you went back to wherever you came from."

He nodded at his outstretched hand and waved the bag.

Lily opened her mouth, but thought better of it when she saw his expression. He had no interest in anything she said. She spun on her heel and stalked out, leaving the bag in his hand.

She returned to the store, disheartened and exhausted. Standing at the front of the empty shop, her isolation settled in and gave added weight to her fatigue. No one to turn to, no one to give her advice, no one who cared whether she existed or not.

"How can I do this alone." Her soft voice fell flat and made the solitude more complete. She ached to hear a kind voice.

On cue, Luke's slow drawl echoed in her mind. Her throat constricted. She wanted to feel his arms envelop her and hear him tell her everything would turn out all right. He wouldn't, though. Not for a couple of months, anyway. Resentment pricked her.

Why does he have to be gone now? She squeezed her eyes shut.

Lily debated whether to keep the store closed. She wanted to crawl into her bed. Sleep beckoned and offered a sanctuary, however temporary. Maybe the marshal had it right, and she couldn't survive in Clear Springs, but she couldn't go back to Jefferson City. Where else could she go?

Nowhere. I have to do this. Alone or not.

With fresh resolve, she swept up the remnants of the window pane and tacked a piece of canvas over the hole. She went out back and dipped a bucket of fresh water from the barrel. Inside, she lit the stove to heat water for coffee, splashed water on her face, and re-pinned her hair. The store opened on time.

CHAPTER TWENTY

Lily slumped at the counter with a stack of mail. She sipped coffee while reading, but her tired eyes blurred the print. Her mind wandered, replaying the long night. Every loud noise in the street made her flinch and set her heart racing. She had given up and pushed the papers aside when the door opened.

A woman paused on the threshold. She wore the clothing of a dance hall girl, better quality and less revealing than saloon girls' attire.

Lily motioned her in. "Welcome. Come in, please."

"You have open hours? I heard we were allowed ...."

"Yes, miss. No restricted hours." She smiled.

The woman returned the smile and closed the door behind her. "Thank you. That's real kind." She shopped for a while and bought several items, thanking Lily again before she left.

The sale revitalized Lily, and the weariness and despair dissipated. More soiled doves came in, most wavering on the threshold as if prepared for flight. Lily greeted each with a smile. She ignored their state of dress and treated them as she would the ladies at church. Some eyed her with suspicion, but most expressed gratitude and told her they would return.

Her spirits lifted. The sales beat any previous day. She reined her hopes in, but the idea to rely on the scarlet women showed promise.

The difficulty came late in the afternoon. A bedraggled prostitute in a grubby outfit, wild, dyed hair, and smeared makeup entered with an unsteady shamble. She ended up at the back of the store perusing the stockings. Bracing herself against the shelves, she stared, eyes wide and unfocused while her head wobbled. Her blouse exposed the top of her corset and a generous portion of cleavage, and her skirt barely covered her knees. Likely one of the crib girls, suffering opium or laudanum addiction.

As the dove rambled through the store, Lily kept one eye on her. She stood to approach the woman and offer help.

The door opened again. A lady in a prim walking dress of the latest style stepped in and surveyed the store. She moved ahead with a stiff gait, back straight, hands clenched tightly in front of her. The woman ignored Lily and stopped to examine a fancy hat near the door.

Lily vacillated, seeing a collision she couldn't avert. For once, she hoped the lady would find the hat unacceptable and leave without a purchase. Seconds dragged into minutes, and Lily remained frozen, afraid to draw attention.

The lady moved first; she picked up the hat and turned toward the counter. Lily plastered on a charmed smile.

"I'll take this hat." She spoke as if she expected groveling appreciation.

Lily bobbed her head and pulled out a hat box. Her hands shook as she stuffed the hat in and wrote out a receipt. The dove hadn't moved.

"How much?"

She murmured, "$7.50, ma'am."

The woman opened her purse and counted out money.

"Hey!" A rough, guttural voice rumbled like thunder through the store.

Lily's heart lurched.

The lady flinched and swiveled her head toward the sound, the tendons in her neck almost creaking. Her mouth screwed up, contracting until the skin around her lips turned white. The dove staggered toward them. She thrust a clutch of rainbow stockings at Lily.

Nothing could salvage the situation.

"I, I'll be with you in a moment," Lily stammered at the dove. She turned to the lady. "$7.50, ma'am." Her attempt to sound chipper came out as a squeak.

The dove reached the counter, billowing the stink of liquor, perfume, and musky body fluids. The lady stumbled backward. She looked from the dove to Lily with saucer eyes as a deep pink stained her pale skin.

"How dare you allow ... that, that *creature* ...?" She abandoned the purchase, snatched her purse from the counter, and retreated several steps. She fired a deadly glare at the dove before her gaze returned to Lily. "We won't stand for this." Her heels tapped out her ire as she bolted for the door.

The dove sagged against the counter and gawked at the lady, eyebrows raised. Her scarlet lips slurred, "What's her problem?"

Lily groaned.

* * * * *

The previous trickle of customers swelled into a steady stream. Within days the shelves stood half-empty, and Lily had a growing list of orders to fill. Shoppers kept her busy during store hours, and she spent evenings writing to suppliers and completing order forms.

As far as she could tell, the rush of business resulted from Beckett's campaign. He'd convinced almost all of the shopkeepers to limit access to scarlet women. His policy would have forced the women to cut work hours short to shop after regular store hours—if not for a few proprietors who refused to cooperate until the law said otherwise. The doves flocked to the outliers.

Lily developed a rapport with them. The girls avoided talking about their pasts—much as she did—but they let slip clues about where they came from and how they ended up in Clear Springs. Some had a middle class background, most were near her age. The connections surprised her.

"My sister would love that color," one dove told her as she looked at a lace kerchief with longing. Her eyes clouded, and she sniffed. "At least she would have when I knew her. Ain't seen her in so long, I wouldn't know now."

Frowning, Lily squeezed the girl's hand. "I'm sure she hasn't changed."

She shrugged. "I'd send it to her, but the folks wouldn't let her have it. They prob'ly told her I'm dead. They send back all my letters."

Lily asked without thinking, "Oh dear, why?"

"I disgraced 'em. Got with child." The dove's face went blank, and she clammed up.

Lily had never given much thought to the occasional streetwalker that stalked the neighborhood around her father's store or ambled along the road near her house with Duncan. She'd assumed the women must be wicked and beyond salvation. As she came to know the doves, her views shifted.

She discovered circumstances beyond their control often drove them to the trade; some found themselves orphaned, sold, or tricked into a job, and many suffered the loss of a husband that left them to support a family. Some doves were married, saddled with a husband who didn't or couldn't work. Even those who chose the work had little alternative. They opted for the illusion of independence rather than the shackles of social convention. Lily had heard of a few who gained ostensible success—wealth, notoriety, leisure—but the price seemed to haunt them. Most had worse luck.

A woman, older than Lily, came in drunk early in the morning. She wandered the store for a long while and at last came to the counter with a plain cloth doll and a wooden toy gun. Her makeup had run under wet trails of tears.

Lily resisted the urge to pry. "Anything else for you today, ma'am?"

"Naw, only got two young'uns. The rest's gone on."

"Oh. I, I'm sorry." Her heart wrenched. "Should I wrap these?"

The dove nodded. "Wrap 'em good. Got to send 'em post. They's with my sister in Saint Lou."

"I'm sure they miss you."

"Reckon they don't. They was too little to remember when I took to the road. Gone five years now." She ran a sleeve across her nose and sniffled. "Might as well be orphans."

Dismay wrung a question from Lily, "Why? Why don't you go back?" She instantly wished she could steal it back.

The woman's sharp look made her flinch. "Think I don't wanna?" The anger melted behind a sob. "Nothin' more I want. But their Pa went an' got hisself killed workin' the railroad. Older boys passed on from fever. Wasn't no way to keep the farm. How's a gal s'posed to keep a family with no money and no work? Had to find a livin'." Her chin lifted. "I couldn't let 'em grow up seein' their ma on her back. I do my bidness far away. Send 'em my earnin's. Best I can do fer 'em." She nodded, as if reassuring herself, and walked out.

Lily sat stunned. Her face burned like she'd been slapped. She hoped she'd never be faced with that kind of choice.

CHAPTER TWENTY-ONE

On Sunday, Lily cleaned the store and stocked the shelves. Clouds hung low over the valley and cool air carried the metallic scent of a storm, making for a good day to stay indoors. Guilt nagged her for skipping church, but she hadn't the nerve to face the gossips.

She knelt on the floor, scrubbing muddy tracks from the rough boards with a stiff brush, and wondered where Luke was and what he was doing. The ache of missing him hadn't lessened, and sometimes she couldn't turn her mind elsewhere.

A tap on the window made her drop the brush and fumble in the folds of fabric at her hip. She found the smooth grip of the gun and lifted her gaze.

Jessie's blurred face peered in the window between cupped hands, looking toward the back of the store.

Lily let out a gust of air and released the small pistol. She pushed herself up, wincing at her stiff back and aching knees. She unlocked the door with a smile, but she grimaced at Jessie's appearance. Dark yellows, browns, and a tinge of maroon tainted half of her face. The swelling had abated, but puffy skin still distended the left side, and the eyelid sagged without muscle control.

"Good morning, Jessie."

The battered dove allowed a small smile. "Mornin', Miss Wright."

Lily tried not to stare at the drooping eye and opened the door wider. "Come in, come in. I'm glad you came."

Jessie limped in. Her body bent to one side in a swaying shuffle, like a wilted flower.

"Do you want to come in back and sit? I'll make some coffee ...."

"No, ma'am. Don't want to put you out. I just came by to thank you for helpin' me the other night."

"It was nothing. I only put some salve on it. Please, stay and visit." She walked toward the rear. "Really, it's no bother at all."

Jessie followed after a moment. In the back room, she let out a soft grunt as she eased into the chair.

Lily set the kettle to heat before pulling two tin cups from a shelf over the washbasin. She left them on the counter and joined the girl.

"How is everything? You look better."

"I'm still kickin'," Jessie said. "My side hurts quite a lot, but I can get around."

Lily pointed her chin where Jessie held a hand against her ribs. "I expect they may be broken. Did you see a doctor?"

Jessie snorted. "That chiseler stole my stash. I ain't got no money to pay a doc. Them parlor girls get their doc paid for, but I ain't no parlor girl. Us crib girls got a place to lay, nothin' more or less."

"I see. Well, I imagine it will heal, too, if you take it easy."

She raised an eyebrow and tucked a lock of drab hair

behind her ear. "Ain't much work layin' on my back."

Lily jumped up to check the kettle. "Have you looked around recently? For a parlor, I mean." She focused on the coffee to hide her discomfort. "They're opening a new one every other day, it seems. Maybe you could find a spot in one. They're … safer. From what I hear, at least."

"They don't want a beat up girl like me. You think the fellas get it up lookin' at this?" She swept a hand around her face. "Ain't had but one poke since I got worked over, and he took it from the backside."

Lily's eyes flew open. Her hands froze in the middle of pouring the coarse-ground beans into the pot. Dark flecks scattered on the counter, and she fumbled to clean up the spill. Her mouth worked to form a response, but embarrassment left her speechless. The silence grew heavy as she finished the coffee.

She turned and caught Jessie smoothing a smirk from her face. Lily frowned and lowered her head, annoyed and a touch hurt. The girl had nerve laughing at her after she'd taken her in and fixed her up, even if she'd only given her a quick bit of salve. Lily poured the coffee and sat, still silent.

Jessie chuckled. "I'm sorry. Just wondered what you'd say. I didn't mean nothin' by it. Anyhow, you got to get noticed to get in a parlor, or have money to pay for the room. I ain't been noticed and ain't got money. Don't figure I'll move out of the cribs unless my luck changes. But they ain't so bad, I guess. Bed, stove, and business comes right to you. Not like street walkin'." She tilted her head and caught Lily's eye. "You don't make much sense, you know. Only ladies I've ever heard bein' nice to us girls for no reason are the nuns down mountain at the charity hospital. You ain't a nun. So I can't figure …." She leaned forward to cradle the warm cup in her hands and watched Lily with a question in her eyes.

Lily licked her lips, unsure how to respond without giving too much away. "I simply don't see any reason you girls should be treated so poorly. You're just doing what you have to do to get along. It's not my place to judge you or anyone else. I've ... made my share of mistakes, I suppose. It hurt when I was judged for them." She met Jessie's gaze and allowed a rueful smile. "And, if I'm honest, it's not entirely without reason. There are a lot of you, and I need the business. If I can help a little along the way, even better."

Jessie tilted her head. "I guess I could see that." She sipped coffee from the side of her mouth, avoiding the scab on her cut lip, and smirked. "I'd gamble there's more to your story, but I'll take that."

Lily averted her eyes and wiped the table. *Am I that transparent?* Her smile felt strained, and she shrugged. "That's really all there is. I'm only trying to get the store going."

An uneasy tension sat between them.

Lily took a drink and studied Jessie over the rim of the cup. She wanted to ask what she wondered about all of the doves. "I answered yours, so here's mine. What are your plans? For the future? What do you really want?"

Jessie ran her tongue over the cracked skin of her lip and gazed at the floor. Her face held no spark of hope or joy. Her voice went flat. "Used to think I could find a fella and have a farm, a family, a place of our own. Nothin' fancy, just somethin' that'd last. Don't guess that'll happen now. I guess I ain't got no plan. I expect I'll just keep on."

The real answer lay in what she left unspoken.

"Maybe that will still happen,." Lily gave Jessie's hand a tentative squeeze.

Jessie offered a weary smile, but it was an automatic response, nothing more than a false front. "I better get goin'. Thanks for the coffee."

* * * * *

Lily lay propped up in bed, a book open on her lap. She'd eaten an early supper and slid between the covers to relax for the first time in days. Wind swirled outside, and the gusts in the trees competed with the creek's low murmur. The stove ticked quietly in the corner as the cast iron heated. The lamp shed a soft circle of light, and she tilted the book toward it. She read only a page before her eyes drifted and her thoughts strayed.

She sighed over the conversation with Jessie. A motherly impulse compelled Lily to rescue her, but she had little to offer.

If the store does well, I'll need to hire someone. That'll be a while before I can afford that, though, and she might have moved on by then.

Maybe Jessie's dream would come true and she'd find a husband and settle down on a farm.

Or maybe she'll be beaten one too many times.

She closed off those thoughts and imagined Luke riding some far away hilltop, watching over a herd of lowing cattle. She put herself in front of him in the saddle, his chest pressed against her. Grass, leather, and sweat trailed on the breeze. The rough stubble on his cheek rubbed her forehead as they breathed. She clung to the contentment, a feeling she barely recognized.

Her eyelashes fluttered against her cheeks, and her breath slowed as she slipped into soothing dreams.

CHAPTER TWENTY-TWO

Lily woke. She lay still, searching the darkened room for whatever had pulled her from sleep. Outside, the blustery wind pitched something to and fro with a muffled tapping. The corner of the book dug into her leg. She breathed in shallow puffs to block out the wind and isolate any other noise. Nothing.

She pushed the book aside and rolled over. The room held no shapes, only inky black impressions. The faint tang of wood and a whiff of fresh bread lingered. The stove had cooled, and goose bumps pebbled her skin. Shivering, she tugged the blankets up.

No hint of disturbance. She sighed and tucked her head into the pillow. Her eyes closed, and she drifted off.

The crackle of a flaring match cut through the quiet.

Lily's eyes popped open. A pale face floated in the darkness. Terror quaked through her. She tried to push herself away with leaden legs.

Duncan—it had to be.

A woman's voice demanded, "Get up!" The figure lit the lamp, shook the match out, and reached for something on the table. A cloaked form brandished a long, heavy knife toward Lily. "I said, 'get up!'"

Lily didn't recognize her. She shrank back, feet pedaling against the mattress, and clutched the blankets to her chest. Her throat constricted, and her hair stood on end.

The woman grimaced, a twisted sneer of disgust. "The whore doesn't want to get out of bed. How typical."

The word stood out and froze Lily. Her eyes narrowed. *The rock. Did she throw it?* It still didn't explain her identity or why she'd broken in. What was it about? Beckett? Jessie? *The gun. Where—under the pillow.* She always put it under the pillow at night. *Can I reach it without her noticing?*

Lily stalled. "What do you want?"

"Move, whore!" The woman jabbed the knife at her.

Lily flinched. She released her grip on the blankets and scooted forward. Her left hand slid under the pillow, fingers groping for the pistol, but came up empty. Blood thundered in her ears.

The woman stepped back, the dagger held steady.

As Lily inched farther, her fingers bumped the barrel of the gun. She stifled a cry of relief. She nudged the weapon around until the grip filled her palm. Her feet dangled over the bedside as she pushed her rump to the edge. For once, the billowing nightgown helped rather than hindered. She tucked the gun behind her bottom in a fold of fabric and stood.

The woman's blonde hair curled from the hood of a long cloak. Tall, but the fabric hid her shape. Her round, cherubic face countered the knife and the glare of hatred in her eyes. She pointed to the chair with the blade.

Lily faltered. She'd lose equal footing. Could she pull the gun fast enough to catch her off-guard? The woman seemed to have an agenda—if she only wanted to kill her, wouldn't she have done so? Lily eased into the chair to bide her time.

The blonde tilted her head and studied Lily. She spoke with a refined accent, almost to herself. "Pretty, at least. That's to be expected—a common girl wouldn't do—but there must be something extraordinary. Intelligence? Likely, but that's not it either." She shook her head, and her mouth twisted. "As far as I can tell, there is only one difference. Only one thing it could be. What do you suppose that is, Miss Wright?"

She knows my name. Lily combed her memory to glean some hint of who and why.

"What are you—"

The woman cut her off with a snort of laughter. "Perhaps not so intelligent after all. Well, everyone makes mistakes. I suppose it could be worse, like the last one. But I won't stand for this one either." Her eyes shifted to the blade.

"If it's money you want, I'll give you whatever I have." Lily's voice turned strident and heightened the sick roll of her stomach. The woman didn't want money, but Lily had to distract her.

"Money?" She scoffed. "Spare me. Money means nothing. What I want is more important than money. Back to my question, though, speaking of giving. What did you give him?" She raised an eyebrow.

"Him? Who? I didn't give anyone anything!"

A smirk. "Oh, but you did. You must have. That's how you lured him away. With your obscene, filthy, whoring sex." Spittle gathered on her lips as she hissed the words.

Luke. She could only mean Luke. Lured him away? He'd mentioned in passing that he'd courted a woman, but Lily had the impression it had ended long ago.

Lily whispered, "Luke? But I thought ... that was over. I, I didn't know."

"Over? It is *not over!* He is mine. You lift your skirts for a man you barely know and think he's yours? Did he propose to you? No?" Her face flushed a mottled crimson and contorted with rage as her voice rose to a screech. "He proposed to me. 'Judith, marry me,' he said. And we *will* be married, and I will *not* let a whore ruin that!"

Lily clutched the gun at her side, beneath the skirt. The woman—Judith, apparently—stood several feet away, still close enough to reach Lily and stab her in a spiraling frenzy. *Did I miss my chance?*

Judith breathed deep and composed herself. "Pardon my outburst. Whores upset me." She continued in a strange, detached voice, "There are two solutions. The simplest requires nothing more than a change of location. You leave Clear Springs immediately and never return." She smiled as though she'd invited Lily to supper.

Shock left Lily gawking, bewildered by the suggestion and Judith's mercurial demeanor. "I, I can't just leave Clear Springs. I have to stay here, I have nowhere to go."

Judith clucked with an expression of sadness and resignation. "I feared you'd say that. That leaves only one other solution." She lifted the knife, staring with vacant eyes.

Lily chose her moment. She drew the gun from beneath her skirt and cocked it. She aimed at the woman's chest, but her hand shook with violent tremors.

Judith's attention returned. Uncertainty flashed in her eyes. She stepped toward Lily.

The muzzle flared with a white light. The bullet flew wide, shattering a jug on a shelf.

Lily's ears rang with the blast, and she couldn't hear, but Judith's lips moved.

"... Whore!" Her eyes bulged as she lunged forward with the knife.

Lily kicked her foot out, slid down in the chair, and tucked her head into her chest. She managed to connect with Judith's shin and threw her off balance.

The knife tip slashed the side of Lily's face. An icy rush of air stung the furrow of exposed flesh. Her breath seized, turning her scream to a strangled whisper. Her arms rose instinctively, and she pulled her head up, expecting another attack. She squinted at hot, blazing light.

No attack came. Judith had knocked over the lamp when she stumbled, and it had shattered at her feet, splashing oil on the floor and her long cloak. The liquid ignited, and a shower of flames crawled up the woman's clothing. Yellow and orange spread like rushing lava. Judith's mouth stretched wide in a soundless shriek. She staggered in a deranged circle.

Horror turned Lily's muscles to liquid. As her hands fell to her lap, the gun clattered on the floor. The spectacle entranced her as Judith spun round, flames whirling with her in an eerie dance. Her instinct to help the woman sputtered when she caught sight of the knife spinning with Judith, a mad, dangerous carousel.

The intruder careened through the door to the front room. The hood fell from her head, and her long flaxen hair singed, throwing off a new, pungent perfume. She clawed at the clasp of the twirling, burning cape.

Lily lost sight of her. In a stunned daze, she watched puddles of fire grow. Time stopped, reality seeping from the room like sand from an hourglass. She felt the rising temperature, the sweat on the back of her neck, heard the sizzling, but it existed in another world. Blood oozed from the gash on her cheek, but its warm trickle seemed trivial in the heat, the fire, the radiance. She barely noticed the acrid odor of burnt oil and hair. Curling tendrils of red, orange, and yellow mesmerized her.

Judith came back into view and tripped over a rack of clothing, pulling it down with her as she fell. She finally screeched. The cloth fed the flames' hungry roar. She scrambled back to her feet, flinging bits of lit fabric aside. She found the open front door by chance and staggered out.

The shrill screams broke through Lily's daze. She recoiled, almost tipping the chair. Fire shrouded the table beside her and had raced along the floor to the bed, blackening the new, yellow wood and consuming the blankets.

Lily shoved out of the chair. Scorching smoke filled her lungs, and she coughed and gagged. Rivulets of sour, clammy sweat dampened her nightgown. Squinting through the black air, eyes watering and stinging, she sought an escape.

The blaze had engulfed the front of the store even faster, fed with her livelihood. Containers exploded and wood crackled, cloth and paper burned hot and bright, ash floated on waves of smoke.

She made for the back door. *The gun!* She turned and ducked to grab it. Flames seared her hand, and she dropped it in a pool of fiery oil. She reached for it, couldn't get to it. Lightheadedness made her sway. *Have to leave it. Go. Get out.*

Fear spurred her through the choking flames. Her fingers fumbled the key in the lock. Her chest wanted to explode, her lungs burned, acid in her throat.

A rasped whisper, "Please!"

She yanked the door open and lurched outside. After several yards, she collapsed. Heat still enveloped her legs, and she focused on them. Large swathes of her nightgown smoldered. Bleating fear and pain, she jerked at the collar, ripped it open, tore the gown away. Smears of slick blood coated her chest. She wiped at them, but her head started to swim. The wind carried sparks around her as she slumped back on the cool grass.

CHAPTER TWENTY-THREE

Fire licked Lily's legs. They burned as if acid dissolved the flesh. She thrashed to escape it.

Someone pinned her arms and murmured comforting sounds. Lily moaned, her voice weak and hoarse in her own ears. Her throat burned, too. Her face—it throbbed and ached from her left eye down to her jaw. It ached the way a bee sting on her neck pulsed with swollen heat when she was seven. *Did I get stung again?*

That pain didn't compare to the searing agony on her legs, like a living thing in her mind. Each time she tried to form a thought, the pain shrouded it in darkness and the idea disappeared. She shivered. How could she be cold when she was on fire? She wanted to open her eyes, but the lids refused to lift.

Something poked and tugged at her face. She whimpered.

Low voices came from far away. "This face will never be the same. Shame. Mary, get that salve on her legs. They aren't awful bad, but we'll have to watch the burns, and they'll be plenty painful."

"Yes, dear. Poor thing."

The flames devoured her legs. *It's eating me alive.*

The fog came back to carry her away, and she spoke to it. "Thank you," she whispered.

"Don't thank me yet, miss."

* * * * *

Lily stirred. Torment riddled her body. Her eyes, dry and gritty, burned as she opened them. A nightstand and chair sat next to the bed, with a dresser on the opposite wall. The sheets gave off the sharp bite of lye. The skin on her face stretched tight, unmoving, and she lifted a hand to it. Bandages covered one side. Underneath, it throbbed with a nauseating rhythm, keeping time with her heartbeat. Her whole head ached as if the contents had outgrown her skull. Her legs stung, but the pain had lessened to a hiss of background noise. Snatches of memory drifted in, followed by remnants of terror. She shuddered.

"Hello?" Her croaking voice didn't sound like her. The effort made her wince. She coughed—daggers behind her eyes—and tried again. "Hello?"

A woman bustled in with a tray of food. "Hello, dear. I'm Mary, wife, nurse, and cook. Doctor will check you shortly. Sit up, now, and have some lunch." The cheerful rush left Lily dizzy.

Mary set the tray on the dresser and helped prop Lily up. She reminded Lily of a doll, with plump rosy cheeks, curly hair, and a permanent smile.

"I'm not hungry, just thirsty."

Mary waved a hand. "You must eat. Just a bit of cool porridge and stewed apples. You need your strength." She fluffed a pillow and pushed Lily back.

With the tray on her lap, Mary gave Lily small spoonfuls of a tasteless mush between sips of water. Lily winced as each bite stretched the inflamed skin under the bandages.

Mary chattered, pausing only for breath. "You don't remember much, I expect? Well, you were lucky. They found you behind the store after daylight. That other girl's screaming brought out the alarm, and the fire brigade had a time with the fire. The wind and all, goodness, it went wild. Your place and the one next door—poof—just gone, and damage to a couple others. Only thing that saved the rest of town was you being on the end of the street. Otherwise, everything but the brick would have gone up in smoke. We've been lucky here, with no fires taking the whole town like some places." She wiped a dribble from Lily's chin and continued, "Anyway, they thought at first the other girl was the proprietor, but then a fellow cleaning up found you out back. That got everyone in a tizzy, I'll tell you. Someone finally decided you were the owner—"

"What of ... the woman?"

"Oh, *that* poor thing. Too far gone, I'm afraid. She passed, right out in the street, no more than a smoldering lump. 'Tis hard to say it, but that's fortunate, too, for those burns would have been an unbearable trial, and little chance of her surviving them for very long, and her history and all." She prattled on as she pushed the spoon between Lily's chapped lips. "The smell! Dear me, I hate when they bring a body in from a fire. It takes days to air that out, make no mistake."

Lily heard little after "she passed." A wave of relief washed over her. She'd never see that face or hear that voice again.

Mary poured a spoonful of liquid and pressed it to Lily's lips. "Laudanum, it'll help."

Lily grimaced at the bittersweet taste and forced herself to swallow. She gulped water when Mary offered the cup.

Mary cleaned up and grabbed the tray as she left. "I'll send Doctor in."

The doctor entered as Lily started to doze. Middle-aged and wild-haired, he moved with the tired shuffle of someone much older.

"Miss Wright, is it? Dr. Andrews. Feeling a little better?" He spoke even slower than he moved.

Lily's feeble smile hurt. "Yes, thank you."

"Let me see how that cut is doing." He removed the bandages and prodded the wound with gentle fingers before wrapping it again. "Not too bad. You'll have a scar, but if I can keep infection out, it will heal. How are your legs?"

He pulled the sheet away from a small, short-legged table over her legs. The gown she wore went only to her thighs. Feverish, blistered skin bubbled along her lower legs. Lily gasped and turned her head.

"Oh, isn't as bad as it looks, miss. They'll be fine. Scarred, but no trouble." He patted her hand and replaced the cover. "You have no family in town?"

"No."

"Well, don't worry. You'll stay with us a bit then. Shame about the store."

The mention of the store struck her like a blow. "It's gone? All of it?"

"Afraid so. Don't trouble yourself with it now. Just rest."

Her head spun. She lay back as numbing despair spread through her.

The doctor rose and paused at the door. "The marshal said he'll be by later to talk to you. Get some sleep."

She slid down in the bed, wincing at every movement,

but couldn't find a comfortable position.

She clung to consciousness, thoughts drifting in broken wisps. Her store destroyed. Perhaps the doctor had heard wrong. What on earth would she do? She quaked with a spasm of shock. Tears streamed from her burning eyes, soaking into the bandages and the pillow. Silent, wrenching convulsions worsened the pain until the laudanum took over and dragged her into a restless sleep, filled with dark, hooded figures engulfed in flames.

* * * * *

Marshal Parker stood at the end of the bed and looked out the narrow window. "What happened?"

"I don't remember much." The lie surprised Lily. It came out before she knew what to say, how to start. She didn't *want* to remember. She wanted to forget the hateful look in Judith's eyes and the sneering contempt in her voice; the crushing disappointment—and relief?—when the bullet landed wide of its mark; the whirling flames as Judith reeled in panic; the hissing, crackling pops of the fire consuming everything in its path; the paralyzing terror that made her bowels loose and watery. Those impressions had seared her mind, but she wanted to carve them out. Perhaps, if she didn't speak of them, they would retreat. She focused on the ceiling, where light and shadow danced as the wind rustled leaves on a tree outside.

"Tell me what you remember, then." He hooked his thumbs in his belt.

"I, I woke up. I saw a light. I took the pistol out." The words came out flat, whether because she told half-truths, or because she had no emotion left, she didn't know. Her voice seemed to come from someone else.

"What pistol?"

"I had a pistol, to protect myself. I must have dropped it."

"Then what? Did you see anyone?"

"No."

"Did you get up, go to investigate?"

"No, I, I froze." She closed her eyes against tears, wishing he would stop.

His eyes darted to her. "How'd the fire start?"

"I don't know. I heard glass break in the store. Then the fire was ... everywhere."

"You hear anything else? Voices?"

"I don't know. I don't think so." Judith's voice breathed in her ear. *Lying whore!* Lily's eyes flew open, and she turned her head expecting to see the face.

"How'd you get the cut?" The marshal watched her closely.

Hesitation as she searched for a plausible answer. "I stumbled, I fell ... against something. I don't know what, I couldn't see."

"And the burns?"

"I couldn't get the back door unlocked. The key—"

"You waited 'til the fire got to the back room before you tried to get out?" His voice turned sharp.

"I, I was scared. I was afraid they might find me. I didn't want to—couldn't move. It happened so fast." Lily's heart pounded in her chest, and clammy sweat broke out on her skin.

"You never saw no one? No idea who came in?"

"No."

She wouldn't—couldn't—tell him. More questions would follow. Why had Judith been there? What connection did they have? If she brought Luke into it, everyone else would call her a whore, too. She couldn't bear that. And what if they didn't believe her? She couldn't prove self-defense. The truth couldn't help her, not now.

The marshal let the silence draw out. Lily waited for him to challenge her account.

"It was Judith Samuels in the store. She's dead. Her daddy is Tom Samuels, owner of the Clear Springs Ranch. He wants to know why his girl got burnt to a crisp. I'm sure you can understand that." Parker bent over the end of the bed and leaned on the footboard. His squinting eyes bored into her. "Nobody seems to know why she would've been there in the middle of the night. Do you?"

"No, I don't know."

Samuels. Where had she heard that name? The zealot at the store with Beckett.

"I guess I'll leave you to rest then, Miss Wright. Maybe you'll remember something. I'll be checkin' in with you again." His pointed look made it a threat, and he closed the door behind him.

Lily ached to cry, or scream, or vomit. She wanted to purge the memories. Nothing came out, and she focused on the blank ceiling, refusing to see the sliver of bandage intruding at the corner of her eye.

CHAPTER TWENTY-FOUR

Lily sat up as Dr. Andrews entered with his medical bag. He pulled the chair up beside the bed and busied himself arranging his instruments. She averted her gaze.

The doctor's slow, labored breathing and the clink of steel instruments made the room close, suffocating. Lily focused on a crack in the worn plaster on the wall. The doctor leaned over, blocking her view, and she closed her eyes.

Her head ached from laying down too long. The sharp sting of crushed glass in her smoke-scorched throat had faded. Her skin had started knitting itself back together, and her face and legs itched with a maddening intensity. The blisters on her legs had subsided, leaking fluid and shedding flaps of skin. Sensitive white blotches of disfigured, shiny new skin emerged.

Her mind wasn't so quick to heal. The fire had destroyed something inside her, just as it destroyed her hard work. She felt much as she did after the birth. Dr. Andrews and Mary had urged her to join them for meals or outings, but Lily refused. She lay in bed or sat in the chair, day after day, asleep or in a half-awake, listless daze, with no desire to talk, or read, or move. She didn't want help, kind encouragement, or bright, cheery suggestions to make her feel better. She wanted everyone to leave her alone in the quiet, bare room—a sanctuary, where she could pretend her world hadn't come crashing down. The laudanum clouded her mind and smothered the haunting memories and grim prospects. As the days passed, she sought out the fog and let it envelop her in its soothing, senseless veil of oblivion.

Andrews tugged at the bandages on her face, picked up a small pair of scissors, and turned her face to the light. Lily pressed her lips tight.

"Lucky this wasn't too deep. Missed most of the muscles. It'll be a thin scar. You can probably cover it up with cosmetic powder." As he snipped each stitch, he tugged at the loose threads, making it hurt, tickle, and itch all at once. "Have an idea of your plans?"

She cringed. The question echoed in her fragile mind and recalled the conversation with Jessie. "No."

He dabbed at a drop of blood. "You going to stay in Clear Springs or head back to—where are you from?"

"Jeff—" A jolt of alarm pushed the fog back. "Chicago. I don't know where I'd go. I suppose I'll have to stay here."

He nodded and cut the rest of the stitches. After the last one, he held up a mirror for her, wet a cloth, and cleaned the series of small holes along the scar. The sting dredged up disturbing memories of the stillbirth, pain and anguish that swirled together in the mist. She fought them, but they lingered like a bitter scent.

Dr. Andrews wrapped his instruments in a cloth and sat back. "Well, you're just about done here. Another couple days to make sure that stays clear of infection."

Lily nodded, but the words didn't sink in.

He stood, releasing a tired wheeze, and picked up his bag. "Let us know if we can help you get settled. I wish I could let you stay on here, but I just don't have the space."

"Thank you, Doctor." She smiled weakly before he closed the door.

Done here. Get settled.

The mist receded. They would turn her out, leave her to fend for herself with nothing—no home, no income.

Where will *I go? How can I pick up the pieces and start again? I'll have to find a job, but where?*

A weight pulled at her, resisting her efforts to emerge from the depression. She struggled to clear her mind and focus. The weight grew heavier. She gave in and let the dark cloud of hopelessness smother her again.

* * * * *

Lily woke before dawn, haunted by confusing dreams where faces—her father, her mother, Duncan, Judith— morphed into one vicious pursuer. The menacing apparition had chased her, cutting her off each time she thought she'd escaped. As she sat near the window, the remnants of terror and frustration colored her mood.

Mary had given her a chemise and drawers, shoes, and a faded blue calico dress left by a patient. The dress wouldn't have fit, but Lily had grown gaunt. Even so, it pulled at her chest and waist, and left her wrists uncovered. Lily fingered the thin, worn fabric.

Daylight came, but the narrow view of trees and wild flowers behind the doctor's house offered little respite. Watching butterflies flitting between blooms would have calmed her in days past. Instead, the tranquility somehow added to her anxiety. The dream had sparked an ember of resentment. She had escaped all of them—her childhood home, Duncan, and Judith. Why wouldn't they leave her alone now? They had already taken everything from her. Hadn't she gone through enough without reliving it all each night? Her jaw clenched, and her hands curled into fists as bitter indignation coursed through her. She faced a bleak future, but if nothing else, she resolved to evict them from her mind.

A sharp knock made her cringe, and she turned to the door with trepidation, as though the demons had come to dispel her determination.

"Miss Wright, it's Silas Barnes."

The name only heightened her tension. She wanted to refuse him entry but knew she had to deal with him sooner or later.

"Come in."

He opened the door and glanced around. When his eyes settled on Lily, they widened in surprise. A twinge of self-conscious embarrassment pricked her as she realized his stare had settled on her scar.

She lowered her head and mumbled, "Mr. Barnes."

He moved beyond the door and leaned against the dresser. "Good mornin', Miss Wright. I hope you're feelin' better. That fire was downright awful. A real tragedy, for sure." He shook his head and sucked his teeth, while his eyes openly raked her form in the clingy dress.

Lily answered in a stiff voice. "Yes, I am recovering. I assume you've come to collect your monthly payment."

His lower lip stuck out. "Not exactly."

"What do you mean, 'not exactly'?"

"Ah, I hate to have to add to your troubles. I tried to wait a bit, didn't want to intrude, but I can't put it off forever, so I figured I better get it over with." Barnes cleared his throat and gave her an apologetic smile, but it didn't reach his eyes. "The terms of the loan are pretty clear. The full payment is required."

"Full payment? What are you talking about?"

"The agreement states that if the property becomes derelict or unimproved—meanin' the value is ruined—it has to be returned to the improved value within thirty days, or the loan's called due." He shrugged. "I wish I could let it slide, but I have to look after my own interests here."

Lily tried to make sense of the words. "I don't understand. As long as I make the payments on time …."

"I'm afraid not. The improvement—the building—was part of the agreement, and without it you're in violation of the contract. If you can't rebuild it pretty quick, I'll have to keep the deed, and the balance will be due."

"But that's not fair!" Tears welled, and she blinked them back. "It's not my fault it burned down. I, I lost everything. I can't afford to rebuild it right away."

He grimaced and reached into his suit to pull out a paper. "And I'm awful sorry 'bout the whole business, but it ain't my fault either. I have to enforce the terms." He held the paper out to her.

The ground crumbled beneath her, taking with it her last tenuous link to sanity. She had given the agreement only a cursory reading—it hadn't mattered what it said, she needed the money and had to take what she could get. She'd known his terms demanded more than anyone should reasonably ask but hadn't understood how unreasonable.

She pushed the paper away. "Please, Mr. Barnes, you must give me some time."

He sighed with regret. "No, I—"

"I'll find a way, I promise, but I need more time. Just a little bit longer. You have to help me, Mr. Barnes."

"There's really nothin' I can do. You have ten days 'til I have to collect." He dropped the paper on the dresser and walked to the door.

"But what happens if I can't pay it?"

"That'd be up to the judge."

Lily abandoned restraint and limped from the chair. She grabbed his sleeve before he could open the door.

"Mr. Barnes, please, isn't there any way you can let me make the payments? I'm begging you."

He cracked the door, craned his head into the hallway, and turned back. A smirk played at the corners of his mouth as he leered at her breasts rising and falling under the too-tight fabric.

His voice lowered, "I reckon I could consider another kind of payment for some of the debt. Would've been better without that scar, but I bet it'd still be worth it." He tilted his head and lifted his hand, grazing the film of cloth over her taut nipple with his fingers.

She cringed away from him, and impulse drew her hand up to slap him. He seized her wrist with a painful squeeze, his jaw tightening. He chuckled.

"You better get friendlier if you want me to take services in trade. I'll be waitin' on payment, one way or t'other." He dropped her hand and left.

As Lily's shock wore off, she shook with humiliation and disgust. She rubbed her hand over her breast, to wipe away his touch. Crossing her arms on her chest, she stumbled back until she sank onto the bed. Saliva filled her mouth as she swallowed back vomit.

That bastard! How dare he?

She squeezed back tears. Trapped, like a scared rabbit in a snare just waiting for a merciful end. She had no money to rebuild. She'd deposited the store's receipts the Friday before the fire, so some money survived in her account, but nowhere near enough. Without rebuilding, she could end up in front of a judge ... or with Barnes. The thought of him touching—*No! I won't let that smug, revolting little man use me.* She straightened and took a deep breath. She wasn't a helpless animal. Strength and determination had enabled her to leave Duncan and elude him. She would get herself out of this mess, too.

Lily searched for a solution. Maybe Barnes had lied about the contract. Perhaps a solicitor could find a loophole, but she couldn't afford to pay one. She needed someone knowledgeable.

The man from the hotel. Mr. Worley? No, Warren. That's it. He might advise me without payment. His card would have perished among my papers in the store, but I can find him, if he hasn't left town. She smoothed her dress. *Hardly appropriate for a call, but it will have to do.* She pinned her hair up, and her hand brushed the taut scar tissue on her cheek.

She hadn't ventured out in public yet. A flash of self-consciousness made her falter, and she fought the urge to crawl back into bed. Her sanctuary. Out on the street, they would stare and ridicule. If she stayed in the Doctor's house, they—Duncan, Judith, Barnes—would win. She set her jaw and abandoned her refuge.

CHAPTER TWENTY-FIVE

On the street, Lily imagined every passerby eyed her with revulsion and pity and would whisper about her when she'd gone. *That's only in your head. That man couldn't even see that side of your face.* She had to muster all her fortitude to press on with a smile. The ten minute walk was an eternity.

She tried the hotel first, in hopes Warren hadn't moved on. Jacob's post out front stood vacant. She hesitated at the doors, dreading a conversation with Mr. Amos. She lifted her chin and forced herself to venture inside.

The proprietor lounged at the desk, leaning back in his chair and smoking his pipe.

"Mr. Amos, how are you?" Lily feigned cheerfulness.

He squinted through smoke and grunted. "Who's that?"

"Miss Wright. I stayed a while back ...."

"Oh. Saw the fire. What—" He tilted his head. "How'd you get that?"

Her smile fell. "An accident."

"Bad one, from the looks. That's a pity. You had a pretty face. You lookin' fer a place to stay again?"

She gritted her teeth. "No. I just wanted to inquire if Mr.

Warren is still a guest."

"Warren." He scratched his chin and grunted. "He moved on a couple weeks ago. Don't recall hearin' where."

"I see. Is Jacob around, then?"

"The boy went to pick up the laundry. Ought to be back a'fore long, if he ain't off loafin' somewhere. What do you need him for?" His eyes narrowed as he settled back and returned to his pipe, a cloud of fumes hanging in the air.

"Just a question for him. Thank you, Mr. Amos. Good day."

She hurried out and leaned against the building. *That fat old man's opinion means nothing.* She closed her eyes and waited until her hitching breaths returned to normal.

Jacob might have more information, but she couldn't wait around. She needed a job, no matter what happened with the loan agreement, and a place to stay. She'd have to settle for a room; she couldn't afford the hotel. Fatigue overcame her, and she was too tired to move.

As she contemplated her options, Jacob staggered out of an alley a few doors up with a large bag slung over his shoulder, looking like his thin frame might collapse.

Lily chuckled. "Jacob, that bag is bigger than you are."

He grinned. "I'll whip it though, Miss Wright!"

She laughed as he dropped his burden and stood with his hands on his knees, gasping.

Once he recovered, he straightened and nodded with his usual bashful manner. "Glad to see you, Miss Wright." His eyes touched on the scar but registered no reaction.

Her tension dissipated, and she smiled. "I'm happy to see you too, Jacob. Mr. Amos isn't working you too hard, is he?"

"Naw, I can handle it." He turned solemn. "I was awful sorry 'bout the fire. I know that store was real important to you."

"Thank you, Jacob. It was. Hopefully, I can start over." A rush of affection warmed her at his disregard for the scar and the earnest concern in his eyes. "You might actually be able to help with that. Do you know if Mr. Warren, the older gentleman who was staying here, is still in town?"

"Mr. Warren? Sure, he went to stay at Mrs. Connor's. He moves around a lot, switches 'tween the boardin' houses and hotel—funny fella. I ain't seen him in a week or so, but I think he planned on stayin' there a while."

"Oh, wonderful! Thank you."

"O'course, Miss Wright. Anytime you need somethin', anything at all ...." He jerked a thumb at himself with a beaming smile.

"I'm sorry to hurry off, but I must. You're an angel, Jacob!" On impulse, she kissed his cheek.

He went crimson and stammered. Lily giggled and hurried up the sidewalk.

* * * * *

Mrs. Connor's boarding house, a hodge-podge of stories and ells, perched near the top of the valley. Lily had heard of her but never seen her. She expected to find Mrs. Connor on the porch, where she held court each day, but an oversized swing on the landing swayed in the breeze, and Lily was relieved she wouldn't have to face the notorious woman.

A man answered her knock and showed her to the parlor to wait for Mr. Warren.

"Good afternoon, miss?"

"Good afternoon, Mr. Warren. You may not remember me, I'm Lily—"

"Wright." He smiled. "I remember you, though my memory isn't what it used to be. You opened a dry goods, I

183

believe?"

"I did. Unfortunately, there was a fire, and my building was destroyed." Her throat tightened.

"That was your building? How terrible. I'm sorry to hear that. Didn't you have a relative in the business with you? A brother or cousin?"

Her heart stopped. "Oh. Yes, regrettably my brother was unable to come. He ... died of fever back home." She changed the topic to fend off more questions. "The building, and the property, is what I came to see you about. I have some questions about a legal document, and I remembered your kindness at the hotel. I'm afraid I'm in a tight position financially, however, and I can't afford a fee for an attorney. I wondered if you might answer my questions. It's nothing too involved, I promise. I really hate to impose on your time, but I didn't know where else to go."

"I'd be happy to consult with you, Miss Wright. If it required a court appearance or research, now that would be different, but I can certainly entertain a few questions."

"Oh, thank you, Mr. Warren. That's so kind of you. I promise I won't keep you too long."

He ushered her to the sofa, and she produced the copy of the agreement. He read it while she explained about the loan, the loss of the store, and Barnes' demand for full payment. She left out the louse's vulgar suggestion of alternative payment.

"Hmm. This appears to be a highly unusual contract. This interest rate is outrageous in itself, but it does also include a clause regarding the restoration of value. I've never seen anything like it in a land agreement, but this isn't my specialty."

"But, is there nothing I can do? I don't have the money to rebuild it."

He shot her a puzzled look. "You didn't mention insurance. They wouldn't issue insurance for the building?"

"No, I'm afraid I didn't ask. Mr. Barnes mentioned that they wouldn't insure a wooden building in a town like this, and I took him at his word." Again, she'd regressed to a naïve child. *How did I ever think I could do this?*

Mr. Warren pursed his lips. "I see. Miss Wright, that puts you in an unfortunate situation. According to this contract, Mr. Barnes is within his rights to call the loan due. You approved the terms with your signature."

Her shoulders slumped, and she put a hand over her mouth.

He removed his glasses and looked at the ceiling, contemplative. "It might be possible to fight the contract under usury law. A judge could set aside the agreement and cancel the debt, or at least modify the contract."

"Really? How would I do that?" A ray of hope.

He held up a hand. "Now wait. I said it's possible. I wouldn't be too optimistic. You would have to file a suit and appear in court to present your case. You need an attorney for that. And still, contracts are difficult to void. You could end up still owing Barnes *and* the attorney."

"Oh. But do you think I could win? How long would that take?"

"You might. It depends on the court's schedule. You'd want to try to get a hearing before the restoration is due, as a judge might put a stay on it."

Warren's cautions did nothing to dissuade her. If she could delay Barnes' demand for payment, she might come up with enough money to pay him, or even rebuild the store. If she won the case, she could free herself from his devious clutches.

"Could I hire you, Mr. Warren? I'd feel better if it wasn't a stranger."

"I don't know if that's in your best interest. As I said, this isn't my specialty. I could ask around and see who would be more knowledgeable." At her crestfallen look, he sighed. "I suppose, if there isn't anyone more capable, I would be willing to do it."

"I would appreciate that. How soon can all this be done?"

"It might take a day or two to find out about another attorney. A few days perhaps, to file the suit."

"You're very kind to go to all this trouble for me."

"No trouble, Miss Wright. I only hope it turns out well for you. I'll let you know in a day or two if I find anyone. Where should I send a message?"

"Oh." Lily frowned. "I'm not sure. I'll be leaving Dr. Andrews' house shortly, but I don't know where I'll be staying yet. I still have to find a room."

"You may be in luck. Mrs. Connor rarely has a room available, but I believe a boarder just left yesterday. I could check with her, if you like. The rooms are reasonable and quite suitable for a young lady."

Her eyes turned to saucers. "My goodness, that would be a lifesaver."

Mr. Warren chuckled. "I'll ask Mrs. Connor. I'm sure she'll assist me as a favor if she can. I'll send for you at Dr. Andrews' when I find out."

"Thank you for all of your help, Mr. Warren." She shook his hand and left, hopeful for the first time in weeks.

* * * * *

Lily scurried into the Doctor's house, out of breath and ready to collapse.

Mary called from the parlor, "Is everything all right?"

186

Lily stopped on her way to her room. "Quite. I found some helpful information, and I may be able to board at Mrs. Connor's house."

"Splendid, dear! It's good to see you up and about and smiling."

"Mary, much of it is your doing. You and the doctor have been so generous. I appreciate all you've done to help me get better. I'm tired, though. I think I'm going to rest."

"Oh, we're glad to help. You do that. I'll call you when it's time for tea." She bent to her sewing but called Lily back. "I almost forgot. A letter came for you. It's on the bureau in your room."

A pang of loss hit. "Probably just another delayed post from a supplier. Thank you."

In her room, she took off her shoes and unpinned her hair. She wanted a quick nap; the morning had left her drained. As she stood to close the curtains, her eyes fell on the letter. It didn't look like a supplier's response. Neat print listed her name on the envelope's front, and she turned it over to find the sender's name. Her breath caught.

Luke's name stared back.

Ambivalence tore at her. She'd avoided thinking of him since the fire. She still harbored a strong affection for him— even love, perhaps. Seeing he was safe set her mind at ease, and she enjoyed knowing he had at least thought of her. Underneath that pleasure ran a current of anger and resentment. Judith's actions weren't his fault, but Lily's involvement with him prompted the tragedy, and he had apparently misled her about the seriousness and duration of his relationship with Judith.

What if he has other women he hasn't told me about? How can I trust him now?

But when she thought of him, her stomach fluttered, and

her heart beat faster. She seesawed between missing him desperately and never wanting to see him again.

She settled in the chair by the window, pried the envelope open, and slid the paper out.

My Dear Lily,

I'm awful sorry I didn't write sooner. We been too far in the hills for mail. Been a long round up, and not done yet. Bad luck is hanging with us wherever we go. The wet spring was worse up here and everwhere there is snow and mud. Had to put down Emmett's horse after it broke its leg and almost crushed him. The rain and wind are a burden. Thunder spooked the herd twice, so we must chase them down agin. A pack of wolves stole some heifers. We catch sight of them but no luck killing the vermin yet.

We should reach Denver in a few weeks, then back to Clear Springs. Most times I like being on the trail, but now I'm keen to get back. I think of you a lot. Ain't never felt lonely on the trail, but now I do. I hope you are good. I bet the store is coming along. I know you will make a go of it. Hope to see your lovely face soon.

Yours, Luke

A lump rose in her throat as the paper fell to her lap.

Am I a trifle to entertain him, or does he really care? It sounds more like the latter, but .... Did Judith lie? Was it part of a delusion? Would she have gone to such lengths if Luke hadn't given her reason to think they would be together?

His letter added a new worry, too. Cattlemen faced danger, but she hadn't dwelled on the abstract concept. The mention of Emmett's accident and wolves in their midst made her shudder. Now she imagined dozens of possible catastrophes.

His last line ... *your lovely face.* She no longer had a lovely face. It had been slashed open and sewn together like a worn out doll. Would he still find it lovely? He might recoil from her. How could he—or anyone—still find her lovely? The anxiety haunted her, and she wondered for the first time if she would spend her life without love.

CHAPTER TWENTY-SIX

The next day, a soft knock pulled Lily from a doze.

"You have a message, dear," Mary called.

Lily scrambled from the bed and yanked open the door. Mary handed her a small card.

"I have a room at Mrs. Connor's." Lily grinned.

"Excellent news, dear." Mary smiled and patted her arm. "A place for you to find your feet again."

Lily embraced her. "I will miss your cooking."

"You'll always be welcome at my table, young lady, so I expect you to come see us. The house is too empty these days. It's been so nice having a girl here again." Her voice broke, its usual cheer dampened.

The couple's daughter, Anna, had died of consumption the year before, and Mary spoke of her often, comparing her to Lily.

"I will, I promise." She smiled and squeezed Mary's hand.

"You'll be going this afternoon then?"

"Yes, I'd like to get settled in so I can look for a job tomorrow."

"I had better give this to you now, in that case. Just a

moment ...."

Mary disappeared up the stairs with a rustle of skirts while Lily turned back to her room. She had little to take with her—a few personal things, a nightgown, spare drawers, and a hairbrush. Even less than when she'd fled her marriage.

I can't think like that. I must stay positive.

She gathered her few items from the dresser and pulled on her shoes as Mary's footsteps tapped in the hall.

"Mary, can you spare a sack to carry my things? I don't like to ask, but I don't want to show up with my nightgown in my hands."

When no reply came, Lily rose to go find her. Mary stood in the doorway with a satchel in one hand, a dark brown cloak over her arm, and a broad smile on her face.

"No need, dear." Mary set the satchel on the bed and lifted the cloak up, holding it against Lily with a critical eye. She tilted her head. "Not the best color for you, and it's a touch short, but I think it'll do."

"Mary, you can't mean to give me these."

"Why ever not?"

"I can't accept them."

"Nonsense. You can accept whatever I choose to give you." She held up a hand as Lily began to protest again. "I won't hear it. This was Anna's cloak. No reason for it to keep rotting up there in my chest when you have a need for one. It's summer now, but it won't be for long. Not up here. It turns cold early and fast. You'll take it. And you just said you need something to carry your things. This will do." She folded the cloak and tucked it into the bottom of the satchel.

"Thank you." Lily fought back tears.

"My pleasure, dear. I am going to make my tea; you come when you're ready."

Lily added the rest of her things to the satchel and sat near the window to wait. She wanted to hurry to the boardinghouse but knew Mary would be hurt if she didn't stay for tea. With Dr. Andrews often gone on calls, Mary spent much of her time alone, and a few minutes to oblige her was the least Lily could do after all they'd done for her.

A rap on the front door interrupted her contemplation, and Mary called down the hall to have her answer it. Lily opened the door, expecting a patient for the doctor or a caller for Mary.

A slight young woman in a worn but fashionable dress waited, hands clutched in front of her. A full bonnet framed her fresh face.

"Good afternoon." Lily offered a polite smile. "The doctor is out. You'll have to wait or come back later."

The woman's mouth twitched, and her eyebrows rose in an expectant look.

Lily assumed she didn't know English or couldn't hear. She leaned forward and spoke slower, "Doctor is out. Come back later."

Confusion flitted across the woman's face before she brayed laughter.

She must be addled. Lily frowned and prepared to close the door.

The woman stammered, "Miss Wright!"

Lily pulled the door back and stuck her head out, mouth agape. "Jessie?"

"Yes, ma'am."

"I, I didn't even recognize you. Come in."

She led Jessie to the bedroom; she didn't dare receive a dove in the parlor. Lily gestured to the chair and sat on the bed.

The bruises had disappeared. The beating had left a small scar below the dove's bottom lip and a heavy-lidded eye on one side, aging her, but no other remnants.

"You look wonderful, Jessie. How are you?"

"Ha! I borrowed this thing," she smoothed the dress over her legs, "so's not to embarrass you. I'm doin' all right. I aimed to visit before but didn't know if you were up for it."

"I wasn't, for a while. I'm feeling much better now. I'm actually moving up to Mrs. Connor's boardinghouse this afternoon, so it's good you came."

Jessie tilted her head to look at Lily's scar and shook her head. "I'm awful sorry you got hurt. Don't hardly notice it now, though. You were real lucky to get out of there. What will you do now?"

"I'm not sure yet. Find work, I hope."

Their positions had reversed, in a sense. Someone had hurt her this time, and Jessie took the role of supporter.

"Aw, shouldn't be hard for a sharp lady like yerself."

"I hope you're right. How is your … work going?" Lily hated to ask but couldn't think of another topic.

"Better. Lots more men in town after that big strike up 'round Davis Creek. I might be able to move up the row. Fiddle Jenny is settin' up a nice place, with a parlor room and a real tub for baths. It ain't done yet, though." She looked down at her hands, picking at the rough skin of a callus. "I even got a fella comin' to see me regular. He's real nice, and he brought me ribbons, and a lace hanky, and a little bottle of perfume."

Odd that she's bashful about a man. She's still just a girl, though.

Lily smiled. "That's very sweet of him. Is he a miner?"

"He works up at a shaft on Four Mile Hill. He comes down a couple times a week. He's aimin' to go to the Fourth of July dance with me, but I told him I aim to work that day. There'll be a whole lot of fellas in town lookin' for company."

"Oh, Jessie, go with him. If you like him, I mean. You never know, maybe it will lead to something good."

"Maybe. I guess I could." She started to speak, but backed off. After another false start, she began in a shaky voice, "I … came by 'cause I got to tell you how much I appreciate you bein' nice to me that night. I was—well, I was real bad off. After I left, that first night, I almost done myself in. Aimed to steal a bottle of laudanum from one of the girls.

"I was havin' a hard time seein' any good things. It started feelin' like nothin' would ever get better for me; like all I had to look forward to was more fellas jumpin' on me and havin' their fun, takin' some swings when they had an urge." She stopped and looked up, eyes wet and bloodshot. "I didn't do it, though, 'cause you showed me somethin' good. Not just bein' nice and all, but I saw you takin' it on all by yerself, with no man proppin' you up. And yer a real person, not one of those uppish ladies spendin' all their time fixin' their hair. I saw you, and I thought—well, I know I ain't smart like you, but maybe someday I could do somethin' like that. When you asked after my plans, I started thinkin' I might get me some." Jessie gave a lopsided grin, shrugged, and looked back down at her hands. "I know I must sound right cracked. But it felt like it was important to tell you."

Lily brushed away a tear and cleared her throat. "You don't need to thank me, but I'm quite glad you're still here. You're a strong girl, and I think you can do it if you set your mind to it."

She wanted to say more, to tell the girl she herself knew little, and understood less, but she couldn't bring herself to expose her own sins. Maybe Jessie was the wiser of them, given all that had happened.

Jessie smiled, a hint of pride flashing in her face. "I won't be a workin' girl forever. I'll get respectable, wait and see." She stood and moved to the door. "Maybe I'll try to come see you at Mrs. Connor's after a while, if you don't mind."

"I'd like that."

She walked Jessie to the entry. The sun shone bright as Jessie ambled down the walk. Lily went to join Mary for tea.

* * * * *

Late in the afternoon, Lily said her goodbyes to Dr. Andrews and Mary.

"I promise I'll pay the bill within the month. I hope to gain a position soon."

Dr. Andrews waved her off. "Don't you worry about that." He handed her a tin of salve. "Keep applying this. It will help. Take care of yourself and come have supper." He squeezed her shoulder, nodded, and left the parlor moving much faster than usual.

Lily smiled after him.

Mary handed her a packet of cookies. "You listen to him, dear. You must visit for some good food. We need to get some weight back on you." Tears dampened her lashes.

"Don't worry, I'm sure the fare at Mrs. Connor's will have me on your doorstep every night." She hugged the small woman. "I can't thank you enough."

"Oh, stop with the thanking." Mary studied her face. "Be strong, dear. You may be tested, but you have the mettle for it."

"I'll try." The admonition sent a strange chill through her and reminded her of what Luke had said.

Mary resumed her normal chatter as Lily took her satchel in hand and promised again to visit often.

She hurried out the door with a wave, eager to settle in at Mrs. Connor's, and wound through the pedestrians on the boardwalk without noticing if anyone looked at her or her scar.

The town had grown considerably since she'd arrived, and more people crowded the rutted street. It almost qualified as a city, with a buzzing hive-drone of urgent activity. Horses and buggies and wagons jingled and clattered. More women strolled amongst the men, and didn't stand out as much—the wives had moved in. The character of Clear Springs had begun its change. The chaotic wildness lay under a veneer of order and decorum. The sordid aspect remained, and she wondered how well it would stay hidden.

She stopped at the bank to withdraw money to pay for her room. She had deposited her funds with the larger Clear Springs bank, rather than Barnes', and realized that move could save her, since he wouldn't have access to her account. It saved her from having to face him, too.

The teller appraised her. "Your account book?"

"Oh. I, I don't have it. It was destroyed. In a fire."

He gave her a dubious look. "I can't simply hand you money on your word."

She glared. "I am Lily Wright. The fire a few weeks ago burned down my store, and the account book. The last deposit was fifteen dollars. Dr. Andrews will vouch for me. What else would you like to know?"

"Very well, I will check with the manager." He sniffed and strolled away.

When he returned, he slid a new account book under the barred window, with a receipt and a smirk.

$115.65.

The numbers swam before her eyes, and she grabbed the counter. *Not enough. Not nearly enough.* She could make the loan payment due in five days, but it left little for the boardinghouse fee and nothing for the doctor's bill and the invoices she still owed on store inventory. She fought a wave of despair and withdrew enough for her board.

She trudged up the path to Mrs. Connor's. Her anticipation had waned, and she wanted to go to her room and relax, alone. A boarder led her upstairs.

The tiny space appeared more like a large closet. From the size and location, Lily suspected it had originated as part of a larger room before renovation divided it for increased rents. She dropped her bag and sank onto the short, narrow bed with an exhausted sigh. The window shed light on a rough bedside table and a wardrobe that looked as if someone had dragged it to Colorado behind a wagon.

Lily shed her clothes, too tired to worry about supper. She fluffed the bedding and looked for evidence of bugs. It appeared clean, and she crawled between the sheets. Melancholy settled in as she assessed her new surroundings. Her precarious situation hit home. Desperation lurked at the edges of her mind.

Perhaps I should just go back to Jefferson City. Maybe Papa would take me back in. She chased the thought away. *No. I won't go back. Even Denver would be better. But for now, I have to stay here. I'll find a job. Mr. Warren will fix the loan problem. No more troubles. Stay positive.*

She fell asleep on a sagging bed in an unfamiliar room, determined to find a way back to solid ground despite the tempest that had cast her adrift.

CHAPTER TWENTY-SEVEN

The clump of boots and men's voices woke Lily as the boarders tramped down the stairs on their way to work. She groaned an annoyed huff and rolled over, pulling the coverlet over her head. Despite her exhaustion, she'd tossed and turned on the uncomfortable bed with worries running through her head. The men departed, leaving the house quiet. She half-dozed, soft morning light spilling in around the curtains, and dreamed of a big, soft feather bed.

Forcing herself out of bed with a sigh, Lily shivered as she tugged her dress on and buttoned her shoes. She pulled out money to pay Mrs. Connor and when she bent to stuff the remaining money back into the bag, the dress seams stretched alarmingly. She hesitated, arguing with herself, but counted out several dollars to buy a new dress. *I'll have a better chance of finding a job if I look more presentable.* She needed every advantage.

Her jaw clenched as she recalled the yards of fabric and dozens of blouses, skirts, and dresses in the store—all gone. The thousands of steps racing back and forth between displays, the ache in her back after lifting box after box, the gallons of sweat—all wasted. All because of that crazy, jealous shrew.

"Goddamn that woman!"

Her cheeks radiated heat in a flash of shame, but she lifted her chin and resisted the urge to repent. Her mother would have been horrified at the oath ... but those chains no longer controlled her. If she wanted to curse, she would. God had punished her enough for a lifetime, and she supposed he'd abandoned her long ago. She couldn't dredge up any real remorse.

I've fallen so far, a curse is the least of my sins. I'm entitled to a bit of anger, aren't I?

A light knock broke through her tirade. "Visitor in the parlor, Miss Wright."

She frowned. "Ah, thank you. I'll be down directly."

After tucking the money into her waist pocket, she dressed her hair and trudged downstairs.

Marshal Parker stood with his hands on his gun belt. His hat lay on a chair.

Lily groaned inwardly. *This is the last thing I need.*

She cleared her throat. "How can I help you, Marshal?"

He swung around, and his eyes passed over her. "Miss Wright, thank you for seein' me. I'm still lookin' into the fire and wondered if you'd remembered anything else?" His expression said he knew she hadn't—and wouldn't.

"No, sir, I don't believe so. It's all still a blur." She gave a helpless shrug.

"Huh." He caught her gaze with hard eyes. "I'll tell you what. I know you haven't told the truth. The doctor said the only thing that could've cut you was a knife—and we both know who was holdin' it. I know somethin' happened that night, but I don't know what or whose fault it was. Some important folks are breathin' down my neck to arrest you.

Knowin' the lady who died, I don't reckon that's appropriate. She wasn't right in the head, and everybody else knows that, but I reckon their grief clouds their judgment. Don't matter the reason, they want someone to pay."

Lily swallowed, waiting for the hammer to fall, but didn't take the bait. *He wants me to flinch.*

Parker scratched his chin, and his mouth turned up in a humorless smile. "That's what I thought. Well, I ain't goin' to arrest you. No evidence to speak of and plenty of hearsay." Settling his hat back on his head, he moved to the door. He turned and wagged a finger at her. "But I'll warn you. I don't want any more trouble from you. Even a hint, and I'll have to do as I'm told, regardless of any evidence." He tipped his hat and pulled the door shut.

She sank into a chair and buried her face in her hands, her nerves shot. After a while, she shook off the tension, reminded herself of her determination, and left to shop for a respectable dress.

* * * * *

Lily walked into the large general store that held the town's postal station. She'd changed into the new, stiff, dark blue dress she'd bought; she disliked the style but believed it far more flattering than the shabby calico. In proper attire, she held her head high and regained some confidence.

"Can you direct me to a board for employment postings?"

A bald, frail man behind the barred counter shook his head. "No, missy, don't have anything like that."

"Do you know of any positions open for a woman?"

His eyebrow raised, and he dipped his head to look at her over his spectacles. "Missy, there's two kinds of jobs for women in this town. I don't think you want either one."

She glared. "There *must* be something else. A teacher or governess, or a clerk—something appropriate for an educated lady."

"If so, no one has notified me."

With an exasperated groan, Lily marched back into the hot, choking dust of the late morning. Summer had descended on Clear Springs. After the wet spring, a pattern of dry, still weather with soaring temperatures left a heavy haze of dirt hanging over the unpaved roads.

Already sweaty and irritated, she loathed the only other plan she'd come up with: plodding to each building—save the saloons—and inquiring after employment from every proprietor. But she saw no other option.

More structures had sprouted since the fire, and evidence of the blaze had largely disappeared. Her empty lot, cleared of debris but littered with small chunks of black ash and charcoal, sat tucked between two large canvas tents. As her gaze followed the street, she contemplated the town's upper end on the south side: the realm of the doves, from high-class to destitute. Brothels and cottages took up two blocks of South Street.

As if their existence renewed her determination to avoid that fate, she turned down the boardwalk in the opposite direction. If she had to call on every reputable business in town, she would.

* * * * *

Hours later, her new dress grayed with a film of dust and dampened by sweat, Lily dragged herself to a small log building under a weathered sign that said "Dressmaker." The cabin huddled at the edge of the trees, away from any roads, with no evidence of active business.

She pushed the door open, and her eyes took a moment to adjust after the bright daylight.

One side of the large room was dedicated to the business of sewing, with bolts of fabric, a treadle sewing machine, a battered privacy screen, and a dress form. A large stone fireplace sat at the other end, with a small kitchen area and rough hewn furniture. Despite the day's heat, ashen coals glowed in the grate. A dark curtain hung over a doorway to a back room. It parted, and a stooped form shuffled in.

The person's back curled in a contorted bow. Lily couldn't see a face. A stark-white clump of hair started well back from a seamed and spotted forehead and lay in a bun at the top of the hunch. A blanket hung from the shoulders and swept the floor, with no hint of what lay beneath.

"Ayuh!"

Lily stepped back, startled, and bent to peer at the figure, now almost sure it was a woman.

She raised her voice as the woman moved toward a rocking chair near the fireplace. "Pardon me, I don't mean to disturb you. My name is Lily Wright. I'm looking for employment."

"No need to holler at me, young lady. Those parts work fine." She settled into the rocker and tilted her head sideways to look up. "A job, you say? What kind of job?"

Lily pointed at the sewing equipment. "The sign outside said dressmaker ...."

"Seamstress, eh? Don't know as I have a need for a seamstress. I can manage that myself, have been for eighty years." The old woman pointed a gnarled finger at a chair opposite the rocker. "Sit, so I can look at you without twisting my head off."

She eased toward the door. "No—thank you. Really, if

you aren't hiring, I won't bother you. I'll be going."

A sharp tone edged in. "You don't listen all that well, not a good quality. I didn't say I wouldn't hire you, young lady. I *did* say sit down so I can get a look at you."

Lily hesitated, reluctant to waste time chatting. She'd wandered from store to office to shop, increasingly discouraged with each rejection, and still had more to canvass. Most told her they had no need, some scoffed at hiring a woman, and one rude man had looked at her scar pointedly and told her he didn't need a troublemaker around. She wanted to go back to her room and hide, but her feet hurt, and the long walk back up the hill to Mrs. Connor's persuaded her to obey the woman's command. Lily perched on the chair across from the woman and pasted on a polite smile.

Rheumy eyes swept Lily from beneath folds of papery skin. The woman tipped back and forth, dirt crunching under the rockers. Her breath came in shallow, wheezing puffs.

As seconds dragged into minutes, Lily's fingers squirmed in her lap, and her smile faded. She broke eye contact. The creaking rocker and rasping breaths grew louder in the stuffy room. She opened her mouth to bleat an excuse, but the woman spoke first.

"Where did you get that brand?"

Lily's brow knit. "Pardon?"

"On your face, the scar. What happened?"

"Oh." The blunt question caught her off-guard. "I was attacked with a knife."

"By who?"

"A w-woman. She was ... deranged."

"You a sporting gal?"

Her eyes popped wide, and she jerked her head side-to-side.

"You aren't married?"

Her tongue slicked her lips. "I was. I left him." A voice in her head berated her for entertaining the crone's tactless probes.

"You're from East."

Lily nodded, though it hadn't been a question. Minutes spun out as Lily directed her gaze anywhere but at the huddled figure. The alternating rhythm of the rocker and thick breathing ratcheted up her unease.

"At least you're truthful, I guess. Better learn to listen though. Sewing doesn't pay well, you know? Yes, I guess you do." She waved a bony hand at the door. "Come tomorrow, seven o'clock."

Lily swiveled her head back to the woman, sure she'd heard wrong. "You'll hire me?"

The woman strained to look toward the rough beams in the ceiling. "Lord, why'd you send me one who can't listen?"

Lily stood, relief tossing words out in a rush. "I, I'm sorry, it just surprised me, that's all. I promise I'll be on time and I'll work hard. You won't regret it."

"Jabbers and doesn't listen." She shook her head and let out a heaving sigh. "Lord, you do try me."

Lily skittered to the door and stopped. "Pardon me, ma'am, but what's your name?"

"Alice Durand."

"It's a pleasure to meet you, Mrs. Durand. I'll see you tomorrow."

As she retraced her path back to the main road, the name rang in her ears. She'd heard it before, it danced at the edge of memory, but she couldn't recall when or where.

Her step lightened. She had at least found a job. Something that paid more would have been better, but with limited options, she had to take what she could. She would keep looking for another position and move up when the opportunity came. Her luck had taken a turn.

CHAPTER TWENTY-EIGHT

As Lily climbed the boardinghouse steps, the delight of finding a position distracted her.

"Evenin', miss. What's yer business?"

Lily jerked her head around. A bloated hunk of flesh sprawled on the bench, the swing creaking with each tortured sway.

"Oh! You startled me. I'm Lily Wright, the new boarder." She moved down the porch and held her hand out.

"Mrs. Connor. So yer the girl."

She examined Lily with a prying gaze, and her meaty paw enveloped Lily's hand with a token pump.

Large, overbearing, and rambling, the woman imitated the house—or perhaps the other way around. Everyone knew Mrs. Connor, and many had told Lily tales of her. She loved to talk and spent her days on her porch swing gossiping; she knew everything about everyone in town and didn't hesitate to use her knowledge when she might gain from it. As Lily stepped back to avoid the swing's arc, the woman's expression turned predatory.

"What's that on yer face?"

"I, I was injured in a fire." Lily lifted her hand to cover the scar.

"Yer that one?" She shook a fist, creating waves in the soft, bloated flesh of her arm. "Durn that Warren feller. He didn't tell me that."

"Pardon?"

"I heard 'bout that whole business. You kilt that Samuels girl."

Lily gasped, shock and indignation rising together. "I did no such thing! She did that to herself, *after* she trespassed in my store." She'd known the gossips would attack the incident with glee, and she understood the marshal's pressure from Judith's parents, but she hadn't really believed the rumor mill had judged her guilty of homicide.

Mrs. Connor snorted. "A good story, no doubt. Might even be a true one, as everyone knows the girl was touched in the head. Syphilis does that. That's what it was too, though of course there ain't a one who'd say it, with Samuels bein' who he is. Wretched thing, her ma bein' afflicted and passin' it to her, but that tells a body what kinda woman *she* is." She stopped short, as if she'd forgotten Lily, and peered at her, her eyes black and furtive like a rat's. "You don't look like a killer."

Lily stood with her mouth ajar during the rant. Having heard the woman's reputation, she'd expected the loose lips, but the unkindness stunned her. Her skin crawled with distaste.

"I, I, I'm not! None of that was my doing. But that's none of *your* business."

The retort shot out, and she snapped her mouth shut. She couldn't afford to offend the woman; board commanded a premium with the growing population.

Mrs. Connor didn't seem to notice the rebuff. She

shrugged. "Ain't no loss in that girl, to my mind. She'd done used up all the sympathy folks carried for her, with her crazy outbursts and that incident with her fella." She narrowed her eyes and jabbed a finger at Lily. "Mind you, though, I ain't fond of women in my house in the usual course, and the first sight of trouble, yer out. I made a deal, and I'll follow it, but you better stay quiet."

Lily's mouth tightened, but she forced a calm reply. "Understood." She wavered, eager to leave the unpleasant hag, but she had to ask. "You said something about outbursts and incidents?"

Connor nodded, doubling and tripling her chins. "'Twas a couple months ago, or was it longer? I don't recall. Anyhow, the Samuels girl ran over a woman with a buggy after stormin' out of her fella's place. Not just ran her over, chased her *down*. Claimed the woman was a witch and had set a curse on her, or some such craziness. They sent her down to Pueblo, to the new asylum, for a spell. She'd come back just a couple weeks before you kilt her."

Lily threw up her hands. "I did not kill her." She squirmed as a question occurred and whispered, "Who was the man? And the woman she killed?" She brushed her hands together, as if she could wipe off the stain of encouraging gossip.

Connor waved a hand. "Hell, I don't know. Some fella from Texas, I think. They was engaged, had posted it in the paper and everythin'. He broke it off, but nobody knew if it was before or after she went crazy." Her voice dropped, and she leaned forward. "The woman was a dove over on South. Ever'body said the fella visited her, but he denied it, heard tell."

Lily thought she'd choke on her tongue, and her thoughts turned to chaos.

She realized Connor was waiting for a response. "How sordid. Oh, and thank you for the room. Good day."

Mrs. Connor continued even as Lily beat a retreat. "That durn Warren. He tried to say it was a nice girl who wouldn't be no trouble. I'll hide him when I see him ...."

Lily brought her supper to her room to eat in peace, more self-conscious than ever after Mrs. Connor's judgment. She'd lost her appetite but made herself down a few bites. She had pushed the table back against the wall and kicked her shoes off when someone knocked.

She winced as she hobbled to the door, vowing to buy new shoes as soon as possible. She opened it a crack to find the elderly attorney fussing with his hat.

"Good evening, Mr. Warren." Too tired and wrought out, she couldn't even muster a polite smile.

Warren wore an apologetic grimace. "Good evening, Miss Wright. I'm quite sorry to disturb you. I wanted to let you know I wasn't able to find another solicitor appropriate to your case." His short, beleaguered sigh showed his reluctance. "I will help you with it, but I will caution you again that I'm not familiar with such issues, and I can't promise anything."

"I understand, Mr. Warren. Truly, I'd rather work with you in any case. I trust you. Do you need anything from me to file the papers?"

"Just the copy of the agreement; I can take the pertinent details from that and get a copy back to you."

"Yes, let me get it." Lily handed the paper to him. "I can't thank you enough. I did want to ask, should I make the payment when it's due? I have the money for it, but it will be a hardship, and I wasn't sure if that was best."

"I would recommend it. The judge may call it back if he decides for you, but I wouldn't risk defaulting in the meantime, if you can help it."

Lily sagged. "All right, I'll arrange it. So you'll file it right away?"

"I should be able to prepare it tomorrow and have it submitted the first of the week." He frowned. "I am sensitive to your situation, Miss Wright, but I do have to charge you. I'll delay the bill until we get a judgment, though, and I'll take payments if that will help."

"I appreciate that. I'll settle it as fast as I can, and if we win, it shouldn't be a problem." She pursed her lips. "I just met Mrs. Connor earlier. She seemed upset. I do hope I haven't caused any trouble for you."

He chuckled. "Oh, don't mind Moira—Mrs. Connor, I mean. She only talks rough." Bright red patches colored his cheeks. "Good evening, then." He turned to walk down the hallway, but Lily called him back.

She tried to think how to word her question. She whispered, "Exactly what is the protocol for baths here?"

"Oh. Ah. There's a wash room downstairs, back by the kitchen. She'll charge a quarter any day other than Sunday." The old man looked away and clutched his bowler.

Lily hid a smile. "Thank you, Mr. Warren. Please let me know when the papers are ready."

Warren scooted down the hall, and she flopped back on the bed, drawn back to troubling thoughts.

The realization that more than a few believed she had deliberately killed Judith made her skin crawl. Worse, she *felt* guilty. She'd had to defend herself, but she couldn't escape the fact that her actions had caused the death of one more person. How could she ever resolve her own sense of responsibility if others blamed her as well? It forced her to question her perception of that terrible night, and those doubts added to the burden of all her other mistakes.

It brought the other deaths to mind, as well—the deaths she'd refused to think of for so long. In the same sense that Judith had died as a result of her decisions, Lily bore responsibility for her own siblings' and mother's death. Her choices had set the wheels in motion.

And what of the baby? Was that my fault, too? Did I doom a helpless child before it could even draw a breath?

The pain of loss welled up until the dam broke and released a suffocating, wrenching anguish. It surged through her body, like snake's venom spreading with each heartbeat. Sobs forced the air from her lungs, and she wished she couldn't draw another breath. When her eyes could produce no more tears, she lay trembling and coughing. Though the crying stopped, she couldn't exile the memories as she always had.

She endured another restless night, filled with guilt and blame, disturbed by shifting visions of her family, her baby, and Judith.

CHAPTER TWENTY-NINE

Lily approached the Durand cottage as the sun crept over the mountain. Her eyes burned from lack of sleep, but she put on a cheerful face for her first day. As she knocked, she only hoped Mrs. Durand wouldn't grill her again.

A voice drifted to her, but it didn't come from inside the cottage. Lily frowned, finding no one about, and thought the wind must have played tricks. The voice came again, and she followed it. She walked to the side of the house and peered around the corner. Her eyes widened.

Mrs. Durand carried two water buckets as she shuffled along a path beside the cottage. A shawl hung over her humped back and trailed on the ground behind her. Each slow, tottering step sloshed water. The old woman had been muttering to herself but addressed Lily without lifting her head.

"Good morning, young lady. You're on time. I like that." She continued her shamble, and the water continued splashing.

Lily rushed toward her. "Mrs. Durand, let me take those."

"Shoo! I can carry my own water."

"Please, let me. That must bother your poor back."

Lily reached for a bucket, but Mrs. Durand wrenched her head up and scowled.

"Listen up, young lady! I'm not an invalid. You are here to sew, nothing more."

Lily stepped back. "I, I'm sorry, I didn't mean ...."

"Don't be apologizing all the time. It'll make people think you don't know your own mind."

They'd come to the corner of the house, and Mrs. Durand stopped to catch her breath. Lily stood by, shuffling her feet and wringing her hands. Mrs. Durand gave a short nod and started moving again.

"I appreciate the concern, but one thing I've learned: as soon as I stop doing for myself, that's when I'll stop being *able* to do for myself. And that's when I hope the Lord takes me home. I have no interest in sitting around, rotting above ground."

Lily grimaced, wondering if the woman would insist on digging her own grave before they put her in it.

After several minutes, and two more rests, they arrived at the front door. Lily hesitated to open it until Mrs. Durand nodded. She stood aside as the old woman went in, set the buckets near the hearth, and swung a crane out from the fireplace.

Mrs. Durand poured water into a kettle and tipped her head toward the other side of the room. "You can get started over there. That pile of shirts needs buttons."

Lily found the stack of blouses beside a tin of buttons. Moving a chair near a small window, she settled in and started sewing. Mrs. Durand sat in her rocking chair, waiting for the water to boil.

While her fingers repeated familiar patterns, Lily appreciated the quiet, but the monotony of attaching buttons allowed her mind to wander, and her shoulders tightened. She'd found a job, but it would take more than sewing to solve everything. Luke, Barnes, a living wage, a home. Impatience nettled her; she wanted it all resolved, but she had little control over any of it. With a huff of frustration, she directed her attention back to the shirts.

The water boiled, and Mrs. Durand puttered around making coffee. She poured two cups and brought them to the bench near Lily.

"Have some. Just don't get it on your business there."

Lily smiled, surprised again. "Thank you."

Mrs. Durand lowered herself into the chair at the sewing machine with a soft groan. She busied herself arranging a piece of cloth, her gnarled fingers moving with unexpected speed. As she started to sew, she started to talk.

"You have troubles catching up with you, I expect. I've seen a few of those myself. Hard not to with my years and all the travel I've endured." She cut Lily off. "Oh, don't think you're keeping them hidden. Plain as day all over your face. You've got a pretty face, but it doesn't hide much."

The old woman's foot worked the treadle, pushing up and down on the pedal, while her hands fed cloth under the dancing needle. The movements flowed at a steady pace, as if her body was part of the machine.

Lily searched for something to say to head off another inquisition, but Mrs. Durand spoke again.

"Don't worry; you don't need to tell me about it. I simply thought I'd point out those are difficult things to keep to yourself. They'll eat at you, haunt you night and day. Pretty soon, they gnaw their way out and show up in everything you do. I learned all about that a long time ago.

"I would wager you're a bit like me when I was your age. I started out in Maine. My papa was a preacher, and mama raised ten children. I was the first of the girls, had two older brothers. Mama insisted I was schooled properly, just like the boys. I don't know if she regretted that or not. It gave me ideas girls weren't supposed to have, lit a fire under my feet." Durand slugged her coffee and turned the cloth. "I couldn't seem to fit in the mold. I always wanted to do the opposite of what they expected. So, when a young man hawking medicines came through our place and asked me to marry him—well, I thought that was a fine idea, since he could take me away from the routine. But what made it irresistible was everybody *else* thought it was a bad idea. Mama and Papa didn't like him a bit. So, of course, I took off with him. And wouldn't you know, everything they said would happen came to pass, and more."

Mrs. Durand cackled and slapped the table. Lily jumped, jerking her attention from the shirt in her lap. She smiled at the old woman's amusement but found it odd she should laugh at something that sounded unpleasant.

The laughter trailed off, and Mrs. Durand paused to cough and catch her breath before continuing. "No, it didn't seem very humorous at the time. I felt quite abused just then. Goodness, did I. I expect I blamed just about everyone for everything bad that happened; Josiah—that was my husband, the quack—I blamed him most; my folks, since they didn't try hard enough to warn me; society, for being so hard on a woman; even God, as he didn't see fit to enlighten me at a younger age.

"I learned about that too, though. I hope you can learn it faster than I did. Took me a while. I had plenty of time for it, plenty of time for thinkin', I guess. Sooner you learn that lesson, sooner you can move on to the next." She nodded once and grew quiet, focused on the rhythm her foot orchestrated on the machine.

Lily kept sewing but threw puzzled frowns at Mrs. Durand. The woman's rambling made no sense and left her with questions she didn't want to ask, for fear of sounding as if she hadn't listened again. The woman seemed to know what Lily thought, and even dreamed, without her saying it. The questions dogged her the rest of the day, since Mrs. Durand didn't say another word until she told Lily to go home at six o'clock.

* * * * *

After supper, Lily got her bath: a dingy rag and tepid water in a dented metal tub. She didn't feel much cleaner, but it did cut the dust and cool her off. While she dressed, Luke occupied her mind. She'd put off writing him for too long. She found some paper and a pencil in the parlor, lit the lamp in her room, and settled on the bed.

She stared at the blank page, baffled by what to say or how to start. She had a million questions but didn't want the answers in a letter. The issue of Judith and his relationship with her, when he'd ended it, the rumors Mrs. Connor had mentioned—no reply could satisfy those concerns without seeing his face when he responded. Besides, the idea of explaining the whole incident made her stomach churn and her hands turn clammy. But what else could she talk about? Anything else seemed disingenuous. After agonizing for an hour, she wrote.

Dear Luke,
I received your letter, thank you. I am glad to know you are safe. I try not to worry for you too much. I hope the weather clears and the rest of the drive passes without trouble.

It has been hot and dry here, and I wish for rain. Clear Springs keeps growing and more strikes bring more people every week. Much has changed, and you will hardly know the place by the time you make it back.
I think of you as well, and am anxious for your return. I would like to write more, but it will have to wait. Take care of yourself and come back soon.

With Affection,
Lily

She wanted to say much more. She wanted to tell him she wished he'd never left, that she resented his absence in her time of need; to explain her apprehension about opening herself to trusting him and about losing him; to reveal her past and nightmares, in hopes he might understand and help heal them. She couldn't write any of those things. She wasn't even sure she could speak them.

He stirred her in ways no one ever had, but she refused to let a man rule her again. Luke didn't seem the kind of man to demand surrender, but he might go to the other end of the spectrum and abandon her when he grew tired of her. She couldn't bear that, either.

She put the letter aside, undecided whether she'd send it or not. She hadn't lied, but she'd held back the things that mattered. Doubts stalked her. She extinguished the lamp and lay awake in the darkness. Silence cloaked the room, but her mind echoed with anxiety she couldn't quiet.

CHAPTER THIRTY

Lily woke feeling battered. Her back hurt, her fingers ached, her eyes had gone puffy and dry. She considered staying in bed and sending someone to offer an excuse to Mrs. Durand, but that would cost her the position, and she didn't dare lose one of the few good things she had left.

With a sigh, she swung her feet to the floor and sat for a moment, brooding over the previous days. Her jaw tightened when she thought of Mrs. Connor and the old wounds the confrontation had reopened.

Maybe that was what Mrs. Durand was talking about. Blame won't help anything, and I have to put it behind me.

She took a calming breath and smiled, determined to have a good day.

At the dressmaker's cottage, Lily sat in the same chair, sewing more buttons. The first day had made her fingers tender, and she asked Mrs. Durand for a thimble.

The old lady sat in her rocking chair, waiting for the water to boil. She inclined her head toward a cabinet of tiny drawers behind Lily.

She chuckled. "Plenty in there. I wondered when you'd ask."

A flash of irritation struck Lily. *If she knew I'd want one, why didn't she simply give it to me?* She took a deep breath and chased the thought away. *No, I won't let trifles upset me today. It's not her fault I'm cranky.* She found a thimble and resumed her work, pushing the needle through button after button.

Mrs. Durand went through the coffee routine and brought two cups over. She took her chair at her table, readied the fabric for the needle, and like the day before, her talk commenced when the machine came to life, as if one powered the other.

"I expect you wondered what blame had to do with what I told you, or with you, ayuh? Hmm. Blame is tricky. Folks always look to place blame when something bad happens, and they're happy to take it when it's something good. In most troubles, there's plenty of people who had a hand in it. I dare say you could connect it to some stranger half the world away, if you put your mind to it. The danger is that it's just a distraction. I'm not saying people shouldn't be held responsible—that's another matter. But blame .... It rots you from the inside out and only keeps you thinking about the past, instead of what's ahead. You'll understand in your own time, don't fret. It's a tough lesson, though.

"My troubles started when the quack decided I wasn't to have any say in where we went or what happened when we got there. He fancied staying on the move, and I didn't mind that, as I had a wandering soul myself. He wanted to run from town to town, though, revisiting the same places. He never liked being too far from other folks, mostly the female kind. Lord, I just couldn't stomach that." She gave Lily a pointed look. "The town hopping or the lady hopping. First time I heard word of his 'cure' for lonely women, I let him know. Then he let *me* know, with a chunk of wood. I wasn't used to that and didn't care for it, but wasn't much I could say about it. After, I guess he wanted to make up and agreed to go west like I'd nagged him for.

"We made it to Ohio, and then Illinois, and finally out to the Missouri Territory. Goodness, I loved seeing new places." She stopped to wet her throat and arrange a new piece of cloth.

Lily found herself enthralled but still didn't understand why the woman had decided to tell the story. It occurred to her that Mrs. Durand might have hired her merely to have an audience, but since it helped the time pass, she didn't care why.

With her foot back on the pedal, Mrs. Durand continued. "By that time, though, I didn't much love my husband. Maybe I never did. I suppose I never forgot that first time he took a club to me, and every time after that just made that anger burn hotter. I'd gotten him to settle on a farm, but it was hard, lonely work. I expect he resented that, and he started drinking and taking his frustrations out on me more often."

A lump rose in Lily's throat. Perhaps they did have some things in common.

"That went on a while, but it turned out I could only take so much. After a bad night, I waited up. He'd passed out. I took a spade—I couldn't find any good sticks—and put an end to his frustration."

A hot wave of nausea hit Lily. Her hand jerked, and the needle slid deep into her finger. She sucked air through her teeth and pulled the needle out. A bead of blood surfaced, and she stuck the finger in her mouth. She found a scrap of fabric and wrapped the wound.

As the throbbing faded, Lily remembered what had caused her to slip. She gaped at the old woman, unable to believe she'd heard right. Her skin crawled with shock and horror. But hadn't Mrs. Durand done what Lily wished she could have?

Could I have lived with that treatment year after year without it coming to that? I doubt it. It only took a few times before I couldn't stand it. How can I judge this old woman?

Mrs. Durand went on with her sewing, giving no indication she noticed Lily's mishap or her distress, never taking her eyes from her work.

"Mrs. Durand ...." Lily needed to hear the rest of the story, but dreaded it.

"In time, young lady. Get those buttons on."

Lily scowled, but Mrs. Durand had finished her talk for the day. Lily returned to her task, but failed to get much done, her work interrupted frequently by uneasy glances at the old lady.

She asked to leave early so she could stop at the bank in order to make the payment to Barnes on time, and Mrs. Durand waved her off.

Lily walked down the hill, sweat dampening her underarms in the glaring afternoon sun. Paying Barnes galled her after his vulgar suggestion, but she couldn't deny a trace of fear lay beneath the disdain. He would use any advantage over her he could find, and her vulnerability made her a prime target. She wished her desperation hadn't driven her to accept his terms, but she couldn't undo the mistake.

At the bank, she wrote the draft on her account and asked the teller to include it with their daily transactions. He agreed, and she heaved a sigh of relief. She couldn't face an encounter with Barnes. With that errand out of the way, her tension dissipated. Her meager account balance still worried her, but she held onto the hope that the lawsuit would succeed.

She stood outside the postal station, arguing with herself. She chided herself for the angst, but she couldn't help it. Nothing in the letter sounded right, and she feared Luke would take it wrong. With a huff, she mailed the letter.

Her anxiety built, and she spent the rest of the evening thinking of him. She tried to push it aside, but he returned like a flash of brightness flickering behind closed eyelids after looking at the sun. She alternated between the sweet memories of their short time together and the unbearable heartache of rejection and loss she feared.

CHAPTER THIRTY-ONE

Lily hurried through her morning routine and almost trotted to the Durand cottage. Despite the unnerving revelation of the day before, she couldn't dampen her curiosity. She'd never met anyone like the old woman. Alice Durand's directness intimidated her, but she wished she had the same confidence to speak her mind and the courage to defend it.

She wanted to ask the woman to continue the story as soon as she entered, but forced herself to sit down to her work and wait while Mrs. Durand's slow, stooped form moved around the kitchen.

Lily had dozens of questions. At the start, she didn't see why Durand had said they had similarities, but Lily couldn't deny the connection—a greater bond than with her own mother. In scarcely a few days, it had crept up on her. A powerful affection for Durand struck her as she realized she hadn't wanted merely the story but also the company. The sentiment felt foreign. Her childhood isolation had followed her into adult life, and she'd never had a woman friend, except maybe Jessie. A rueful smile twisted her lips. How had two such unorthodox women become her closest companions in such a short time?

Mrs. Durand brought the coffee over and sat.

"Thank you. Mrs. Durand ...."

"Alice. No need for formality at this late hour."

Lily smiled. "Alice, then. I just wanted to say I appreciate you hiring me and being so kind."

Alice flapped a hand at her. "You can thank me by finishing those buttons."

The old woman drank her coffee and rubbed her swollen knuckles for several minutes, and Lily had to bite her tongue to keep from prodding her.

The old woman sounded tired when she finally began. "I spent the rest of that night—after dispatching the quack—on the porch, wondering how I'd gotten where I was. I'd never expected to find myself alone, a widow and a killer, out on the prairie.

"We'd had a couple of babies, but the poor things both died before they made it out of diapers. I sometimes wonder if it would have changed things if they'd lived. Maybe Josiah would have learned how to love, or maybe I would have learned how to forgive. I expect it was a blessing God took them, though." She nodded, as if to reassure herself.

"So, there I sat; my dead husband not twenty feet away, and the nearest neighbor ten miles away. I felt pretty bad, even though I was glad to be rid of him. That night was my low spot. Some folks would figure it was later." She stopped sewing and looked at Lily, her eyes almost accusing, and slowly shook her head. "No, that was it. That was when I decided everyone else was to blame for all my trouble; if my parents had stopped me from running off; if my husband had been a better man; if God—or anyone else—had been a better teacher. Not once in that long night did I think where

I ended up was my own doing.

"Now, I'm not saying that husband of mine didn't deserve what he got. I expect that's for the Lord to decide." She grew quiet, and her foot stopped on the treadle. She glanced at the beams overhead, sighed, and sipped her coffee.

A burst of frustration escaped Lily. "But how could you have known? You may have made mistakes, but that didn't mean you deserved a bad husband."

The old woman snorted and restarted the needle on its steady path. "Your ears are failing again, young lady. What you deserve and what your choices come to don't often match, but that's how life is. That's not the point. Pay attention, and you'll find it.

"I wrapped the man up and prepared to put him in the ground. I spent all the next day, digging on the hill above the house. I wasn't exactly worried 'bout the law; there wasn't much law in those parts then, and after he was buried they'd have been hard pressed to dispute whatever story I told. No, I was worried about getting myself off that farm. It wasn't a place for a woman to be alone.

"The Sioux were making trouble in that area. We'd been on decent terms with ours, but you never really knew what they might do next. Well, I found out. They showed up as I was hauling him to the grave. It didn't take them long to judge the situation and figure out I was on my own. So, they took me captive."

Lily gaped. "You were kidnapped? By Indians?"

Alice nodded. "I spent five years with them, wandering all over. They set fire to the farm, burned my husband's body. I don't know if anyone came looking for me or not, but they sure didn't find me. It was a small band, stayed on the move a lot. I was no more than a slave. They didn't treat me real bad, but it was a hard time. I begged them to kill me. I prayed to God to let me die. Nobody listened. I just kept on living."

"But you got away ...." Lily had stopped sewing.

"Yes, I finally did. They'd stopped near a town to do some trading. I escaped, and they fled. I told the townsfolk the Sioux killed my husband and took me. It was far enough away from the farm that they hadn't heard of me or my husband. I stayed there a bit, getting used to being civilized again. I found I liked civilization even less than I had before. I moved west, and I've just kind of kept moving further out ever since. I came to Clear Springs some years ago, when it was still quiet. It's about ruined now, though."

"I don't understand," Lily said, shaking her head. "Being held captive wasn't worse than killing a man in self-defense? And you're saying you blame yourself for all of that? That's ridiculous!"

Alice let the machine wind down, and a deep breath brought on a coughing spell. She waved her hand when Lily half-stood to help. The woman's worn joints creaked and popped as she pushed herself up from the chair. She shuffled the few feet to Lily's seat, and her watery eyes pierced Lily with an intense gaze.

"Under the circumstances, that man may have needed killing, but I didn't think before I did it. I never considered the consequences of my choices, not fully. Not when I ran off with him, not when I ran off at the mouth about his women, and not when I whacked him over the head with the spade. I cut off my nose to spite my face, time and again, and I paid dearly for it.

"But this is the important part, Lily. If I hadn't blamed everyone else for my troubles, I would have realized I was the one controlling my destiny. When you blame others, you give up the power to do for yourself. I could have escaped sooner, from the husband and the Indians. I was so caught up in my misery and feeling sorry for myself, and worried about who I should blame for it, I let opportunities pass me by. Bad things happen, ain't many who will avoid that. But when they do, focus on the opportunity—not the misery and blame." She nodded once. "I have to make water. Get those buttons on."

She shuffled to the door, on her way to the outhouse.

Lily sat perplexed, trying to reconcile all the old woman had said.

Alice went to lie down after a while, and Lily spent the afternoon in silence, with the buttons and her thoughts.

She could understand how the suggestions might apply to parts of her past. Her own elopement with Duncan paralleled Alice's in some ways. She'd found herself trapped in an unhappy and violent marriage, like Alice. But Lily had left Duncan, not killed him—and she hadn't waited years to do it. Granted, she hadn't had the best laid plans, but she had succeeded in escaping and starting a new life. She couldn't have foreseen or prevented the confrontation with Judith and the fire, not really. She believed she had taken what opportunities she could.

What about the blame? It had eaten at her, precisely as Alice said. Lily had buried the anger, but her heart still held the moldering remains of her reproach. She blamed her parents for abandoning her. She blamed Duncan for tricking her into loving him, and somehow for the loss of the baby. She blamed Judith for the fire. Now, she could blame Barnes for stealing her dream. None of that blame had helped her, had it? The bad things had happened—had she focused on blame or opportunity?

She was afraid to answer those questions. She wanted to

justify her decisions. Her mind produced unassailable rationale for her own innocence. She could defend her actions, but what good would that do? Alice might say none at all.

Regret and anger bubbled to the surface as she contemplated the path her life had taken. The unfairness of it all made her want to run away, reinvent herself anew, but how many times could she do that? Alice had learned to accept the injustices she'd encountered, it seemed. Lily searched her heart but couldn't find that peace yet. She still railed at the wrongs committed against her, and she couldn't put aside the anguish. Perhaps she would never find the strength to leave it behind. The prospect distressed her, and she wished Alice hadn't brought it up.

CHAPTER THIRTY-TWO

Lily left the cottage distraught. As she walked down the hill, she looked forward to retreating to her room and planned to find a discarded book in the parlor and lose herself in the pages. She wanted to be alone.

She turned onto the main road. The commotion of wagons, horses, and pedestrians had quieted at the end of the workday, and the nightly carousing had yet to start. Few people walked or loitered on the boardwalk, and Lily appreciated the lack of traffic.

Crowds had made her uneasy since her flight from Duncan—a sea of faces might hide danger. That apprehension had abated, but her anxiety sharpened again under the strain of comments on her disfigurement. Now that she knew the town believed she'd killed Judith, she felt even more conspicuous. She told herself she didn't care what others thought—they had no right to judge her—but the self-conscious torment lingered.

As she passed a narrow alley between frame buildings, a burst of raucous laughter echoed from the far end. Several older boys stood near the rear of the buildings, gathered around something she couldn't see. Lily dismissed them and walked on. As she neared the other side of the gap and prepared to mount the boardwalk again, a feminine voice rose above the boys' guffaws.

"Leave me be!" The inflection signaled annoyance, but a harsh edge betrayed a hint of panic.

Lily stopped and craned her head. Though the boys blocked her view, a glimpse of a colorful skirt showed between their legs. She frowned, tired and anxious to get home.

"I said I ain't workin'," the woman continued, "and I ain't got no interest in green tadpoles anyhow."

Lily's eyes widened, and the voice spurred her into the alley. As she approached, the boys' voices grew louder.

"Didn't ask if you was workin'. Since when do cats get a break?"

"Ain't no tadpoles! Better watch that sass."

"I got a pole for you!"

Laughter broke out again. The four boys looked to be in their middle teens. Though not yet grown, all but one stood taller than Lily.

Lily raised her voice, "What are you boys up to?"

They all balked and turned toward her, guilty surprise painting their faces. Their quarry stepped away from the wall and confirmed Lily's hunch.

Jessie stood among the wooden crates in a shabby dress, arms crossed over her chest. The women's eyes met, and Lily caught a flicker of relief.

The boys wavered, miming a polite, chastened manner.

One boy, who looked younger, spoke up, "Nothin', ma'am. Just chattin' with this gal."

"It didn't sound like she was enjoying your conversation," Lily replied.

The tallest boy shook his head and shot his companions an insolent grin. "She just don't know us good enough yet." The others snickered.

"Somehow, I don't think that would improve her opinion." Lily threw him a withering glare. "I think you boys ought to be going home now."

Jessie stepped closer to Lily, trying to edge around the group.

A short, stocky boy with a brutish mouth moved to block her path. He trained his gaze on Lily, and she spotted the narrowing of his eyes when he noticed the scar. A frown subdued him until something came to him.

"I know who you are. You're the one started the fire and killed Miss Samuels." His nostrils flared, and he turned to the other boys. "It's all right, fellas. She can't get us in trouble. Daddy said she's no better than the cats she chums with. Nobody will pay her any mind." He smirked at Lily. "How'd you like the message Daddy sent? Rock should've knocked some sense into you."

Lily's stomach lurched as if she'd taken a physical blow. Her mouth worked to find a response, but her throat offered only a soft wheeze.

Jessie stopped moving away from the group and rounded on them. "Hey, you can't talk to her like that. Miss Wright's a lady!"

The stocky one shot Jessie a look of contempt. "Aw, shut your trap, whore."

The three other boys lost their indecisive looks, seeming to find courage in his audacity.

"Beckett, we could get 'em both, and it'd go quicker," the tallest pointed out. He eyed Lily and chuckled.

"I'm taking this one. You take that one, if you want. I wouldn't risk it with a killer," the stocky boy replied.

He moved to grab Jessie's arm, but she stepped back to avoid him. The circle closed tighter around the dove.

Lily tried to think of a way out. She couldn't let them get away with their assault, but they held the upper hand. *Beckett's boy is right. The marshal will believe the boys over me and a prostitute.* The lawman's warning echoed in her ears, but the greater risk lay in the boys' numbers and size. Though young, they would easily overpower the women if it came down to it.

"Stop!" Lily stood straighter despite the blood thundering in her ears.

Their attention swung back to her.

"You nasty little guttersnipes, don't you dare touch her." The words came out in a low snarl, but her trembling made them weak and uncertain in her own ears. She set her jaw and pointed at the stocky boy. "I know who your papa is, Beckett," she said, spitting out the name, "and I'll make sure every one of you answers for this."

The younger boy backed off a couple steps. An almost imperceptible recoil disrupted Beckett's bravado at the mention of his father. Lily stared him down, unblinking, praying he wouldn't call her bluff.

After a moment, his lip curled, and he adopted a tone of indifference. "Come on, boys. These whores aren't worth the trouble."

Beckett shot Lily a final sullen glance. Pushing Jessie out of his way, he stalked around the corner of the building. The other boys followed.

Lily let out a gust of air and waited for her heart to stop pounding. Nausea made her tongue feel thick, and her mouth filled with saliva.

A peal of laughter burst from Jessie. "Mercy! You see their tails 'tween their legs?"

Lily sagged against the side of the building. "Jessie, it's not funny. They could have hurt us."

Jessie smirked with annoyance. "I would've gave 'em what they wanted if they'd kept on about it. Why'd you get in it? You should've went on by if you was so worried."

"What?" Lily glared. "They don't have the right to force you. I risked my own skin, and you don't even care, you can't even say thank you? Perhaps I should have let them have you!" Lily let her anger reach her eyes, to veil the hurt.

Jessie looked away. "I didn't ask for no help," she mumbled.

"What's the use?" Lily threw her hands up and turned on her heel, stomping back toward the road.

When she'd nearly reached the boardwalk, Jessie called her. Lily stopped but didn't turn around, gritting her teeth and blinking back tears. After a moment, Jessie touched her arm.

"I, I'm sorry, Miss Wright," Jessie said. "I didn't mean ...."

Lily whirled on her. "How dare you! I opened my door to you. I thought," she swallowed to steady her voice, "I thought we'd become friends. But you don't care about me. You don't even care about yourself." The last came out in a weary murmur.

Jessie looked down at her feet. She spoke slowly. "It ain't that. I ... I was ashamed you saw me in trouble again. And I just, I've never had nobody who would do for me like that. The girls, well, they don't stick up for each other, 'cause they can't afford to. Ain't nobody ever cared if I was in trouble, or what I want. Takes a bit to get used to, I guess." Her gaze came back to Lily, and she shrugged. "I never had a real friend. I'd like to try havin' one ... if you ain't too mad at me."

"Jessie ...." Lily sighed and softened her tone. "I'm not mad. Well, I am, but only at the life you're living—and the fact that you accept it."

Jessie folded her arms over her chest. "What do you expect me to do? Ain't no way for me to change it. At least not yet. I do what I have to, what I need to get by."

"I understand that. I do. But you have to stand up for yourself and take it more seriously. Don't let them treat you that way. If they know you'll give in, they'll keep pushing and taking."

A lady in an elaborate walking habit stepped off the boardwalk and walked past. She surveyed them with a critical eye. Giving a disdainful sniff, she held her lace kerchief to her nose and quickened her pace.

Humiliation burned Lily's cheeks, and she stood straighter in defiance. Jessie glanced at the woman but showed no sign she noticed the slight, looking past her with disinterest.

"You don't get it. They'll take it anyway. I'm just practical." Jessie looked toward the setting sun. "Speakin' of, I gotta go be practical. Maybe I'll see you at the festival."

"You're going? I thought you planned to work."

"Well, that fella promised he'd make up for it. So I might as well have some fun, too." Jessie grinned.

"I hope I'll see you, then." Lily smiled to cover her frustration and sadness at the girl's fatalism.

"All right. And thanks for the help." Jessie flashed a sheepish smile. She turned back down the alley, walking toward the street dominated by parlor houses and cribs, the dove's cage.

CHAPTER THIRTY-THREE

Mr. Warren caught up with Lily the next morning, calling to her from the parlor as she passed in the hall. She joined him, and he set aside his newspaper.

"Good morning, Mr. Warren. How are you?"

"Fine, Miss Wright. And you?"

"I'm well. I've been working as a seamstress, until I'm able to find something better."

"Good to hear. I filed the complaint yesterday, so we should have a date with the judge soon; within a week, I would hope. I'll let you know when it is." He removed his glasses and polished them with his kerchief. "Will your employer give you leave to attend the hearing? It may not be necessary, but it's better if you can."

"I believe so, but I'll have to ask. I'm anxious to have this behind me."

He replaced his glasses and looked at Lily over the top of them. "We'll do our best, but prepare yourself, in case he decides against us. It is difficult to cancel a contract."

"I understand." She grimaced. "But surely the judge will see Barnes has taken advantage of me. The terms are so unreasonable, especially in light of the fire."

"We can hope. I will do everything I can." His sympathetic smile didn't make her feel better about their chances.

"Well, thank you again, Mr. Warren. I better be going, or I'll be late. Good day."

"Good day, Miss Wright."

Despite his pessimism, Lily walked up the hill in a good mood. The claim would work, she insisted. She would go before the judge in a few days, and he would see how Barnes had manipulated a desperate, naïve girl. If the lawsuit ruined him, all the better. She relished the idea that she might make him feel helpless, as she had when he'd invaded her room and abused her.

Arriving at the cottage, she found Alice in her rocking chair, waiting on the water to boil.

"Good morning, Alice. I finished the buttons. What should I do today?"

"I expect you can put some fasteners on those skirts. Later on, I'll need you to go down and do some shopping, if it isn't too much trouble. I have most of my supplies delivered, but I need a thing or two I hadn't planned on."

"I'll be happy to. Do you mind if I take a day of leave, likely sometime next week? I have some business to attend to." Lily sat down to the large pile of skirts awaiting finishing touches.

"That will be fine. Not much of a rush for anything here."

"Thank you." She hesitated but forged ahead, hoping she wouldn't irritate the old woman. "Alice, I thought about all you said. I think I understand most of it—or some, at least—but there are still a few parts ...."

"Ask your questions, young lady." Alice moved around the kitchen, preparing the coffee.

"You never married again? Or ... had a spark?" Heat lit her cheeks at the implication Alice might have had a lover, but she had to ask.

Alice cackled. Once she caught her breath, she replied, "No, never did. A few gentlemen tried, when I still had some bounce in my skirts. I decided I simply wasn't cut out for having a man around. I enjoy my own company well enough, I suppose. I expect if I'd run across a good one, who could keep company without being a pest, I might have. But I never saw one. I've had that option—to be independent of a man—and I hope you'll have it, too. Mayhap you'll come across one you like, but make sure you pick one 'cause you want him, not 'cause you need him. And never forget that if he's the right kind of man, he won't require a shackle."

Lily smiled, but the words made her wonder. It took courage to live alone. She didn't think she had that courage, to endure a life without a companion or a family. When she'd left Duncan, it hadn't occurred to her she might never find another man to love. After being on her own, she realized she wanted to find love again and create her own version of the family she'd lost over and over. She might survive without it, but would she ever be happy with that life? Alice didn't mind it, apparently.

Maybe Alice didn't actually choose it ... and maybe it won't be a matter of choice for me.

Lily picked up her sewing. Alice brought her a cup of coffee, but instead of settling at the treadle, she returned to the rocking chair and sat quietly.

Lily started to ask why but decided it wasn't her business if the old woman didn't want to sew.

After a few minutes, Alice prodded, "Finish your questions."

"Oh. Well, I guess really just one." She tilted her head.

"I'm afraid I still don't understand why you say that time was your worst. I mean to say … of course it must have been dreadful, what you had to do, but you didn't know what was to come—though your experiences afterward were horrible too—and you had freed yourself. You couldn't know the consequences. Didn't you feel some kind of … triumph or liberation?"

Alice sat with her coffee in her lap, rocking with her head down. Lily assumed she'd fallen asleep and held back her frustration.

Alice's voice came low and quiet, as though she had to drag it from her raspy throat, "I've traveled, seen a lot. I've been through storms and droughts, winters that never seemed to end, summers hotter than Hades. Times we didn't eat more than a few crumbs for days. I worked until I thought my back would break, until my legs gave out, until my fingers were bloody. One summer, I broke my ankle and had to hobble around the house leaning on a chair, on dirt floors, with a cryin' baby and a little one runnin' around— and that with a husband who was supposed to be a healer but wouldn't make his own wife a crutch. I buried my own children and helped with more than a few others. Tried to bury my husband. I lived with people who saw me as a dog and fed me scraps. They beat me when they felt like and ignored me the rest of the time. None of it compared to that one night.

"I lost myself. In killing him, I'd made my own freedom of sorts, ayuh. I didn't do anything with it, though. I gave up. Long before the Indians came and long after they'd gone.

"I came to realize, after I'd smacked his head to a pulp, I'd done it for the wrong reasons. I didn't do it to be free of him or the beatings, or even to save my own life; I did it for revenge. I wanted revenge, to punish everyone else for my life, my failings, and to punish myself, too. I wanted it for the part of me that wanted him to hurt like he'd done me.

"Revenge—well, that's just another flavor of blame. I had let that anger take me over, and it changed me. It ruined that part of me who loved. That night was when I finally saw that it was gone. It's been near fifty years since. That piece of me hasn't ever come back. That's what I killed."

Lily swallowed hard, struck by the empty regret in Alice's words. She laid her work aside. Hesitant, she walked to the rocking chair and knelt in front of the old woman. She put her arms around the hunched figure and held her. Alice made no move to reciprocate, but Lily stayed.

With a sigh, Lily rose and looked around. She found the small bag of coins and the list with uneven, shaky writing.

"I'll go do the shopping now," she said.

As she closed the door behind her, a patch of wetness on her shoulder touched her skin, and her tears joined Alice's.

She followed the list and purchased paper, ink, a brush, and a blanket. By the time she returned, Alice had gone to take her nap. Lily put the purchases aside and continued her sewing. The silence in the cottage gave her relief, allowing her time to think, but it accentuated Alice's solitary existence.

The quiet cabin reminded her of the tiny house in Jefferson City. She'd spent her time there alone, day after day, while Duncan worked. It wasn't much different when he was home. Their relationship was a charade, a bargain neither could fulfill. She'd ached for conversation and companionship. Imagining years of that loneliness—a lifetime—made her shudder.

I can't live like that. I can't surrender myself, but I still want to love and be loved. What about Luke? A warm flush of tenderness and passion enveloped her.

Is it still possible? Maybe ....

Her hands worked while her mind rambled, and she sought the strength to face whatever the future held.

CHAPTER THIRTY-FOUR

The Fourth of July dawned hot and muggy. Miners, ranchers, and cowboys left their camps in the hills and spilled into the valley. The hotels reached capacity, more tents sprang up, and the streets rang with the clamor of carriages and excited voices. By ten in the morning, the celebration had begun.

Lily ventured out at eleven, finding a spot near the start of the parade route, away from the crush of people farther down. She'd almost stayed in but scolded herself for her qualms. She deserved a day of fun, and the Fourth of July—the biggest event of the year—brought out the entire community.

Red, white, and blue decorations lined the streets. Wagons and buggies, bearing fanciful signs and flowered statues with American themes, waited to start the parade at the edge of town. Organizers had erected a podium for speechmakers and music. After the orations, the clearing would transform into a dance floor for the evening. Vendors attended their stalls and tables to hawk food, goods, and games.

Men in bowlers, wide-brimmed felts, and straw Natties, all in their best dress, loitered in groups along the dirt road. Calls of "Happy Fourth!" and "God Bless America!" sounded, followed by clinking cups raised in salute. High spirits and alcohol boosted their volume and fueled tension.

Small clusters of women and children stood out in the crowd. The women drew polite attention as they promenaded down the boardwalk or stood under umbrellas near the road. A few wore elaborate walking outfits with large bustles and frilled skirts, trimmed with silk and lace, and others eyed them with envy.

The road served as a clear border; the respectable wives and families kept to one side, attended by their gentlemen; on the opposite quarter, the doves flirted with lively, unfettered men.

Lily sat on the family side but didn't feel like she belonged to either realm. Surrounded by people, she remained alone. She'd hoped the revelers would lift her spirits, but they made her uneasy, leaving her hands clammy as she scanned faces, both hopeful and wary of recognition. She pushed aside her detachment and forced a pleasant facade, but no one spoke to her.

The parade began with war veterans marching and social organizations carrying signs and waving flags. They trudged along the road, wiping sweat from their faces and whipping up clouds of dust. A hint of forced gaiety hung in the air with the soot, a frenzy of merriment that couldn't quite overcome the stifling heat as the sun reached its zenith. A middle-aged man marched past in his faded Union Army uniform, his ruddy face darkening to purple, and he collapsed halfway down the course. His comrades carried him to the boardwalk and splashed water over him. The parade continued without pause as banner-laden wagons rumbled along the path. A few children joined in, scampering behind the last cart, which carried a miniature Liberty Bell.

The crowd drifted off to play games and find dinner before the afternoon speeches. Lily held back until the street quieted. A dull ache had settled behind her eyes, and her room beckoned. Her stomach rumbled, insisting she find something to eat first. As she reached the booths, someone called to her.

"Miss Wright!"

Mary, the doctor's wife, darted over, cheerful as ever.

"Happy Fourth, Mary." Lily smiled.

"And to you, dear. How've you been?" Mary took Lily's arm, and they strolled toward an open area, away from the path.

"Good. I have my room at Mrs. Connor's. It's not bad."

"I'm glad it's working out. You must come have tea." Mary patted her hand.

"I will, soon. I'll have to wait until I have a day off."

"Oh, you found a position? That's wonderful. I knew you'd land on your feet, smart girl like you. In one of the shops?"

A group of boisterous young men bounded past, yelling and laughing.

"No, for the dressmaker, up on the hill. Mrs. Durand."

Mary's eyes widened, and she tucked her chin. "You don't say? How did that happen?"

"I just stopped in and asked for a position. Why?"

"Well, it's rather odd. The woman hasn't spoken but a handful of words to anyone in town. Not in the ten years Doctor and I have been here, anyhow. Lots of talk about that one."

"Talk? What kind of talk?" Lily frowned. It came back to

her: that was why Alice's name had seemed familiar. She'd heard of her soon after arriving. The stationer had said Mrs. Durand refused to see him when he delivered to her and only communicated with him through notes. He'd called her "crazy as popcorn on a hot stove."

Mary leaned in, lowering her voice. "No one seems to know where she comes from, but they say she's crazy. Is she?"

Lily chuckled and waved a hand. "Goodness, no! She's a very nice old woman. Aloof, perhaps, but she has a keen mind."

With a doubtful look, Mary patted her hand again. "Just you keep an eye for yourself."

"All right." Lily chuckled.

Mary excused herself to go help the doctor and bid her goodbye.

Lily wandered among the stalls but her self-consciousness kept her from enjoying the revelry. She couldn't help thinking quick glances and bursts of laughter might pertain to her. After buying a snack, she walked back to the boardinghouse, thinking of Alice.

The old woman wasn't crazy, but Lily wondered why Alice had hired her. After years of apparent isolation, the decision did seem odd. When she thought about it, the whole thing unsettled her.

An urge to see the old woman made her pause. As any other day, Alice would be sitting in the empty cottage, rocking or sewing. Lily started in that direction, intent on asking more questions, but each breath of sultry air was like pulling butter through a rye grass straw, and sweat trickled down her back. She resolved to visit the next day, even if it was Sunday. She escaped to the boardinghouse, shed her damp clothes, and laid down to rest until evening.

* * * * *

Sharp reports woke Lily as the sun descended behind the trees and bathed her room orange and yellow. Panic sent ice through her. Memories of wet wood popping and screaming and the ghastly glow of fire paralyzed her before she remembered the fireworks. She let out a stuttering breath and sat up. She pulled the dingy curtain aside, and brief flashes exploded within a circle of figures standing in the road. Her irritation faded as her pulse slowed. She couldn't begrudge them their fun just because she had troubling memories.

Her stomach grumbled, but she had no desire to go out. She wanted to stay in her room, quiet and calm—where no one stared, whispered, judged, or ignored her. She hadn't enjoyed the earlier outing, had only watched as everyone else talked and laughed with friends, chased after children, and took pleasure in the community. None of their enthusiasm penetrated her isolation.

It hadn't always been that way. When her parents took her to the fair as a child, before Peter and Sissy died, she'd loved the excitement of finding other children to play with, the giddy wonder of the circus man with his horse and monkey, the pure joy she felt when her father played a bottle game and won her Dolly. Peter and Sissy played hide and seek with her among the trees. They had spread a picnic under the oak, and her parents stole a kiss when they thought she wasn't looking. She had giggled, and they'd scolded her for spying, but their eyes sparkled with laughter and their fingers remained entwined.

Lily pressed her lips together, holding back the longing ache, and wished she could find that happiness again.

If you want that happiness, you have to do something to find it. Hiding won't help.

With a sigh, she rose and dressed. She would ignore the contemptuous looks and titters behind hands. She would go down to the dance, socialize, and enjoy herself. She would leave the cage she'd built for herself.

CHAPTER THIRTY-FIVE

As Lily walked to the clearing, smoke and sulfur floated like a mantle in the still night air, overpowering whiffs of food and making her eyes water. Crackles and bangs made her flinch. By the time she approached the gathering, the firecrackers became smothered pops, less noticeable under the hum of music and the boisterous crowd. The odors intensified, joined by the sharp tang of alcohol and sweat.

She skirted the edge of the dancing area. Oil lamps cast circles of wan light in the clearing. As a band played a ballad, several women danced with men. A ring of anxious hopefuls awaited a turn with the ladies. Pairs of fellows who couldn't wait cavorted on the dirt dance floor. Lily smiled at their antics. A large bonfire lay to one side, surrounded by benches. Most of the benches remained empty while the music played.

Lily found a seat with a view of the dancers. She escaped notice for a while, but soon a young man approached with his bowler in fidgeting hands.

"Pardon, miss, but might I beg a dance?"

Lily hesitated. The band had started a vigorous rendition

of "Yankee Doodle Dandy," always popular for Fourth of July. Her mother had thought dancing and such songs wicked, and forbid her to go anywhere the guests might engage in it, so Lily had never learned.

"Please, miss?"

His pleading smile tugged at her. Her eyes shifted to the couples hopping through the matted grass. She couldn't decipher a standard step to their movements, only a swinging and stomping back and forth, with arms linked or holding hands.

Alice's voice popped into her head, goading her: *Go! Stop being such a ninny!*

Lily chuckled. "Oh, very well."

She rubbed the nervous perspiration from her palms, stood, and took the arm he offered. He stuffed his hat back on his head and straightened, his chest puffing out as a wide grin split his face. Two other men stood nearby, watching them and mocking him with glee.

"Don't pay them no mind, miss," he told her. Glaring at the jokers, he raised his voice, "They ain't fit to dance wit' goats!"

Lily laughed as he led her out, but her heart raced. "A goat might be a better partner than I."

"It's easy, and yer a sight prettier."

"You might not think so once I've broken your toes."

The man laughed. "A few toes is a small price. I might cotton to it."

With that, he tucked her arm into his. He called over the music, "Ready?"

Lily jerked her head to the side, but he'd already begun circling. He lifted his knees, skipping forward and hopping back. Her feet tangled, and she almost stumbled. She feared everyone would laugh, but he grinned and waved her on.

She tried to imitate him, holding her skirt with her free hand as they moved back and forth.

He yelled over the music, "See, it ain't hard!"

She grinned back, unable to resist his cheer. They wheeled around, he grabbed her other arm, and they switched directions. The tempo sped up. They moved faster to match it, whirling and skipping. Her heart pounded in her chest, and she forgot her awkwardness. He let out a whoop and yanked his bowler off, waving it in the air. She laughed as she gasped for breath, and the band played the last notes.

"By gum! I wouldn't trade ya fer a goat."

Lily tapped him on the arm in reproach, but her cheeks ached from smiling. "I might," she panted, "trade you."

He chuckled. "I couldn't fault ya fer it." He led her back to the bench, pulled his hat off, and bent over in a deep bow. "If'n ya ever need a goat, the name's Justice."

"Thank you, Justice."

Lily offered her hand, and he kissed it with a gentlemanly flourish.

"Much obliged, miss." He sauntered back to his friends, who clapped him on the back.

The band paused for a drink. The voices of the gathering rose during the break, the fire licked at the sky, and Lily's apprehension drained away.

After a bit, the musicians picked up their instruments and played an Irish jig Lily remembered from her childhood. Men crowded around in a circle, with a few dancers in the middle who traded out after a few wild steps. The group clapped and yelled, urging the band and the dancers faster. Lily clapped with them, giggling as a man fell on his rump.

Jessie appeared and joined her on the bench. Her dress, more modest than usual but still revealing, hung limp and showed a fresh stain on the bodice.

"Howdy, Miss Lily!" She raised her voice over the noise. "A right good frolic!" Her eyes glittered in the firelight, and her lopsided grin teetered.

Lily smiled. "Hello, Jessie."

As the girl leaned close, her breath fell on Lily with a reek of liquor. Jessie licked her lips and propped herself on a wobbly arm.

"My feller's been treatin' me real good."

Lily nodded but leaned back with a frown. "I can see that, Jessie. A might too good, maybe?"

Jessie swung her head back and forth. "He says nothin' too good fer his girl. You ought to find yerself a feller, Miss Lily. You could land a real fine one, I wager."

"I suppose. Are you all right, Jessie? Don't get too crazy."

"Aw, I'm right dandy. Just celebratin'."

Lily caught Jessie as she toppled. "Just take care, please?"

Jessie's head wobbled in assent. "Will do. I gots to find my feller 'fore some gal ropes him. I'll bring him to meet ya."

"I'd like that," Lily lied.

She sighed as Jessie stumbled off. The man couldn't be much good if he encouraged such excess, but it wasn't her business, and if he could get her away from working, it might still offer an improvement.

A slow melody drifted out from the players, pulling couples back to the circle. A man asked Lily to dance, and she acquiesced. He wore a businessman's suit, though it fit him poorly and he hadn't shaved. He held her at a respectful distance as they turned amongst the other dancers. Lily maintained a courteous smile, but her mood faltered. Concern for Jessie distracted her as she followed her partner's motions.

The song ended after an eternity, and the man brought her back to her spot on the bench. After he thanked her, Lily waited for him to move along, but he lingered. His eyes kept returning to her scar.

"I don't aim to be a pest, miss, but might I have the pleasure of knowin' your name?"

"Lily Wright." She tried to act gracious, but it came out curt. "And yours?"

"John Parks. Pleased to meet you, Miss Wright." He moved next to her on the bench.

She smiled politely and nodded.

"Can I bring you somethin' to eat or drink?" When Lily didn't respond, he continued with a suggestion of reproach, "If I'm botherin' you, just say the word, Miss Wright ...."

The words succeeded, making her cringe at her poor manners. She shook her head. "Not at all, Mr. Parks. My apologies, I was wool-gathering. I would enjoy a drink, if you don't mind."

He smiled. "No apology needed. I'll be back with a drink directly."

Lily heaved a sigh after he'd gone, relieved to have a minute to think. The urge to protect Jessie weighed on her. The encounter with the boys in the alley told her Jessie acted carelessly around men. A nagging alarm in the back of her mind told her the girl needed help. She wanted to find her and watch over her until the alcohol wore off. That would take hours, and she didn't know where to take her. It would likely make Jessie mad, and Lily doubted whether she would agree to retire anyway. But if it saved Jessie's skin ....

No, it's not my place to mother her. She's a grown woman, and as she said, she hasn't asked for help.

She suspected it would mean the end of the friendship if she tried. Perhaps she could simply speak to Jessie's man, to make sure he'd take care of her. She'd feel better if she could meet him and talk to him, and maybe let him know Jessie had someone who cared.

As she made up her mind to seek them out, Parks returned, carrying two drinks in tin cups.

"At your service, Miss Wright." He gave her a broad smile and a mock bow.

"Ah, yes .... Thank you, Mr. Parks." Lily groaned inwardly. She'd forgotten him and wished she had excused herself earlier.

"Not a teetotaler, are you? Beer was all I could get, hope you don't mind."

Her nose wrinkled, but she took the cup and smiled. "No, that's fine." She took a drink and hid a grimace. The brew in her cup tasted worse than usual.

The dancers whirled past, and Parks attempted small talk.

"What brings a purdy lady like you up here? Come with family?"

"No. I came to open a business."

"Oh. Which one's yours?"

"I don't have it anymore." Lily gulped the beer, hoping to end the conversation so she could search for Jessie.

"Oh. That's a shame. Why not?"

Her mouth tightened as she shot him an irritated look. "It didn't work out."

"I'm sorry, I didn't mean to pry." He shifted uneasily and looked at her cup. "I can get you another, if you like."

"No, thank you. This will do." She finished the cup and handed it back. "I'm obliged for the dance and the drink. I need to go look for a friend, if you'll excuse me."

His face fell, and he glanced about, as if searching for something to say. "I can walk with you."

"Really, that's not necessary."

A pang of remorse needled her at the stricken look in his eyes. She didn't want to hurt his feelings, but she also had no interest in entertaining him. She wondered if she shouldn't have come to the dance. Her feet hurt, and despite her nap, she was tired. She wanted to find Jessie and get back to the boardinghouse.

"Please, miss? I just like talkin' to a purdy lady. Don't get much chance up here."

"Oh, all right. I'm only going to look for a moment, though. I'm feeling a bit under the weather."

His eyes slid over her. "Sorry to hear that. I hope I ain't the cause."

Lily faked a half-hearted chuckle as they started walking. "No, it's not you at all, Mr. Parks. It's just been a long day."

While they wove their way through the tents, her gaze turned to the crowd, seeking out the few women. Faces blended together in the dim light. Shadows skittered between them, tricking her eyes. Feminine forms stood out, but none of them matched Jessie's features. The buzz of laughter and music intruded. She found it hard to concentrate.

A wobbling man and his dove staggered past. Lily peered myopically at the girl, hoping to recognize her. The face blurred before her. Lily stumbled on a clump of grass and bumped the man, who showered her with a happy grin. She flailed and grabbed Parks' arm to steady herself. He pulled her away from the man.

"You sure you're good to walk, Miss Wright?" His voice sounded tinny and far away.

Lily nodded, and the motion made the ground tilt beneath her. "I'm fine. I think I just need to sit down."

"Sure thing, Miss Wright."

Parks ducked a boisterous group of men, and somehow she lost him in the throng. The noise had grown to a roar in her ears. Her vision doubled and trebled. Her mind focused on Mr. Parks. She had to find him. She spun around, desperate.

His face loomed before her. "Sorry, Miss Wright. Those fellas bowled me right over."

Walking directly behind her with his hands on her arms, he pointed her away from the commotion and pushed her along.

Her stomach pitched and rolled. She spoke to hear her own voice. "I feel very strange." It came out slow and slurred.

"Don't worry, miss, I'll get you to a place you can rest."

He steered her through the mass of people and past the bonfire. Whispers tickled her mind, and it rebelled.

This doesn't make sense. There are benches all around us. We could have sat at the fire. Where is he taking me?

Lily pulled her arms away, but dizziness hit her in a wave and left her reeling. He reached out to hold her up, grinning. She shook her head.

That isn't right. I can't stand up. Why would he be smiling at me? Why isn't he worried?

The questions echoed in her mind as her vision shrank to a narrow tunnel. She pushed the hands away and started to turn back. She had to find Jessie.

His arm blocked her, sliding around her like a snake.

She screamed, "No!" Her mouth formed the word, but the sound failed to follow.

The tunnel closed around her.

CHAPTER THIRTY-SIX

Lily's head throbbed with dull waves of pain. She groaned and rolled over, eyes closed tight. The muscles in her abdomen quivered. She wanted to sleep for days.

Do I have to work today? No ... it's Sunday, thank goodness.

She couldn't work if her life depended on it. A surge of vertigo rocked her, and she clutched the pillow tight. Why did she feel so sick? She only remembered one cup of beer and nothing else to drink. Nothing to eat, either, so that might explain some of it, but one cup? She didn't have alcohol often, but one cup shouldn't make her feel this awful. Disconnected pieces of memory flashed behind her lids.

Dancing. The bonfire. Jessie. More dancing. A man .... What was his name?

It wouldn't come. They'd danced, and he'd brought her a drink. Then what? She'd gone to look for Jessie, the man following along. Something about the man—odd, polite but insistent, and he looked at her strangely.

Did he walk me home, or did I get here on my own?

She thumped her forehead with her palm, trying to jog the answers loose. She couldn't remember. She swallowed hard, but her tongue stuck to the roof of her mouth.

Water, I need water. So thirsty.

She rolled to the side of the bed and opened her eyes a slit. Muted light filtered in through a gauzy curtain. She let her feet fall to the floor and pushed herself up. Dizziness made her sway. Closing her eyes, she reached to the wall for support, but her hand swiped at air. She took a small step and reached again. Nothing. She scowled and opened her eyes.

The wall had moved, it stood several feet away, and an upholstered chair sat in the corner next to the window.

She blinked and squeezed her eyes shut again.

Imagining things. What on earth is wrong with me?

She took a deep breath and opened. The same view. She jerked her head to the right, expecting the door and the armoire at the end of the bed.

Instead, a much larger room accosted her, appointed with a dresser and mirror, a cedar trunk, and a privacy screen at one corner.

Lily's breath wheezed out, and she sank back on the bed. Why wasn't she in her room at the boardinghouse? How had she come here, and where *was* here, exactly? Her hands went to her temples and pressed, as if she could force the memory to the surface.

Nothing came to her. She had finished her drink and left the bonfire to look for Jessie—then, a void. The man, or someone, must have brought her here.

She fought off the spinning sensation and lurched to the only door. She turned the knob, but it wouldn't open. Trying again, she pulled hard. The door merely rattled in the frame.

"Hello?" Her voice sounded dry, cracked. "Hello!"

She scanned the room again, anxious to find something familiar.

The furnishings had signs of age; the brass frame showed tarnish and dings; the mirror on the dresser had a crack near the bottom; the cloth on the screen blighted by tears and stains. The wood floor had a shiny, worn path from the door to the bed, and nothing adorned the walls.

Nothing sparked recognition.

She stumbled to the window and pushed aside the thin curtain.

A clapboard frame building stood close, across a small gap. The building blocked everything but the sky. The sun sat out of view, so she couldn't guess the time. By the height, it looked like the second floor.

She tugged at the handles on the window, but it wouldn't budge. Her hands explored the frame. Nails held it shut.

Lily crossed back to the door and pounded it with her fist.

"Hello! Is anyone out there? Let me out!"

Silence replied.

Blood pulsed behind her eyes, its sickening rhythm matching her rapid heartbeat. She bent to the keyhole and squinted. A plain, yellow-white wall stared back. She stepped away, frowning at the door in confusion.

As her eyes moved over the room again, a pitcher on the dresser reminded her of her thirst. She seized it and drank. Flat, stale water, but it quenched the dry itch in her throat. She returned to the bed and sat. Her eyes closed tight, face twisted with pain, as the booming in her head escalated. The unfamiliar room baffled her, but a bigger question loomed.

Why did someone lock me in?

Her fingers clutched the fabric on her legs, and for the first time, she realized she wore only her chemise, corset, and drawers. Dress, shoes, stockings, hat—all removed. Her stomach heaved. She yanked open the dresser drawers. Bare. Flipping up the lid of the chest, she found only a piece of blackened oil cloth. Nothing behind the screen, either, except an empty chamber pot.

Someone had taken her clothes off and left with them. Someone had locked her in a strange room, and she had no idea who, where, or why.

The stark breakdown hit her like a train.

Reeling with shock, she pounded on the door again. She banged until the side of her hand hurt and switched to using her palms. Her hands turned red, stinging and throbbing.

No one came.

Lily shuffled back to the bed and collapsed. Silent tears dampened the pillow.

CHAPTER THIRTY-SEVEN

It seemed Lily lay there a long time, but she couldn't know how long. The light remained the same. No sounds penetrated the room, nothing except the soft rustle of the bedclothes or the sniffles from her running nose.

There must be a reasonable explanation. Someone brought me here because I was sick, and they accidentally locked the door. Or maybe they locked it for my own safety. But from what danger?

She refused to consider other possibilities.

While she contemplated breaking the window, the click of a key in the lock brought her back.

She bolted from the bed. Her heart flew into her throat as relief and fear battled in her mind.

The door opened, and Silas Barnes sauntered through, tucking a key into his pocket.

"Good mornin', Miss Wright."

Lily blinked.

"I hope you got a good night's rest." He looked around the room. "Hell, I reckoned she'd spruce the place up for you. I told her you were my special guest." He chuckled. His eyes came back to her, taking in her form under the thin fabric of her underclothes, and he grinned. "Yep, a real special one."

Lily took a faltering step back, and her legs hit the bed. Her mind went blank, incapable of processing what her eyes showed her and her ears took in. She opened her mouth, but words wouldn't form.

"I reckon you got some queries for me, huh?" He sniggered as if he'd told a dirty joke.

The sound made her skin crawl, and hatred overcame her shock. She glared, swallowing a rush of nausea before she could speak. "You vile snake! Whatever you think you're doing, you won't get away with it."

"Snake? That ain't no way to talk to your employer." He made a stern frown, pushing out his lower lip, mocking her. He couldn't hold the look and shook his head and cackled. "I ain't doin' nothin' wrong. I just came to see the newest girl in my parlor house."

"What on earth are you talking about? I am not one of your 'girls,' and you are certainly not my employer."

"Says who? You? You're a crazy, murderin' arsonist who runs around with whores. Lost everything and had to turn to sportin', just like her friends. They done ruint her, dragged her down with 'em in sin. Damned shame, it is." He clucked with regret.

A glimmer of understanding seeped in.

"That man—Parks. He works for you. He drugged me." Her eyes popped wide. "You think I'll be a prostitute? For you? You've lost your mind!" She crossed her arms over her chest and set her jaw. "You can't keep me here. And you most certainly can't make me engage in prostitution. Bring me my clothing. I'm leaving." She projected disdain and confidence, but underneath her heart pounded, painful stabs in her chest.

"Afraid I can't do that. Our girls got to be ready for guests. No need for any unnecessary encumbrances that might slow down their business."

"Damn you, you will not keep me here!"

Lily stomped past him to the door and yanked it open. His eyes followed her, but he made no effort to stop her. As she moved into the hallway, a large figure stepped in front of her. A man glowered down at her with one good eye.

"Miss Wright, meet Deadeye Dan. He's our box herder—keeps the girls from gettin' uppity. He's kinda cranky, so I wouldn't offend him if I was you."

The tangled nest of hair covering Deadeye's jowls split with a grin. Her head came barely to his chin. His girth could have made three of her, but it looked solid. A black patch covered his left eye, his other eye almost as obscured under a heavy, dark brow. Musk and sweat flowed off him in almost visible waves.

Lily backed away and turned to Barnes. "This is outrageous. You can't do this. I'll tell the first one who comes in. I'll escape."

"Aww, that ain't no way to thank me. I reckon you'll get used to it real quick. It'll calm you right down. Woman like you could use a good fuck."

Lily slapped him with all her strength. The rough stubble on his cheek raked her palm. His expression remained neutral. Her nostrils flared, and spit bubbled on her lips. With the speed of a snake, his right hand struck her cheek. The blow wasn't hard, but it stung. She gasped and fell back a step.

"We'll learn you some manners, one way or t'other." He nodded to Deadeye, and the beefy man turned and thumped down the hallway. "I'll give you this evenin' to yourself, so's you can get used to the idea. You better rest up. Startin' tomorrow, you'll have plenty of entertainin' to do. Deadeye'll bring you some victuals every day, and he'll be on hand to make sure you treat guests real nice." He wagged his eyebrows and grinned.

Deadeye returned with a cup and handed it to Barnes, who nodded and offered it to Lily as she rubbed her cheek.

"In the meantime," Barnes continued, "this ought to cool off that temper of yours."

Her lips curled. "I'm not taking anything from you."

Barnes huffed an exaggerated sigh and inclined his head toward Deadeye. Deadeye's hand went to the holster at his waist and pulled out a revolver. He pointed it at her head, the barrel not a foot from her face, his features blank.

Her heart stopped, and a scream shot to her lips, but she snapped her mouth shut and glared at Barnes.

"I'd be real disappointed if he had to use that, since I want to recoup my investment, but it'd still end some hassle for me."

Her jaw quivered. She snatched the cup from him. Clear, amber liquid. "What is it?"

"Just a bit of laudanum to put you in the right state of mind," Barnes said.

Deadeye held the weapon steady. She pursed her lips, flicking her eyes from the cup to Deadeye's gun. She drank. Warmth followed the bitter taste and spread through her chest and into her belly, and she thrust the container back at the huge man. He took it and holstered his gun, moving back to the hallway.

Barnes clapped his hands once and rubbed them together. "Good. Glad yer beginnin' to see reason. Deadeye'll bring you some paint tomorrow—see if you can't cover up that scar, damn shame that ruint a pretty face. Our guys ain't all that particular, though, I reckon." He chuckled, then turned serious. "Don't give Deadeye no trouble; he ain't the forgivin' soul I am." He turned to leave.

A cry burst from Lily, and she couldn't keep the shakiness from her voice. "Why? Why are you doing this?"

He rounded on her with a steely gaze. "I don't take kindly to bein' cheated. We had a legal bargain. You got to keep your part of it, one way or t'other—this'll pay that off. Reckon you can make me a good deal of coin. But my real beef is that I get awful testy when someone slanders me in the courts. I got a reputation to uphold, or my business is ruined. You shouldn't have sued me."

Rage rose in her as he ambled out, and she let out a strangled snarl of frustration.

Barnes ignored her, and Deadeye closed the door. The lock thunked.

She stood in the middle of the room as tears came again. Her knees buckled, and she sank to the floor.

CHAPTER THIRTY-EIGHT

Lily huddled in the middle of the room, rocking back and forth. She cursed Barnes over and over. She couldn't chase his hated face from her mind. He mocked her, and her bitterness flared. She envisioned his face destroyed, his voice distorted by screams. She would find a way to make him regret his despicable plot.

As the laudanum took effect, the familiar fog rolled in, still low and flimsy, but it distracted her from the violent musings. The purpose of Barnes' plan came back to her.

She would be used; men would put their rough, dirty hands on her skin and force themselves inside her, violating her body; they would leave their seed and toss her aside; she would exist as nothing more than a vessel for their lust.

A powerful shudder ripped through her. She retched, bringing bile up her throat. She swallowed it back, but it left a burning residue that made her tremble.

Lily shook her head and whispered, "No, no, no, no."

I can't be a whore. I won't. I have to find a way out.

She seized on the idea and bounded to her feet. Distorted by the drug, the room shifted each time her eyes moved. She swayed before regaining her balance.

The window! She stumbled to it and pushed the curtain aside. Clouds had built in the sky, and she still had no hint of the hour. She pushed her face against the cool glass, hoping to glimpse people below or in the other building. She couldn't see a street or the alley below. The adjacent building sat too close. Curtains blocked its few windows, with no evidence of people inside. Trees at the back of the buildings obscured that view, as well. She tried to recall the layout of South Street and which buildings had two stories, but she'd seen too little of it to guess which held her.

I could break the glass and call for help. Likely no one around to hear in the middle of the day, though. I can wait until dark; there will be lots of people on South Street then. She slumped. *No, the music and noise might drown out my calls then. And there's still Deadeye.*

The cold detachment on his face as he'd pointed the gun sent a chill through her. He wouldn't hesitate to hurt her— or worse. He might hear her break the window, and he'd surely hear her yelling.

Which fate do I choose? Does it matter now?

Her lips parted with a moan, and she turned from the window. She examined the room for some tool to use, any possible escape. She moved to the wall opposite the door. Cupping her hands around her ear, she pressed close. No sound came.

Someone will realize I've gone missing, won't they? Alice will, but she might not have the chance to tell anyone or might assume I've caught sick. Mrs. Connor won't care until the rent isn't paid, another week, at least. Mr. Warren will notice—but perhaps not for days, and he might assume I skipped town. Luke won't return for a week or more. He might look for me, but what chance would he have of finding me?

The room spun faster, and Lily fumbled for the bed. Clutching the pillow, she curled into a ball. She forced away what was to come and let the fog roll in. The thick mist comforted her. She embraced it, grateful for the shroud.

* * * * *

Lily opened her eyes and sucked in air.

Deadeye stood at the side of the bed. The light from the window had faded, leaving his face an empty shadow, but his head inclined toward her, and his eye crawled over her.

Tremors took over as she fought the urge to flee, her breath a hitching moan.

His body tensed.

She waited, certain he intended to take her.

After an agonizing moment, he tilted his head toward the dresser. He turned away slowly, and his heavy steps rumbled out the door.

She lay shaking, afraid any movement would bring him back. The minutes stretched out. The blood stopped thundering in her ears. She sat up. On the dresser, a plate sat next to the pitcher. Her stomach contracted and spit welled in her mouth, drawing a cramp in her jaw. With nervous checks toward the door, she crept out of bed and tiptoed over the worn floor.

The shadows deepened as Lily wolfed down dry bread and a small hunk of tasteless, boiled meat.

When did I eat last?

She couldn't remember, couldn't even determine the day. After the meager meal, she gulped stale water from the pitcher.

Eyes fastened on the door, she went behind the screen to relieve herself in the chamber pot. Her legs trembled as she squatted, her muscles weak and sore. With a grimace, she wiped herself with a grimy cloth hanging next to the pot. A pungent odor wafted from it. *I doubt that's had a wash recently.* She stood on shaky legs and ran a hand over her brow.

It reminded her of the sticky sweat clinging to her skin. She found a scrap of a washrag in the dresser and wet it to scrub off the worst of the grunge. As she hung the rag to dry, the door opened.

Deadeye entered, and Lily skittered backward. He ignored her, plunking a cup on the dresser before moving to light the lamp on the wall. The wick sputtered and brightened, throwing soft light on the room.

A hissing voice in her head goaded her, urging her to grab something, anything, and attack the lumbering guard. She clutched her hands under her chin to resist the impulse.

Deadeye pulled a bottle from his pocket, poured a dose of laudanum into the cup, and held the vessel out.

Lily's mouth tightened, but she eased forward to grab the drink.

No, no drugs. I have to keep my wits if I want to find a way to escape. But ... it would ease the anxiety ....

A wave of revulsion hit her as she realized she craved the drug's oblivion, a different kind of escape, to save her from the violations to come.

He grunted, and his hand moved to the butt of his gun.

Lily flinched, almost dropping the cup. She closed her eyes and drank. Her lips curled at the bitter taste, and a shudder rippled through her.

She sneered. "Can I keep the cup, at least?"

With a shrug, he picked up the plate and plodded to the door. She glared after him. He turned as he pulled the door shut. A low growl came to her, but as his face cracked into a grin, she caught his laughter.

Fear darted back in, nipping at her resolve, while her feet slid back and forth along the worn path from the door to the bed.

She guessed she had a day before Barnes offered her up for the men—if it was still the first day. She didn't think she'd slept longer than that. A day to find an escape, somehow. She strained to think, willing her mind to stay sharp as the laudanum dragged her into the abyss.

Without a weapon, she couldn't overpower Deadeye. The room held only a few things she might use to arm herself; but nothing she wouldn't have to hide, or that wouldn't require breaking something. She feared the noise might draw Deadeye's attention before she had time to prepare.

That left trying to leave the room, either through the window or the door. She wouldn't know where to go, even if she made it past the guard into the hall, and she had no doubt others in the house would stop her. She could break the window and jump, but would she survive the fall? With luck, maybe, though injury seemed almost guaranteed. With an injury, her keepers might apprehend her before she could flee to safety.

If I manage to escape, what then? That bastard will come after me, one way or another. The marshal might not believe my story. No, Barnes won't risk that if he can help it. He'll make sure I never have the chance to tell it.

The air had thickened until every movement seemed like swimming through soup. The poor oil in the lamp sent wisps of sooty smoke to the ceiling. Dizziness forced her back to the bed. She resisted the sleepy tug on her eyelids and searched for another way out, but her mind kept coming back to one thought.

Whether I attempt escape or stay—even if I endure the worst and earn the money he demands—will he ever let me go? No. But I'll find a way out. I have to.

CHAPTER THIRTY-NINE

The door burst open and banged the wall. Shadows chased fingers of fading light as they crawled over the walls and ceiling. A murky figure floated into the room.

Lily frowned, clawing at the thick mist in her mind. Delusion or reality? The laudanum still held sway, and she couldn't decide.

"Time to try out my new goods." A familiar voice, but gruff and slurred.

The door closed.

Lily rubbed her eyes and squinted.

Silas Barnes reached the end of the bed, holding a whiskey bottle.

She mumbled, "What?" A vague sense of peril slithered out of the fog. She rose up on one elbow, but fell back, too sluggish to retreat. "Go away, Barnes."

His heavy breaths cut the silence. He snickered. "Naw, I want a good poke afore it gets ruint."

The words jumbled in her ear, carrying no meaning. *Must be a dream.* With a huff of dismissal, she flapped a limp hand at him.

Barnes took a swig of whiskey and set the brown bottle on the dresser. His bowler landed next to it.

"Ain't had fancy pussy in a long while. A'course, it won't be fancy for long." Wiping a dribble of liquid from his chin, he chuckled and reached down to his trousers.

Her eyelids wavered, weighed down by the drug, and she fought to keep them open. She wished the dream would end.

He moved closer, swaying. His grin widened. The feather mattress sank under his weight. Humming under his breath, he stroked himself.

Lily turned her head and closed her eyes, but the room tilted and spun. A hand fell on her and squeezed her breast, fingers digging in. A whimper parted her lips. She railed at the fog, desperate to flee the nightmare. Time slowed to a crawl.

Barnes stretched out beside her, his breath puffing bitter spirits. He yanked the top of her chemise down and exhaled a titter of delight, like a boy with a long-anticipated present. As his hand snaked down her body, he lowered his mouth to her nipple and bit.

The pain whisked through the fog, as a gust of wind clearing a smoky hollow. Lily flinched and tried to pull away. Her mind sharpened, but her body still lagged. Her weak effort to push him away fell short.

He smacked her hand aside and laughed. "Behave, or I'll let Deadeye after you. Heard tell he kilt a whore with his pole once."

With an ungainly jerk, he pitched his body atop her and pushed her legs apart with his knees. He groaned, fumbling to find her entrance. A blunt jab worked his member into her.

The intrusion sparked a jolt of surprise and thrust Lily into awareness. She twisted and shoved her palms against his head.

"No!"

Barnes ignored her protest. His mouth slathered her breast with spit while he battered her.

Bile rose in her throat, and her desperation flared. She grunted as he bucked atop her. Instinct and anger drove her hands to his face, and her fingernails flayed the skin.

The scratches cut through his ardor. Growling, he wrenched his head away.

"Bitch!"

He rose up on one arm and struck out with the other. His fist caught the side of her head. Pain bloomed, a kaleidoscope of colors flashing before her. She went limp. Barnes loomed above her as she struggled to stay conscious. He wiped his cheek and glanced at his bloody fingers. His lips twisted in a sneer.

"Was gonna take 'er easy on you. Reckon you want it hard. More to my taste anyhow. Teach you some respect."

Barnes rolled her over.

Flashes of memory, of Duncan pinning her face-down, rutting on top of her. She shuddered and shook her head to banish the terror rising with the image.

Barnes chuckled, reached down to prop her knees up, took hold of her hips, swift despite the alcohol, and forced his shaft between her buttocks. With a grunt, he invaded her.

Lily screamed, and her body went rigid. As her knees slid back, she fell, but he followed. She squirmed, whimpering a desperate plea.

He pinned her and steadied himself before grabbing a chunk of her hair and twisting it around his hand. He yanked her head back and pressed his mouth against her ear.

"You ain't gonna like this."

He rammed forward, tearing a path deep inside her. Pain, far worse than any Duncan had inflicted. Lily screamed again.

"Not too loud, now." He chuckled and shoved her face into the pillow.

Searing agony ripped through her, and her arms waved in a useless bid for a handhold. He panted hot breath against her neck. Her muffled sobs seemed to heighten his excitement, spurring him to greater viciousness.

Lily sought to separate herself from the torment. A drop of musky sweat fell on her jaw, and she focused on its wet trail down her chin. His grunts echoed, rising in pitch. She reveled in the darkness behind her lids, trying to lose herself in it. She concentrated on everything but the pain.

A gasp burst from him, and his climax drove him forward. With a shudder, he relaxed on top of her, panting. When he'd caught his breath, he shoved himself off and stumbled to the dresser. He grabbed the bottle, flopped on the bed with his back against the headboard, and took a long gulp.

"What you runnin' from? You wasn't a virgin. Got yerself a husband?"

The pain radiated in hot waves. Vomit filled her throat, and she swallowed it.

"Girls like you don't show up for no reason. Seen dozens of you. Always runnin'. Always more trouble than yer worth." He drank deeply and coughed. "Can always tell who's runnin'. I know that look, that smell. Desperation. Hell, had it my own self."

He lifted her head up by the hair. She bit her tongue to keep from crying out, coppery spit filling her mouth, and let her face fall slack. He dropped her head and snorted.

"Fuckin' passed out. Gotta tell Deadeye to cut back on the dose."

He quieted, and Lily hoped he'd fallen asleep. She almost peeked, but he spoke.

"Yep, I was runnin', too, when I came west. Kilt a cheatin' bastard in Boston. Easy to disappear out here, but won't never have a home. Once ya get runnin', ya can't ever stop." His voice cracked, and he swallowed more from the bottle. "Unless ya got money. When you got money, you can do whatever you want. Like that bastard Samuels. His girl kilt my Molly, just kilt her out in the street like a dog, but they didn't care. They up and let her go. Asylum, my ass. They let her go. She got hers, though." He snorted. "I told her about you and that cowboy. Worked better than I coulda dreamed. Kilt two birds with one stone. And now I'll earn back way more on that loan. That's how ya get even *and* make a profit. I'll have my fortune, go out to Californy, and they won't never find me. Teach them dandies to spurn me."

Barnes drained the bottle, tossed it on the floor, and staggered to his feet. As Lily lay motionless, he tucked his clothes back into place. He retrieved his hat and let himself out. The lock clicked behind him.

Lily lay still for a long time. She waited until the burning turned to a throbbing ache and lifted a shaky hand to wipe his sweat and spit from her cheek. A cry slipped from her as she rolled over and pulled her legs up. Her buttocks felt slick, sticky. With a shuddering wheeze, she lunged from the bed and stumbled behind the screen. She retched into the chamber pot until nothing more came up. Wincing, she used the cloth to clean herself. It came away streaked with blood. Dizziness threatened, and she crawled back to the bed.

The lamp's flame flickered as it died. The room fell into darkness. The throbbing faded.

She wanted to cry, but her eyes produced no tears. She tried to dredge up anger, or fear, but she felt nothing, a numb shell. Her eyes stared into the shadows, and she waited for oblivion.

CHAPTER FORTY

A flat, muddy light seeped in the window. Clouds smothered the sliver of sky visible from the bed. Lily hadn't slept, hadn't moved. The hope she'd clung to withered, and weary resignation edged in with the morning chill.

She had fought too long, lost too much. *Too long? No, not that long.* Less than two years before she'd had a life of ease, ensconced in her parents' comfortable house, unaware of the misery that lay ahead. Leisure had filled her days; hours spent sewing silly decorations, learning useless trivia, planning dinner parties, daydreaming of romance and adventure.

None of that will help me now. How did it all go wrong so fast? My family, my home, my baby, my marriage, my business. I've nothing left and no way out.

Luke? Miles away. His face flashed before her. What would he say when he saw her, saw what she'd become? A whisper, cold and harsh: *Whore.*

She uttered a sick moan and buried her face in the pillow. Soiled, scarred, and broken—how could he love such a woman? She would lose him, too.

You're on your own.

The whisper in her head spoke of the window. She had a way out. An enticing thought. Break the window and jump. If she survived the fall, she might gain her freedom. If she didn't .... Well, that was a kind of freedom, too.

Her head shifted on the pillow, eyes rolling up to the panes of glass. The gray sky beckoned. Like the fog, it offered an escape. Her head fell back.

Not yet. Tired, too tired to move, too tired to escape. Time enough for that later.

The key clicked in the lock, and the door swung open. Deadeye poked his head in and ducked back out. He returned with a tray, boots thumping across to the dresser. Lily didn't move.

She had lain awake as the night and morning wore on, exhausted but unable to find the comfort of sleep. Her only attempt to move had drawn a wretched cry and left her gasping as every muscle protested. She'd sunk back and willed away the urge to urinate.

Deadeye set the tray down and plucked a box from it. He grunted, holding the box up. Lily gave no response. His beady eyes narrowed while the other hand moved to rest on the butt of his gun. He stared at her for a long minute before he dropped the box back on the tray and stomped out.

A bowl sat next to the box. She had no appetite—and no desire to discover how badly Barnes had damaged her when the need to empty her bowels came. She might discard the food, but Deadeye had made it clear she'd better use whatever the box held.

Lily held her breath and steeled herself. Pushing up on one arm, she gasped and bit her lip as her weight rolled onto her backside, stiff limbs trembling and screaming, shot with ropes of fire. She forced her body up and leaned against the bed. She fought the urge to lie back down. Eyes squeezed shut, she slid her feet forward with small jerky steps until she could grab the dresser. She stood panting until the internal ache subsided.

The box contained a brush, pins, and several tins. She picked a metal box to open. It held a thick, glossy ointment, tinted deep red. She dropped it and pulled her hand back as if bitten. The tin rattled on the metal tray.

Cosmetics. They would force her to paint her face, to wear what the doves wore.

She closed her eyes and fought back a wave of nausea.

It doesn't matter. No different than medicine. It doesn't make me a whore.

Barnes' snickering voice replied in her head: *Damned straight, it's the fuckin' that'll make you a whore.*

A throttled screech erupted from her. She snatched a container and hurled it in a blind rage. It struck the mirror with a loud crack, crazed lines bolting across the hazy glass, and drew her gaze to the reflection.

A stranger stared back at her. The woman's hair flared in a wild tangle about her head and shoulders. One side of her jaw had bloated where Barnes had struck her. Dark, puffy half-moons under her eyes made them appear bruised. Her skin held a ghostly tone, and the scar stood out in a stark purple streak on her cheek.

Lily sucked in a breath and turned away. Tears stung her eyes as a shudder rippled through her. Swallowing her disgust, she faced the mirror again, forcing herself to pick up the hairbrush to smooth the unruly mane. Rattled by tremors, her hands fumbled among the tins until she found the pancake. She managed a passable look after several tries and followed with light rouge and lip color.

When she'd finished, a different stranger gazed at her from the cracked mirror. Her shoulders slumped. Despite her denials, the final blow came down; she had permanently transformed, even if the colors faded.

Her eyes cut away.

There's still a way out.

The leaden sky brought a shiver.

When she couldn't endure any more, she would break the window—but something held her back. Not yet.

She wrenched her gaze from the window and tucked the containers back in their box. With a grimace, she took the bowl, limped behind the screen, and dumped soupy porridge into the chamber pot. She tossed the bowl aside and propped herself against the wall, lowering into a squat, sore muscles threatening to give out. Her stream began and seared the tender, abraded flesh with a bolt of fire. Barnes had torn more than she knew. A whimper escaped her as she tried to push the flow faster. The last hot liquid left her, and she cringed as she wiped. She covered the pot with the rag. Her thighs refused to push her back up, and she crawled to the bed once more.

Lily hissed as she sank onto the mattress, the burning between her legs still intense. She prayed she wouldn't have to relieve herself again for a long while.

The door opened. Deadeye glanced at her face and chuckled before he pulled the laudanum bottle from his pocket and went to the dresser. Lily sighed with gratitude, craving relief from the pain, and reality. Deadeye poured her a dose and moved to pick up the tray.

"What's that round thing? In the box?"

He paused but took the tray. "Womb veil, for not getting' a baby. Put it inside, up by the womb. Stops the seed. You'll want to wash it every day."

Her cheeks lit with fire. "I see." She stopped him. "The pot needs emptied." She hid a smile at his impatient grunt. Small satisfaction.

He grabbed it and went through the ritual of locking the door. After several minutes he returned the pot, gathered the tray, and backed out.

He paused at the door. "Be ready. It'll be a busy night." Tobacco juice dripped onto his beard with his grin.

The lock turned.

A baby. She hadn't considered the prospect. *A baby by some stranger. I wouldn't even know who.* Another idea slammed into her like a train. *Barnes could've already ....*

She dove for the dresser and pulled the small box from it. The rubber cone inside flexed easily. Horror overcame distaste, and she inserted the device, cringing with pain. It was uncomfortable but eased her mind.

The drug carried her into the fog and held the hurt at bay. At last she slept, lulled by raindrops ticking on the window.

* * * * *

Thunder rolled through the valley, pulling Lily from her dream. Edged in deep shadows, the room filled with twilight, but gave no hint of the hour. For the first time, a faint tinkle of piano music drifted up from the parlor. She shivered and rose on an elbow to tug the blanket closer. Music meant customers. Dizziness returned. She shook her head, denying the spurt of cold dread erupting on her skin.

No. I won't be afraid. It's only sex. I've had sex before. The doves do it every day. If they can endure it, so can I.

The words rang hollow, but she ran them through her mind over and over.

LAUREN GREGORY

As dusk faded in the window, a sliver of light glowed under the door. The piano player banged out more tunes. Footsteps sounded on the other side of the door, and something blocked the light.

Lily swallowed and pulled the blanket closer. An involuntary plea slipped from her lips in a whisper. "Dear Lord, please help me." Her mother would have clucked her tongue and told her to expect no help from a God Lily had disobeyed. She repeated it anyway, while the key turned in the lock.

Deadeye entered, moving faster than usual. He brought in a spittoon and another lamp, set them on nightstand, and lit the wall sconce with a match. The lamps chased the shadows into the corners. The box herder poured a dollop of laudanum into her cup and thrust it at her. Lily balked at the large measure.

"You gonna want it, no doubt." He nodded. "Boss got 'em lined up, waitin' fer ya."

She took it, but his comment alarmed her. How many? Tears threatened, and she swallowed them with a gulp of the bitter liquid.

He left a jar of ointment and a rag on the nightstand and opened the trunk to spread the section of heavy oil cloth over the end of the bed.

"What on earth is that for?" The question came out before she could stop it.

"So's their boots don't ruin the beddin'."

Lily groaned and buried her face in her hands.

"Don't go messin' the paint up. Boss done promised these boys a fine piece."

She held back an angry scream, resisting the urge to spew curses at him.

He yanked the cover from the bed and stuffed it into the trunk.

Lily let her hands fall to her lap, where they curled into fists.

Deadeye loosed a stream of tobacco into the spittoon, surveyed the room, and seemed satisfied. His eyes settled on her.

"I'll hold 'em back a few 'til yer physic kicks in, but they'll be chompin' at the bit." His jaw tightened, and his voice went lower. "No trouble, ya hear?" He turned to leave.

Lily spoke through clenched teeth. "How much?"

He stopped and looked back. "How much what?"

"How much is he selling me for?"

With a snort, he said, "Prideful, eh? Ten bucks. It'll go lower later after the first rush."

She shot him a disgusted glare. "I'm not vain. I simply want to know how long until I earn enough to get out of here."

His bushy eyebrows rose, and he opened his mouth but closed it without a word. He gave a slight shake of his head as he left, for once not locking the door.

CHAPTER FORTY-ONE

The minutes spun out like molasses. In the darkness beyond the window, the clouds thinned, leaving tattered veils around the naked moon.

Lily's eyelids grew heavy as her fog billowed in, cloaking reason, misery, and fear. She was torn between wanting to stay vigilant and welcoming the stupor. Which state offered release?

The men would come and take their pleasure with no interest in her beyond her ability to make them feel powerful and virile, to release the spirits corrupting their bodies and inflict the poison on their subject. That poison would fester—the same impurity the community would use as an excuse to cast her out. The customers would pay the fee and continue on their way, never knowing what price she paid.

If she could remain alert, she might deflect their advances and save herself ... and draw Deadeye's wrath. The daze would allow her escape to a senseless void where their touch meant nothing.

Soon, it no longer mattered what she wanted. She thought of the window again, wondered how it would feel to fly, but the time had passed. The warm, floating sensation overcame her resistance and fetched her along a lethargic river of indifference. The door wavered with bleary vertigo, while the smooth cotton chemise wrinkled between her fingers, a strange calm found in compulsive rubbing. She sat with her back against the headboard, legs curled under her, and waited.

A sharp rap sounded like a gunshot, but she didn't flinch. A man pushed the door open and entered quickly, closing it behind him. He moved with precise efficiency, no wasted actions.

"Good evening." He turned toward the screen in the corner.

His gaze averted, he unbuttoned his suit jacket and hung it on a hook behind the divider—how had she not noticed that hook? His straw hat followed the jacket, laid carefully atop the point.

"Ready yourself, miss." He had the clipped tone of the Eastern upper class.

Lily heard the words but didn't move. His eyes still avoided her as he turned toward her and unfastened his trousers, the fabric tented at his groin. An elaborate mustache curved over his cheeks, like her father's. She dragged her gaze from it.

"Quickly, miss, I'm not here for flirtations."

Her eyes slid back to him. "What are you here for?" The words came thick, flat.

"Business." For the first time, his sharp glance landed on her. "I trust I won't need to make a complaint."

With a humorless laugh, she moved her head side to side.

A complaint. No, that wouldn't do. Not with Deadeye at his post outside the door.

Her legs moved on their own, jerking out from under her and pulling her bottom down the mattress until she laid flat.

The music from downstairs .... What is that song?

He uncovered his member, holding it between two fingers as if loathe to touch it, and crawled onto the bed, kneeling with legs tightly clamped. He'd grown erect but gave no other sign of anticipation. His mouth a tight white line, his eyes flat but determined, shoulders square.

He appeared ready to engage in a tense trade negotiation. A surge of nausea joined wicked laughter in her throat, and she forced both down, turning her head. Her eyes slipped closed. Warmth brushed her thighs, and they parted as the man moved over her.

A quick thrust. She clenched her jaw, soreness tearing through the fog, the man tearing through her indifference.

Luke. Oh, Luke .... Why did you have to leave?

Piano music, happy and boisterous, mocked from far away, until his breath hissed fast and ragged in her ear. As he trembled almost imperceptibly, a soft groan left him with his poison.

He dressed with urgency while she fought her heaving stomach. After the door closed, Lily realized he'd made sure no other part of his body touched her, his fussy nature repulsed by her. He saw her as unclean—yet, he had made her that way.

The truth sank in slowly. She'd become a soiled dove.

* * * * *

Another knock. Lily pulled her legs together and tensed as she sat up. Boots echoed on the wood.

"Hot damn, worth the wait!" This one sounded Southern. Tall and lanky, but with an odd, high-pitched voice. He wore the miner's standard of heavy trousers and a thread-bare shirt under his jacket. After shimmying out of the coat in a flash, he flopped beside her.

She tried a smile, but it faded when his hand assailed her breast with a clumsy squeeze.

His grin wobbled. "Sumpin' wrong?"

Low laughter bubbled up in her throat. *What an absurd question.*

"Wrong? What the devil could be wrong?" Slurred and bitter, her voice grated on her ears.

He apparently took her words at face value and smiled again. His eyes drifted down, glazed with lust.

"Boys said I was plumb crazy spendin' most my strike on a whore," he breathed, "but I ain't seen a finer pair o' tits in years."

He ducked his head, tugged her top down, and lapped at the milky skin. Stubble on his jaw rasped against her chest, his salty sweat smell surrounding her. She wanted to push his head away, but he found her hand before she could and nudged it over the hot lump in his pants. A quick shudder ran through her, pumping acidic spit over her tongue.

No, I can't vomit. I can't.

Feeling her quake, he lifted his head. "Whoo, yer a hot one, huh?" His slick tongue darted out over his lips. "Don't worry, I'll scratch that itch."

My God, he thinks I want him, that I'll enjoy this. The revelation stunned her, even more than the other man's disdain. *Never.* But she hid her scorn and closed her eyes, determined to slip back into the fog.

His calloused hand still on her breast, the bed jiggled while he slipped his pants down and positioned himself. Her body tensed when he pulled her hand over his rigid piece, but she let him guide her hand to stroke him.

Lily blocked out the man's low moans, his pungent odor, his fingers digging into her hips as he pulled her toward him and entered. She imagined the rhythmic rocking of his plunges as the steady sway of the old pony her grandfather had bought her when she turned five, rather than a disgusting act of violation. The man panted his lust over her chest, but she pushed it to the background and focused on the comforting mist in her mind.

He finally spilled his seed and collapsed atop her. Opening her eyes, she turned her head away from the stringy hair tickling her chin. As he caught his breath, his hand lay beside her head on the pillow, and a gold band on his third finger glinted in the lamplight.

* * * * *

Lily retreated into the fog, conscious but detached. The knock came after each man left, one after another; tall, short, fat, thin, old, and young, blurring together over hours. Some spoke to her, and she spoke back but had no idea what she said. All of the men appeared to have taken their courage from liquor, and the air grew thick with spirits and musk.

The pain intensified with each entry until one of the men smeared some of the ointment between her thighs. She sighed with relief—it reduced the friction and let her endure their rough assaults—but after a few more men, even the salve couldn't ease the pain in her raw, tender skin.

She moaned under the men, and they took her agony for pleasure. Her body soon wilted like warm taffy, limp and soft. They positioned her as a doll, moving her to suit their needs. One man slapped her when she didn't move quickly enough. Another cried with his release. Another used her mouth, and when he left, she grabbed the spittoon and retched.

Late in the night, instead of a customer, Deadeye followed the knock. Lily worked to pull herself up in the bed.

"I can't .... I can't take another," she mumbled.

"Naw, Boss is lettin' you off, bein' a beginner an' all." He stowed the oil cloth back in the trunk. "Only fer tonight, though. When it gets busy, you'll have thirty or forty."

He left to empty the pots. When he returned, he laid a fresh sheet on the dresser.

"Clean yerself up an' change the beddin'. I'll bring vittles in the mornin'."

Her head wobbled in agreement, but she fell asleep before he'd left the room.

CHAPTER FORTY-TWO

Lily woke to the echo of her father's voice ringing in her ears.

She'd stood in the parlor doorway with her Dolly. Papa stood next to twin caskets laid out on the dining room table. Her brother and sister had sat up in the boxes, waxy and pale, with flies buzzing in loops around them. Peter in his best suit, Sissy draped in satin and lace. All three stared at her with revulsion.

Her father pointed at her. "You killed them. Whore!"

The word tore fresh wounds with its icy contempt.

She blinked, afraid to find him standing before her, pointing, horrified reproach in his eyes.

No one there, dust motes floating in rays of sun her only attendants. The bright light threw spikes of pain into her temples, and she closed her eyes and pressed her palms against them. Fragments of the night's disgrace floated up until she pitched off the fouled mattress to vomit into the chamber pot. She rested against the wall, wiped her mouth, and waited for her stomach to settle.

Her muscles protested, but she stood on shaky legs and hobbled to the wash basin. Grime stained her chemise and drawers. Someone had torn one of the straps in his haste, and it hung from her breast like a shriveled, gray flower. She wet a rag and wiped the dried crust from her thighs and the wetness from her backside. Tears stung her eyes as she bathed the swollen flesh burning between her legs. She'd never feel clean again.

Still exhausted, Lily ached to return to bed, but the soiled sheet repulsed her. She yanked the old sheet off, wadded it up, and threw it at the door. It landed with a wet smack, and bile rose again. Her body trembled, quaking and ripping the fabric from her fingers while she stumbled around the bed, trying to tuck the clean sheet at the corners.

The fragile façade of detachment slipped. She stood beside the bed, lips quivering.

How will I survive another night like that ... or worse? I won't. At least not with my sanity intact. It'll drive me mad. I can't.

Panic drove her to the window. She pulled the handle at the bottom with every ounce of strength she had left, but it wouldn't budge. Blood pounded in her ears, and her lungs refused to draw air. The nails, she'd forgotten them.

Turning back to the room, she scanned every item to find something that might pry the window open. Nothing strong enough, unless she could break something.

Might as well break the window. She needed something heavy enough to shatter the thick pane of glass. The box of cosmetics, perhaps, or the water pitcher. *Yes, the pitcher!*

She dashed to the dresser and laid her hands on the jug.

The door opened, and Barnes intruded.

Lily turned, consumed by hysteria. She released the pitcher, and it thudded back on the bureau. An incoherent screech of rage spewed from her, and she rushed the man as his face transformed with shock. When she reached him, he thrust an arm out, and she collided with his hand. His palm hit her chest, and the heel ricocheted up against her throat.

The scream cut short with a rasping hitch. Her head jerked back while her feet pedaled on the slick floor. She went down and clawed her throat, chest locked in a vise. Barnes moved over her and settled a boot on her neck.

"Don't do that again."

Her heart hammered and muffled his voice, but it couldn't suppress the malice in his dark eyes. The foot pressed harder, and an inky pool flooded her vision until it blocked out his glare.

* * * * *

Water splashed Lily's face, and she gasped. Her throat ached. Still on the floor, she sputtered and struggled to sit up. Deadeye stood over her with the pitcher and chuckled.

"Damn women jus' don't learn." He gestured toward the bed. "Get on back. Boss says you abused yer privilege."

Rage overcame her again, and she lunged at his leg with her mouth open wide. She bit down, but the layers of fabric dulled the impact. Deadeye grunted, bent to grab her hair, and yanked her up.

"Ouch! Let go of me, you bastard!" Her voice had turned raspy. Lily flailed her arms and legs, scratching and kicking.

He held her writhing body away and, with an air of nonchalance, set the pitcher on the dresser. He turned and sunk his fist into her belly. The blow knocked the wind from her with a groan. Her body crumpled as her stomach turned inside out, and she convulsed.

Deadeye dragged her to the bed and shoved her down.

"Done bein' nice."

She wheezed, a hot lump of pain radiating through her abdomen. He jerked her wrist up and tied it to the bed with a length of rope that appeared from nowhere. His hand found her hair again, pulled hard, and wrenched her head back. Her tears blurred his face as he leaned close.

"Listen up. Boss don't want no more trouble outta you. Or else."

His eyes glinted with eager tension. They told her she'd gone too far, and he'd revel in putting her in her place. Sour tobacco juice dripped onto her chin, but she held still, and her eyes widened.

He'll kill me without a second thought.

He released her, stalked out, and brought in a tray of food, which he dropped on the bed with a clatter. The door stood open when he left, but she knew he wouldn't go far.

The sliver of blue sky shimmered through the window. She left the tray untouched while her bound hand, hanging from the headboard above her, went numb.

No more choices. I'm stuck here. The realization struck hard—harder than Deadeye's fist, or Barnes' blows, or even the stinging ache still centered between her legs.

My only escape is death.

She examined the idea, considered how she might accomplish it. The rope, perhaps ... but there was nothing to hang from. A shard of glass would work, but they might find her too quickly and save her. A fire? She shuddered. Maybe as simple as pushing Deadeye far enough. They would hurt her, first, though. She hated to admit it, but she feared that.

But all of those things would allow Barnes to hide his deed. They would bury her in the night, and no one would ever know their crimes. She refused to let that happen.

If I sacrifice myself, I'll be damned if I don't take them with me.

A strange calm came over her ... until the memory of her mother's face—silent and mottled purple, floating under the noose—sent a chill up her spine. *History repeats itself, right?*

The voice in her head turned plaintive: *But I can't face this. I can't. How many more men? They've ruined me. The pain ... humiliation ... the way people will look at me, if I ever get out of here. They won't care that I was raped.*

No. I won't be like her, and I won't let them get away with this. I don't care what anyone thinks. If he kills me, so be it, but I won't give up. I'll bide my time. And I'll make sure they are punished.

Her lips set in a grim line. The decision made, she forced some food down in gulps.

Deadeye came back to take the tray and give her the laudanum. She averted her eyes. A trickle of fear slid down her neck as she remembered the look in his eyes.

I'll do what I have to do. I'll survive this. I have to.

* * * * *

Deadeye returned after nightfall to untie her.

The men came again, one after another. The fog couldn't keep them out, but it clouded her mind enough to bear it. Lily fought the urge to scream, to fight them off. She laid still, dug her nails into her palms, and kept silent.

After an eternity, the night ended, and she fell asleep, exhausted.

The pattern repeated: sleep late, eat, and "entertain" customers. Barnes didn't return. Aside from customers, she had only Deadeye for company. He kept a close eye on her when he entered, and she suspected he wished she would misbehave again. She did her best to ignore him, determined not to give him the satisfaction of seeing her fear.

To resist the lingering lure of the window, Lily retreated and smothered her demons. She endured the rough hands, unwashed bodies, drunken tempers, and poison. In her mind, she repeated her new-found mantra:

I'll survive this. I have to.

CHAPTER FORTY-THREE

Spurs jingled, cutting through Lily's tired desolation. The unexpected noise competed with the faint piano music. When had she last heard the clinking signature of a cowboy? The days ran together, time meant nothing; each sunrise passed as she slept, and each sunset only heralded further corruption of her mind and body. She had trouble remembering more than a few hours past or thinking beyond a few hours ahead.

"Howdy do, miss." His slur stretched the final word to a hiss.

In the low light, his hat brim hid his rough features, but she made out a heavy growth of blond beard. His clothes spoke of the trail and carried the scent of cattle and campfires. She shrugged off his question with a vague mumble and slid down the mattress. Her eyes stayed on him. Something about him nagged at her, but other than the rarity of trail men, nothing stood out.

He braced himself against the wall to work the buckle on his holster. He cussed in a low voice, pulled the belt free, and tossed it on the dresser. With a grin, he moved toward the bed while he unbuttoned.

Lily scowled. "Take your damned hat off." She decided the sound of spurs had thrown her off. *Just another drunk. Hope he's the last for tonight.*

He laughed and laid the hat aside. "Sorry, didn't peg you for high class," he muttered.

When he turned around with a bare head, Lily's heart stopped.

He looks like Luke. She blinked and squinted. *No, not really. It's just the hair, and the fact he's a cowboy.* She took a shaky breath, closing her eyes. An ache gripped her chest. She hadn't thought of Luke in days ... or was it weeks? The ache sharpened into resentment. *So what? He didn't come for me. He's gone.*

The man fell on the bed and leered at her while he groped to free her breasts.

Lily gritted her teeth, wrinkling her nose at the bitter stink of his breath. She found her way to the sanctuary she'd built in her mind, but once she'd summoned Luke, he refused to withdraw. Memories of him mingled with the hands and mouth on her skin. Tears came, and she moaned softly, a maelstrom of regret, anger, and desire welling in her core.

The man's head rose, and he grinned. "Now there's a good filly." The words melted together, washed in whiskey.

He returned his attention to her body, but the moment had passed. Lily seethed with frustration and disgust, refusing to accept she'd started to respond to the drunken stranger.

Have I fallen that far? Her skin crawled with his touch.

His excitement grew, and he mounted. Hunched over her, panting and groaning, he found release and went limp with a gasp.

Lily lay beneath the hot, sweaty weight, berating herself for her lapse. A rumbling snort broke the stillness.

"Oh hell! Another sleeper." With a heave against the body, she wriggled out from under him and sat on the edge of the bed.

She would have to bring Deadeye in to haul the man out, but she waited, grateful for a few minutes of peace. If she waited long enough, the detested box herder would come anyway and she could avoid talking to him.

She yawned as she pushed herself up on wobbly legs. She moved to the dresser to wet the rag and clean the night's musky residue from her thighs. Her eyes caught her reflection in the mirror.

Mesmerized by the disturbing image, she searched for traces of her old self but only saw the disparity. She'd lost weight, and her skin stretched tight over the sharp points of bones. The opiates made her itchy, and her skin had suffered with irritated spots rough from scratches. After the long night, the bright paints had run and smeared, blurring her features. Twin smudges of color stained her neck, despite a layer of powder.

Barnes had returned the night before, drunk and belligerent. She didn't say a word. She resisted the screaming in her mind, refused to obey the instinct to fight, retreated into the fog. It didn't dampen his brutality. Her lack of response seemed to infuriate him just as much as resistance. He had used her roughly and, near the end, coiled his fingers around her throat. She'd thought he intended to squeeze the life from her, but he laughed and released her before she lost consciousness.

She couldn't quite convince herself he would let go the next time, and her hatred burned hotter at the memory.

Another loud snore came from the man on the bed. With

a shaky hand, she poured a cup of water and drank. As she set the cup down, her arm brushed the cowboy hat, knocking it off the dresser. She froze while sweat glazed her face.

The smooth leather of the man's holster gleamed in the lamplight.

A weapon.

She checked the cowboy. He lay where she'd left him, mouth open, eyes closed, rattling away in his stupor. She slid a drawer open, wincing at the creak of wood against wood. After another nervous peek at the man, she tugged the gun from its sheath, tucked it in the back of the drawer, and eased the bin shut. She pulled a couple tins from the cosmetics box and slipped them in the holster. The weight wasn't enough, but it would have to do.

How long before he notices the gun missing? More important, will Deadeye notice the empty holster when he drags him out?

She shook her head. The questions didn't need asking. The risk didn't matter. It was her only chance.

Lily twitched at the token knock.

Deadeye stuck his head in. "What's the hold up?"

She stood at the dresser, wiping smears of paint from around her eyes, and jerked her head toward the bed.

"Hell's bells, why dintcha get me? Been standin' out there waitin'," Deadeye grumbled.

Her eyes followed him in the mirror. The box herder hauled the cowboy over his shoulder and shot her a black look on his way out. She glared back. When he reached the door, she cleared her throat.

"What?" He whirled on her and narrowly missed bashing the cowboy's head against the wall.

Her lips twisted with an insolent smirk. She stuffed the holster into the hat, careful to keep the length of belt on top to hide the empty pocket. With effort, she held her hand steady and thrust the hat toward Deadeye, while her heart pounded in her chest.

He snatched the hat away and moved to the door. "Damned women."

The door slammed. Lily let out a rush of air, wiped a cold trickle of fear from her temple, and leaned against the dresser. Her heart hammered while she listened for returning footsteps.

He hadn't noticed the light weight of the hat right away. A good sign, but not a guarantee. It would take Deadeye several minutes to carry the man outside to dump him on the street. He might discover the missing gun at any time, or the cowboy might wake and cry foul.

Seconds slipped by, stretched out as if the world had stopped spinning. The piano music tinkled, and a door shut somewhere. She stood, waiting with her heart in her throat, until her legs cramped, and she sank to the floor. The lamp burned out, cloaking the room in black.

CHAPTER FORTY-FOUR

The sun had risen hours before, but Lily didn't know how many. Time had stopped. She'd fallen asleep on the floor and woke when the darkness began its retreat. The parlor house lay quiet at dawn, and she sat in silence, immobilized by the drug and her fear. Shadows recoiled and grew sharp edges as faint light brightened into day.

Fighting the fog, she tested various ruses and ambushes countless times to find the flaws that might doom her escape. Even with the gun, her chances seemed slim. She had to catch Deadeye off-guard, and she could only count on one shot. If she stayed in the bed, surprising him seemed unlikely. He could see her every move, and she had nowhere to conceal the pistol. If she hid, her absence would draw his attention as soon as he entered and force a quick shot.

She still had to escape the house. She didn't know who else she might run into or where to go. The idea of jumping from the window left a ball of hot acid in her stomach.

None of the scenarios seemed plausible as she played them out in her head. Every time, something went awry, and she envisioned Barnes' black eyes boring into her as he punished her. Her confidence weakened, and she almost talked herself out of the attempt. A part of her still hoped for rescue of some kind.

A small voice whispered a cruel taunt: *You're a whore now, escape won't change that.*

"No!" Bitter, choking bile filled her throat. Anger welled.

It's not my fault! How could I fight back? I couldn't stop them. Hot tears spilled onto her dingy corset. *They've taken everything. They set out to destroy me, and they've succeeded.*

In the stillness, Alice's gruff admonition rumbled through her head: *Focus on the opportunity—not the blame.*

The words echoed, dampening the storm of resentment. Alice spent years with her captors, letting chances for escape slip by. Lily could wait for rescue, but even if she survived, what kind of life was that? She had to take a chance.

She beat back the fear and waited as the shadows moved inch by inch.

* * * * *

Lily crouched. Beads of sweat surfaced and rolled down her neck. The thick, humid air, charged with the static that came before a storm, pressed close. She changed position when her feet tingled, never taking her eyes from the door.

She'd moved the chamber pot in front of the door, hoping it would distract him long enough, perhaps give her an extra fraction of a second. With her back against the wall, she'd pulled the screen close to provide a narrow opening with a view of the entry. She should have a good shot before Deadeye found her. Panic threatened with every minute, each creak of the house, any slight evidence of others.

It's late. He should have come by now.

Her sweaty hand cramped. She loosened her grip on the pistol and took a deep breath. When the fear overwhelmed her, Alice's image floated up, and Lily's resolve strengthened, but her heart thumped a broken cadence.

Familiar footsteps finally scraped and thudded along the hall.

Breath seized in her chest. Her hand tightened on the grip as she raised the gun. With a supreme effort, she quelled the tremor in her weakened muscles.

The key rattled against the brass plate.

Wait! I'm not ready. I'll miss.

The door came open with a clang of metal. Lily jerked and blinked at the loud toll—she'd forgotten the pot. The vessel swished rancid waste over Deadeye's boots and onto the floor.

His attention veered to the wobbling pot, and he bent toward. The path his eyes took grazed her hiding spot. He squinted and focused on her.

She fired.

Deadeye twitched but started toward her.

Terror raced up her spine. Her fingers fumbled to cock the pistol as he batted the screen away. With the divider flying over the bed, a jolt pushed Lily up, and she dove to the side. She landed on top of the screen, scrambling to aim again.

The move left Deadeye charging at the empty wall. He tried to change direction, but his bulk drove him forward. He hit the plaster with a grunt, his head crashing against it. A dark spot bloomed on his shoulder and smeared the whitewashed wall with red.

Frozen, Lily held the gun on him. She thought she'd missed. The stain of blood drove home the brutal reality: she'd shot someone. The barrel wobbled as a ripple of horror tore through her.

The impact had stunned the big man, but he turned on her with rage as hot as the blood on his shirt.

"No!" Her mouth opened in a strangled croak; a demand, a plea, a hopeless cry to make it all stop.

It's him or me.

The gun jumped in her hand, and a curl of smoke flew from the barrel.

Deadeye's face went slack as he stumbled backward. A huff of breath escaped him, his knees buckled, and he sank to the floor.

She rolled off the bed and staggered to her feet. Standing again, she trained the gun on him while she shuffled to the door. He sat propped up, head lolling to the side, and his breath came in hitching gurgles.

After two shots in the small room, pain throbbed in her ears with a high-pitched whine. Loud voices drifted up, questions shouted from below that snapped her attention back to the plan.

In the puddle of urine by the door, she found the skeleton shape. Footsteps clumped on stairs. Her fingers groped for the key while she kicked the pot aside and pushed the door shut.

The key slid home in the lock, and she twisted it.

She whirled and raised the gun again. Deadeye hadn't moved. Someone rattled the door knob and pounded on the wood. Head spinning, Lily tried to remember the next step.

The window!

She hefted the pitcher and turned her face away. The pitcher hit the window with a crash. Slivers of glass and chunks of ceramic scattered.

The voices in the hall rose with alarm, but the pounding on the door stopped.

Ragged breaths seared her throat as she ripped the sheet from the bed. Sharp barbs pricked her bare feet, but she tiptoed to the window and knocked out the jagged remains of the pane. As she wrapped the sheet around herself, a last glance at the box herder sparked another wave of dread.

You've killed again.

She swallowed and set her jaw.

Him or me.

"I'm taking the chance, Alice," she whispered.

Throwing a leg over the windowsill, she ducked her head out. Glass littered the weeds and grass in the alleyway. Clouds had bubbled up on the horizon, advancing on the valley, but blue sky reigned overhead.

She breathed deep and jumped. The sheet fluttered around her as she flew out the window.

CHAPTER FORTY-FIVE

Pain jolted up Lily's leg, and a twig-like snap came from her arm. She collapsed and couldn't hold back a yelp. The gun dropped from her limp hand as a grimace contorted her face. She gulped in her first breaths of freedom.

A few discarded barrels and crates littered the alley, but no people. Stars sprinkled her vision, and she shook off a wave of dizziness.

"Damnit!"

She pulled her dangling arm close, and the pain flared hotter. A bulge slithered under the skin above her left wrist. She tucked her arm in the folds of the sheet and tried to think what to do next.

Her plans had mostly ended at the window. Sitting in the alley, she didn't know where to go. With little faith she'd come out alive, she hadn't considered what came beyond the escape.

A crash sounded above, and loud voices echoed between the buildings. Barnes' face appeared in the empty window frame. He looked down at her, his features twisted with rage.

He called to someone behind him, "She's down there, go git her!"

Her heart stalled. She hopped to her feet, but her ankle bloomed with fire as she stumbled against the house. With light pressure, she tried the foot again and decided it wasn't broken. She limped toward the street, breath whistling through clenched teeth.

The view of the road opened up when she neared the end of the alley. As the late morning sun reached its zenith, South Street lay barren. A couple of doves looked out from small windows, jaded boredom on their faces. Their ramshackle cribs lined the opposite side like the stalls of a stable. The women's eyes sparked with curiosity when Lily emerged from the passage, but they merely watched her struggle into the road.

She stood in the dirt ruts and turned one way and the other. A door burst open on the front porch of the parlor house. Without looking back, Lily screamed and broke into a shambling run. Her ankle protested with bolts of agony, mirroring the painful grinding of bones in her arm as she clutched it tighter.

A deep voice yelled behind her and drew cackling laughter from the doves.

Lily pushed herself faster. Terror overwhelmed her as she rounded a corner onto another, smaller lane. Her sobbing gasps for air failed to keep up, and her lungs burned. She careened through the maze of clapboard, brick, and canvas.

She recognized where her feet had carried her only when she saw the sign: Dr. Andrews, Physician. Pounding on the door, she cast panicked glances at the road, expecting the lumbering owner of the deep voice to appear.

Mary opened the door with a smile, but her eyes went wide. "Lily! Land sakes, child .... What?"

Lily whispered, "Inside!" She pushed past the plump woman and collapsed on a chair in the doctor's office.

Mary rushed in carrying a cup of tea. "I was just getting ready for lunch, dear. You look dreadful! Whatever happened? Where have you been? I asked after you at Mrs. Connor's, and they said you'd run out." Her eyes went to the dingy sheet and chemise.

Lily flushed, shocked she'd forgotten her lack of clothing. "I didn't run out. I was kidnapped. Barnes, that bastard—" She stopped when Mary flinched. "I'm sorry, excuse my language. I, I just didn't know where to go."

"Oh, nonsense. You can always come to us. Doctor is out on calls, but he would say the same."

The adrenaline faded, and Lily slumped in the chair. "My arm is broken, I think, and my ankle .... I'm so tired." She jerked as her eyelids drooped. She clutched Mary's hand with her good one. "Fetch Jacob, at Mr. Amos'. Tell him to bring a horse."

The pain and fatigue closed in and darkened her world again.

* * * * *

Lily woke to a sickening crunch. "Oww!"

Mary stood near her head, holding her elbow. Jacob gripped Lily's wrist tight. At her cry, he flinched and let up on the tension. The bones in Lily's arm settled back together, and she moaned as throbbing pain flared.

"There, dear. Drink this. Quick!" Mary put a cup to her lips.

The familiar heat slid down her throat. Mary worked to

splint the arm without bumping it. A clean sheet covered her from head to toe, but Jacob had turned away as soon as he released her hand and kept his back to her. She closed her eyes and clenched her jaw, determined not to cry out again.

When the doctor's wife finished wrapping the arm, she offered the cup again. Lily shook her head and pushed it away.

"No more. I won't be able to ride." She struggled to sit up, but Mary held her back.

"Ride where, for Pete's sake? You can't go anywhere." She adopted her sternest face.

"I have to leave. He'll come after me." Lily asked Jacob, "You brought a horse?"

He nodded and mumbled, "Yes, ma'am."

"Lily, who will come after you? What is this about?"

"Mary, I don't want to get you involved, and I don't have time to explain. He's dangerous. I shouldn't even have come here."

"The marshal will take care of it, dear. I already sent for him."

Her eyes turned to saucers. "You didn't! Mary, no. He won't help." She threw Mary's restraining hand off and fought to stand. When her weight hit the bad ankle, she winced. Mary had wrapped it, too, but the swollen joint still hobbled her. "Jacob, make sure the horse is ready."

The boy nodded again and left.

Mary wrung her hands. "Listen here, young lady, this is ridiculous. You can't ride with those injuries; you'll break your neck. And why on earth wouldn't the marshal arrest someone who kidnapped you?"

"I killed a man!" Lily burst into tears and covered her face with the sheet. "It wasn't my fault. I had to escape. But the marshal already thinks I killed Judith, and now I've killed someone else. They'll lie. He won't believe me." She lowered the sheet.

Mary's mouth dropped open, and her hand came up to cover it.

"Please ... just help me get out of here."

"Well, I—of course, I'll help, dear." Her eyes filled with worry, a look Lily hadn't seen on the jovial face before. "But where will you go?"

"I don't know yet. Far enough to forget this town." Bitterness twisted her face. "I thought I could make a new life here, but this place isn't what I expected. It's not what it seems. It'll kill me if I stay."

Mary's eyes misted. "I hate to see you go." She shook her head. "But if you must, you can't go like that, and you'll need food." She turned and bustled from the room, as if welcoming a chance for action.

Lily fell back in the chair and let out a shaky breath. The laudanum slowly took the edge off the throbbing ache in her arm, but riding under its influence made her nervous. She hadn't ridden enough to feel comfortable one-handed and drugged, but she had no choice.

Arms draped with clothes, Mary returned in a flurry. She tossed the garments down and pointed to them.

"Some old things from patients. Put them on as best you can while I pack you something to eat. I'll help when I get back."

Lily picked up a piece with a bewildered look. "Mary, but these are pants ...."

"Young lady, there's no way you can ride sidesaddle with one hand. Besides, you might draw less attention if people think you're a man—at least from a distance." She nodded and hustled out again.

Lily eyed the trousers with distaste but appreciated the woman's practicality. She struggled to pull them on over her drawers with awkward tugs. They hung loosely on her thin frame, but still made her uncomfortable, like she was on display. She sighed and slid the shirt on. It took several minutes to manage the socks and boots, and she barely noticed the whispered curses she flung at them.

Mary brought a hat and hairpins and, after fastening all the closures on the clothes, deftly tucked Lily's hair close against her head. She gave her a critical once-over and shrugged, chuckling.

"It's not fashionable, but it'll do. I sent Jacob out to put the food and more clothes in the saddlebags."

Dismay settled on Lily. "Oh goodness, I just realized .... I haven't paid the board. He'll be held responsible for the missing horse. I can't pay for it."

With a wave of her hand, Mary dismissed the worry. "Don't worry about that. I'll make sure that old skinflint Amos gets paid anything he's owed."

"Mary, I appreciate this. You've done so much for me. I can't begin to repay your kindness, but I promise I'll send money when I can." Tears stung again, and she hugged her close.

"I'm not worried about money, dear. I only want you to take care of yourself."

Mary helped her hobble out to the back of the house. Jacob waited, holding Charlie's reins, and his face flushed as he gaped at her.

Lily chuckled. "Your stomach will fall out with your mouth like that."

He snapped it shut and lowered his head.

"I'm only teasing. I know I look a frightful mess."

"No, Miss Wright, that's not it at all! Just surprised me ...."

He grinned when he looked up again.

"Oh, you brought Charlie! He looks so much better than when we arrived." She patted the horse's neck. "Jacob, you're the sweetest boy I've ever met, and I thank you for all your help. You're a true gentleman."

He flushed. "I got some good weight on him and worked him a little. He'll ride smooth for you." He paused, and rushed the rest out as though afraid he'd lose his nerve, "Miss Wright, I sure hope everything works out. You're a real fine lady."

"I think I'll be all right." She smiled. "Can you help me mount?" She turned and hugged Mary once more.

Jacob laced his hands for her good foot, and she stepped up, gingerly sliding her leg over the saddle. She cringed at having to ride astride with the soreness in her private parts.

Jacob checked the girth and nodded. "Mrs. Andrews had me tie a pistol on there. Hope you don't need it, but just in case. I better be off before Mr. Amos pitches a fit. Good luck, Miss Wright." He loped toward the street and waved as he went beyond the house.

"You be careful, Lily." Mary's eyes filled, but her lips held a straight line.

"I will. Mary ... if Luke Jackson comes back, tell him ... well, just tell him I hope I see him again."

"I'll make sure he gets the message." The woman shocked her with a pert wink.

Lily blushed. "Goodbye, Mary."

Mary held a hand over her mouth and waved.

Lily rode across a field toward the trees that ringed the valley floor, avoiding the roads and people. The sky had turned gray as clouds rolled in like waves, and a stiff breeze threatened to blow her hat off. When she reached the timber, she turned halfway in the saddle. The town appeared peaceful, with a few wagons on the streets and ordinary people going about their business. To her, the town wore a mask, hiding a core that had festered and bred horrifying nightmares. She shuddered, faced forward, and hoped she could leave them behind.

CHAPTER FORTY-SIX

Lily eased the horse along a narrow deer trail through a spatter of rain. The sky grew darker and rumbled. Cold, fat drops pelted her felt hat, saturating it and sending trickles down her back.

She'd ridden for hours and winced with every step Charlie took. Her arm throbbed, and her rump ached. Her thighs, quivering under the strain, had rubbed raw where they gripped the saddle. After not riding for months, she'd lost the rhythm of the horse's gait.

The triumph of her escape faded with the daylight. She had no destination. She had only a vague idea of the locations of other towns and camps in the region, and anyone looking for her would check those places first. She didn't dare look for sanctuary too close to home. How long could she wander before she had no choice but to seek out a community? Despite her successful getaway, she hadn't escaped the trap.

As the rain fell harder, Lily looked for a spot to camp. She wanted to keep going and put more distance between her and any pursuers, but the rain-soaked ground had turned slippery, and nightfall crept closer. They descended into a small creek bottom, and she steered Charlie toward a large boulder.

"Whoa, boy."

She halted him alongside the rock and slid off onto it. Pain shot through every inch of her body and left her gasping. Mary had fashioned a sling for her arm, but every move jostled the injured limb. Her legs wobbled, threatening to give out. Exhaustion hit like an avalanche. She stumbled and leaned against the rock for several minutes. Charlie tugged at the reins, seeking grass, and she gathered strength to move again.

"All right, all right."

After tying the reins to a tree, she worked to loosen the moisture-swollen straps on the pack with the cold fingers of her good hand. Charlie twitched with impatient stomps, jostling the load and forcing her to start over.

"Damnit, stand still. I'll let you eat in a minute."

Charlie danced away as the pack finally came loose and started to slide, and she lost her grip. It plopped into a shallow puddle.

"Nooo!" She snatched it back, but the bundle was soaked. "Great, just great."

With a sigh, she tossed it under the boughs of a large pine where the rain had barely penetrated. She dug out a hunk of bread from a saddle bag and nibbled on it as she untied the horse and led him to a patch of grass. She wished she had hobbles and could unsaddle him, but with her arm, she'd never get the saddle back on him. The chill of her wet clothes made her shiver as Charlie grazed.

As the last light faded, she secured the reins to a tree. She tried to loosen his girth, but couldn't manage it one-handed and gave up. Cold, wet, and exhausted, she crawled under the umbrella of the pine and leaned against her pack. The damp blanket lent no warmth, but she curled up and sleep overtook her.

* * * * *

Night passed with chilled sleep and fitful dreams. When the first glimmer of light spread in the eastern sky, Lily rose and managed a smoky fire with pine needles and rotten deadfall. Her battered body protested after stiffening overnight, and she sighed with relief when she found a small bottle of laudanum in the pack. A sip only dimmed the pain, but she forced herself to limit the drug. She ate some bread and grazed Charlie again, waiting for dawn to advance.

Birds called and chipmunks barked as they eyed the interlopers. She led Charlie to the boulder and clambered back in the saddle. The clear sky belied a nagging chill in the air, and her teeth chattered as they set out.

They wandered over hills and through meadows, following animal trails, and rested often. By noon, Lily had little idea how far they'd traveled or in which direction. It no longer seemed to matter. The throbbing in her arm, the bone-deep cold she couldn't shake, the fatigue, and above all, a growing despair at ever finding a safe haven—all grew into a crushing weight, and she rode on only because she had nothing else to do.

Clouds built again as the sun slid beyond tree-lined ridges surrounding a grassy basin. Lily slumped in the saddle as Charlie plodded along a cattle trail. A stock pen sat atop a rise halfway down the valley, with a rough lean-to perched on the hill, and she nudged him toward it with a feeble kick.

"Almost there," she mumbled.

The tremors of the deep chill had quieted, chased away by fever. A ringing in her ears matched the tempo of a heavy pounding behind her eyes. In a bleary daze, she used the boards of the corral to dismount, nearly falling under the horse. Vertigo spun up and twisted the world into swirling chaos. Nausea doubled her over, and her stomach's meager contents heaved onto the grass. Stumbling, she used her last bit of strength to open the gate, steer Charlie into the pen, and close it behind him. She staggered to the shed and sprawled in the dirt, consciousness drifting in and out as dusk settled.

*   *   *   *   *

She came to with pain flaring in her arm. Drums boomed in her head. Her stomach had shriveled. When she sat up, a grimace cracked her lips as queasiness stirred. Thick, heavy clouds smothered the valley, leaving shadows in the flat morning light while drizzle soaked into the meadow grass. She fumbled through her pockets for the bottle and drained it. The bitterness curled her lips. Fever-heat radiated from her skin, eclipsing any warmth from the drug.

I have to get up. I can't stay here. She struggled to summon the energy to move, but slumped back on the ground. *Just a little more sleep ....*

Screams broke through the fog, and fire singed her skin. She bolted up, slapping at her clothes to smother flames. When she opened her eyes, she found no blaze. The weathered lean-to swam into focus. Panting, she leaned against the rough logs while sweat soaked her heavy men's clothing.

Another scream pierced the wet air, and the sweat turned to ice on her skin. She clapped her hand over her mouth, smothering a cry, and pulled herself up. The horse whinnied again as he paced the fence, his attention on the top of the basin where the cattle trail entered. She sighed as her heart slowed to normal.

Only Charlie. What's he going on about?

Up the valley, the black smudge of a horse and rider stained the gray-green grass.

A gasp hissed through her fingers, and she blinked to clear her vision, but the rider still approached.

"No ...."

How could they have found me? I have to get out of here. He'll have seen Charlie already. Where can I go?

Her thoughts scattered as Charlie whinnied again. She slid along the wall until she reached the open front. The rider's horse had picked up its gait as it came down the draw, and she squinted to identify him. Through mist and intoxication, the apparition shimmered, obscuring distinct features. Her gut told her it was Barnes or someone sent by him. Acid stung her throat.

I won't be at his mercy again.

The rider had come within a couple hundred yards. She looked toward Charlie. She'd never get him out of the pen in time.

The pistol! On the saddle. *Oh God, no.* She'd left it in her delirium. Now, it was out of reach. She was trapped.

Fear overrode caution, and she burst from the shelter and scrambled around the side. Pain flared in her ankle, but she drove herself to limp up the hill behind the lean to. She dodged clumps of grass, rocks, and the sharp spikes of yucca plants, weaving a clumsy path toward a group of tall pines. With dizziness shooting stars before her eyes, she focused on the shadowy maze and resisted the urge to look back.

Have to get to the trees. He won't find me in there. Just get to the trees.

Mere feet from the boughs of the nearest ponderosa, her foot slipped on a rain-slicked granite outcrop. Her ankle twisted, and the ground rushed up. Tears mixed with raindrops, coursing down her cheeks as she pulled her broken body forward on her knees. She reached the bed of needles under the tree and collapsed.

CHAPTER FORTY-SEVEN

Lily wrinkled her nose. Acrid smoke floated by, and the stench of soured, damp leather surrounded her. She closed her eyes tighter against the vertigo as it pitched her in crazy circles, but the pounding behind her eyes worsened. Heat enveloped her, baking her dry skin, until she gasped for breath. In the thick haze in her mind, an alarm warned of fire.

A voice in the fog urged: *Get up! Run while you still can!*

She gave a feeble push, but something held her down, a heavy cocoon suffocating her.

It's no use. Trapped. No more escapes.

The voice insisted: *Don't give up. Take the opportunity.*

I'm too tired. I can't run any more.

Her companion snapped: *Tired? Young lady, haven't you listened? Tired isn't an excuse for giving up.*

Recognition dawned on her. She frowned. "Alice?"

She opened her eyes to a blurry wall of logs. A fire popped and crackled somewhere, casting a diffused orange glow.

"Alice!" She strained to sit up, struggling weakly against

a thick cover.

A face appeared and floated above her.

"Luke?"

"It's all right, Lily," he drawled.

"The fire .... We have to get out. Save Alice." Her tongue refused to obey her mind and jumbled the words. "The fire!"

"Just rest, darlin'. There ain't any danger."

She thrashed, marshalling all her energy, and threw off a heavy blanket and sat up. "No, we have to run."

Luke moved closer and laid his hand on her forehead. "Hush, now." His voice remained strong, but mild. He pushed her back. "Ya can't run anywhere. We'll go in the mornin'."

"Too late!" The pounding in her head intensified when she rose. Vertigo sent her into a spin. Rough logs surrounded them, lit in wavering firelight—wood to feed the hungry fire. She struggled. "We can't stay."

He shook his head and smiled. "It's just the fever addling yer senses." His hand firmed against her and pressed her back. "Yer safe. I ain't goin' to let anythin' hurt ya."

She fell back, protesting, but the dizziness overwhelmed her resistance. Her eyes slipped closed, and the fog rolled in again.

* * * * *

Bright sunlight burned Lily's eyes as she opened them. She blinked and squinted. Luke cradled her, and the swaying gait of a horse lulled her. She closed her eyes again, sure she'd never left dreamland, but something was missing.

"Where's Charlie?" She sat up.

"Right behind us."

She lifted her head and sighed with relief. The horse plodded along on a lead in their wake. She relaxed against Luke. Her fever had abated, but her limbs had turned to lead. Her arm ached, and she shifted it away from Luke.

He glanced down at her movement and smiled. "Mornin', darlin'."

"Good morning. How long have we been riding?"

"Couple hours. Wanted to try to get back to Clear Springs by evenin', in case it rains again. Don't want ya out in it."

"Clear Springs? No! We can't go there." A shudder rattled her teeth.

"No cause to worry. Mrs. Andrews said the marshal put it to rest. Ya ain't wanted for nothin'."

"What?" She grabbed the reins from his hand and pulled the horse to a stop. "What about the man I ... shot?"

"Accordin' to the marshal, he didn't make it but admitted Barnes kidnapped ya before he went. Said ya were held against yer will and were only tryin' to escape."

Lily shook her head, incredulous. "Deadeye said that? No. He'd never ...."

"That's what the marshal told Mrs. Andrews." He shrugged. "Guess he was in a lot of pain and feared he was on his way to meet the devil. Called for the Reverend and wanted to clear his slate. And I reckon he wanted to stick it to his boss, seein' as how ol' Barnes ran off and left the sucker to die without even callin' the doc."

The news left her dumbstruck, and she hadn't noticed they'd started moving again.

She halted the horse and scowled. "I said no! I can't go back there. It's ... not only the law."

"Well, the other fella ran out as soon as you got away." Luke frowned. "What else is there?"

Lily averted her eyes. She couldn't let him see the pain,

fear—and accusation—in them. She stayed quiet, unable to think of a reply.

He sighed and tipped her chin up. "I know other stuff happened but don't know what it was. Wherever that scar came from, it's been long enough to heal." He paused when she flinched, and his lips set in a tight line. "I've been dressin' myself down since I found ya and saw that. I never should've left. But I damned sure won't make it worse by lettin' ya die of fever now."

At his mention of the scar, a knife of humiliation and heartbreak twisted in her. She thought she'd prepared herself for his rejection, but the pain of it caught her off-guard.

It bothers him, then. He doesn't want me. He hasn't even tried to kiss me.

"That doesn't matter now," she muttered, "but I don't want to go back there."

"Lily, we got to. That doc's wife—she was real worried and asked me to bring ya back. Ya need a doc, and it's by far the closest town with one. We ought to get there by sunset." He spoke with a tone of finality.

Resentment rose in her, but she had no choice. In her condition, she'd never make it to another town by herself. She *did* want to see Alice and Jessie. If Barnes had left, and the marshal had said he wouldn't charge her, she had no reason to stay away.

"I rode for two days. I went slow, but it should take longer than one day to get back." She made no effort to hide her irritation.

"Yup, but ya went in circles a lot." Luke failed to hold back a smile and nudged the horse on with his spurs.

Fuming, she glared, unable to think of another argument. She soon slept again, rocking in the saddle with his arms around her.

*   *   *   *   *

They stopped at midday to eat and rest, but Lily vomited as soon as she ate.

Laudanum withdrawal set in. Muscle aches and cramps racked her in cycles, the fever came back, and sweat soaked her clothes. The pain made her restless, and Luke barely held her in the saddle once they moved on. He dabbed her face with his kerchief as she alternately shivered and perspired.

A stiff breeze ruffled the aspen leaves as they left a canyon. Heat radiated through her clothes, but Lily quivered with chill and opened her eyes.

She didn't recognize the man holding her. She grimaced, searching for memories and context. She remembered men—many men who touched and prodded and hurt her.

She pushed away with a flash of terror and anger, clawing at the arm wrapped around her.

"No, don't you touch me!" Panic turned her voice to the bleating scream of a lamb at slaughter.

The man sat immobile, staring with wide eyes. When Lily started sliding from the saddle, the spell broke, and he pinioned her arms.

He pulled her close. "Lily, stop!"

"They won't stop. They keep coming. I couldn't stop them." She sobbed, horror and shame colliding.

Lily fought to release his hold. The horse shied from the commotion, dancing beneath them. He tried to steady the horse while keeping a firm grip on her.

The pain and fever worsened and dizziness overtook her. *Tired. So tired.*

The man whispered her name over and over. Her whimpers subsided as she retreated into the mist.

CHAPTER FORTY-EIGHT

The couple rode into Clear Springs under the pallid glow of a rising moon. Lily had lain limp against Luke for hours as the fever raged. She faded in and out of sleep and consciousness, never knowing which was which. When they arrived, she thought it must be a dream.

Luke called out in the dooryard, and the doctor shuffled out.

"Doc, she needs help quick." His voice held a tremor, and the last word came out in a sob.

Andrews let Luke slide her thin frame into his arms and waited while the distraught cowboy bounded from the saddle.

Luke reclaimed her as soon as he hit the ground and brushed past the doctor. The doctor and his wife settled Lily into a bed. Mary shooed Luke out so she could remove Lily's clothes and bathe her.

Lily was imprisoned in her mind, half-awake, hearing and feeling, but intense muscle cramps stole her ability to move or talk. While Mary wiped sweat from Lily's body, voices came from the hall, Andrews and Luke.

"Calm down, young fella. She'll be all right. The missus told me what the poor girl went through. As long as we can keep that fever under control, she'll recover from the withdrawal within a few days."

"But that's worse than any withdrawal I ever heard of. She was ravin' mad."

Mad? They're saying I'm insane again. Just a mad, scarred whore. He'll toss me aside for sure. Anger built at that thought, anger toward the injustice, Barnes, Judith, and even Luke. Lily tried to speak, but only a faint moan came out.

The doctor's calm voice spoke instead, "It can be quite severe in some. Depends on the person, the circumstances. I've seen sicker. She'll be all right."

Luke asked, "Doc, what about ... her mind? Is she goin' to be the same or ...?"

"Time will tell, son. She's been through a lot."

"Can I sit with her?"

"Wait for the missus to finish."

"Obliged, Doc."

Mary finished washing her, covered her with light sheets, and called Luke in. Lily lay still, eyes closed, caught between reality and the hell in her mind.

"She's a strong girl, Mr. Jackson."

He whispered, "Will she rest quiet for a while?"

"I think so, but I'll be close by in case she has trouble."

The squeak of the door hinge, followed by a chair scraping across the floor. Luke's scent came to Lily, the familiar light aroma of leather and grass, carrying memories that calmed her. Quiet settled, Luke's soft breaths the only sound, and soon it pulled her into the abyss of a disturbed sleep.

He sat with Lily the first night, but when she awoke the next day in another hallucination and attacked him again,

Mary sent him away. Lily lay in bed for four days, occasionally coherent, often sleeping, sometimes thrashing and raving.

* * * * *

With his hat in hand, Luke entered the sickroom. Lily sat up on a pile of pillows against the headboard, her hair neatly pulled back. A fresh splint cradled her arm. His eyes slid away, and he moved to the chair opposite the bed, staring at his hands.

His voice was rough, "Glad yer feelin' better. I was real worried."

She nodded. "I'm still a bit weak, but the fever's gone."

He responded with a slow bob of his head.

The silence lengthened until Lily cleared her throat. "I want to thank you for coming after me. I don't remember much. I ... well, I was pretty sick. Sorry to put you to all that trouble."

Luke grimaced. "It wasn't any trouble. Just glad I found ya." He blew out a heavy sigh, his gaze shifting to the floor. "About the fire and all ...."

"I'd rather not talk about that." Her tone sharpened.

With the sheet gripped in tight fists, she glared at the familiar wall with her jaw clenched. *I won't cry. I won't.* A lump filled her throat.

"I, I understand that, I just need to—"

"I know what you're going to say. Please, don't." Her lips trembled.

He kept his gaze on the floor. "I'm goin' to say what I came to say, and then I'll go." He cleared his throat. "Listen, a lot has changed—"

"Oh, how dare you!" Her voice went low with ire, but

faltered. A sneer twisted her lips. "I appreciate the rescue of the wayward woman, but you didn't need to come here only to give me some excuse. You've done your duty. You don't have any other obligation to me."

He finally looked up and his eyes widened, his head jerking back as if ducking a blow. His lips moved but nothing came out as confusion and shock played over his face.

She rushed on, quavering, "I know very well things have changed! Your face says so, and so does mine. You can't bear to look at me—and I don't blame you—but I don't need your pity or your excuses. So just go." Her stoicism collapsed as she buried her face in a pillow.

"Now hold on!" His voice boomed in the small room as he moved to the side of the bed. "What the devil are ya talkin' about?"

Her shoulders trembled with each muffled sob.

He sighed. "Lily, I ain't got any excuses to give ya." He touched her shoulder, but she flinched, pulling away, and he let his hand drop. "I only wanted to say I'm sorry for all the trouble I caused *you*. Mrs. Andrews told me 'bout the fire and all. Ain't none of it would've happened if it weren't for me. I should've stayed, don't know why I didn't.

"On the ride, thinkin' bout ya interrupted everythin' I did, and I dreamed 'bout ya every night. I've cared for a few women, but none of 'em settled in my heart, I never fell in love with any of 'em. But I fell in love with you." He paused, an audible click in his throat. "I almost left the outfit early to get back here to ya. Quittin' a ride gives a man a stain, though, and I thought I was just bein' a love-sick cow, bawlin' my loneliness for all the world to hear. So I stayed and tried to ignore how bad it hurt thinkin' of ya. Darlin', I wish I'd come."

She mumbled into the pillow, "Oh, how big of you."

He pounded a fist on the bed table. "Damnit, I'm tryin' to apologize. I shouldn't have left. I should've been here. A city girl doesn't know how to keep clear of the vultures out here. Yer so strong and smart, but that ain't enough sometimes. I knew that and left anyway. I could've protected ya." His voice cracked. "Judith attacked ya 'cause of me. She couldn't accept it when I called off the marriage. Her mind went. She killed a girl before, too, 'cause she thought I'd bedded her. Wouldn't listen when I told her I hadn't. I still can't reckon why the devil the asylum let her out. But I'm sorry she dragged ya into it. I never imagined ...."

Lily lifted her head enough to spit out an oath. "To hell with your regret! And I don't need your protection." She buried her face again.

Luke sighed. "I reckon ya can't forgive me now, and you've got no reason to. I only wanted to let ya know how sorry I am for what Judith did and all the rest. I blame myself. I should've been here to stop it, and now yer payin' for my mistake." Lily didn't move. He stepped back and cleared his throat. "All right. I'll leave ya alone. I know what I think don't matter much to ya, but yer a real brave gal, and I'll always love ya."

What? He still loves me? That and one word—blame—echoed. He wasn't to blame, for any of it.

Lily tried to hold her resolve but couldn't. "Wait."

Luke's footsteps moved away, slow and shuffling.

Realizing the pillow had muffled her command, she lifted her head. "I said, 'Wait!'"

Lily sat up, head hanging. Luke halted but didn't turn around. Her fingers picked at a thread on the sheet. The clock ticked while the tension tightened like a corset stealing her breath.

She whispered, "What about ... my face? And ... what happened ... with Barnes. He made me—I was a whore. I heard what you told the doctor, that I'm mad. You can't even look at me now." Tears dripped onto her hands with each shaky breath.

Luke's shoulders slumped, his head dropped, and he exhaled as if he had taken a punch. He stalked to the bed. Dropping beside her, he tossed the hat aside and took her hands in his.

"*That's* what yer worried 'bout? Darlin', no." He reached up to tilt her face to his and shook his head. "Why would any of that matter? I hurt for ya, Lily, for what ya went through, but wasn't none of it yer fault, and it don't change how I feel 'bout ya.

"Whole time I was gone, I cursed myself for leavin' when I'd found the most special lady in the world." He smiled and wiped a tear from her cheek. "Yer the same lady to me now as ya were then. I couldn't look at ya before ... 'cause I can't stand that ya got hurt and, if I'd been here, I could've helped. Not 'cause I don't like lookin' at ya. Yer prettier than ever, darlin'. And whatever else happened, all I care 'bout is that yer safe."

Lily made a face and dropped her gaze. "You aren't to blame. But ... you don't care what everyone else will say? I'll never be ... respectable again."

"Don't care a damn. If they can't tell a lady when they see one, devil take 'em. That would never keep me from bein' with ya."

"Why didn't you tell me about Judith?" She raised her eyes and searched his face. "She said ... you lied. That you two were still together."

Anger turned the angles of his face severe. "Lily, we was done long before I met ya. I did propose, but I broke it off before she ran that woman over. Judith wasn't a very good person, even before her mind started goin', but it took me a while to see it, and I'd had doubts before that. After she went away to the asylum, I sort of wanted to forget about her. It was an ugly thing I wished I'd never been involved in."

"And the dove she killed? What was that?" The words came out an accusation.

He winced. "I didn't even know her, never seen her before. Judith killed her for no reason but her own insanity. She imagined things, got paranoid. I paid to bury the girl proper, but that's 'bout all I know of her."

"Oh." Lily frowned.

Could she believe him? What he said made sense. *And if he intended to leave me, he'd have no reason to lie.* Her anger dissipated, and guilt needled her for doubting him.

"I reckon I should have told ya 'bout all that. I just didn't think to. I thought Judith was locked up for good. And when I met ya, I reckon I kind of lost my head." He shrugged with a sad smile.

She couldn't help but smile back, and when he held his arms out, she embraced him. She relaxed, sinking into the calm, like coming home.

But his words brought to mind her own omissions.

CHAPTER FORTY-NINE

Luke reserved rooms for them at the fancy new hotel and moved Lily the next day in a hired buggy, despite her insistence that she could walk a few blocks. He told her he would take her wherever she wanted to go once she recovered enough to travel. She protested, desperate to leave Clear Springs, and contended she could travel right then. Explaining he had business that would take a week or so, he convinced her to stay put.

With reluctance, Lily rested two more days. Early on the third day, a knock interrupted her breakfast.

She opened it to Luke holding out a large package.

"What is this?"

He grinned. "Good mornin', darlin'."

She laughed and ushered him in. "Good morning. What did you bring?"

"Open it and see."

After untying a string, she pulled the lid off the box. Inside laid a new dress, fancier than any she'd owned since childhood.

"Luke! You can't—"

"Don't tell me what I can't. I want ya to have a nice dress, so's ya can go out without frettin' over whether yer presentable."

"Luke, it's too much ... but I appreciate it." She held it up, and her eyes watered.

He winked. "Just don't go thinkin' I'll outfit ya like the queen."

She brushed away a tear and hung the dress over a screen in the corner.

Turning back, she glared and wagged a finger at him. "You waited to give this to me. You wanted to make sure I wouldn't ignore Dr. Andrews' insistence on rest."

He played an insulted look. "I didn't. I had to wait for it to come in on the stage."

"Oh?" She raised an eyebrow. "So if I ask at the store ...."

He laughed. "Honest!"

"I doubt it, but I suppose I can't complain. Anyway, I would like to call on Mary."

"Then ya hire a buggy. Don't go walkin' all over town. Ya don't need to wear yerself out."

"I will, I will."

He gave her a kiss on the cheek and left. She dressed and left, too. On foot.

The crisp morning warned fall lurked around the corner, and her breath hung in the air. She shivered and almost turned back for her cape, but the sun promised warmth later.

She strolled up Main Street, resting often. The town's growth continued. New businesses and residences spread further at the edges; a few brick, most wood, and a scattering of canvas quarters had popped up to house the steady stream of newcomers since her own arrival.

Turning onto a side street, she walked slower. Her heart fluttered with an uneven pace, and she found it hard to breathe. As the buildings lining the cross street came into view, she stopped in mid-stride. Her feet refused to move, and hot spit filled her mouth as her stomach rebelled.

South Street lay behind an invisible wall, a prison without bars. The doves on the other side lived in chains of fear, pain, and despair, wings clipped, unable to fly out of their cage. Squat, rough boxes at one end led to small clapboard houses, and the three large parlor houses rose above at the other end. The women still slept, and their customers had drifted off to nurse hangovers or return to work.

Lily stood frozen.

What am I doing? I can't be seen here. What if Barnes came back? He might have spies, someone on the lookout. It's stupid of me·to come. I'll go back to the hotel and just send a messenger.

She breathed deep, nodded, and turned on her heel.

That's better. It's quite simple.

As she pictured herself paying the messenger, the look on his face when he saw the address made her cringe.

He'll wonder what I'm doing corresponding with one of them. He'll see it and know. He might even recognize me.

She halted again, swiveling her head back to the cribs.

I can't send a message. But I can't go back there.

Another voice broke into her thoughts, low and scolding: *Young lady, you'll do what you put your mind to. Or do you not have one now? They'll talk no matter what you do, so you might as well do whatever needs doing. Get on with it.*

Her tongue flicked out to wet her lips, and she swallowed. It was true. They would talk. Did it matter? She planned to leave Clear Springs soon and never return.

Still, Barnes ....

But he wouldn't have returned already, and even if he has spies, what could they do to me now?

Lily straightened her back and lifted her chin. Her feet moved once more, and she denied the hammer of her pulse.

She knocked on the weathered door of a crib. No one answered. Another, louder knock still brought no reply. She frowned. With the heel of her hand, she pounded.

"Hey lady, give it a rest."

Lily jumped and turned to the brassy voice. A head of wild hair jutted through the small window of the neighboring shack. The woman was bare-chested, but for a shawl thrown indifferently around her shoulders. She eyed Lily with distrust.

"That one moved on. Better if you do, too."

Lily almost bolted. Instead, her hands curled into fists, and with a steady gaze, she pressed on.

"I'm looking for my friend, Jessie. Do you know where she went?"

The dove raised her chin. "What you want with Jessie?"

"I told you, she's a friend. I just want to see her before I leave town."

The woman considered a moment. "Well, yer too late. She beat you to it. She went off with her feller a few weeks back, day or two after the Fourth. Headed for Nevada."

Lily sagged against the door.

After a moment, the dove spoke up. "You wouldn't be a Wright, wouldja?"

Lily bobbed her head.

"Oh. Then she said to tell the Wright woman she'd be in touch and not to worry 'bout her 'cause she was gettin' married and gettin' a farm."

A bittersweet smile surfaced. "Thank you."

The woman shrugged and pulled her head back in.

Lily walked back to the main road deflated and tired. She felt cheated at not having a chance to talk about the changes in their lives, and though she doubted she could bring herself to talk about her captivity, she had a better understanding of Jessie's life. She was happy for Jessie but wondered if the marriage would fulfill the girl's dreams.

I hope so. She deserves some good in her life.

After crossing Main Street, she trudged toward the hill. The cabin, alone in the shadow of the tall pines, looked over the burgeoning town.

As she approached, a light breeze whispered through the trees, and sunlight dappled the walls under the clear sky. The small house gave her a sense of strength and family in spite of its solitude. She smiled, eager for the voice that had echoed in her head. Her steps quickened.

A water bucket lay on its side near the door, and she picked it up to carry it in. She rapped on the door, entering without waiting for an answer. The cabin looked as it always had with Alice's rocker next to the fireplace and the kettle on the crane. The sewing machine held a piece of cloth under its needle. An empty cup sat nearby. Lily breathed in the familiar scents with a smile and set the bucket aside.

Early still, too early for Alice's daily nap.

"She must be out back," Lily muttered.

Exiting the cabin, she followed the well-worn path around the side, calling the old woman's name. She peeked around back and checked the small root cellar. With no other sign, she reluctantly knocked on the outhouse door. Silence answered. She pulled the door open. Empty.

Maybe she wasn't feeling well and lay down early.

She walked to the front of the cabin and went back in. She wouldn't wake her; a stack of shirts and a cupful of buttons would keep her busy until Alice woke. A flutter in her stomach made her shiver, and she tiptoed to the curtained doorway to the back room and pulled the cloth aside.

Alice rested on top of the covers, clothed, hands laced over her chest. Eyes closed, face calm. Her skin had contracted, sunken, like a mummy.

She might have simply slept, but the faint decay wafting from the room carried finality.

Lily stood on the threshold a long time, completely still as she studied the creases and lines of the old woman's face, the bony knobs on her hands, the frail form beneath her clothes. Silent tears slid down her cheeks, leaving wet patches on her new dress.

With a heavy, wavering sigh, she stepped into the room and let the curtain fall behind her. Standing at the bedside, she bent and gently kissed Alice's forehead. A salty droplet fell on the wrinkled, parchment skin as she straightened.

She whispered, "I'll find the opportunities, not the blame. Thank you, Alice."

Lily walked back down the hill.

CHAPTER FIFTY

Lily knocked on Luke's door.

When he opened it, his eyes went wide. "What's wrong, darlin'? Yer white as a ghost." He pulled her inside, sat her in a chair, and kneeled before her. "What happened?"

"Alice. She's gone. I didn't get to see her again or say goodbye. Why? Why do I have to lose everyone?" The last came out in a sob.

"I, I'm sorry." He took her in his arms, and her tears dampened both of them. After a bit, he pulled back. "Who is Alice? And what do ya mean, 'lose everyone?'"

She sniffled, and he offered her a kerchief. "An old woman, up on the hill. I worked for her after I lost the store. It was only a short time ... but she showed me so much. Her life—she went through a lot, and helped me understand how to overcome some things."

Lily ran a hand over her face. *I must tell him, no matter the consequences.*

"Luke, I have to explain some things. A lot has happened, not only here in Clear Springs."

In halting words, she relayed the death of her brother and sister, her parents' retreat afterward, her father disowning her, and her mother's death. All the while, she defied the fear that the revelations would make Luke think less of her, drive him away.

Her chest tightened, and the tears flowed again when she arrived at the worst—Duncan, the baby, her escape.

"My baby. I lost him." She shook her head. "I don't know if it was a boy. They wouldn't tell me. But I think it was. No, I'm sure of it. But I lost him, like everyone else. I, I don't understand why. I've hurt so many, and ... they died because of me." Her body trembled. "Duncan didn't care about the baby. Not really. He just wanted status, a way to tie me to him and get Papa to take me back. He didn't care that I couldn't .... I wasn't ready for another baby, but he wanted it right away, thought a grandchild would make my father forgive me. He, he forced me." She turned away, her face burning, anger and shame rising.

Luke's voice filled with disgust, "Damn him." He pulled her back to him, hands on her shoulders, and waited until her eyes met his. "Lily, none of that's yer fault. Ya didn't cause them to die. Ya can't hang on to that."

She nodded. "I, I know. I'm trying. But—"

"No. No buts. Death is part of life. Ya got to take it as it comes and quit blamin' yerself."

A smile tugged at her mouth, despite the pang in her heart. "That's what Alice was trying to help me understand. Blame, regret. I hear her voice, still. She helped me survive."

He tilted his head and raised an eyebrow. "That's a smart ol' woman then. I'm sorry I didn't get to meet her."

"You would have liked her." She lowered her head. "I, I want to tell you about the fire ... and Barnes ... but I don't think I can, just yet."

"Darlin', ya don't have to. When yer ready, I'll listen, but none of that matters to me." He tipped her chin up. "You stole my heart the first time I laid eyes on ya. I love ya, and that ain't gonna change."

She hesitated, afraid of the power of the words. "I love you, too."

He leaned in, pressing his lips to hers with a light touch. His gentleness touched her, but a thought made her pull back as her cheeks flushed.

Will he expect me to lay with him again, now? She couldn't, not yet. It wasn't like the brothel, but she knew the memories would come back and taint their lovemaking.

She forced herself to voice the fear. "I can't be with you yet, though—like that, I mean. I don't know when I can face that again. I, I understand if you don't want to wait for me … if you want to go on without me." Her heart ached at the words.

His head dipped, and she winced, at once sure he'd reject her.

When he looked up again, tears wet his eyes. "Ya think that little of me, Lily?" He shook his head. "I know ya went through hell. I enjoyed our lovemakin', more than I could say, but that ain't why I love ya or why I want to be with ya. I'll wait, long as it takes."

A weight lifted, and she smiled. He held her again, and his warmth gave her hope.

Luke left to notify the doctor of Alice's death and let Lily rest. He returned in the evening and escorted her to dinner in the hotel's dining room. The long day had drained them, and they retired early. Before they parted, he told her to wait while he ducked into his room. He came back grinning and held out a small, rectangular silver box, decorated with fancy etchings.

Lily balked. "What is this?"

"Somethin' that'll make me feel better."

"So, it's a present for you?" She laughed.

"Open it."

She undid the clasp and lifted the lid with a gasp. A gleaming silver pistol with a pearl grip lay inside on black velvet.

"Luke! It's lovely, but it's too much. I can't accept this, especially not after the dress. You've spent too much on me already."

"I hope you'll never need it, if ya let me hang around," he smiled, "but I want ya to have it. Just in case. And maybe it'll help ya feel safer."

As she prepared to protest again, an image of Barnes flashed in her mind, and she shuddered as the objection died in her throat. "All right. I'll feel safer, I suppose." A frown crossed her face. "But please, no more presents. You don't need to buy me things to impress me."

With a playful wink, he said, "Can't depend only on my purty face."

Lily laughed and swatted him. "Goodnight."

"'Night, darlin'."

* * * * *

The next afternoon, as she contemplated her debts and how she might earn money to pay them, the maid notified her she had a visitor in the parlor.

As Lily entered the small sitting room, Mr. Warren rose from his seat and held out his hand.

"Mr. Warren?" Lily smiled and shook his hand, but unease sent a tingle up her spine.

If Barnes has gone, why has he come to see me?

"Hello, Miss Wright. You look well. I, ah ... heard of some of your troubles." He cleared his throat, clearly uncomfortable, and gestured to a seat. "I hope you've recovered."

Lily swallowed as she sat, and her smile faltered, but she kept her voice steady. "Yes, quite. What may I do for you?"

"Well, when you ... went missing, the judge decided in Mr. Barnes' favor."

Her mouth dropped open, and her stomach shriveled. "But—"

Mr. Warren held his hand up and went on, "There wasn't anything I could do. But when the, ah ... circumstances around your absence came to light, I asked the judge to reconsider, and he reversed the judgment."

"I should hope so." Her shoulders relaxed. "There's no more debt to him, then?"

"None at all. I don't think Mr. Barnes would try to collect now, anyway, but I brought the papers for you, for peace of mind. If there's ever any trouble, you show these and tell them to contact the judge." He handed her a packet of documents.

"Thank you, Mr. Warren. Please send me the bill for your services. I will be leaving Clear Springs, but I'll have them forward my posts. I appreciate your help. Was that all?"

"Not quite. We do have one other matter to discuss."

"Oh?" Her relief turned to worry. *What now?*

"Mrs. Durand designated me as her solicitor. I was very sorry to hear of her passing. You worked for her, correct?"

"Yes, briefly."

"Well, it seems she wrote her will shortly before she died, and the doctor delivered it to my office this morning. I've had several dealings with her, and it appears legitimate. It was dated July 6, and the doctor seems to think she passed that day."

"I see." *If only I'd gone to see her on the Fourth.* "Did she mention me?"

"She did." He smiled. "She left you her estate."

"The cabin?" Lily softened. "Why, that was very kind of her. I came to care for her a great deal."

"Quite. Yes, she left you the cabin and some other things." Warren opened the other packet of papers he held and began reading with a mischievous quirk to his mouth, an odd look on the fussy man. "'I leave to my employee, Lily Wright of Clear Springs, Colorado, all of my earthly possessions, my home and land, and any money I have left, as a gift of independence, so she can make her choices on want instead of need. She may not listen good, but she's learning.'"

Lily laughed softly, despite the tears filling her eyes.

"Now, I won't go into detail right now—that will have to wait until the estate is inventoried—but I can tell you, Mrs. Durand had a large sum of money."

Lily grew still. "A large sum? You must be mistaken. That's not possible. She was a dressmaker."

"No mistake. She owned quite a bit of land all over and sold it all a few years ago. She never spent any of the money, and the land the cabin sits on is worth a good amount now."

"I see." She couldn't say more. Her mouth had gone dry. She expected the man to admit it was a hoax.

Mr. Warren smiled wider, as close to a grin as his prim face would allow. "I'll contact you with more information later, and you can decide what to do with the property and goods. I simply wanted to inform you before I lost track of you."

Lily nodded. "I, I'm sorry. I don't know what to say."

She tried to stand on wobbly legs when he rose, but he waved her off.

"Please, sit. I will be in touch. Good afternoon, Miss Wright. I wish you all the best." He offered a hand, and she raised her own, shaking it without feeling the contact. He walked out with a comical spring in his step.

She sat in the parlor, bewildered and dazed.

Perhaps my luck really is changing.

CHAPTER FIFTY-ONE

Lily set out for a walk as the sun hovered above the valley in a clear sky. Solitude lured her, and she wanted time to think. She'd left a message for Luke to join her for a picnic lunch when he finished with his dealings. The hotel cook had made up a basket, and Lily carried it out of the hotel, without once worrying whether anyone had stared.

She climbed the rise to the cabin and laid out a blanket on a nearby outcrop. A light breeze played with the long, late summer grass on the hill. For a while she stood in the sun, considering the cabin and thinking of Alice. Doctor Andrews had removed the old woman's body and arranged for the funeral the following day. Lily didn't want to go inside yet, but the house comforted her.

She hadn't slept well in ages. She felt caught in a cyclone, unable to find her bearings. Nightmares intruded at any hour. A sound or smell, or nothing at all, could transport her back to the parlor house, or the store, or the cattlemen's lean-to. Her own mind betrayed her and rejected reality to replay the hideous memories like a cruel theatrical diversion that left her quivering and drenched in sweat.

Dr. Andrews had said it would pass with time, but she wondered how much longer she would have to suffer.

She turned her attention to the town below. The vantage point showed the movement of people and horses on the maze of roads. From above, Clear Springs seemed an idyllic haven among the towering peaks, but she couldn't wait to leave it.

Worries about Luke still nagged. She loved him and thought she could be happy with him, wherever they went, but anxiety whispered in the back of her mind.

What if I can't shake the nightmares? What if the hell stays with me and tortures me until I lose all semblance of sanity? Is it fair to put my burden on him? No. No, but I'll get better. He'll help me get better.

She lowered herself on the blanket and tried to enjoy the valley's beauty. The mid-day warmth made her sleepy, and she sighed and stretched. Below, a rider turned off the road and headed up the path.

Good, I'm hungry.

She pulled her knees up and rested her chin on them, drowsing while she waited for Luke.

The horse's hooves clopped and crunched on a patch of bare granite, drawing her back from the precipice of sleep. She yawned and rubbed her eyes. The mount had stopped next to the blanket, and she tilted her head up to look at the rider, but the sun threw streams of bright light from behind him. She blinked and squinted at the black silhouette.

"It's about time. I thought you got lost," she said.

"I did get lost, but I knew I'd find ye."

The voice wasn't Luke's, and it turned her heart to ice. Her breath wheezed out with a slow leaking hiss.

The man slid off the horse, moving with slow deliberation, his eyes fixed on her.

Lily scrambled to her feet and backed up a few steps. Without the sun blinding her, the man's features came into focus. She faced her husband for the first time in months. She swallowed, trying to draw some saliva as terror strangled her. He smiled, but the charm failed to reach his eyes.

"Duncan, I don't want to see you."

"Charlotte, what sort of greeting is that for yer own husband? Or should I call ye Lily?" His smile morphed into a sneer, and he eyed her critically. "Nay, I dinna think Lily suits ye."

The world started to spin. Lily slowed her breathing to stave off the vertigo. The ground steadied beneath her.

"That's not your concern any more. I left because I don't want to be your wife. That hasn't changed."

He shook his head slowly. "I dinna agree wit' ye there, lass. It *is* me business. I think when we have a chance to talk, ye'll realize things have changed." He glanced at the basket and quilt with an insolent grin. "Since ye made up a nice dinner, we can have ourselves a picky-nick and chat."

"I don't want to chat. The food is for a friend who will be here any moment. He knows about you, and he won't let you hurt me."

She had no guesses for what Duncan planned but hoped to keep him distracted long enough for Luke to arrive.

"Who? Yer rough and tumble cowboy? Dinna worry, I know about him, too, and I'll be takin' care of him proper." He shifted and pulled a pistol from the back of his waistband. Lily cringed. "I have a feelin' this'll be mighty persuasive for both of ye, and it won't abide argument." He chuckled and shook his head. "I followed ye all the way from our home. Tracked ye from Philly. Woulda got stuck there, but the station man remembered that ya said two names—

gave him yer real one and then changed yer mind. Could nay even remember to do that right, eh lass?" He clucked with regret. "Took a while, went to a couple other Godforsaken cesspools up here in these hills first, but I finally found the right one. And here's me faithful wife." He smirked.

Her hopes sank. She had her pistol—Luke had insisted she carry it—but with her right arm still in a splint, she couldn't count on aiming and shooting fast enough to hit anything.

"Duncan, why? Why follow me? Why would you want me when you know I don't want you? I won't go with you. Even if you drag me back, I'll leave again. You can't force me to stay with you." She softened her tone. "We were not happy. I can't give you what you want. You married me for status and influence, and I don't have that now. I lost it as soon as I walked out of my father's house, and he won't change his mind for anything, not even a grandchild."

Duncan's face turned dark. "I dinna care 'bout yer pa. I married ye to do the right thing, 'cause of yer full belly, and provided a home for ye when ye had no place to go. And we were happy, until ye started actin' as if I was no better than the dirt beneath yer feet. Ye're my wife, and ye always will be in God's eyes, until one of us dies. No other God-fearin' man would want ye, and they won't have ye. I'll make sure of it."

Lily searched for some way to convince him to give up on her. Only one might work. Or it might push him too far.

She gave him a slow smile. "You're a bit late for that. Do you know how many men have had me? I've been a whore, Duncan. I've been fucked by dozens of men, had things done to me not even you would imagine. I'm not the same woman who left you. I've changed. Do you really want a whore for a wife?"

Duncan laughed. "Ye, a whore? Ye couldn't manage a decent lay if ye tried." His eyes narrowed, and the muscles in his jaw worked. "Ye're lyin'."

"Am I? Ride on back into town and ask some of them. They can tell you how decent I am."

"Ye filthy, lyin' ...." He studied her, raised the gun, and aimed it at her chest. His shoulders lifted in a shrug. "Have it yer way."

"Lily?" Luke's voice yelled from below, with a touch of alarm.

Beyond Duncan, Luke appeared, riding toward them.

Duncan spun toward the sound.

No!

CHAPTER FIFTY-TWO

Lily's hand darted into her pocket. She expected to find the gun turned upside down, knew it would snag on the fabric as she pulled it out, but her hand closed on the pearl grip, and it slid from her pocket with ease.

As Luke came up the hill, he spurred his horse faster.

She screamed. "Luke!"

Time slowed down and sped up, all at once. Her hand weighed a thousand pounds as she raised it, so slow and sluggish. Luke moved as if flying and reached for his gun. Duncan had set his sights.

No, Luke, go back!

She aimed the gun with her left hand and braced her arm with the other, clumsy and too slow. Her hands shook like leaves in a breeze. Her thumb pulled back the hammer.

Duncan fired, and Luke cried out as his horse shied.

Lily flinched as Luke's bellow echoed off the trees. The movement sparked a fire inside her. Time stopped. She breathed out slowly. She aimed at Duncan's heart.

It's not revenge. It's to take my life back. One chance. One opportunity.

The gun fired as Duncan turned toward her. Her aim failed, and the bullet went high.

The slug hit Duncan's neck. He flinched, dropped the gun, and fell back, hands clutching at his throat. An eerie, sickening squeal rent the air and trailed off.

Lily stood frozen as blood sprayed from the body.

She walked around the blanket and stood over her husband. Her hands trembled. Her heart fluttered like a trapped bird.

His glazed eyes stared back without blinking—eyes Lily saw in her nightmares, eyes once filled with lust and domination, anger and hatred. They'd sparked a fear that had driven her over a thousand miles, spurred her to find independence, and cost her so much. She tried to find sadness or regret, but she felt only relief.

She shuddered, and time started again.

The blood had slowed, and his skin had lost its ruddiness. She waited, sure he'd move again, but the body lay motionless. She tucked the pistol back in her pocket. A movement at the corner of her eye caught her attention.

Luke sat in his saddle, his face drained of color, a hand pressed over a growing red stain on his thigh. He leaned over, peering at the body on the ground and back at Lily, and let out a heavy sigh.

His voice came out strained, but steady. "Good shot."

She helped him off the horse, laid him on the blanket, and tore a strip of her dress for a bandage.

Luke stopped her hand. "Don't blame yerself for this, ya hear?"

Lily raised an eyebrow. "This isn't my fault." She jerked her head over her shoulder. "It's that bastard's."

He burst out with a belly laugh, and Lily grinned as she wrapped his leg and put pressure on the wound.

Luke pointed at his horse. "Mind makin' sure she's not hurt?"

She checked the animal for wounds, finding the bullet embedded in the saddle.

The marshal rode up the hill a few minutes later, followed by a gaggle of the curious. When he reached the outcrop, he dismounted and waved the onlookers back. The group huddled at a distance. Parker surveyed Duncan's body, Luke, and settled his eyes on Lily.

"Where's your gun, Miss Wright?"

She pulled it from her pocket and laid it on the blanket, her gaze steady on the lawman.

"I thought so. Who's the dead man?"

"My ... ex-husband. I left him when he beat me. He shot Luke. He would have killed me if I refused to go with him."

Parker took off his hat, scratched his head, and put it back. "Aw, hell. You've killed three people in my town. I can't keep givin' you the benefit of the doubt. I admire your spunk, Miss Wright, but you're makin' my job real difficult."

Luke shook his head. "It wasn't her, Marshal. I shot him. He shot me first."

The marshal stared at Luke, his face blank. "That shot didn't come from your pistol."

Luke started to protest, but Parker waved him off.

"I don't figure it matters, though." Parker jerked his thumb toward the group of townspeople, and his tone turned harsh. "They ain't gonna let this slide, no matter who shot who. I'll make a show of an investigation, but I reckon both of you better head on out of town, real quiet and real soon."

* * * * *

Luke gritted his teeth while Dr. Andrews cleaned the wound. Lily paced, wringing her hands. Luke's face was ashen, and she knew it hurt more than he'd admit.

Andrews poured carbolic over the hole. "The bullet went all the way through, so it ought to heal well—lucky your horse didn't throw you—but it'll have to heal from the inside out, so you have to keep it open. Don't let infection get in there, or you'll lose the leg."

"Don't worry, I'll make sure it's taken care of," Lily said.

Luke grumbled, "Ain't my first shootin'. I can manage."

Lily tapped his arm. "Oh, nonsense. You can't even see the backside of it. How are you going to manage that? Taking help won't kill you."

Andrews rolled bandages around the leg and secured them as Mary popped her head in.

"You two will stay for supper." Her invite brooked no argument.

Lily smiled. "Only if you let me help."

Mary waved a hand, but Lily followed her out.

They enjoyed a quiet evening visiting before saying their goodbyes. Lily promised she would write and cried on the way back to the hotel.

CHAPTER FIFTY-THREE

In the morning, they took a buggy to the cemetery for Alice's burial. Mr. Warren attended as the only other mourner, and the reverend offered a short prayer. The others drifted off with small talk as Lily stood by the grave.

She knelt and laid a bunch of flowers by a rough wooden cross.

"Oh, Alice. I wish I hadn't missed the time with you. I had so much more to talk to you about, to ask you. I suppose you'd say there wasn't much else left to ask with all my jabbering and questions. I'm trying to listen better, honest." A grin cracked as she nodded. "You taught me a lot, though. I think I understand more of it now. I hope. I wish you could have stuck around. I have a lot more to learn.

"Mostly, though, I wish you hadn't been alone. I know, I know—you liked it. But you had a lot to give … and you needed some in return, too. One of the things you taught me is that it's all right to be alone, but it's better to have more than that, a family and people who care. I, I think I've found someone I can have that with. I love him, and he loves me." She wrung her hands and sighed. "I'm torn, though, and afraid. I know he won't hurt me, it's not that. I want a family, but I want to be independent, too. I'm still learning who I am. I never got to do that. I need to feel like I'm my own person, not an accessory or instrument for someone else. Can I do that and still have a family? Will he understand that? What do I do? I wish you could answer." Lily sighed and stood, brushing dirt from her dress. "Thank you for everything, my friend."

Lily walked back to Luke and asked him to take her back to hotel. He helped her into the buggy, and they descended from the hilltop cemetery. The pine-covered peaks surrounded the narrow valley with Clear Springs below, pockets of aspens shimmering as their leaves swiveled. Beautiful, but too confining.

She turned to Luke. "I want a spread where I can see for miles. I want a nice, open valley."

"Yes, ma'am. I'll find one for ya." He laughed.

* * * * *

Lily arranged for horses and supplies through the afternoon. They knew which direction they would go, but hadn't yet decided where they would stop. She worried about the weather turning, but Luke assured her he'd know when they needed to hunker down. On their last night in Clear Springs, she kissed him goodnight, went to her room, and slept well—the first night in weeks without a nightmare.

Lily emerged from the hotel in men's pants as the first few dying leaves tumbled by in a brisk breeze. The eastern horizon had begun to brighten, but the sun still slept.

Luke hobbled on his injured leg, double-checking the saddles and packs with the light of an oil lamp. Her boots clomped on the wooden sidewalk, and Luke turned. Raising his eyebrows, he looked her up and down and whistled.

Lily twirled. "Are you sure you want to ride with a fallen woman?"

"Only one."

They smiled, and the warmth in his eyes gave her goosebumps.

She looked over the stock and frowned. "What's the extra horse for? I only arranged for three."

"Miss Wright?" Jacob walked up behind her, red-faced, and avoided looking at her pants.

"Jacob! How good to see you." She stifled a laugh at his embarrassment. "I didn't think I'd have a chance to say goodbye."

He smiled and shook his head. "No, ma'am, you won't. I'm comin' with you."

"What?" Lily whirled to Luke.

Luke nodded. "I hired him on as a ranch hand."

Lily clapped her hands and laughed. "That's wonderful!"

Jacob's face turned redder, and he spun around to ready his own horse.

As the sun peeked over the pass, they mounted and rode west on Main Street. Lily and Luke rode side-by-side, Jacob following on his mount with an extra pack horse. They reached the last of the buildings with the sun at their backs. Pink light drifted through patchy fog, painting the peaks in brilliant purple.

Luke halted his horse. Puzzled, Lily stopped and backed up until she pulled even. As Jacob approached, Luke nodded him on.

Luke's blue eyes settled on her, direct and probing, a dazzling smile on his open face.

"Will ya marry me?"

Lily held his gaze, pondered the idea, and smiled back.

"No. Not yet. Someday."

He let out a soft sigh and nodded.

The flare of disappointment on his features tugged at her heart, but she needed more time. She needed time to be her own—not a daughter, a wife, a dove. No cage, gilded or not.

She leaned across the gap to brush her lips against his. Turning toward the mountains, she flicked her reins, and they continued up the road as a collared dove's song faded behind them.

THE END

ACKNOWLEDGMENTS

I must thank my writing groups and beta readers, who endured critiques, questions, and angst; my editor, Randall Andrews of JaCol Publishing, who taught me to see the forest and the trees; and my mom, who believed and nagged. Finally, thanks to my kiddo, who ate a lot of late dinners and heard a lot of desperate pleas for peace and quiet.

Lauren Gregory, who was raised on a horse farm, discovered a love for writing in sixth grade when she learned she could move people with words. She misplaced that love for a couple decades and traveled the world in the Navy, floundered through two college degrees, and embarked on raising a rowdy son who's too much like her. She found that love again on a cold November morning in 2013, and they've been locked in a tortured embrace ever since.

These days, she writes novels, maintains a history blog, and herds poodles in her native Colorado.

www.authorlaurengregory.com
www.authorlaurengregory.blogspot.com
www.thehistoryscrapbook.com

Thank you for reading.
Please support the author by leaving a review.